P9-CQJ-169

DISCARDED

RIGHT WHERE I LEFT YOU

Julian Winters

VIKING

VIKING
An imprint of Penguin Random House LLC, New York

First published in the United States of America by Viking,
an imprint of Penguin Random House LLC, 2022

Copyright © 2022 by Julian Winters

Penguin supports copyright. Copyright fuels creativity, encourages diverse
voices, promotes free speech, and creates a vibrant culture. Thank you for
buying an authorized edition of this book and for complying with copyright
laws by not reproducing, scanning, or distributing any part of it in any form
without permission. You are supporting writers and allowing Penguin to
continue to publish books for every reader.

Viking & colophon are registered trademarks of Penguin Random House LLC.

Visit us online at penguinrandomhouse.com.

Library of Congress Cataloging-in-Publication Data is available.

Book manufactured in Canada

ISBN 9780593206478

10 9 8 7 6 5 4 3 2 1

FRI

Design by Lucia Baez
Text set in Stempel Schneidler Std

This book is a work of fiction. Any references to historical events, real people,
or real places are used fictitiously. Other names, characters, places, and events
are products of the author's imagination, and any resemblance to actual events
or places or persons, living or dead, is entirely coincidental.

The publisher does not have any control over and does not assume any
responsibility for author or third-party websites or their content.

To all the Black and brown LGBTQIA+ readers who haven't seen their version of a happy ending anywhere yet—sometimes we have to create our own. I believe in you. Until then . . . this one's for you.

One

Two things: This is the worst idea you've ever had.
And I'm glad it's you I'm stuck here with.

—Reverb, *Disaster Academy* Issue #10

Spoiler alert: I'm in love with two boys.

Head over heels, smiling-at-nothing-while-walking-into-walls kind of love.

But they're not *real* people. They're comic book characters. Also, they might be in love with each other. Huge emphasis on the *might*.

"You're doing that thing again, Isaac."

I tilt my head. "What thing?"

Diego, the virtuoso of bad imitations, gives me this exaggerated smile with wide, Disneyesque heart eyes, sighing loudly. One of those I'm-helplessly-in-love sighs.

"Shut up," I say halfheartedly.

"It's very distracting. And annoying."

"You're annoying," I tell him.

I'm lying on my back, my head resting on the edge of Diego's bed, reading last month's issue of my favorite comic book, *Disaster Academy*. He's next to me, sitting upright, tongue between his teeth, focused on a video game.

Diego's right—I'm making The Face.

I can't help it, though. The chemistry between my favorite characters, Charm and Reverb, while they're crowded in an air vent, awaiting the signal to attack the villains below, is too much. It's the proximity of their shoulders. Their easy banter. The way Charm's eyebrows lift when Reverb says he wouldn't want to be stuck with anyone else.

My heart would run through a brick wall for these two ridiculously-in-love teen superheroes.

Diego has heard all this before. He's too chill about everything—except video games—to complain about my obsession with this series. Like now, with my officially licensed *Disaster Academy*–sock-covered feet propped against the wall, squinting at every panel, searching for the barest hint that Charm is finally going to confess his feelings to Reverb.

It doesn't happen.

Diego's bedroom is pure chaos. Posters of his favorite video game, *Beyond the Valley of Stars*, and a few vintage ones—*Super Mario Bros.*, *Final Fantasy VI*, *Kingdom Hearts*—layer three of the pool-water-blue walls. Pinned high above my feet is the Puerto Rican flag. The rest of Diego's room is mountains of clothes on the floor, sneakers in the corner, a plate of tonight's half-eaten dinner on a cluttered desk.

Framed below the wall-mounted TV is a photo of us

from five summers ago. Clunky-glasses-wearing Diego Santoyo and acne-attacked Isaac Martin. Our arms are wrapped around each other's shoulders. We're beaming at the lens, Diego wearing a BORICUA PRIDE T-shirt while I have on an old-school *Justice League* one.

Since that photo, Diego's lost the glasses, and a biblical miracle—also known as the Aftermath of Puberty—cleared up my skin. We both have curly hair. His is soft and swoopy on top while mine, thanks to my mom's side of our family, is thick and sponge twisted, the sides of my head shadow faded. Diego is lean and long but still two inches shorter than me. Genetics decided that I'd be muscular but not toned, because I dare not engage in anything athletic besides riding my bike everywhere, a consequence of not learning to drive yet.

"No, you can't just bust the door down!" Diego groans, a hand covering his eyes. "We need the Key of Tonatiuh."

He's not talking to me.

He rants into one of those gaming headsets, the right earphone tugged sideways so he can occasionally acknowledge me.

"That's not how it works, Level_Zero," he says as if one of the characters on-screen is a real person, not controlled by some rando gamer probably halfway across the world eating Doritos while slurping on a Baja Blast. His frequent fights and jokes and mildly deep discussions with other online gamers are odd to me.

I nudge his knee. "Have you escaped the nightcrawlers yet?"

"Almost." His thumbs repeatedly jam the buttons on the controller.

I roll over onto my stomach. "What level are you on?"

"BRB," he says into the headset before tilting his head at me, smiling. "Thirty-two. There's seventy-five total."

"So I'll be minus one best friend this summer?"

"Three weeks tops," he teases, then returns to his Gatherer's Guild.

I scan the pages of *Disaster Academy*.

Thing is, the thought of being without Diego for more than a day this summer is numbing. When mid-August rolls around, I'll be at the University of Georgia in Athens—alone.

In retrospect, it's kind of absurd, our situation. Diego finished in the top ten of our graduating class. Smashed the SATs. Aced every test with zero sleep and only two hours of studying. He's also got mad coding skills. College was built for kids like him.

Suffice to say, his parents aren't down with his decision to take a gap year and pursue his dream of designing the ultimate inclusive video game.

To be honest . . . neither am I.

A blob of sweat dribbles from my hairline to my cheek. Summers in the South are unbearable. Also, the circulation of cool air from Diego's vents sucks. The endless scent of boys sitting in their own perspiration coats the air. Luckily, Diego's mom loves adding extra fabric softener to their weekly wash.

Diego takes a sip of his energy drink. Cloud Strife, the Santoyos' fluffy orange tabby, purrs at his feet. He absentmindedly scratches behind her ears.

"Another all-nighter?" I eventually ask.

"GTG," he says into the headset. There's only two people Diego abandons playing *Beyond the Valley of Stars* for—his mom when she's yelling, and me. Frozen onscreen is his favorite character, Delmar, a tall, elf-like character with light brown skin similar to Diego's and blue hair. He stands with other characters from the game I don't recognize.

Before he tugs off his headset, Diego winces, cheeks darkening. "Whatever, Level_Zero. Catch you tomorrow." I raise an eyebrow as he lowers his controller. "I have to find the second Imperio Stone before Valencia locates the Death Stone," he explains.

I don't understand any of that, but I get Diego's obsession with video games in general. That earnest look in his eyes as he plays. The need to be immersed in something so different from your own reality.

He motions toward my comic. "So what, you're gonna spend the night pining over those two?"

"Pining is an *art*, Diego. It takes practiced discipline."

He smirks. "Which means you're gonna practice all that disciplined pining by whacking it to poorly written fanfics again."

Blush heats my cheeks like a nuclear explosion. It's nearly undetectable against my deep brown skin, but I still cover my face with the comic. "It happened one time!"

"But it happened."

"I hate you."

"I'm your best friend, dude." *Dude* is Diego's favorite word. "I'm your *only* friend."

It's a fact that burns coming from him. For a few years, I counted my older sister, Isabella, in the friend category until it started feeling kind of silly. We're *family*. And I wish this were a strategic choice—my lack of friends—but it's not.

I'm awkward with new people. Most times it's hard for me to relate or open up to them. There's no natural flow to our conversations. No easy silence like you can have with a person you've known for more than a year. I can't remember when it started, but the moment I'm introduced to someone, a barrier appears. It prevents them from getting too close. They can't hurt me, and I'll never disappoint them.

On paper, branching out sounds nice. But I've never done it. Diego and I *found* each other. We were both reaching for the same swing at a park while our parents watched from afar. Our bond was so instantaneous and natural, something that hasn't happened for me since.

"Don't give me shit right now," I warn, refocusing on *Disaster Academy*. "Charm is three seconds away from confessing his undying lo—"

"No, he's not. He didn't last issue. The three issues before that—"

"Haven't you heard of slow burn?"

Diego shoots me one of those "sure, Jan" looks he's been perfecting since we were kids. His eyes are light brown as if there's a constant glow behind them.

Mine are plain, tree-bark-brown eyes.

"It's called queer baiting," he says. "Happens all the time."

"Whatever," I mumble.

I recognize my own fixation with the idea of Charm and Reverb being a thing. I've waited so long for them to finally admit their feelings on-page. Seeing them kiss has been my secret hope since Issue #3 when Charm came out as gay to the other students at the Webster Academy for the Different. Since Issue #4 when Reverb and Charm became roommates. And Issue #5 when Charm gave Reverb that smile—you know the one—and Reverb blushed.

Issue #6 . . .

I can't even think about that moment without having heart palpitations. Issue #6 is a milestone in the fandom.

"You'll see at Legends Con." A flood of confidence washes over me. "Jorge and Peter will confirm it's canon once I ask them about it."

Peter Heinberg and Jorge Prados are the writer-artist duo behind *Disaster Academy*. In a few weeks, they'll be here in Atlanta taking audience questions during their private panel at Legends Con.

I plan to be one of those lucky fans.

For the last six months I've worked for my mom on the weekends, saving money to afford con passes. You can't just purchase them on the internet either. Legends Con is so exclusive you have to enter and win an online lottery to get a unique access code before you even get the *chance* to buy entry-level badges. On the day badges are released you have a ten-minute window to log in and purchase up to a maximum of three before you're locked out.

It's seriously some *Hamilton* level ridiculousness.

We both entered the lottery, but guess who won? Yup. Isaac the Obsessed.

All that's left is logging in and securing our passes tomorrow at 1:00 p.m.

"I can't believe you're really doing this," Diego says, smiling quietly.

"*We're* doing this," I remind him.

He's been saving up money since last year when we

watched online clips of the con from this very bed.

I elbow his thigh. "You're going to meet your girl soon."

Saturday is all about my quest to meet the Two True Legends, but Sunday is Gameathon, the convention block dedicated to gamers. It's Diego's opportunity to see his own idol, the creator of *BtVoS*, Elena Sánchez.

Diego winces. This is another one of his looks I know, though it's a more recent development.

"Is your mom still giving you shit?" I ask.

"She drops daily reminders about how this is a big mistake."

Diego's been excited for months at the prospect of pitching his video game ideas to Elena. The last half of senior year was dedicated to him talking about it. It's his dream.

Cloud Strife paws her way through a pile of clothes. Cool moonlight blankets the room from the window behind the bed. Silvers and blues glow against his skin as Diego runs his fingers through my hair. He's the only person allowed to do this besides my mom and Isabella.

My phone buzzes. I yank it out of my jeans to check the display name in case it's Mom.

It's not her, though.

It's Carlos.

I don't answer. If I haven't spoken to him the other three hundred times he's called in the last five years, I don't know why he thinks I'll start now.

Diego snatches the phone from me. I don't put up a fight. We don't have secrets. He reads the name on-screen before tossing it facedown onto the sheets. The MADE IN AMERICA WITH MEXICAN PARTS phone case my grandpa bought me is all that's visible now.

"¡Mi culpa!" Diego says, turning back to the TV to start a new game.

I slip back into my comic. On the page, Charm and Reverb are clumsily plotting their escape from the air shaft. It's the perfect moment, with their heads so close, to confess how absurdly in love they are.

My big, hopeful heart dies a little when they don't.

Two

How can I save the universe? How can I save
anyone when I couldn't even save my dad?

—Charm, *Disaster Academy* Issue #6

The next morning, laughter and the soft hiss of steam-ing milk greet me the second I stumble into the kitchen. I sneeze once. Then again. My sinuses and summer air are sworn enemies, battling a war I often lose.

A watery film over my vision paints countless wavy, gold streams of sunlight across Mom's face. She stands over her latest freebie product—one of those overly-expensive-but-sure-to-break-in-a-month espresso machines.

We're on week two.

Mom's a social media manager at an agency that handles a small but exclusive clientele of Atlanta-based celebrities. The perks? Our house is a museum of every trendy invention, clothing line, this-will-kill-you-or-shrink-your-waistline dietary tea in existence. She tests the products, her clients rave about them on Instagram as part of their sponsorship deal, and we get to keep this cozy house that just the two of us have occupied ever since my brother and sister left for college.

"Morning, Isaac," Mom says cheerily.

I grunt a "morning" while attempting to tame my hair.

Mom and I have an unspoken rule—she initiates our pre-breakfast talks and I agree to actively participate in the discussion of her choice. She grew up in a Black American household where loud, animated discussions in the morning were frequent. On the other side of my family is a lineage of famously non–morning people I relate to more. I've been told the Martíns from Monterrey, Mexico, never rose from bed before 10:00 a.m. when it wasn't required. Once my grandpa's parents moved to the States, they changed to "Martin" so people wouldn't mispronounce their last name everywhere they went. José Martin, my grandpa, is also the rare early riser in our family's bloodline.

"¡Chiquito!"

My grandpa sits at the breakfast table like he always does when he comes to visit—legs crossed, an open newspaper between his hands, a mug of coffee topped with cinnamon getting cold by his elbow. There's something about reading how our world is in perpetual crisis that prevents him from ever finishing his coffee.

Despite being six foot one, I'll always be his Chiquito. His little one. Maybe because, other than Mom, I'm the shortest in the family.

"Morning, Abuelito."

"How are you?"

"Moody and full of postgrad angst," I reply, kissing his temple.

"What is this angst?" Abuelito asks.

"Life," I sigh.

"Boredom," Mom teases.

"All of the above." I smile, and Mom does, too.

"Latte?" she offers, bouncing around the kitchen in a fluffy blue robe and yoga pants, her standard "work" attire, considering she conducts business from home.

"Gross." I skulk over to the fridge. After taking out a two-liter ginger ale, I drink right from the bottle. Since I'm the sole ginger ale consumer in the house, Mom doesn't fuss. The carbonation tickles my nose. Another sneeze.

"Take your meds," Mom insists.

The cabinet over the espresso machine is stuffed with all kinds of medication. Pain relievers. Day and nighttime cold relief. Anxiety prescription. Blood pressure. Upset stomach. Today-is-Monday-good-luck pills.

Mom has a cure for almost everything. Everything except heartache, betrayal, and the swift spiral that follows. But we don't talk about that.

Not to each other.

I chase two allergy tablets with another mouthful of soda.

Mom finishes her latte and cocks her head at me. "Have you started that checklist I gave you?"

"Not yet." I pause to thump my chest, turning my head

so I don't burp in her face. "I have other goals. Priorities first, Mom."

"Goals?" she wonders. "Like packing for college?"

My throat tightens, but not from my allergies.

Truth is, I'm kind of avoiding that. There's a solid 50 percent of me that's excited about UGA. I'll be in a different city, hopefully shedding the Isaac everyone thinks they know and becoming the Isaac I know I can be. But college means more than leaving Diego. I'm leaving Mom too.

We won't have these daily moments, not in person, anyway. Once I'm gone, it'll be just her in this house. If she breaks down again . . .

I hate thinking about that.

I hate knowing I've seen the scars under her armor.

"And what are these other goals?" Mom pokes me in the chest, at the wrinkled *Disaster Academy* T-shirt I slipped on this morning. "More of Lucky and Echo?"

"Charm and Reverb," I correct her.

"I was being funny."

"And you failed."

Mom stands in front of the kitchen window, golden rays soft against her dark brown skin. Her hair is pulled into a messy ponytail, loose springy curls resting against her cheeks. She's five foot eight but has this way of making me feel short. It's her big personality. It towers over everything.

"Today's the day, right?" she inquires. "You have the money on your debit card?"

I nod.

She helped me open a bank account at the start of senior year. I've never really had any money in it until this past January, but now it has all my savings for Legends Con. As of last night, it has the funds Diego gave me for his pass as well. I've been obsessively practicing entering in my card's sixteen-digit number and expiration date on my phone.

I'm ready.

"Isaac, please don't let attending this convention be your only plan for the summer." Mom sighs, turning back to the counter.

"It's not. I, uh—" I hesitate, then whisper, "I'm going to Pride at Piedmont Park too."

Besides Diego, I know I can tell Mom almost anything. When I was fifteen, I casually came out to her over burgers and milkshakes. Just an *I'm gay* between bites. Her response was *Wonderful. Pass the ketchup*. I'm not stressed about discussing Pride around Abuelito either. He took the whole coming out thing as an invitation to pivot from introducing me to the girls at his Catholic church he wanted me to date to introducing me to all the openly queer people instead.

I know I'm lucky.

"You're going to Pride," Mom repeats.

"*Teen* Pride. Adult Pride is in October," I quickly clarify. "There's a parade and music and movies. I'll be with Diego. I just want—"

To hang out with other people like me without my mom hovering nearby.

That's the part I can't get out. Mom isn't one of those helicopter parents. It's not as though she'd embarrass me. But I want—no, I *need* my first time at Pride to be solely about the experience, not worrying how my mom is taking it all in.

The thing about coming out is you're so focused on making sure who you are doesn't hurt or change your relationship with your loved ones that you never really think about yourself. About your moment. About how wonderful it is to just . . . be.

At Pride I want to be myself without any extra anxiety.

Mom has this look on her face. The *I'm thinking* look. "You'll be careful, right?"

"Of course. Diego's got my back."

"Fine." She turns to the espresso machine. It hums and clicks and buzzes. "We can discuss details later."

That's code for: *What time will you be home? Do we need to have The Talk again?*

Abuelito clears his throat, refolding the newspaper. "Summer is when all the best love stories begin, Chiquito."

I roll my eyes, laughing.

Abuelito, the hopeless romantic. He fell in love with

my grandma in the summer during the early '80s. Weekend coffee dates at a small café. Slow dancing to Gloria Estefan's "Anything for You" at their wedding. Naming their first son after their favorite musician, Carlos Santana. It's all a beautiful fairy tale starring two first-generation Mexican Americans.

"Didn't you and Flaco begin dating in the summer, Lilah?" Abuelito's smile is outlined by a thin, cement-gray beard that matches his wavy hair and complements his medium-tawny complexion.

Mom grins tightly. "June." Then, to me, she says, "Your dad was such a romantic."

"Carlos," I mutter.

She doesn't bother correcting me.

I stopped referring to him as "Dad" five years ago. That was one summer where love didn't flap its meaningful wings and soar. Instead, it crashed and burned when Mom caught Carlos kissing another woman in a gas station parking lot. Those romance genes clearly skipped a generation.

After, he packed all his belongings and moved out.

It was no longer Carlos, Lilah, and their three children. It was Carlos, Kate, and their English bulldog, Valentine.

Not exactly an ideal summer love story.

"Chiquito," Abuelito says gruffly. He sips his cold coffee, then grimaces.

Mom's already brewing a fresh cup. She does that—

takes cares of others without them asking. Even though Carlos is gone and Abuelito's only her father-in-law, Mom still looks after him. Her own parents, who were born and raised in Georgia, just like her, now live in their dream retirement city, Cape Coral.

When I'm gone, who will take care of her?

Abuelito points a wrinkled finger at me. "You'll find the right one too," he says. "He'll be right under your nose. Like in *The Princess Bride*."

I snort.

Me and Abuelito don't agree on a lot of films—we're both picky—but there are three we love unequivocally: *Black Panther*, the only Marvel movie Abuelito likes; *Coco*, in my opinion the best Pixar movie; and *The Princess Bride*.

Nothing compares to our obsession with that movie.

We've watched it twice a year since I was five years old. That summer, I caught the flu. Abuelito took it upon himself to babysit me daily while Mom and Carlos worked. I don't know if that made it more magical—that I was living out the same story in my own life as the grandson in the film—or if it was just the opportunity to spend more time with Abuelito.

For two weeks, he fed me homemade chicken soup and ginger ale and put on *The Princess Bride* until I fell asleep.

Abuelito's fondness for that movie is deeper than comfort food and cuddles. He saw it with my grandma when it was in theaters. They watched it yearly until she died. She was his Princess Buttercup. And, not to brag, but Abuelito could teach farm boy Westley a few things about charisma.

He wants that same kind of storybook love for me.

I do too. But I haven't seen many non-white queer teens, let alone Afro-Latinx queer teens, get that kind of fairy-tale love anywhere—definitely not in movies or comics.

"As you wish," I say to Abuelito, quoting one of his favorite lines.

He smiles.

"Make sure to leave room for Bella's visit in all these summer plans," Mom reminds me, pouring Abuelito a fresh cup of coffee, then adding cinnamon. "She's coming before the baby is due. Iggy wants us all to go to dinner."

Tension tightens my jaw. "I don't—"

"None of that while Bella is here," Mom interrupts. "All of you will have to pretend to be, I don't know, *real siblings*."

Ignacio, my older brother, is right under Carlos on my No Longer Exists list. He's the eldest and, by birthright, the most stubborn. Iggy didn't cease and desist all contact with Carlos after what happened. It's the reason my sister and I have a silent pact when it comes to our brother—his Team Carlos makes us Anti Iggy. We don't speak to him unless it's mandated, usually by Mom or Abuelito.

"Don't forget the things he's done for you," Mom says, warm but serious.

"Things?" My face scrunches. "You mean ridicule me for following Bella around?"

Mom sighs. "The other things."

There are no other *things*. Just a thing that hangs in my bedroom. A reminder of who Iggy could be and who I'm confident he's not.

"Whatever," I say under my breath.

Before Mom can scold me, a *doot-doot-doot* echoes in the kitchen. It's her phone. Her mouth stretches like a softened Airheads candy as she scoops it off the counter.

"Speaking of an *angel*," Mom says to me, obvious snark behind her voice, before answering the FaceTime call. She aims the camera so we're both on the screen. "Hello, Bella!"

"Hi, Mom. 'Sup, Isaac."

There she is, my sister, flopped across the peach sofa in her apartment. Bella lives in Savannah, a four-hour drive from here, which is why it feels like years before she visits. She makes it home for birthdays and holidays with her husband, Chris, but not as often now.

"How are you feeling?" Mom asks.

Bella angles the camera until we get a full view of her hand resting on a very pregnant belly. "Does this answer your question?"

"Thirty more days," Mom reminds her.

"Shit," Bella hisses.

"No cussing in front of my grandbaby!"

"Blame Isaac." Bella smirks in a very Lilah Johnson way. "He's a bad influence."

"What?" I shout. "Oh, hell n—"

Mom's head snaps in my direction. My mouth clicks shut. Bella's laugh comes in tinny through the phone's speaker.

I peek over Mom's shoulder. Bella looks exhausted, her dark curls pulled into a giant onyx crown on her head. She's a nice combination of our parents. Whereas Iggy's all hard lines and fair pinkish-gold complexion like Carlos, I'm soft and round features like Mom. But Bella's curves and angles with smooth brown skin.

"Blame all those R-rated movies you watch at night," comes another voice before Chris's head pops into view. "'Sup, Isaac. Hi, Mom!"

"Hey, Chris," Mom says in that singsong voice she only uses with him.

Chris is mostly cool. A bit dorky with a slicked back, almost copper quiff, along with wide hazel eyes and freckles spilled like gold paint across his pale white skin.

"Yo, Chris," I say, waving.

"We were just talking about you two," says Mom.

"And Iggy," I add, scowling.

On-screen, Bella rolls her eyes. "Hard pass."

"Right?"

"Enough of this, troublemaker," Mom says, hip bumping me away. "Go talk with Abuelito."

I let Mom dance around me, unhurt by being ejected from the conversation. Bella and I typically FaceTime every other day. I have other plans, anyway. T-minus four hours and eight minutes until registration for Legends Con.

I need to get out of here. If I stay at home, I'll only end up lying on my bed, reading more Charm-Reverb fanfic and, well . . .

That's *one* way to kill time, but I have a better idea.

Three

I know it's weird to say this now, especially since we're all about to do something big, but: I'm gay. I've never told anyone that. Only my mom. She's cool. And I've never had a boyfriend. Does coming out make anyone else hungry?

—Charm, *Disaster Academy* Issue #3

I don't actually live in Atlanta, the city.

Our house is in a suburb of Alpharetta, outside the Interstate 285 perimeter, which is the highway that forms a giant loop around the city. Alpharetta is twenty-six miles from Atlanta.

Twenty-six miles separate me from Iggy.

As a web designer he can afford an apartment downtown above some gentrified shopping district even though Iggy's the opposite of hipster and cool. Also, Mom says his latest live-in model girlfriend books a lot of gigs in the city.

The universe knows I need exactly twenty-six miles from Ignacio Martin to feel like I'm finally my own person. I'm no longer "Iggy's little gay bro" or "Iggy's lost puppy," the nicknames kids from our high school gave me. When I hung around Bella and her volleyball friends, no one bothered me. She was Bella; I was Isaac. No extra titles necessary.

I hate that not only Iggy's traitorous choices but also everyone else's opinions have ripped this seam between us further apart.

I hate a lot of things, I guess.

The best part about Alpharetta is there are two major comic book stores to satisfy a true geek's heart.

Heroes for Hire in downtown Alpharetta pulls in all the farmers market and food truck crowds along with the locals who love tradition with modern upgrades. The employees dress in clean uniforms and bright nametags. Soft rock plays overhead. Flatscreens advertise the newest comics releasing on Wednesdays. Compulsory greetings and farewells are shouted with a generic smile for every customer.

The other bookstore, Secret Planet, is vintage comic book shop awesomeness. Dingy gray carpet, spinning wire racks with all the newest issues, action figures hanging from the ceiling like guardian angels. The back room is crowded with towers of boxes stuffed with comics sleeved in plastic. Employees that look—and act—like customers wave or nod at incoming patrons before returning to whatever their latest read is.

Heroes for Hire is tailored for the Met Gala. Secret Planet is dressed for a sleepover at a friend's house.

Since the age of Stan Lee, they've been vicious rivals.

I'm a proud member of the Secret Planet squad.

"Welcome back, Captain Incredible!"

I wince as I hang in the entryway.

My nickname came from one of those generic Hero Name Generators on Google. Part of a cheesy promotional thing Secret Planet did for National Superhero Day a year ago. Unfortunately, it stuck with the one staff member who appears to be working today.

Behind the front counter, in an orange blossom–print, short-sleeve button-down shirt, is F.B. His lazy smile is exaggerated by a fine shadow of stubble and intense blue eyes. He's the only person I know who can get away with that hair in Secret Planet. It's dyed a wild burst of aquamarine. Somehow, it works with his long face and deeply square jaw.

I up-nod at him, trying to casually sneak to the new releases section, but he waves me closer. Hesitantly, I shuffle in his direction.

F.B.'s scuffed Vans are kicked up on the counter. I'm not sure how he became Secret Planet's assistant manager. Once, during a typical F.B. ramble session, he told me he's originally from Santa Barbara. *SP is as close to an adequate, low-stress lifestyle for a twenty-one-year-old that I can find 'round here. Luckily, I had weak competition*, he'd said.

He licks jam from his thumb now. Flaky pastry crumbs stick to his lower lip. "Sorry. Got the munchies," he explains.

Another thing I know is that F.B. is a frequent advocate

of a certain type of herbal therapy. But that's not classified information. Even Big Winston, Secret Planet's owner, is aware.

"Oh." I don't really know what else to say.

That doesn't stop F.B., though. "Some wicked bad stuff's brewing 'round here." He tosses an unfinished donut into a pink pastry box.

"Uh."

The back of my neck itches. That familiar, uncomfortable buzz moves into my arms and legs.

"I know. You're wondering what happened," says F.B.

But I'm not. Not really.

He peeks over his shoulder at a mahogany-brown door with a giant poster of Storm from the X-Men and Black Panther in an embrace pinned to it. Big Winston's office. "I can't—" He pauses to slurp from a can of Mountain Dew. "It's top secret news. But it's Ben-Affleck-as-Batman bad."

I almost laugh.

Over time, I've learned that even in the most cataclysmic situations F.B. finds a way to be inappropriately funny. From birth he's had to learn to laugh at his own misfortunes. His parents unironically named him Frances Bean, after the daughter of rock royalty Kurt Cobain and Courtney Love.

The fondness for green stimulants is strong in that family.

"Anyway," F.B. says, grinning. "How's the fam?"

"Uh. Fine."

"Are you excited about UGA?"

"Kind of."

"Yeah, I hear you. I haven't finished my undergrad yet." He finally dusts the crumbs from his mouth with a crumpled napkin before tossing it in the box. "I'm gonna, though. Soon."

I nod. My eyes bounce from F.B.'s Mountain Dew to Big Winston's door to the pucker of gray carpet meant to edge up against the base of the front counter. Even with Secret Planet's modestly updated AC system, I'm hot all over.

"So, Captain Incredible, you obvi didn't stop in today to hear my low-key complaining about our hella demanding educational system," F.B. finally says in his semiprofessional voice.

I shake my head with a sympathetic smile.

"Of course not. It's new release day!"

"Yup," I confirm.

The thing about F.B. and me is we share a rare gene—the geeks-out-over-heroes gene. Our relationship is completely comic book based. At least on my end. For months he's tried to discuss other topics whenever I visit, but . . . I don't know.

It's weird to let others in. People who aren't my family or Diego. How do strangers just openly talk about personal things like school or relationships or their fears?

Thankfully, F.B.'s never made it awkward when I don't reciprocate his openness.

"Let me guess." He reaches under the counter before slapping a comic onto its soft woodgrain. "You're here for the latest *Shrapnel* comic. He barely survives this one, you know."

I roll my eyes. "He *always* survives."

Shrapnel is everyone's favorite antihero. He's a mercenary with an excessive case of toxic masculinity. Every issue he does inconceivable things like chugging a beer while slaughtering a roomful of trained operatives. I guess his superpower—accelerated healing—is kind of cool. Technically, he can't die. Not unless someone decapitates him. Even then, no one ever stays dead in comics.

I glare at the comic and say, "I'll never support him."

"Why?"

Before I can answer, someone else responds.

"Because Shrapnel's story is far too layered with cues about our societal power dynamics, our uneven fight with mortality, and the psychological solitude created by worshipping vigilantes as heroes."

I spin around, scowling.

If the commercial, robotic vessel of Heroes for Hire is the mortal enemy to F.B. and Secret Planet, then Alix Jin is my Lex Luthor.

She sits cross-legged on the floor in a corner of the store with an open graphic novel in her lap. Her dark brown hair is pulled up in a knot. Loose strands fall across her rose-beige face. It's the start of a fierce Southern summer, and she has on a baggy sweatshirt. Probably to keep herself warm since her soul's obviously dead and decaying.

She watches me through the chunky curtain of bangs that hang just below her brow.

Alix and I went to the same high school. Well, she still goes there. She'll be starting her senior year after summer break. We shared a few of my senior courses last semester. She's only seventeen, but she's one of those AE kids—advanced *everything*. We both tended to sit in the back of the classroom, avoiding eye contact with each other and everyone else. Never raising our hands to answer questions, even though I'm almost certain Alix knew all of them.

She had this thing where she'd exhale softly whenever someone shouted out the wrong answer. Like she was disappointed in their ignorance.

Maybe she was frustrated that they were breathing the same air as her.

But inside Secret Planet, acknowledging her existence is almost unavoidable.

"Here again, I see," I comment.

"Just like you," she points out, lowering her eyes. "Still trying to fit into that imaginary shell of a self-deprecating hero in the plotless narrative of your own life?"

There it is. The reason I never attempted to joke with her in class. Why I avoided her for group projects.

Alix Jin is *ruthless*.

"You need a hug."

"You need to stop obsessing over a fictitious, non-existent relationship as a thesis for your own romantic deficiencies," she replies dryly.

I turn back to F.B. He's laughing behind his hands. "I'm here for the new issue of *Disaster Academy*," I announce.

"The latest issue of *It's Not Going to Happen, Fanboy*," Alix says.

"This isn't a library," I hiss at her, as if I don't do the same thing any time I'm here. My favorite spot to read comics is a corner under the giant rainbow Pride flag.

Alix doesn't respond to me. She's already forgotten I exist. A simple tug of the cuffs on her sweatshirt until they cover her knuckles, a careless brush of stray hairs behind her ears, and she's reading again.

I wish I had that power—to pretend people or things didn't exist.

Like the twenty-six miles that separate me from Iggy.

The one-sided silence that protects me from Carlos.

The fact that this summer won't be like anything else.

The shop's motion-sensitive electronic door chime goes off. It signals whenever someone enters or exits. When I was younger, it used to be this welcoming chime as I barreled through the door. Now it whines and perishes with a clang. The batteries have long outlived their expiration date.

I look up.

A boy stands in the doorway. He appears to be around my age, but it's hard to make out the details of his face with the sun backlighting him. His skin is a warm fawn. A white T-shirt pulls almost too tightly across his chest. He plays with his deep brown, springy curls.

After stepping inside, he scans the store as if he's looking for something or someone.

Recognition knocks the wind out of my lungs.

It's him.

Our eyes meet. He gives me one of those crooked do-I-know-you smiles.

Why would Davi Lucas, star right wing of East Middleton High School's ice hockey club and future American Hockey League Hall of Famer, remember me? The social structures of our high school wouldn't dare allow an athlete protected by the laws of popularity and rigorous dedication to sports to know the president—and sole member—of the Comic Books Society. The laws of every early aughts teen movie have taught me that in order to date the hot guy, one can only be marginally geeky.

Like a band or student council member.

"Hey." Davi cocks his head.

My ears tingle. I cough up a "Hey," then, clearer, "Hello, Davi."

"Isaac, right?" His smile bunches his eyes. "We went to middle school together."

"And high school," I mumble. "I was—"

"You were my tour guide when I moved here," he says, nodding.

Davi and his family, originally from Brazil, relocated here from a small town in upstate New York. I was the first person to navigate him around the bright and smelly halls of our school. Turns out, in middle school, most sixth graders opted out of showering daily. Being appointed Davi's official chaperone was pure luck. Our last names fell in line—Lucas and Martin—on the roll call.

"We also had a class in ninth grade, right?" he says.

"Tenth," I correct him. Heat blisters my ears. Damn it, why did I even open my mouth? I don't do things like this—talk to semi-acquaintances.

"It was biology." Apparently I can't shut up.

His smile widens like he's not bothered by my edits of our history. "Can you believe high school is over?" he asks, still wearing that curious expression.

"Nope." Sometimes I catch myself randomly rolling over before sunrise, expecting my phone's alarm to go off.

Davi pushes his curls back. "Prom was sick, though."

"Uh. Sure."

Prom wasn't that special for me. One of those social situations I felt pressured into doing because Iggy and Bella did it. How could I disappoint my mom?

I went solo, sharing a rented SUV with Diego and two guys from homeroom. Less than an hour in, Diego spilled cherry punch on my white Chuck Taylor All Stars. Some kid named Travis upchucked behind the bleachers where I was casually spectating everyone dancing to The Weeknd.

Diego and I skipped the after-parties. I thought he'd reject the idea of going back to his house for our usual routine, especially when Leah and Lamar, classmates from Diego's Environmental Science course, invited us to a post-prom slumber party. People always wanted Diego to show up at some kickback. But he gave me this easy grin over his shoulder, then gently turned them down. I couldn't hear what he said over the loud music, but it was enough for Lamar and Leah to nod, trade looks with me, then walk away.

Later, at Diego's, we drank sparkling cider as I watched him play video games until 5:00 a.m.

When Mom asked about the night, I shrugged it off. I was too embarrassed to tell her I didn't engage in the classic after-prom escapades. I didn't get drunk. I didn't hook up with anyone.

I was the typical socially anxious Isaac Martin.

Truth is, there's another part of prom I remember vividly: staring at Davi for a solid five minutes as he danced with Callie Hernandez. He looked incredible in his dark wine-colored tuxedo. Our fated encounter in middle school was the unknown beginning of something that has woven itself into my DNA. This inescapable lightheaded sensation. A knot in my stomach.

Bella calls it Crush Syndrome.

"This is a cool place," says Davi. "Hang out here much?"

Before I can respond—not that one logical sentence fills my scrambled brain—F.B. says, "Secret Planet is the bomb dot com! Captain Incredible is here all the time."

I squint at F.B., hoping my underdeveloped telepathic abilities will silence him. No such luck.

"Wow. I wish I had that kind of time." Davi's eyes run over the store. "Might be a little overstimulating, though."

My mouth twitches into a grin. It's not the only thing twitching. Or overstimulated. "You don't have time?"

His laugh sounds weighted. "Nah. It's always hockey season for me. Twenty-four eight. I'm either on the ice or doing dryland drills."

"In the summer too?" I ask, shocked that I'm managing to navigate a conversation with someone that's not Diego or family, let alone *Davi Lucas*.

"I spend summers at a hockey camp," he says. "After Pride, I'm leaving for Tampa Bay."

"That sucks," I say, looking down at my shoes.

It's a good thing I didn't shoot my shot, right? Who am I kidding? Like I'd ever had the nerve to—

Wait. His words recycle through my head: *After . . .*

"Pride?" squeaks out of my barely open throat.

Davi grins awkwardly. "Didn't you know? I came out right before graduation. I'm bi."

"Bi." I don't mean to say it like it's a foreign term. But it's just . . .

Davi Lucas is bisexual.

"I thought—" He pauses, his eyes roaming my face. "I mean, you're out, right?"

Coming out in high school wasn't monumental for me. It's not as if I had a large friend group to tell. I only mentioned it to people who asked. I just wanted it known. But I didn't think anyone paid enough attention to me to make it a big deal.

Obviously Davi did.

"Um." I can't figure out why, right now, saying this is suddenly so big. "Yes, I'm gay."

"Cool," he says with that same wide grin. "I'm going to Pride and then—"

I don't even let him finish. "Me too!"

"Cool," he repeats.

We stand there, silent. I don't know what Davi's thinking. But I know my brain is a minefield of possibilities.

What if I were bold enough to ask Davi to hang out?

What if we were friends?

What if I just go for it, be that Isaac I plan to be in Athens?

"Anyway." Davi pivots to F.B. "I came to grab a birthday gift for my best friend. It's a new graphic novel about his favorite character. Debris? Shard?"

"Shrapnel," F.B. and Alix both say, his voice coated in enthusiasm, Alix's monotonous.

"That guy!" Davi laughs again.

"This new one is set in the early years where Shrapnel nearly died, like, *three times*," F.B. says. He dusts donut crumbs from his shirt, then walks around the counter to escort Davi toward the graphic novels.

I watch them. Well, I watch Davi and try to shake off the dizziness. Crush Syndrome has taken full possession of my thoughts.

What if I went to Pride with Davi?

But . . . there's Diego. He wouldn't want to hang out with me and my crush, right?

Diego. Shit. Diego Legends Con Diego.

On the wall above F.B.'s head is a digital clock. *Fuck, I'm three minutes late.* My hands shake as I scramble for my phone. The Legends Con homepage gradually loads. I scroll to the lottery access link.

This is it. Peter Heinberg and Jorge Prados and me. Diego meeting Elena. All our dreams happening in one weekend.

I try to log in with my secret passcode.

ACCESS DENIED.

No, no, no. It's only 1:04 p.m. I can't be locked out already. I try again and again. It's the same result—a vicious, red error message:

WE'RE SORRY, YOUR PASSWORD HAS EXPIRED.
ALL AVAILABLE PASSES FOR LEGENDS CON HAVE BEEN CLAIMED.
WE HOPE YOU'LL JOIN US NEXT YEAR. THANK YOU!

Four

No Capes! Reviews Blog

Top reviews for *Disaster Academy #7*

@PicaSays

★★★★☆

The latest DA is filled with humor and action and disaster teens. We get more of Halo Boy trying (and failing) to be a leader. Boomstar and Solaris shenanigans. (Evil) plotting from Dean Charles. Loved the deep dive into Pica's background! There was one problem: not enough Charm and Reverb. Where's the impact of Charm's actions last issue? Are we supposed to ignore how selfish he is? What does Reverb think? WHY IS HE STILL CHARM'S FRIEND?

What am I going to do?

I've been standing outside the Santoyos' front door for five minutes. My phone's buzzing nonstop in my back pocket. I know it's Diego. I know what his texts probably say: *Did you get the tix? Where are u? HELLO ARE ALL OF OUR DREAMS ABOUT TO COME TRUE???*

Every time I try to find a response, a way to tell my best friend it's not happening, I come up empty. I can't avoid him. I can't tell him what happened in a text either.

It's a miracle I survived the bike ride over here from Secret Planet through all the tears. The second I closed out the Legends Con tab on my phone, I left. All those heroes hanging overhead, the posters on the walls, the newest *Disaster Academy* staring at me from the front counter as F.B. hyped up *Shrapnel* to Davi—it was too much.

Now I'm too chickenshit to knock on Diego's door.

Fortunately, I don't have to. Summer's air, dense with pollen, gets the best of me and I sneeze three times.

The door swings open. "Dude, did you stop to get a celebratory ginger ale or—" Diego pauses, his grin and crinkled eyes quickly vanishing as he sizes me up.

I sniff hard. Fat, salty tears smear against my fingers as I wipe my eyes. After what I've done, I don't deserve to cry in front of him.

"Diego," I squeak.

His expression goes neutral. He jerks his head toward the stairs behind him. "Come on," he whispers, almost smiling. "It's cooler in here."

I hesitate, blinking, but then he shoots me that impatient look he used to give me when we were younger and I didn't immediately get excited about an idea he had. It eases some of the tension out of my shoulders.

I follow him inside and up the stairs to his bedroom.

Diego's bedroom floor is just clean enough that I can pace from the window to the door without tripping. Cloud

Strife makes it difficult as she crosses my path on the way to her throne—a comfy pile of Diego's winter hoodies. I keep my head low. Fists clenched at my sides. I'm hovering somewhere amid disappointment, anger, and waves of ache.

"Dude, you looked disturbed," Diego teases. He lies on his stomach on the bed, playing *Pokémon* on one of those portable video game consoles. The whole world could end and Diego would be fine if he could lose himself in a video game. "¿Qué pasa?"

Guilt shreds my stomach like a starved lion devouring its prey.

"Diego." I sigh so hard my ribs hurt. Then I say, low and trembling, "I messed up."

"You messed up?"

"We're not going to Legends Con."

It was all right there: Peter Heinberg and Jorge Prados and Elena Sánchez. My chance to ask the question: "Is the love between Charm and Reverb real?" This endless confidence that I was The Chosen One. Eat your heart out, Frodo. I was destined for this.

But destiny laughed in my face and said, *This never happens to people like you.*

"What happened?" Diego finally asks.

"I-I got distracted."

"How?"

This is the part I'm most ashamed of. The part that

cracks my soul into six million pieces. I force my way through the gross shame swallowing me whole to tell him. I mention going to Secret Planet. F.B. talking my ear off. Seeing Davi—though I leave off the parts about being preoccupied by his face—until those earlier tears blur my vision again.

"Dude." Diego's fingers, warm and cool at the same time from gripping the console, circle my wrist. The touch surprises me. He tugs. "Sit."

"No, Diego, I messed up."

"Fine. I get it," he says, concerned. "We're not going. But you're freaking me out, so please sit down and breathe."

The fight has exited my body. The flight too. I flop carelessly onto his bed.

Diego leans against me. The video game chimes from the forgotten console between his legs. "Maybe we could try BadgeCon?"

"No. I checked."

"GeekPass?"

"They're already selling the basic passes we wanted for a grand."

"What about Backstage Buys?"

"Two grand."

"Two grand?" Diego's voice is small.

"Every ticket resale website is advertising passes for way more than we have saved up." Slowly, I repeat, "We're not going."

Diego is silent for too many heartbeats. Part of me wants him to yell at me. Just be ruthless. I selfishly ruined not only my dream, but his, too, fantasizing about a boy. But Diego doesn't.

I stare at the ceiling. Late afternoon light maps orangey circles across the white paint. Diego's window is cracked. The taste of early summer—young peaches and trimmed grass and chlorine from the neighbor's pool—layer the inside of my mouth.

In my periphery, Diego's silhouette blurs. His hair is in rare form today, tall and swirly. It reminds me of Reverb. If I had Charm's metahuman abilities to alter reality, then I'd be at the Webster Academy.

I could ask Reverb if he felt the way about Charm that I *hope* he does.

But if I were like Charm I wouldn't have full control over my abilities. It's one of the many things I love about him—he's an eighteen-year-old superhero who doesn't see himself as "super." He's not this morally perfect role model. He screws up. He makes bad choices.

Charm's also the first openly gay, Black superhero around my age. His sexuality isn't a plot device. A reason for his existence. It's simply another cool facet of his identity. The fact that Reverb, his Pakistani American roommate, is his possible love interest is kind of unheard of.

And although Charm's not Afro-Latinx, so much of him still feels like . . . me.

His story has always felt like mine.

Fact is, all I see in comics are in-your-face romances for straight heroes. If a character is queer, they're generally clichéd and faded into the background. Or eventually dead.

It's rare for queer teens in comics to have clumsy rom-com happy endings, especially if they're anything other than white.

On the windowsill, Diego's phone buzzes. It's been serenading his neighborhood with a '90s R&B playlist since we walked in. His foot wiggles against mine in rhythm with Lauryn Hill's "Can't Take My Eyes Off You."

Since childhood, we've been like this—unfazed by our physical closeness. Knees touching. Hands overlapping. The Santoyos are an affectionate family. They're all hugs and cheek kisses and snuggled together on the sofa for movie nights.

I nod toward his phone. "Are you gonna check that?"

"Nah. It's probably just Zelda."

"Who?"

"Gamer friend. I've mentioned them before."

He might've. I don't know. My brain is slush and mud and that crust in your eyes after a long nap right now. The raspy voice coming through the phone's speaker tell us, "You're just too good to be true."

"Change the song," I almost demand.

We both know I'm not categorically opposed to the brilliance of Lauryn Hill. But this song—about love and longing and someone too good to be true—is a little too ironic for my mood.

Diego reluctantly shuffles up the bed. The song he chooses triggers an involuntary tug at my lips.

"Dude," Diego the Vicious Manipulator says, the smile in his voice punching me in the chest. "You know you love this."

"I don't."

I *do*, but I can't admit it. Ever.

"Remember . . ." He doesn't have to finish. This song is so saturated in warm memories and *feels* for us, I'll never forget.

This is teenaged Isabella Martin's fault. Her obsession with Bruno Mars obliterates all versions of Crush Syndrome Isaac. She had a bedroom shrine. Owned every album in digital and vinyl format. Once, to buy concert tickets, she worked *two* summer jobs: babysitting and assisting Mrs. Garcia, our neighbor, with her garden project.

Bella's exhaustive fangirling also led to mandatory live performances of Bruno's music in the Martin living room—starring preteen Diego and Isaac. We'd sing along to "Just the Way You Are" like our voices weren't obnoxiously loud and off-key. It was a big deal. Carefully selected wardrobe and choreographed routines. Mom styled Diego's hair into Bruno's classic pompadour. Mine is biologically opposed to that much product and brushing. TV remotes were our microphones.

Diego's already standing on the bed, crooning the first verse down at me. When he gets to the part about Bruno's girl's beauty, he jokingly strokes my cheek, wiggling his eyebrows. Blush spreads from my forehead to my neck. He goes all out, shoulder shimmy and uncoordinated hip swinging. It's awful, but a laugh bursts from my mouth.

The chorus hits. Diego throws his head back, putting as much rasp into his singing as possible and that's it. I can't let him suffer alone.

This is *our* song.

I get to my feet. He lets me take the lead, even though between the two of us his vocal range is marginally better. Credit his mom for that. Camila Santoyo has a beautiful voice, a gift she obviously didn't pass on to her children.

The bedsprings jostle our dance steps. We croon until our throats ache. Warm tears cling to my eyelashes. Tears like a storm in the middle of July—unexpected but soothing.

Some tears aren't for wounds. Some are for healing.

The music begins to fade. Diego holds my hand, twisting and turning me. I almost lose my balance, but he catches me, a hand steady along the small of my back.

We flop onto the bed, wheezing with laughter, as the door creaks open.

"Hey. Isaac. Mijo. Don't break anything."

Camila leans in the doorway, arms folded, still in her pale pink scrubs. But her smile is as endless as a clear blue sky. She has these big brown eyes, and inky black hair braided loosely.

"Sí, Mamá," Diego says through a long exhale.

"Remember the last time you two—"

Diego gives me a look. I return it. We know what's coming.

Camila lists every incident—tree climbing, fence climbing . . . a lot of *climbing*, because we both thought we were Miles Morales as kids—that has either led to breaking an object or one of our bones. Mainly me; I've inherited zero coordination skills from the Martins or Johnsons.

"Sí, sí, Mamá. We know," whines Diego.

"Don't use that tone," Camila warns, shaking her head.

Diego's jaw tenses, then releases.

Since graduation, the friction between Diego and his mom has intensified. Every tease and laugh they share is accompanied by a glare or a wrinkled nose. Every "I love you" is undercut by a quiet "You're ruining your future."

"I think they get the point, amor."

I've never been able to identify what it is about Oscar Santoyo that has always made me comfortable. Maybe it's his eyes. They scrunch up like Diego's, even when he's not laughing.

Maybe it's his easiness, even when he's upset about something.

Maybe it's because he's nothing like Carlos Martin. Nothing at all.

"Cariño," Camila hisses, but the corners of her mouth upturn when Oscar kisses her temple.

"Yes, we know." Oscar pins us with a stare and flat mouth. "No breaking stuff."

"We'll chill out," Diego finally agrees, eyeing the ceiling. I can tell he wants to say more but doesn't.

Oscar brushes a careful hand across Camila's cheek. "Dinner almost ready, amor?"

Camila nods, her shoulders sagging. Oscar's arm circles her waist, pulling her in. Her head rests against his collarbone. Everything about them is peace. They're tenderness and affection.

My stomach swishes in a weird pattern. I can barely remember a time when Mom and Carlos were like that.

Were they ever this happy together?

"Isaac." Camila's voice seems distant. I blink at her. "Shouldn't you be getting home? Won't your mom want to have dinner with you?"

I smirk. "I doubt it. Mom's pretty busy these days."

"She's told me. I'm glad she's staying . . . occupied."

There's something hidden in Camila's tone. It's not

that usual sadness she has when we talk around the topic of Mom and those months where she was just managing to survive every day. This is different.

"You're welcome to stay for dinner," Oscar offers.

"Dude." Diego bumps my shoulder with his. "She's still on that healthy lifestyle kick. But you won't die."

A year ago, Oscar had a minor health scare. He spent a week in the hospital while they ran tests. Doctors suggested more rest and better eating habits. Now Camila inspects every product's label before buying. She refuses to stock their pantry with any candy or sweets or snacks that didn't come from the bland aisle of Whole Foods.

"Organic. Non-GMO. Low salt. No sugar. No bueno." Diego lists everything on the hand he doesn't have tangled in my hair.

"I'm watching you, mijo," Camila warns.

"You're not even wearing your reading glasses," Diego teases.

"You're going to be wearing this size-seven Nike—"

"Amor, amor," Oscar interrupts, his own body experiencing a malfunction in composure. "Is that your world-famous arroz con pollo burning?"

Diego perks up.

"Your favorite, I know," Camila says with an almost cruel grin. "And yes, it's a lightened version for your papá."

Oscar tugs gently on his wife's hip. "Come. I'll help you finish up."

"Cariño, you're a catastrophe in the kitchen."

"Maybe I can help you with other things, then?" he says, squeezing her side. "Things too *hot* to handle by yourself." The wiggle of Oscar's eyebrows is borderline pornographic.

Diego shudders. "Please don't talk that way around us."

"Why not?" Camila asks.

"Uh, because it's disgusting? Parents do not"—Diego flails a hand around, as if trying to shake the words out of his fingers—"*do that.*"

"Oh, we do," Oscar says. "You know, Ollie wasn't conceived—"

"¡No más, no más! You win!" Diego shouts.

"No más," I repeat much slower.

Diego grins at me before tossing a dirty sock at the door. It's too late. His parents' laughter is a dim, haunting sound as they walk toward the kitchen. They're replaced in the doorway by a boy with dimples, fluffy brown hair, and eyes darker than a moonless sky. He bites his thumb-nail. There's a red stain on his Star Wars T-shirt.

"Hey," I say, and he flinches.

Oliverio Santoyo is a much quieter version of his older brother.

"Ollie!" Diego waves him in. "Let's play a round of *Spider-Man*. Vamos."

It takes Ollie less than five seconds to wedge himself

between us on his brother's bed. Diego passes him a controller before queueing up the game. I recline, hands folded behind my head. Diego's fingers return to my hair, skimming lightly against my scalp.

"I know it sucks we're not going, but," he whispers over Ollie's head, "that's not all this summer's about, right?"

I nod solemnly.

It's about spending as much time with my best friend as possible, doing all the things we've both wanted to but didn't think we could until now. But I know how much meeting Elena meant to him. He needs this piece of the puzzle to convince his parents he's not screwing up his future.

And I'm the reason that opportunity is ruined.

"Right," I whisper, closing my eyes.

I don't add on the "I'm going to fix this," but I stuff the remaining hope and confidence I have left in myself behind that one word.

Five

Isaac @charminmartin · May 15

Im not saying every one should be reading #DisasterAcademy for CHARM—Black + GAY + smart + funny hero who has a dope relationship w his mom but Im not NOT saying it! Peep DA11 preview in @jorgepradosofficial tweet we stay winning!!! #morequeerBlackheroes

I love sunsets. Even if it's only in my periphery, there's something about knowing it's happening. The pulse of swirling oranges and reds. Heavy creases of light dancing across my knuckles as I read another issue of *Disaster Academy*.

Something is slowly ending but also beginning.

Sunsets are this well-known secret: soon, everything resets.

The curtains on the large window in our living room are still open. Every few pages, I look up to watch the sky transform. In the comic, the background bleeds down the page as Charm tries to rearrange time to bring his father back to life. He was thirteen when his dad, a pawnshop owner, was murdered in a standoff with a thief. His reality-altering abilities had not fully manifested back then.

Thirteen, like I was when Carlos fragmented my reality.

On this page, Charm is so close to changing history. But every time he manipulates time and space, his fingertips inches from his father's reach, he's jolted back to his dorm room. Anguish ripples across his face.

I think about what happened at Secret Planet. I was *so close*. But close is never enough.

"You really think you're cute, don't you?"

Mom's softened giggle floats from upstairs. Our house is old; voices constantly fill all the empty spaces. From my bedroom I could always hear Ignacio—that's who he was when flirting with a girl—on the phone down the hall. Or Carlos and Abuelito arguing over a football game in the kitchen. On Friday nights when Bella came in past curfew because her "study sessions"—code for dates with a varsity basketball player—ran long.

Feet pad down the stairs. The third, seventh, and eighth steps groan with the slightest pressure. No one can sneak around in this house.

"I have to go. Yes, we'll talk later," Mom says hurriedly, ending her call as she walks into the living room.

I lower my comic.

"Hey," she says, almost breathily. She sits on the arm of the cream-colored sofa I'm stretched out across.

"Hi, Mom." I cock my head at her, an eyebrow lifted. "Who was that?"

She's fresh from a shower, her skin looking soft and scrubbed. Her complexion, like mine, is dark enough that the blush doesn't show. But Mom's smiling, dressed in an old UGA T-shirt and sweatpants. Her curls are hidden under a headscarf decorated in sunflowers that belonged to Abuela.

"No one," she replies.

"Bella?"

"No."

"Diego's mom?"

"I said no one," she repeats, her voice clipped in that end-of-discussion tone parents use.

I shrug, flipping the page on my comic.

"You're extra distracted," she says. "I thought you weren't going to spend the summer just reading."

I exhale. "That's kind of my brand."

When she scoots down onto the cushions, I pull my knees to my chest to make room for her.

"Want to talk about it?"

Mom has always had a better relationship with me than with anyone else in our family. Sometimes I think that's why Iggy clings to Carlos. And why when I was younger, my siblings walked around me rather than with me. As if they held this secret grudge.

"It's just stuff," I whisper.

"Does this stuff," Mom says, more nonchalant than condescending, "have anything to do with Legends Con?"

"Kind of."

I haven't told Mom what happened yet. I'm too embarrassed.

Earlier, I searched every ticket resale and auction website available. That dust-sized hope inside me grew into a ball of enthusiasm. Maybe there was one badge available somewhere that I could afford for Diego.

But the prices were even higher than yesterday.

"Not everything is about that convention." Mom folds her legs under herself. "Some stuff can be about college. The future."

You mean my future at a school almost an hour and a half away with no friends. I fight against the urge to say it out loud. It's the other reason I haven't mentioned my Legends Con failure. I know she trusts me, but she's worried too. How will I manage being in a new place without anyone to lean on in a bad situation?

"Nah, it's not that." I clear my throat. "It's other stuff."

She squints at me. "*Boys* stuff?"

I refuse to disclose my current boy situation to Mom. All crush-related things are shared with Bella and Diego only. Right now I can't tell either one of them about Davi. Especially not Diego.

"Yeah, no." I shake my head, verging on a laugh. "It's not boys."

"Because if it is, we can talk about cond—"

"Mom!"

"Protection is important," she says earnestly. "So is mutual consent. You need to know if you or your partner want to do those *things*."

My chest feels tight.

"Not everyone wants to be physically intimate. That's totally okay," she continues. "You can be with someone and not do anything sexual."

"Yes, Mom. I know."

"Or if you need to discuss . . . what you might, uh, enjoy physically with a partner . . ." She's fidgeting and stumbling. "We can discuss how you can approach that."

After a very awkward breath, she adds "Once you've moved out from under this roof, of course" with a smirk.

Holy shit. No. This is a line Mom and I cannot cross. We're close, but I don't want to be *that* close.

Thanks to Coach Saleem's sex education course sophomore year, I generally understand the way condoms work. There was even a *brief* discussion about sex outside the usual heteronormative dialogue. The internet has been quite "helpful" in discovering the other imperative topics. Another concept porn has helped me discover: I don't have to feel pressured to assume any particular sexual role. I'm still learning my body. Slowly figuring what might interest me. Subscribing to the idea that I have to solely inhabit one role—or like just one thing—is nowhere in my plans.

But that's not a discussion for Mom and me.

Thing is, Carlos and I never got around to The Talk.

Mom sat me down for it. It wasn't as bad as I thought, especially since we discussed what might come after liking someone or the validity of not finding anyone sexually attractive. I know not every kid at school has adults in their lives who aren't too embarrassed or uninformed to talk about sex like Diego does. They're forced to learn everything from locker rooms and Netflix and Twitter.

"It's not about boys," I say, unable to meet her gaze.

"Then what is it?"

My index finger traces the bold font on the *Disaster Academy* cover. This is something I can't explain to her. Not that I've tried. I don't know if she'd understand what it's like to not see yourself in the world, even in a comic book. To know you're guaranteed the same thing everyone else gets.

I mean, on some levels, maybe Mom does get it. There aren't a ton of non-stereotypical portrayals of Black women portrayed in books or media. If there are, it's extremely limited, especially when it comes to dark-skinned Black women.

"I just . . . really want this summer to be memorable."

I leave off four very important words: for me and Diego.

Honestly, during my badge search, a part of me hoped I'd find two. A second chance for me even though I don't deserve one. I still want to meet Peter and Jorge.

And now a piece of me wants my Charm-Reverb happy ending to be with a boy like Davi.

"Before you, I wanted things too," Mom says. "Working in insurance was so boring and repetitive." She looks off into the sunset. "So I went back to school. In the middle of getting my Master's out comes this bowling ball named Isaac."

I laugh.

"I was terrified. How the hell was I going to finish my degree *and* take care of an infant? Bella was a four-year-old terror. Iggy was starting kindergarten. Your dad—"

"Carlos."

"We tried. Abuelito helped." Another sigh breaches her lips. "This one thing I wanted for myself . . . it felt impossible."

I nod, my thumb sticking to the comic book page it's bookmarking.

"Not a single thing went as planned, but that didn't matter." She grins at me. "I did it."

I nudge her with my foot, grinning back. "Proud of you."

There's a shine in Mom's eyes. "Come on." She pats my knee, then stands. "We need a nonthinking moment. There's only one place for that."

Without asking, I know exactly what she means. The sudden burst of relief that saturates my bloodstream carries me to the kitchen with her.

According to legend, Mom was a culinary-school-worthy cook before she met Carlos. All things Southern cuisine was her specialty. Her baked mac and cheese is my favorite. It's right above her from-scratch sweet potato pie. But *after* marrying Carlos, she became godlike in the kitchen. That, on the authority of Abuelito, is thanks to him appointing her as his sous-chef for all family meal preparations. Mom does not dispute this claim.

She has made it a high priority to pass this family gift down to me.

Once, she explained, "If you don't know how to cook as an adult, you'll die. As your mother, I cannot carry that guilt on my shoulders."

I've theorized Mom loves teaching me to cook because Bella hates it and Mom's one attempt at schooling Iggy to bake ended tragically. When the recipe said, "Mix by hand," he took it literally. Iggy shoved his big paw into the bowl and began mashing the ingredients together.

Thankfully, I'm not a clone of Iggy's ineptitude.

Cemita poblana is one of the first dishes my grandpa taught Mom. It's this delicious sandwich of fried cutlets, a pile of queso fresco, onions, and jalapeños on a cemita, a roll covered in sesame seeds. We always spread avocado on the bottom bun. Sometimes, Mom marinates the beef or chicken in a special chile sauce overnight for an extra bite of spice.

I love the way Mom hums old tunes while she slices the avocado and I fry the meat. The *pop-sizzle-pop* of the oil underscores her voice. I listen closely.

Sade, her favorite.

She calls out instructions without looking at me:

"Too much oil."

"Don't turn it so soon. Let it cook."

"I can't smell the seasoning. Did you use enough pepper? Flavor, baby, flavor!"

"Don't burn down the kitchen. I can't convince Abuelito to remodel it again."

She has peak mom instincts.

To my left, our new fridge hums as it makes ice. This house used to belong to my grandparents. It was built sometime in the early '80s, at the height of gentrification in Atlanta. It's strange how, now that Mom and Carlos are divorced, Abuelito insists she keep the house instead of selling it. Even though Mom, by law, isn't a Martin anymore.

Not all families are created by blood. Some families are made through love and companionship.

Once we're done cooking, Mom pours us glasses of lemonade while I build our sandwiches. She says, "One day, these gifts I've given you are going to make someone very happy."

I roll my eyes. "Yeah. Me."

"Stop being selfish. Having amazing skills in the

kitchen is one way to keep a partner around."

Really? Because it didn't seem to work for you. I don't say it. I'm worried I might one day. Like, my Carlos resentment will reach full boil and I'll say something ugly to Mom or Abuelito.

"I'll never use these gifts for that."

Mom purses her lips. "Oh?"

"Why do people spend their entire relationships trying to impress the other person?" I shrug. "If they love you, flaws and all, then things like this should be a bonus. Not a prerequisite."

"Think so, wiseass?" Mom pokes my cheek. "How did you get so smart about love?"

"Comic books," I say with an almost believable grin. "And watching *The Princess Bride* five billion times."

With the careful precision of an architect, I layer jalapeños over the cheese. Mom smacks my hand. "Not too many. You know what spicy stuff does to your digestive system."

I do. It's another thing Mom and I don't need to discuss out loud.

An accomplished subject changer, Mom says, "Your movie rewatch with Abuelito is soon, right?"

"Yes."

It's a biannual tradition. We watch *The Princess Bride* on the first day of summer and again around Christmas. Abuelito cooks chicken tacos and Mexican-style corn. We camp out in my bedroom, shoulder to shoulder, eating and drinking Jarritos I pick up from the nearby corner store. Abuelito recites half the dialogue while I quietly swoon over all the kissing parts.

This year Pride falls on the official start of summer. Legends Con is the day after.

"I got news today that they need me in New York that weekend," Mom says. She takes a small bite of her sandwich. "I'm helping to launch some new clients."

"Oh." I blink a few times. "Is Abuelito coming to stay?"

Sometimes Mom's job requires her to travel. She's been all over the United States for things. Since Iggy and Bella moved out, Abuelito has always come to stay with me during her trips.

"Nope."

"Ugh, do I have to go stay at his house?" I make a face when my voice cracks. "I'm eighteen! I—"

"Can take care of the house by yourself?" Mom finishes.

I lick a blob of avocado off the corner of my mouth, nodding.

"I know," she whispers. "I'm leaving you in charge, Isaac Solo."

I snort at the Star Wars reference even though it's not that funny.

"I think you can handle it." The harsh angle of Mom's left eyebrow signals there's more. "I doubt you'll be throwing any parties—"

I gasp, half annoyed. "I could!"

"Who would you invite? Diego?"

The heat beneath my cheeks nearly melts my face off.

I know she's unaware that her words cut sharper than one of those handcrafted swords forged by Hattori Hanzō in *Kill Bill*. My own mother believes I'm incapable of being one of those reckless, formulaic teens from the movies.

That's me: Isaac Martin, socially awkward enough to trust with the house for a weekend.

Thanks for cosigning, Mom.

Six

Am I supposed to be shocked? I thought it was obvious to everyone you liked him. Everyone except *him* of course.

—Boomstar, *Disaster Academy* Issue #8

Wednesday night is a great night for Twisted Burger.

Correction: *Any night* is a good night for Twisted Burger.

It's neon-light-filled interior perpetually smells of grease and heaven. Every burger is a double patty shoved between soft buns, drooling with sauces, smoky cheese, and wilting lettuce. The fries are consistently hot and golden. But the nuclear core that makes Twisted Burger an epic life choice is the Mondo Shakes—extra thick milkshakes in a variety of flavors, from chocolate brownie to dulce de leche. If you don't get a brain freeze or stomachache from it, it's not a Mondo Shake.

Also, the menu has a prime selection of vegetarian options, which makes this a Camila Santoyo–approved dining establishment.

She's not here. Tonight's her monthly meet-cute with Oscar. Diego thinks it's kind of weird that his parents still have a Date Night. They "randomly" meet up at various locations around Atlanta, acting out scenarios: a blind date, a chance encounter at a coffee shop, a missing puppy run-in in front of Dairy Queen. Then they have dinner before strolling hand in hand through their neighborhood.

To be honest, the Santoyos are relationship goals.

"Don't forget the Lava Chocolate Mondo Shake for Ollie," Diego shouts over Twisted Burger's one flaw—the loud, awful music. It's a relentless rotation of one-hit pop wonders or hip-hop-lite jams. "And extra jalapeños!"

"Duh." If there is a person that lives for spicy foods and an uncooperative digestive system, it's Diego. "And no cheese on your burger."

He has a strict belief that cheese is not meant for burgers.

"You're strange," I tell him with a small grin.

"Says the dude who dips his fries in his Mondo Shake."

He's got me there. Then again, isn't that what having a best friend is about? Accepting each other's indecencies when it comes to dietary selections?

I spy Ollie in the arcade corner while we stand in line waiting to order. On Date Night, Diego babysits. He doesn't seem to mind tonight. Being away from Camila's disappointment and the weight of his decisions must be a relief. He hasn't told them he's not going Legends Con yet. No doubt he's avoiding the *I told you so* he'll get from his parents for putting so much of his plan into meeting Elena.

Ollie's short for a twelve-year-old. He stands on his tiptoes with his tongue out, clicking the plastic buttons on the old *Ms. Pac-Man* arcade machine as he tries mercilessly to flee the pastel-colored ghosts.

"Rookie," Diego comments. "I was the shit at his age."

"No," I say, nudging his ribs. "You *were* shit." Diego still owes me a month's allowance for all the money he borrowed trying to beat the vintage *Street Fighter II* game they used to have in that same corner. It was fun watching him, though. That identical earnest energy he has now, only in the comfort of his bedroom. "You got your ass handed to you by Sagat at his age."

"I'm gonna go help him," says Diego.

I turn back to the slow-moving order line. At the front, an elderly woman, sparkly pink glasses hanging off the tip of her nose, inspects the menu. Behind the register, a white boy experiencing a major acne breakout texts on his phone, sighing.

In front of me are two girls who can't be older than fourteen. Fifteen in the right lighting, which is not Twisted Burger's hip-but-efficient standardized commercial lighting. They are wearing twin ponytails and tie-dyed T-shirts and yellow flip-flops.

"If I get the Special Gravy with my fries—"

"Becca, there's no *if* when it comes to Special Gravy."

The first girl, Becca, has auburn hair and a smirk that could kill kittens. The other has large blue eyes like one of those demon-possessed dolls in horror movies.

"But I'm going to see Troy later, Casey. What if we . . . hook up?"

"Ohmygod, Becca." Casey groans. "Just say 'sex.'"

Becca's cheeks, already sunburned, glow as bright as Twisted Burger's neon red sign. "I don't want gravy breath!"

"Then come prepared." Like a magician, Casey materializes a toothbrush from a small pink fanny pack.

"You carry a toothbrush?"

"I carry an entire just-in-case emergency kit," Casey says. She begins unloading item after item. The depths of that bag are limitless.

"Ohmygod." Becca's skin is almost purple with embarrassment. "How many brands of condoms do you have?"

"Not enough."

I bury my face into the crook of my elbow, coughing to mute my laughter. I don't know. It's weird to overhear people talking about sex. Maybe because Diego and I don't really discuss it. We talk around it quite a bit.

He knows about my solo activities after reading fanfics.

I'm quite informed about him forgetting to lock his door before "studying anatomy" on his phone when he was uncertain about his own sexuality.

But our conversations don't extend outside the walls of our bedrooms.

Is it abnormal to be an eighteen-year-old gay boy and not have sex as a twenty-four-seven priority?

"Martin?"

I don't realize that someone's talking to me until I hear it again: "Yo, Martin."

I pivot around, mouth open, eyes wide.

It's Davi. His hair is damp and slicked back, his skin glowing with drying sweat. He's wearing a soft-looking scarlet and gold East Middleton High T-shirt and black basketball shorts.

"Didn't mean to scare you, Martin."

I never got why athletes refer to everyone by their last name. Even the complete non-jocks. As if we're all teammates playing on this imaginary squad.

"Isaac," I mumble, then wince. "Everyone used to call me Mini-Martin because of my older brother. I hated it."

"Sorry." He rocks back and forth on his heels. "It's a habit after being on the ice."

"It's okay."

"No, it's not, Isaac." He smiles warmly. But it's the way he says my name. Sincere. Joyful. As if he likes the way it feels in his mouth.

That's the thing about these crushes—I'm used to imagining kissing whichever boy I like. From Kevin in elementary school to Jase in sixth-grade gym class to Brent in geography and Davi all throughout high school. It never fails. I catch myself studying their hands, wondering what our fingers are going to look like interlocked. *What will our first date be like? How will I introduce them to Abuelito?*

Will I be able to coax that smile from their lips the same way Charm does from Reverb's?

Imagining these things is easy. That version of Isaac is bold. He doesn't stumble on his words. His heartbeat isn't erratic because he can't carry a conversation. He makes eye contact.

Imaginary Isaac is a boss.

But that's not who I am.

I'm the Isaac who stares at Davi's lips—pinkish, a little chapped—without a follow-up to what he said last.

"Anyway." He laughs awkwardly. "My friends would murder me if they knew I was here."

"Why?"

"The Redhawks' strength and conditioning meal plan for training camp doesn't include Twisted Burger." Davi's headed to Miami University in Ohio in the fall. East Middleton High's administration made such a huge deal about it when he signed his National Letter of Intent, you'd have thought he just inked a pro contract. "My friends say I'm lucky so I shouldn't blow my chances."

I don't know how one burger and a Mondo Shake will destroy any opportunities coming his way.

"I guess I'm kind of lucky." He shrugs. "Guys playing hockey in Georgia don't really get noticed. Scouts certainly aren't checking the ice for a Brazilian American pardao boy who doesn't come from a rich, influential family."

"But they *chose* you. That's not luck," I say, smiling. I'm gently slipping into that imaginary, bold Isaac who talks to Davi. "Screw 'em. Get a burger."

He leans toward me. The scent of sweat and minty body spray waft off his skin. "I think I'll get two."

"Two sounds good," I say, my voice rising sharply.

We stare at each other for a few seconds. It's enough time for me to identify at least one shade of brown in his eyes—honey. A galaxy of what-ifs exists in those eyes.

I'm caught on one thought: this moment is like Charm and Reverb squeezed into that air vent, so close to—

"Ollie changed his mind. He wants the Cookie-licious Mondo Shake."

Out of nowhere, Diego swings an arm around my neck. "I convinced him not to go megasize. He can't even put away half of a regular shake."

Davi retreats a few steps, smiling clumsily. My eyes shift to Diego, who's still rambling. Oblivious is his default state. In a room full of people, Diego could talk to me for hours as if no one else was there. Most days, I like that. When you're one of three children, it's hard to get that kind of attention. Just . . . not with Davi here.

I clear my throat, raising my eyebrows in Davi's direction until Diego notices.

"Oh." He blinks a few times. "'Sup, Davi."

Davi does that little what's-up head nod. "Santoyo."

"Am I interrupting?" Diego trades looks between us. "I can order if you . . . ?"

"No, it's cool." Davi shrugs. "We were just shooting the shit."

"Catching up," I confirm.

Davi's expression brightens. "You know how it is. Can't always keep up with everyone between all the classes and homework and stuff."

"Tell me about it." Diego laughs.

I'm hot and flustered, speechless. Watching Diego and Davi talk about senior year is strange. Alternate-universe weird. As if all three of us could've been friends at any point in those four years. We could've hung out on the weekends.

"Doing anything cool for the summer?" Diego asks Davi.

"He's going to Pride," I say before Davi can respond, excitement taking my voice even higher. Davi's eyebrows shoot up and I want the words back. "I mean . . ."

"Yeah?" Diego gives me a quick look.

I smile stiffly.

But Davi grins. "It's my coming out thing since I technically didn't have one. The guys on the team and my family know, though."

"He's bi," I tell Diego. But I don't know why. It's like

my brain's trying to make this happen—a Davi and Diego friendship—and this is the one common thread that will solidify it: them both being bisexual.

Except I hate it when people assume me and another gay person are destined to be instant friends because of that connection. As if successful friendships are born out of one commonality.

"That's . . . cool." Diego chews his lower lip.

"It is," I say softly, fighting a frown.

"Sorry. Are you two," Davi's index finger wiggles back and forth between us, "a *thing*?"

The weight behind his stare awakens this awareness inside me. Diego's arm is around my shoulders. My own arm is curled around his waist. His fingers are knotted in my hair.

Heat rushes my face. "What?"

"It makes sense." He shrugs. "Best friends usually end up together. Or at least hook up."

Words fail to reach my mouth. Even if they could, they'd probably get trapped in my throat. My lungs squeeze painfully around nothing.

Diego and me?

DIEGO SANTOYO AND ME?

Objectively, I can fully admit Diego is handsome. When he laughs, his eyes get scrunchy. His curly hair requires almost as little maintenance as mine. And he's funny in that not-trying-too-hard way.

He's Boyfriend Material, I'll give him that. Just not for me.

"No, no, no." I shake my head vigorously.

Diego's eyes catch mine. Beyond his long, dark lashes is a dim spark. A revelation. He comprehends that the reason I'm point five seconds from hyperventilating is because I'm in full-blown Crush Syndrome mode.

"Nah, we're not a *thing*," he says emphatically, turning to Davi. "Strictly platonic. I don't want *anything* to do with his junk."

My head snaps in his direction. "Wait, did you just friend zone me?"

"When did I ever un–friend zone you?"

Davi chuckles, hands up, palms out. "Cool, cool. You're just friends." He drops a hand on my shoulder, squeezing. "Well I better order, but we should hang out more, Isaac."

I cough. "That'd be sweet."

Then Davi's hand is gone. He is, too, stepping around Diego and me to get to the front counter. I shift away from the line. I can't think about food right now. I can't think about *breathing* right now.

Diego follows me to the *Ms. Pac-Man* corner. "Davi Lucas, huh?" His mouth slides sideways. Not a grin or a frown. Somewhere in the middle. Then, he jabs my shoulder. "That's bold, new territory. Didn't think you had it in you."

I can't tell if he's teasing or disappointed that I didn't

tell him about Davi. We don't keep secrets from each other. Not of the Crush Syndrome variety anyway. He's known about all six previous crushes—one girl in fourth grade and every boy since I came out. I know about his one major crush—the García twins, Lola and Pietro—sophomore year.

"So . . ." Diego's eyes narrow. "He's going to Pride."

I nod, twisting the ends of my curls. It's a nerves thing.

Why is it so hard to admit to Diego that I want to see Davi at Pride? Or that I want Davi to *want* to hang with me at Pride?

"And you like him?" His eyebrows scoot up his forehead.

"It's kind of—"

"Crush Syndrome," Diego says before I finish. I don't know how to *lie* to Diego. Omission is one thing, but lying tastes sour and forbidden when it comes to our friendship. He rolls his eyes, but there's a small smile on his lips. I think he gets it.

"Seriously, we're just reconnecting," I say, my throat dry.

Before Diego can interrogate me more, Ollie stomps up to us, fitting himself between our bodies. I've never been happier to see an agitated Santoyo before. His arms are folded, his pursed lips rivaling twelve-year-old Diego in the prime of his I-hate-being-an-older-brother phase.

Ollie glares at us. Mostly me. Diego's busy texting.

He pockets his phone, then says, "I think we all need a megasized Mondo Shake and extra jalapeños on our burgers." He scrubs a hand over Ollie's hair, then flashes a credit card with Oscar Santoyo's name on it. "I'm buying."

We walk to the now customerless counter. Davi's long gone. It's just us—Diego and Ollie, then me a few steps behind them.

I keep my eyes straight ahead, avoiding the urge to see if Davi's still somewhere in the corners of Twisted Burger. What kind of friend am I, thinking about a crush while I'm out with my best friend? The friend who's summer I royally screwed up. The friend who still hasn't given me shit about that. The friend I'll be leaving behind in August.

Over his shoulder, Diego gives me this look. He's smiling, but his eyes aren't holding it. Still, he reaches back. His fingers circle my wrist and tug me forward. I go willingly.

Because Diego's a Level Two Hundred Best Friend and no one turns down a Mondo Shake.

Seven

GEEKS NATION FORUM

Re: CHARMVERB FANS ONLY

ACharmingReverb: WHY DO I CRY EVERY TIME I READ DA#6? WHY AM I LIKE THIS??? The connection between charm and reverb jumps off the pages fam! When their foreheads touch . . . kermitthefrogfainting.gif

DA12345: BRO. Enough. We get it. Ur obsessed. Issue 7 was better.

ACharmingReverb: That one barely had c & r in it!

DA12345: exactly!

ACharmingReverb: HATER

Disaster Academy Issue #6.

The single greatest comic book cover ever.

Superior to *Batman: The Killing Joke*. Above *Spider-Man (1990) #1*. The artwork exists on universal levels equal to the cover of *Superman #75* where Superman's tattered cape flaps in the wind with the caption: THE DEATH OF SUPERMAN.

Nerds Anonymous, a prestigious and well-respected online comics blog, lists it as their number one cover of all time.

Number one *LGBTQ* comic book cover. A minor detail. No, it's an annoying detail. I hate how anything that has queer content is immediately dismissed from the regular lists and relegated to its own secondary division. As if—as a community—we're nothing more than a subcategory of normal. As if "normal" even exists.

Anyway, the cover—and everything inside—is iconic. It's the only one to feature solely Charm and Reverb. None of the other students at Webster Academy for the Different appear on it. No villains either.

Charm and Reverb stand back-to-back in their school uniforms, heads tilted skyward, surrounded by an infinite sea of black space and glittering white stars. Reverb is scowling, but Charm wears this almost-smile as if he wouldn't want to be anywhere else with anyone else.

In Issue #6, Charm loses control of his powers, transporting himself and Reverb from their dorm room to a noiseless, empty cocoon of shadows. He can't teleport them back. He tries and tries. Reverb's own ability to absorb nearby sounds and convert them into intense vibrations through his hands is useless. Ten pages in, tears are streaming down Charm's face. It's the first time I saw a young Black boy cry in a comic without it involving violence or death.

Then Reverb grabs his hands. He pulls Charm close. It's this one, singular moment where their foreheads touch—Charm's eyes squeezed shut, Reverb's chestnut-brown eyes wide and promising. He whispers five words into the hollowness of space: "I believe in you."

As straight up corny as it is, I always think it's like when Westley says "As you wish" in *The Princess Bride*.

For me, those five words made Reverb more than a friend or teammate.

Their hands didn't unclasp until the last page, even after Charm transported them back to Webster Academy.

On my bedroom wall, there's a framed, poster-sized version of Issue #6. It's signed in gold sharpie by Jorge Prados. A seventeenth birthday gift from Iggy.

I still don't know how he got it. But I love it. I also hate that it's a reminder that Iggy is and will always be the superior brother. I'll never be able to top that gift. I'll never be the hero everyone sees him as.

As if my thoughts conjured him, I feel a disturbance in the Force. Noises from the kitchen wake me from my daydreams. An old enemy has returned.

"Ma!" Iggy shouts. "It's summer. Why is there no peach cobbler?"

"Why are you invading my fridge like you still live here?"

"I do. My stuff's upstairs in my room."

"Iggy, your things were donated to charity. It made a lovely tax deduction. Your old bedroom is a yoga studio now."

Mom's giggles echo into the living room where I stand, rubbing sleepiness from my eyes with the sleeve of a snug UGA hoodie. She's teasing about Iggy's old room. Yes, there are a few yoga mats and scented candles in there now. But his stuff remains untouched.

It's a chilly morning. Last night, the sky split open for a storm that lasted for hours. A thin blanket of cold still lingers in our house. I try to tug the hoodie's cuffs over my knuckles, but my wide shoulders pull the sleeves tightly against my arms. It used to belong to Mom before I hijacked it.

It's the one she wore in late fall while walking to classes on UGA's campus. I've seen dozens of vintage photos of her, scanned and recently uploaded to her Facebook page. Mom studying in a corner at Carnegie Library. Dancing at football games. Holding a plastic cup high with her friends at a party.

She was a different person then.

No Carlos. No broken heart. Loud as ever, but with a lighter energy.

Part of me hopes that like that version of Lilah Johnson, I'll be okay by myself too. I'll find my footing in an unknown place.

Mom's at the espresso machine humming Sade. Her curls are hidden beneath a teal scarf today. She's dressed in robe-and-yoga-pants chic. Whenever Iggy visits, she's always extra happy.

Meanwhile, I'm between wanting to vomit and throw an orange at his head.

Physically, Iggy isn't much like me. He has a square face

with dark eyes, his features sharp as if cut from stone. His skin tone is an almost gold hue. Like all Martins, he's tall but doesn't have the curls Bella and I have. Instead, he has a drop fade haircut with perfectly kept waves on top.

He shuffles around Mom with a small pink Tupperware in his hands.

"Hands off," I say, voice still thick with sleep.

Iggy pops the top off to sniff the contents. The last slice of cheesecake Mom baked two days ago with the new countertop convection oven she's testing is inside that container.

"Don't you have your own food at your own apartment?" I scowl at Iggy.

Again, he ignores me.

"Morning, Isaac," Mom singsongs.

Before I can grumble my customary "Morning," Iggy says, "Why're you sleeping in? It's eight a.m. Most adults are halfway through their workday by now." He sips black coffee from an old SUPER DAD mug Mom got for Carlos years ago. "What kind of future college freshman doesn't have a part-time summer job?"

"Me," I deadpan, lazily walking to Mom's side. She rubs a hand over the top of my sleep-wrecked hair.

"You'll need money when you're at school," Iggy continues.

"Is that why you're here?" I retort. "To borrow money from Mom?"

He scoffs. "I'm quite financially stable." After another gulp of coffee, he adds, "I live downtown. It's not cheap." Because he's the kind of guy who likes to remind you how successful he is, how much his rent costs, who his girlfriend is.

"Thanks for the update," I say flatly.

"Is this your plan for the summer? Sleep in?" Iggy narrows his eyes. "Be a total asshat?"

"Congrats, you're hilarious. You can leave now, Ignacio."

I smirk triumphantly when the wrinkles in his forehead deepen.

"Boys," Mom says in that warning voice we've heard since childhood.

"I have plans," I say, sagging against the counter behind me.

"Like what?"

None I'm sharing with you.

It's not that I can't tell Iggy about things like Pride or Davi Lucas. That I desperately need to make up my failure to Diego. It's just that we've never had that kind of relationship. Maybe it's the five-year gap between us? Or that he's a pathological dick.

"I'm doing stuff," I finally say.

"Translation: bumming around Secret Planet for the next two-and-a-half months."

"No." *Yes.*

Iggy shakes his head. "You should visit Dad—"

"Carlos," I cut him off.

Iggy has this talent for speaking to me while simultaneously pretending I'm invisible. "All that effort to spend time with you and you treat him like crap."

"How am I supposed to treat the man who—"

I stop myself. All this talk about Carlos frustrates me. I hate how the memories—before and after his poor life choices—float in my stomach like that film of scum that gathers on the surface of pool water when it's left uncleaned.

"Why don't you answer his calls?" asks Iggy.

"Why don't you mind your own damn business?"

"Isaac," Mom says, her voice clipped. "Enough. You, too, Iggy."

A thick silence falls on the kitchen. The espresso machine drones and gurgles. The fridge hums. Iggy's phone pings with texts. A constant *Why don't you answer?* loops through my brain.

Mom refills Iggy's mug. She smiles softly at him, then at me. As if she's saying *I love you both equally* and *This is my fault.*

Carlos's existence isn't her fault.

I wish she'd stop thinking otherwise.

"Morning!"

Diego strolls into the kitchen, half smiley, half zombie-like. He's probably been up all night playing *Beyond the Valley of Stars*. A red-and-white striped shirt one size too big and loose basketball shorts devour his slight frame. He twirls a set of keys on his index finger, indicating he swiped his mom's Jeep to get here. His parents have tried multiple times to bribe him with his own car in exchange for attending college in the fall, but not even a new ride could persuade Diego Santoyo to abandon his gamer dreams.

"Morning, Diego," says Mom as he hugs her.

"Buenos días," Iggy says, fist-bumping Diego, before slipping into a fast-paced conversation in Spanish I struggle to keep up with.

Another annoying Iggy fact: He loves to flaunt his fluency in Spanish with Diego in front of me. Because he's great at it, and I'm not.

I can comprehend some of what people say. From being around family and the Santoyos, I know basic phrases. I can reply here and there to simple questions. Of course, Diego taught me swear words too. But I still struggle with verb tenses, gendered words, accents.

I'm not confident when I speak it.

It's not effortless for me like it is for my siblings.

Technically, I'm the reason they even learned the language. They're only a year apart in age. But I'm four years younger than my sister. When I was born, they temporarily moved in with Abuelito so Mom and Carlos could readjust to life as parents of an infant again. Carlos worked full-time while Mom struggled to balance school and all the attention I required.

Abuelito insisted on Iggy and Bella using Spanish for everything: conversations, reading, ordering McDonald's after school. On Sundays, they had dinner with his church friends, who all spoke it too. They were submerged in our culture while I cried, napped, and spit up on Mom.

Carlos and Abuelito didn't purposely skip over those same experiences for me. It just happened. By the time I was old enough to understand, Abuelito was older too. It was easier for him to tuck into my side for *The Princess Bride* than it was to teach me how to conjugate a verb. Carlos tried a few times, but he lacks Abuelito's patience.

Sometimes I wonder if I'm more of a Johnson than a Martin. More of my mom than Carlos. If this one thing I lack defines whether I'm enough of one identity to claim it as my own.

"Okay," Diego says, turning to me with a grin. "¿No más, Isaac?"

He does this—includes me in conversations when Iggy tries to leave me out. It's not a sympathy maneuver. Though sometimes it looks that way. He's the only one who knows how I feel about never learning the language the way my siblings did. And he never corrects me in a mocking or terse way, like Carlos did when he tried teaching me.

It's Diego's way of making me feel even more connected to who I am.

"No más," I agree, smiling nervously.

But Diego's eyes brighten. He pivots back to Iggy. "We have plans."

"With this one?" Iggy jerks a thumb in my direction.

When Mom's not watching, I flip him off. Iggy sticks out his tongue. Devolving into adolescent form is a Martin specialty.

"Let's go upstairs." Diego tugs on the sleeve of my hoodie. On the way out of the kitchen, I swipe the cheesecake from Iggy, along with two forks.

There are house rules. The first one: Any substance infused with a high dosage of sugar belongs to Isaac. No exceptions.

Eight

"I can change the literal fabric of reality. But all I
want is to do normal teen stuff. Drink iced coffee.
Go to a concert. Shoot hoops. Attend Pride. I'm
weird, right?"

"Yeah. But I'd still do all those things with you."

—Charm and Reverb, *Disaster Academy* Issue #5

The Diego Santoyo definition of "plans" is being lazy in
my bedroom with no intention of talking about Big Issues.

There's no way I'll complain about that.

My room's quite different from Diego's. It's carefully
organized. The bed's next to the window so I can catch
that harsh morning glow in case I ignore my alarm and
oversleep. Below the autographed poster Iggy got me is
a clean desk with only a MacBook, some pens, wireless
earbuds, and an orderly stack of my favorite comic books,
fifty percent of which are *Disaster Academy*. No clothes on
the floor. My shoes are lined up by the closet door.

The only real clutter is in the corners: boxes and trans-
parent storage bins, some half packed with clothes, others
with graphic novels.

Otherwise, it's the perfect chill space, made even better

by one of those wall plug-ins Bella bought me. I love the scent of citrus. It erases the obnoxious cocoa butter aroma of Iggy's hair product.

I wish getting him out of my head were that easy.

From my spot on the floor, I sigh while staring at one of the unfinished boxes. "My dorm will never smell like this."

Stretched out on the bed, Diego asks, "Like what, my feet?"

I'm greeted by five wiggling toes when I rotate my head. "Hell no!"

He routinely wears shoes with no socks, a bold choice considering he has exceptionally sweaty feet.

I twist in his direction. He's staring at my ceiling, morning sunlight brushed against his face like glittered paint. His profile is soft, even his triangular jaw. I pull up my phone's camera app while he hums Drake's "Hold On, We're Going Home." It takes a few attempts, but I get a respectable snapshot.

Diego, Sun God Among Mortals.

I save the photo because I'll need the memory. When summer ends, I won't wake up to his smelly feet or soft profile in the sunlight. Four months ago, that wasn't the plan.

Diego got into UGA before I did. Like I said, he's a lazy genius. His grade point average guaranteed him an automatic ride. But in January, the doubts started for him. He'd make a couple of halfhearted what-if, instead-of comments whenever the topic of college came up. I'd ignore them, laughing, because that's Diego—easygoing, never too serious.

By early March, just as I got accepted into UGA, Diego decided he wanted to chase a different goal—one that didn't include Athens anymore. I remember sitting on this floor with him, the thrill of the welcome letter scrunched in my right hand fading as Diego said he wasn't going with me.

I'm taking a gap year, he whispered, sniffling.

He never cries.

It's okay, I whispered over and over to him.

It's the only lie I've ever told Diego.

"Mom keeps adding to the pile." I wave a hand at the boxes and storage containers.

"How many times have you been to Target in the past month?"

"Five," I reply dryly. Our mothers share a DEFCON level obsession with Target. For them, back-to-school shopping is a national holiday.

"That's a lot of . . . uh, boxes," comments Diego. He barely meets my gaze, focused on the packing tape and cardboard.

"Bed sheets. Bath towels. A mattress pad." I list every item on a finger. Mom has already acquired *four* different pairs of shower shoes for me. I lost count of how many new packs of boxers she's purchased. Also, Mom buying me underwear? Not cool anymore.

"Can you fit all of that in your dorm?"

I shrug. "She says I can." Then, with a wry smile, I say, "I could probably fit some other stuff, like—"

But I stop myself before I can add *You. Please come with me.*

I'm not going to guilt trip my best friend into abandoning his dreams to keep me company in Athens.

"She's ready to get rid of you," Diego whispers. It's supposed to be a joke, but there's nothing humorous in his tone.

Mom hasn't shed one tear while packing. No frowns or worry lines. It's as if she's unbothered by the fact that she'll be *alone* alone in this house.

There's this part of me that wonders if maybe she's excited about me going to college. Not in that I'm-so-proud way. More like she's ready to have some space.

With school being done, I'm always at home. Occasionally I'm with Diego or at Secret Planet. Iggy and Bella were never like that. They had their social groups or relationships. They've been independent since forever.

I stare at the boxes, my vision clouding.

Maybe Mom's ready to have back what she had before Carlos?

Iggy didn't move back in with us once he graduated college. Bella met Chris while at school in Savannah, and now they're living together, married, having a baby. I'm the last one.

Am I the thing holding her back?

You're not supposed to think that about your parents, right? Like you're the wall keeping them from their future.

Somewhere in my head, I imagined Diego and I would share an apartment post-UGA. Get a dog. Find jobs. Read comics and play video games.

Just be us.

Now it feels like the future I envision for us is being dictated by what we do in the upcoming days, weeks, the next two months.

The thing about summers is they start slow and glorious. Everything's gold and blue in the day, heady and warm at night. The days stretch for what seems like weeks. You can't walk five feet without smelling the chlorine from a community pool or something cooking on a grill or freshly cut grass. There's an unnamable magic everywhere.

By mid-July, though, it feels like a fireball racing downhill. All the magic is replaced by a constant countdown: "what was" rather than "what could be."

August is just a graveyard of the hope early summer gave.

Diego exhales softly. His breath is so close to my temple, I can smell the orange juice he had during breakfast.

"How are . . ." I hesitate. "How's the game planning going?"

Asking that question was much easier over a year ago. We'd sit in the back of SAT Prep pretending to take notes while Diego mapped out the virtual worlds he wanted to build on a refurbished iPad. Even though Diego wants to work in the story development side of gaming, he'd whisper about the new coding tricks he learned from some fourteen-year-old Black girl's YouTube channel. I'd smile because every game idea featured a playable character based on me: Isaac the mage, the vigilante, the student killing zombies with a broadsword.

"Cool, I guess," he says.

"Nothing new?"

He shrugs. "Not really."

"Luis Diego Santoyo," I say, thudding the back of my head against the mattress so he can see my serious expression. I can tell he's holding something in.

Pink blush spreads outward from his cheeks. Luis is his given name. Growing up, he complained that all his cousins were named Luis. So he started going by his middle name.

"Is this about . . ."

Shame prevents me from finishing. Guilt dries my

throat. It's been a morning of avoiding all the Big Issues, but here I am, wondering if my best friend truly hates me for wrecking his life.

"About?"

"You know." I still can't say it out loud.

I'm a coward.

Diego slides off the bed. He grabs my MacBook from the desk. It's covered in stickers of Mexican flags, unmasked *Into the Spider-Verse* Miles Morales, and Charmverb fan art. Diego fits himself next to me on the floor. He grins as I pop the Tupperware top. I use the side of one of the forks to cut the cheesecake into pieces. When the laptop's screen comes to life, Diego taps in my password.

Zero secrets between us.

Except the Davi thing . . .

"Can I be honest?" he asks.

I nod, feeding him a cheesecake chunk with extra graham cracker crust, his favorite part.

"Legends Con probably meant more to you than me."

I almost drop the fork.

"I mean. I wanted to go with you. Obvi," he quickly corrects. "But even if I met Elena, there's no guarantee I would've had the opportunity to make an impression."

"What do you mean?"

"Cons are loud and big. There are so many damn people!" He sighs loudly. "Do you know how many gamers want to meet her?"

Elena Sánchez is one of the youngest, most talked about game creators. She's also pretty much a ghost. Rarely makes public appearances. Doesn't even run her own social media.

Diego shakes his head. "I wouldn't have had a real chance to talk to her. It'd be over in a second. Then I'd be forgotten. *Diego who?*"

I chuckle. How could anyone in this world forget Diego Santoyo?

He logs on to Google Docs. I feed him more cheesecake as he explains his latest story idea. He goes on and on, but I don't really hear him. I'm stuck on the excitement etched into his face. The way his eyes light up, his smile never ending.

"This." He taps the screen. "I couldn't tell her all of this at the con."

He's right.

I had only planned to ask Peter and Jorge one question while they autographed my armful of *Disaster Academy* merchandise. But Diego . . . he has a whole presentation. There are docs for characters, storylines, all the quests and arcs for his game. He was going to ask Elena for a recommendation letter for an internship at one of his top three indie game publishing companies, Stage One Digital, in Atlanta. They only accept four interns a year, but a letter from Elena would guarantee him a spot.

How could he accomplish all that in thirty seconds?

I hadn't even thought of a way to pose my question to Peter and Jorge outside of "Are they real?" or showing them that black-and-white "NOW KISS!" stick figure meme.

The rush of nausea hits me when he whispers "One day" like a promise.

Once, I tripped on a chord connected to his gaming system—because, per usual, his bedroom floor was a danger zone—and knocked out whatever game he was playing before it saved. He screamed at me, had a meltdown, then wouldn't respond to any of my texts for the rest of the day. It was the worst.

But this Diego? The one who hadn't yelled when I told him. Who's been cool ever since.

It freaks me out.

We sit quietly. The thick, soft hairs on his calf tickle me. Cheesecake is smeared at the corners of our mouths, but we don't care.

"Besides," he says, bumping our shoulders hard. It hurts me more than him since Diego's mostly lean muscle and sharp bones. "We still have Pride. We have the whole summer just for us before you . . ."

This time, he doesn't finish.

"Yeah," I whisper.

I don't mention to him how, without the anticipation of Legends Con, there's more time to stare at the boxes piled in the corners. More time to wonder about who my roommate at UGA will be. And why their name isn't Diego Santoyo.

"Pride's gonna be great," I say, hoping he doesn't notice the thickness in my voice.

"Dude, you have no idea."

Diego points to a banner that says COME JOIN THE ATLANTA TEEN PRIDE CELEBRATION at the top of the organizer's webpage.

Simultaneously, smiles burst across our faces.

One of the things I love about our friendship is these calm moments where the things that excite or scare us the most aren't said out loud. They simply exist between us in a safe space. Sometimes we talk about them. But most of the time we just know what the other is thinking.

I know Diego is looking forward to Pride as much as I am. We haven't had any heart-to-heart discussions about it. I remember the nonchalant way we came out to each other.

In the middle of a field at this park we used to go to all the time.

I'm bi, he said randomly.

Sweet. I'm gay.

We were fourteen and each the first person the other told. Neither of us made it a big deal.

But it's different now. Even if Diego hasn't said it, he wants to live out loud in the same way I do. I want to wear the word QUEER across my face in rainbow paint.

Watch the parade. Feel Diego right there next to me in a sea of shameless joy.

In the deepest part of my marrow, I want to know all the odds stacked against me—being gay, Black, having a family that isn't known for being lucky in love—doesn't prevent me from getting the W.

"You're not going to cockblock me, right?" I tease while feeding Diego the last of the cheesecake.

He laughs. "Isaac Jaime Martin, as if you're going to meet anybody."

"You never know," I reply. "It could happen."

"It could happen," he repeats slowly, blinking at the carpet.

Our bare feet nearly overlap, his left over my right. I almost let Davi's name slip from my lips. But something in the way the corners of Diego's mouth inch up, the way he's looking at me from beneath his eyelashes, tells me I might not have to.

He clears his throat. "Did you already have someone in mind?"

Diego Santoyo knows me. He gets me.

I shrug. Then shake my head. As much as I want it, Davi still feels a bit like a naptime dream. One of those images that is blurred around the edges, cloudy and uncertain because you had too little time with it.

But I want the full HD version.

"If you met someone, I'd never cockblock," he pauses,

brow furrowed. I can't read what passes over his eyes. Then he's beaming, bright and warm again. "I don't want to miss out on this big thing for you."

"For us."

His leg stretches, his foot bumping one of the empty boxes. "For us."

He goes silent again, so I do too. There's a buzzing coming from his pocket. He pulls out his phone, taps in the passcode, then exhales. "Sorry. I'm getting shit in the Gatherer's Guild group chat for abandoning them. We found the Earth Imperio Stone earlier."

"Oh *no!*" I say mockingly.

"Shut up. You've never faced the wrath of Level_Zero before."

Level_Zero is his online nemesis. Diego's a big thing in the gaming community. Not just the Georgia one either. The *Southern* gaming community. He's slowly becoming nationally known too. Or digitally known? Whatever. He's up and coming.

Everyone loves KonamiCode—Diego's online gamer-tag.

He tried to explain the name to me once. Something about a master code for old-school video games to gain extra lives? I have no clue.

"Hey." His knee nudges mine while he types. "I'm linking up with a few of the other gamers tomorrow. Do you wanna hang?"

I stare at the ceiling. *No.* I hate the idea of being around total strangers. They'll just talk around me with their inside jokes. Also, for all I know, all Diego's online "friends" are forty-five-year-old, mansplaining dudes who live in their moms' basements. Or maybe they're ten-year-olds hyped on cherry Coke with two million YouTube followers.

But I think about Diego's words: *We have the whole summer just for us before you . . .*

I owe him for fucking up Legends Con. Also, at this point, I'll take any available opportunity to hang with him before I leave for Athens.

"We're going to the diner," he says. "Food's on me."

Already, my pulse is thudding loudly in my ears.

"They're cool, I swear." His fingers drum on my knee. He starts humming, and instantly, I recognize the song. A certain Bruno Mars melody.

"Okay, fine," I say to the ceiling, holding back a sigh.

But there's something about the way he sags into me, as if he thought I wouldn't want to be around him. As if that's not the only thing I want for the rest of the summer.

I turn my head to look at him. My heartbeat finally slows.

Diego's smile is so bright, I forget the sun exists.

Nine

SHRAPNELS #1 STAN @lovefelixeverafter · Jan 12

WOW PICA REALLY SAID #NONEWFRIENDS TO CHARM IN DA2!!! 🔥 #sickburn #DisasterAcademy #thedisasters

Isaac @charminmartin · Jan 13

Replying to @lovefelixeverafter
Delete your account! Charm only needs Reverb

Cosmos and Java is my favorite diner. The name is partially misleading, though. They don't serve fancy cocktails and overpriced coffee. The cosmos part is a reference to the diner's theme: outer space. Plastic 3D planets hang from the ceiling. Every server wears this weird, Star Trek–like uniform. The jukebox is loaded with sci-fi theme songs, along with the usual classic rock.

It's a seamless harmony of nerdy and strange.

In the middle of a galaxy-printed carpet, our group has pushed two square tables together. Most of the booths surrounding us are occupied by elderly diners lazily enjoying their meals. Outside, the golden hour is sneaking up in the sky. Gilded sunlight corkscrews into a swirl of corals and blues.

DJ, our waitress, stands over the table. "Drinks, or are we ready to order?"

"I am!" F.B. announces, slamming down his plastic menu. He has a nice pink sunburn across his nose to match his newly dyed hair.

Technically, he wasn't part of Diego's original plan for today. I stopped by Secret Planet earlier, needing someplace familiar and comforting before I stepped into this fire. F.B. was going a mile a minute about his latest emo, might-voluntarily-listen-to Twenty One Pilots mood. I had to mention the meetup with Diego's gamer friends before I was late.

Oh.

He kept blinking at me from behind the front counter, our silence intensifying the awkwardness.

Do you want to . . .

Do you want me to come? he asked. It was hard to miss the hopefulness in his voice.

Uh. Sure. That'd be cool.

It wasn't a complete lie. I love talking to F.B. about comics. It couldn't hurt to have a buffer between me and Diego's other friends.

But now that he's here, none of the uneasiness is gone. If anything, it's louder and more visible.

"And the chicken fingers." F.B. is rattling off different items from every section of the menu. Either he's stoned or hasn't eaten in two weeks.

"And you?" DJ says in a flat tone, pivoting to face the boy to the left of F.B.

"What're your vegan options?"

I don't know what to make of Blake. He has brown hair that's brushed up and back like a future daytime TV journalist. His gray-blue eyes accentuate his round baby face. He's been mostly quiet, cracking his knuckles, smiling a little whenever Diego makes a joke. Occasionally, his gaze drifts in my direction, sizing me up.

Friend or foe?

"Do you have root beer? Or can you make a Roy Rogers?" he requests.

Definite foe. What is he, twelve?

Next to Blake is Zelda. They have a shiny, rich umber complexion with big, wavy, dark hair. Neon green eyeshadow sharpens their features. They're wearing a white I ♥ WHITNEY T-shirt and the freshest pair of Jordans I've ever seen. Everything about them is kind of badass.

"Ginger ale, Isaac?"

I grin up at DJ, nodding.

DJ's worked at the diner for as long as I can remember Abuelito bringing me here. I'm pretty sure she's in her late forties, early fifties. Her hair's cut into an asymmetrical bob with an undercut, colored crime scene red—that deep crimson of a victim's fresh blood.

Iggy and Bella might've had McDonald's and learning Spanish over Sunday dinners, but I have a lifetime of watching Abuelito read the newspaper, drink lukewarm coffee, and explain—in detail—all his favorite plot points from *The Princess Bride* inside this diner.

Maybe it's not a fair trade-off, but it's mine.

"We have one more coming," Diego tells DJ as she collects the menus.

One more?

I raise an eyebrow at him but he's too busy laughing with Zelda to notice.

There's already so much noise and chatter happening at our table. Even F.B.'s involved in the discussions. I can barely keep up. My right leg hasn't stopped bouncing under the table since Zelda and Blake arrived. If it doesn't halt soon, I might vibrate so fast that I pass through time and space like Flash.

That wouldn't be so bad.

But I'm here for Diego, so I try to relax.

I zone in on the discussions about memes and YouTube channels and games. It turns out that both Blake and Zelda are in Diego's *BtVoS* Gatherer's Guild. Zelda's also this big name in the cosplay world, which is how they know F.B.

"I can't believe you're *the* Misty Munroe," F.B. says, awed. He has Zelda's Instagram account pulled up on his phone to show everyone.

Zelda's looks are on another level. Everything from Wonder Woman to Vixen to the Winter Soldier. Each costume is smartly designed and extremely accurate.

Their latest look, a husky and proud Maleficent, slays.

I clock their follower count.

"Ten thousand," I whisper, my cheeks prickling when everyone stares at me. I clear my throat, thankful when Zelda's melodic laugh recaptures the attention.

"It's NBD."

Yeah, right. I'm barely touching two hundred followers on my Insta. Most of that is from *DA* fan art reposts. #Charmverb. It's not the greatest ship name, but we're a strong following.

"I'm just trying to live up to my heroes," Zelda continues. "Misty Knight and Storm."

"You're a legend," Diego says, fist-bumping them.

Zelda huffs. "I wish someone would tell that to my dads."

Quietly, I try to piece together what that means. I'm not good at asking follow-up questions with new people. It feels as if I'm prying, no matter how nice or open they're being. But it doesn't matter, because Diego says "Oh, there goes number six," and my entire universe implodes.

Walking toward our table is Alix Jin. Her hair is piled into a sloppy ponytail on top of her head. The loose-fit black sweatshirt she wears has a HOUSE OF JIN logo printed in fading white script on the left side of her chest. She glares at me for a moment before reluctantly flopping into the last empty chair.

Diego Santoyo is the one thing separating me from the demon Azazel.

"So." She crosses her arms. "This is happening."

Under the table, my leg jumps at light speed. My fight-or-flight has never been any good. In situations like this, it's always flight.

I never expected dark-hearted Alix Jin to have *friends*. Or acquaintances. She's so unapproachable with everyone. But here she is, talking in her usual monotone with Blake and Zelda. She listens to F.B. ramble about *Shrapnel*. She maintains eye contact with Diego anytime he speaks.

She fits in.

Unlike me.

I slouch in my chair. It's as if an entire solar system is pressed against my chest. I tug out my phone and click on the Geeks Nation app, scrolling to the latest *Disaster Academy* discussion. No one notices me frowning at my lap.

Not for the first time, people are arguing over who would get a solo series first—Charm or Reverb? It's a silly debate. The answer is neither. Not only are Charm and Reverb roommates and teammates—and in love (fight me on this)—but they're best friends. You can't have one without the other.

I add my own thoughts to the discussion: "THEY'D HAVE A SPIN OFF TOGETHER YOU COWARDS! WHY WOULD YOU BREAK UP 2 BFFS?!"

Next to me, Diego laughs. The heat from our shoulders pressed together is welcome. For a second, I consider snapping another photo of him like this: head tipped back, eyes scrunched, curls everywhere.

Why would the universe want to break up two best friends?

DJ returns with drinks and an extra server just to pass out all the food. The chaos of hands reaching and "Careful, that's hot" and silverware clinking disrupts my thoughts.

Before she leaves, DJ turns to Alix. "What're you having, love?"

I wait in anticipation for Alix to order the heart of a baby deer or something. But before she can respond, DJ says "The usual?" and Alix's eyes drop as she nods meekly. "Thanks."

DJ pats Alix's tense shoulder before sauntering back toward the kitchen.

I almost fall off my chair. Alix Jin is a regular at the same diner I come to with Abuelito?

In what universe is that possible?

Fleetingly, I wonder if I'll ever know Alix like that. Enough to remember her usual and what makes her speechless the way she is now.

Probably not.

As we eat, our table devolves into the loud chatter from earlier. Everyone except me and Alix. I trade stares between my phone and Diego, while Alix maintains an air of apathy, picking sesame seeds off her hamburger bun.

Zelda rants about why Okoye from *Black Panther*—and, by default, the Dora Milaje—deserves her own film while sampling Blake's mac and cheese. "Is this made of plastic?"

"It's nondairy."

"It's *gross*." They wipe viciously at their mouth with a paper napkin.

Blake explains how he's already beat the latest *Kingdom Hearts* game—twice—even though it's only been out a month. "Figuring out the coding in their games is way too easy."

Diego rolls his eyes. "Blake's a hacker. And a cheater," he tells the table.

"*Level_Zero* is a hacker," says Blake smugly. "You're just mad I've broken through the coding of all the games you can't beat."

"Like I said, a cheater."

"An intellectual strategist," Blake says with a dignified air.

They continue to argue, but I ignore it to rewind the conversation in my head. Something clicks.

Diego's halfway into a bite of his second chicken taco when I sputter, "Wait, your greatest competition, the one you're always going on about is . . ." I point in Blake's direction. "A *toddler*?"

Seriously, he can't be older than thirteen.

"I'm fifteen," Blake snaps.

I stand corrected.

"This is the almighty Isaac the Savior?" He wiggles a fork with questionable-looking macaroni noodles falling off the tip at me. "You abandoned the Gatherer's Guild's trek through the Cavern of Desolate Souls for *him*? That's wack, bruh."

"Okay, privileged white boy, you don't get to use *bruh*," Zelda warns with the slightest curl to their mouth. *"Ever."*

Blake maintains his scowl. "I could annihilate him any day of the week in *COD*, KonamiCode."

I arch my right eyebrow at him. "Uh, I don't know what that is."

"*Call of Duty*," Diego whispers to me.

"I prefer *Overwatch*," F.B. says, which opens a brand-new discussion that I'm once again not part of.

I squeeze my hands shut, nails digging into skin, so that my leg doesn't wiggle.

This is for Diego.

"Do you game at all?" It's Blake, his full attention directed at me again.

The others watch me silently. My throat goes dry. My leg jumps once. Twice. Then it stops when Diego's hand gently squeezes my knee.

"It's not really Isaac's thing," he answers for me, smiling. "But you should see his comics collection. Dude owns every single issue of *Disaster Academy*."

"It's true," F.B. mumbles, his mouth stuffed with fries. "Captain Incredible might as well be SP's Employee of the Month."

"OMG, I love *Disaster Academy*!" Zelda exclaims. "Boomstar's my fav."

I grin at them. Boomstar's an underappreciated character. She's all blonde-and-pink hair and sarcasm and can control gravity. People literally have no choice but to bow to her coolness.

"I was gonna cosplay her at Legends Con this year . . . if I could've afforded a badge," says Zelda, a frown overtaking their expression.

"Same," Blake says dejectedly.

This strange quiet air wraps itself around us. The diner's gradually filling up with noise. Silverware falls from a table. Someone slurps their soup. The staff funnels out of the kitchen, one waitress holding a slice of chocolate cake with a single lit candle as the others hum "The Imperial March," a birthday tradition around here.

I sink down in my chair. Heat prickles my ears. My stomach tightens even though I've barely touched my food.

Zelda and Blake probably entered the Legends Con lottery just like me. But, had they won, they wouldn't have missed their opportunity to purchase a badge. There wouldn't have been a Davi Lucas to distract them.

F.B. stirs a fry in the lake of ketchup on his plate before

popping it in his mouth. "Can you imagine the six of us taking over the con?"

It's this instant can't-miss moment. Around the table, eyes light up. Even Alix's mouth twitches like a smile might breach her force fields and intercept her dark, crystalized soul.

Legends Con is so much more than a hub for comic book geeks or gamers. It's a haven for people from every corner of nerdiness. A harbor for lost souls searching for a family after their favorite sci-fi show has been canceled. A giant step into the outer realm for cosplayers, paranormal enthusiasts, and fantasy fanatics.

I want to say all of this to them. Explain why I want to meet Peter and Jorge. Scream about all the things I planned to do at the con. But there's this invisible hand that covers my mouth. It shoves every word back down my throat.

How can I discuss something so deep and personal with people who don't even know basic, Google-searchable facts about me? People other than Diego, that is.

"Hey," Diego finally says. "Who cares, right? Let's make the best of this summer."

Under the table, his knee is pressed to mine. It feels intentional. He's telling me we're okay.

And I believe him.

"Nice try, KonamiCode," says Blake, snorting. "Not going to Legends Con still sucks balls."

Diego chokes on his Coke. Everyone around the table chuckles. All but Alix, who huffs, then glares at the ceiling.

But, in this moment, she doesn't count.

As we wait for the carrot cake slice F.B.'s ordered for dessert, everyone around me discusses things like the hardest games to beat. Single-player versus massively multiplayer online games. Their favorite characters. This leads to Diego informing most of the diner about the ways Delmar is the superior gaming character. It's kind of cool the way he explains it all as if he's giving a TED Talk.

He leans so hard into his nerdiness.

I admire how he's so fearless, even while talking to people who mostly know him as KonamiCode. They don't know he's allergic to shellfish. Or that he has sweaty feet. That his first name's Luis.

None of that matters to him.

He gets an energy from these kinds of interactions. He feeds on the way everyone responds to him.

Usually, it's too much for me to watch. Extroverts in action. "Energy thieves," Bella once called them. It's ironic because the whole Martin family, Mom included, is a pack of socializers.

But Diego's so genuine when he's engaging with other people. It's hard to explain the hint of jealousy inside my chest when I watch him. I don't mean for it to exist. But, sometimes, I wish I had that. I wish I could see a stranger wearing an officially licensed *Disaster Academy* T-shirt on the street and look them in the eye to say "That's cool."

A warm hand covers my knee. "What would make the better comic book movie: *Shrapnel* or *Disaster Academy*?" Diego asks with this casualness that I love.

Just like that, opinions are being tossed out. Most of them are wrong. Everyone's loud again. I remind myself to drop a few extra dollars in DJ's tip. But none of the conversations are happening without me.

I'm involved. Kind of.

I shut F.B. down before he can suggest Shrapnel join the Webster Academy.

Then, I lean against Diego. I don't say "thanks," but I hope he sees it in my eyes.

I hope he doesn't sense how miserable I'm going to be when he's not there in a few months.

Ten

GEEKS NATION FORUM

Re: Best Teen SuperTeams?!

BrimonSpierfeld: when Halo Boy said "Adults think we're a joke. They think we're unsure. We can't handle anything. But we can. We're the ones who are gonna save the world. Together" I felt that. Teen Titans WHO? Young Avengers WHAT? The Disasters baybee!

ACharmingReverb: ONCE A DISASTER. . . . . . . ALWAYS A DISASTER!

We step into the diner's parking lot just as the sun begins to hide behind tall buildings in the distance. Cars fill the streets with blaring music. Rap songs battle to be heard over country and EDM. A twinkle of waning sunlight sweeps over a giant mural of smiling blue aliens painted up the side of an empty café.

The air has this aura of unpredictability to it. Magic exists beneath the orchid sky. You can break all the rules. A boring night could turn into a wild adventure. A star could fall to the earth.

Anything could happen.

Diego whispers, "Wow."

I follow his gaze to all the shops stretched out across the main road.

In almost every window or hung above a door, dancing in the light breeze, is a flag. Rainbow ones. Bright pink, lavender, and blue flags. A few are made of soft blues and pinks with a white stripe in the middle. A large black, gray, white, and purple flag is draped across a manne-quin's shoulders like a cape.

My mouth curls up. "It's kind of epic."

Diego and I are two weeks away from going to our first Pride.

I try not to think about how all this—the flags, the #LOVEISLOVE stickers slapped on streetlamps, the air soaked in "Born This Way" vibes—is just a formality for some of these businesses. Part of me knows that come July first, the support disappears. The EQUALITY FOR ALL banners are removed. The queer community returns to being invisible to most people. We're no longer here to uplift anyone's profit so they won't uplift our voices for another year.

Places like Heroes for Hire won't display all the promi-nent LGBTQIA comic book characters like Batwoman or Iceman or America Chavez in the front window. The staff will discard their rainbow buttons in favor of standard-issue nametags. Troye Sivan will be replaced by boring, adult-friendly music while customers shop.

Heroes for Hire, your capitalistic gay-friendly comic bookstore for an entire month.

But there's one guaranteed safe place for me in this city of polished queer support: Secret Planet.

My favorite spot is a corner near the front door where a wall is decorated with flags. *Our flags.* It's a reminder: We're here. You're here. You belong.

It's why I'll always be Team Secret Planet.

As Diego points out more banners, I wonder what life will be like in Athens. *UGA isn't as large as some schools; will Pride be as big there? Does everyone go all out to celebrate? Or will I have to find some sort of off-campus queer support group for these things?*

Maybe I can find a way back for adult Pride in October so Diego and I can march in the parade.

I love that possibilities exist.

From now on, Diego and I get to decide how big or small this is for us.

My silent reverie is broken by Blake crowing at the sky. "I'm so wired! Let's stay out. KonamiCode's right. We need to enjoy the summer."

Alix squints at him. "Don't you have a curfew?"

But he's already on his Android, thumbs tapping the screen. "Texting my mom now. She's a manager at a coffee shop. She won't care as long as I don't wake her up when I get in."

"Must be nice," says Zelda, typing away on their own phone. "Summer or not, my dads won't let me stay out past eleven."

I grin in solidarity. Not that Mom was ever on my case when I was seventeen, since I didn't go anywhere other than Diego's house. But she still had rules: No coming home later than 10:00 p.m. during the week, eleven on the weekends. Text or call when I arrive. At least one contact number of whomever I'm with. Turn on the Find My Friends app.

It's 8:33 p.m., but it feels later. Trying to keep up with all these new personalities is exhausting.

"I'm in," Zelda says with a sigh. "But if I break curfew, my dads are gonna break me."

F.B. goes to give Zelda a high-five, but they stand, arms crossed, offering him a healthy dose of yeah-no side-eye.

Without hesitation, Diego agrees to hang out longer. Then, shockingly, Alix does too. Diego nudges me, and he has this look on his face—pleading determination—that reactivates the guilt in my stomach.

Finally, I say, "I hate you."

It's such a lie. But I try to put my full disdain at the thought of being anywhere with Alix for five minutes more into those three words.

Diego hooks an arm around my waist, then grins at the others.

"I know a place."

One look and I can already tell what he's thinking. I groan before shooting my mom a quick text to inform her that I might be home late. I make sure to include that I'll be with Diego, so she doesn't completely freak out.

But I don't mention where I'm going.

There's a high probability that we're all getting arrested tonight, and the last thing I need is my mom being held liable.

Memorial Park is less than three miles from my neighborhood. It's tucked into a corner near an elementary school, the public pool, and one of those newly built subdivisions where all the houses look identical.

I can't remember why Diego and I stopped coming to this park. Did we outgrow the swing sets where we met and the looping slide and lying in the grass while the sun washed over us? Did we find new ways to escape the secrets we kept from the rest of the world but not from each other? Or was it just high school and the constant pressure to perform? Continuously having to "act mature" when, really, you've barely stepped into this new transition without falling on your face.

A chain-link fence separates the park from us. Beyond it is unending grass, a darkened pavilion, and the vague shape of a lake reflecting light from the scattered stars in the sky.

"This," Zelda says, waving a hand toward the fence, "is your idea of fun?"

Diego smirks, nodding.

"Are we even allowed to be here?" Blake whispers.

Technically? No. Most Alpharetta parks close around 8:00 p.m. At least one squad car patrols the neighborhood past operation hours, searching for trespassers or horny teens having sex in their parents' SUVs.

Diego's knobby fingers slip through the gaps in the fence, giving a strong tug. "Come on. Let's live a little."

"Or die trying to climb a fence," Alix deadpans.

"Wait. We have to *climb* it?" Blake squeaks.

Seriously? This is the infamous Level_Zero? I'm wholly unimpressed.

"The cops are probably watching the main entrance," F.B. says as he sidles up to Diego. "The only way in is up."

The fence wraps around the majority of the park. It's just long, flimsy stretches of metal rusted by rain, but still imposing in its own way. Diego discovered this backside entrance when we were still in our we-can-climb-anything phase. It's blocked from neighborhood view by a thick bundle of trees.

I glare at the fence like an old nemesis.

We have history. A messy one.

Diego and I were only ten years old when we tried to conquer this beast. Two fearless Miles Moraleses. Actually, Diego the Fearless. I was more like Isaac the Do What Diego Says back then. And now, too, I guess.

Anyway, we managed to climb over the top and half-way down the other side before my foot got snagged on a severed piece of fence. I panicked. The jagged metal was trying to eat my ankle. Diego, smiling like I wasn't about to die, reached a hand toward me. But he slipped and the splintered teeth sliced his chin.

There were blood and tears.

The tears were all mine, of course. I hated that my best friend was bleeding because of my clumsiness.

Diego refused to go home once we were on solid ground. He was on a mission. It was our last day of summer vacation. He wanted every breathable second of freedom to be spent lying under the sun on the green field at the heart of the park. I wanted it too—minus the blood.

He used his T-shirt to stop the bleeding. I used mine to mop up my tears. We lay there, bare-chested and grinning, for hours.

We owned that day.

My fingers curl around the links of the fence. Diego's already climbing, F.B. right behind him. Blake, head tilted back, looks as if he's trying to pray to the video game gods to give him a few extra lives. Alix has already made it to the other side and is glaring at me. I didn't even see her scale the discolored monster. Maybe she walked through it via some demon dimension.

Silently, I count to five. Then I climb.

Blake is winded and trembling when we both drop to the ground. F.B. claps him on the shoulders. "Hella brave, little toaster." It hardly returns the color to Blake's cheeks, but at least he smiles wearily.

Rust-orange marks crisscross over my palms. I try to rub them off on my joggers.

Zelda saunters up. They're not sweating or breathless like Blake and me.

"Hey," Blake says between wheezes, "you didn't climb?"

"I'm a fat diva," Zelda announces. "We don't climb fences."

"Then how'd you get in?" I ask, confused.

"I have my secrets," Zelda replies. "My Lord and Savior, Whitney Houston, shined a light on me."

"Come on," says Diego, his hand pushing against the middle of my spine. "Let's get to the best spot."

The premier part of Memorial Park is the lake. At night, there's a soundtrack of roaring frogs and noisy cicadas filling the open space. The water's glassy, obsidian surface is the perfect mirror of the sky above, the reflection only interrupted by rare breezes. A sun-warped wooden dock extends ten feet into the water.

Tonight, the moon's out, painting the area a pale silver.

Diego is stretched out on one of the gazebo's benches with me. His bare feet rest in my lap. I have no idea when he took off his shoes. His back's propped against Alix, who's on his other side.

"Whatever just happened, it was boss-level incredible," F.B. says, flopping onto the bench opposite us. He's pleasantly buzzed, which must've happened on the drive to the park. I rode shotgun in Camila's Jeep with Diego. Alix and Zelda sat in the back. Blake braved F.B.'s West Coast defensive driving skills in his burnt-orange Toyota hatchback.

Watching him swerve and speed through the residential streets was horrifying.

"My followers are gonna love this," says Zelda gleefully as they sit next to F.B. They mess around on their phone. Blake joins them, giggling and breathless again.

I'm not sure how F.B. was coordinated enough to record Zelda and Blake doing a TikTok dance to a K-pop song, but I'm impressed it's not a shaky mess when Zelda rotates the phone so we can all view the result.

"This is not a flex, but my curls are popping despite this humidity," Zelda observes.

It's true. Not a single strand has frizzed out of place. Under the gazebo, hovering fireflies cast a greenish crown around their head.

"My papa says, 'The bigger the hair, the closer to God,'" they say with the kind of snort that persuades people around them to laugh too. "Papa was raised hardcore Catholic in a huge Latinx family. Everything with him is religion, fam, or food related."

"Same." Diego meets Zelda halfway for a fist bump.

He gives me a look, and I can't help but smile.

The Santoyos aren't overly religious. Neither is my family, other than Abuelito. But Camila wrangles Diego into the same navy suit and tie he's had for three years—

he's finally grown into it—for Midnight Mass. And my mom insists we all watch some form of church service on Easter and Christmas. We even pray before we open gifts. She was raised Baptist. Carlos and Abuelito are Catholic. I haven't fully committed to either.

Is that weird?

To be eighteen and not know *what* or *if* you believe in anything?

Zelda says, "Daddy tells people, 'If I'm going to spend this much effort on my hair, imagine what I can do with the rest of the world.' He's spent enough years on the drag circuit to know what he's talking about."

"Your dad's a drag queen?" I say, then shrink a little when Zelda grins.

"Both of them. Anita Grand and Havana Niceday."

F.B. nearly chokes. "As in *the* Anita Grand and Havana Niceday?" he asks.

Zelda sighs, nodding exhaustedly as if they've seen this reaction a thousand times before.

Without missing a beat, F.B. launches into an abridged version of the Legend of Anita Grand and Havana Niceday. He's such a fanboy. But his story comes with photos from Google and YouTube clips.

It's amazing, really. The hair, the makeup, the outfits. The comedy and . . . *drama*.

Anita loves voluminous wigs and sequins and everything from disco to Cardi B.

Havana is into soft color palettes and contour cheeks and anything by Shakira or Jenni Rivera.

One look at Zelda's indifferent expression tells the part of the story F.B.'s missing.

"They're always in the spotlight." Zelda's tone isn't like the one from the diner when they talked about their cosplay life. It's guarded. "But when a new batch of queens start at the club, Daddy lets me design their first costumes. On weekends, I get to watch rehearsals. Give feedback."

"That's cool," F.B. says with the right amount of awe I can never manage while talking to someone new.

Something about Zelda makes me wish I could do that instead of just sit here blinking at them as they talk.

"I really want my own thing," they say. "I'm building a portfolio to apply to SCAD."

Savannah College of Art and Design is a serious deal. It's historically challenging to get into.

"Legends Con was going to be my way to break out of their shadow."

Again, a shame spider walks down the back of my neck. I don't make eye contact with Zelda. Or Diego. I think we're okay. But I still want to find a way to make this right with him. Something bigger than spending tonight with his friends.

F.B. nods at Zelda. "I get that. Being in someone's shadow all the time totally sucks."

"Relatable content?" they ask.

"Yeah, so . . ." His smoke-raspy voice trails off. He tilts his head in my direction. "Remember that bad news I said was brewing last week?"

I nod robotically. Most of that day is still just a haze of failure and Davi Lucas.

"Usually, all the local comic book stores help organize pieces of LC. It's hella fun." He grins at the moon. "This year, Big Winston was letting me take the point. Set up our contribution. Next thing I know, SP was left out of the equation, thanks to Vee Johnson."

"Who?" Zelda almost shouts.

Vee Johnson, assistant manager of Heroes for Hire.

F.B. gives us a play-by-play of what happened. For months, Vee sent out emails glorifying Heroes for Hire by tearing down its competitors, including my favorite comic book store. She included sales figures and graphs and an entire PowerPoint dedicated to the ways Francis Bean Lowell and Secret Planet failed to carry any clout in the comics community.

"You know, Vee originally applied for a job at SP," F.B. says. "She used to be a *regular*. But she bailed after finding out there was an opening at Heroes for Hire."

"No loyalty," Diego sneers.

"None." F.B. sighs. "I just wanted a chance to prove myself."

We all nod solemnly. Everyone except Blake. He's

turned toward the lake, and there's a pale strip of moonlight resting across his face. His short arms hug his legs to his chest. He's quiet for a few breaths.

"I'm an only child in a single parent home," he finally says. "I haven't talked to the biological gene donor called Dad in years. Mom's always working. Everyone at school is a dick."

"Spoiler alert: the kids at every school are dicks," Alix says.

Blake bites his lip. "Gaming is the only place where I get to be—"

"A privileged white boy with even more power?" Zelda says, a thick eyebrow raised.

"An asshole?" Diego teases again.

Blake laughs. "All of the above." Then, with a pinched voice, he says, "I was going as Level_Zero, but also Blake. I was going to belong . . . if my mom could've afforded a badge."

Something familiar shifts in my chest. It unfurls, then stretches until the pressure weighs on my lungs.

Diego tosses one of his shoes at Blake. "Maybe next year."

Blake fumbles to catch the shoe. "Maybe."

They share these smug smiles. I'm almost jealous of their connection. But Blake's not me. He'll never attain Tolerates the Smell of Your Sweaty Feet Daily friendship bonus points.

"This is really . . . gross," Alix comments dryly.

"Shut up." Diego, still propped against Alix, nudges her, guffawing. "We all have valid reasons for being disappointed by this."

"Whatever."

Alix's cruel indifference strikes again. I stare at the back of her head as the breeze sweeps over us. The ends of her hair move freely while the rest of her is perfectly motionless.

I wonder if she was ever interested in attending Legends Con. *Is she losing anything by not going like the rest of us are? It doesn't matter. She'd never tell me, and I probably wouldn't ask. Why bother trying to build any civility between us? I'll be gone in less than two months.*

My gaze shifts to Diego. His grin-scrunched eyes are a reminder that there's only one person here I want to maintain any kind of relationship with. No offense to his gamer "friends."

But this—Diego's sweaty feet in my lap, F.B. and Zelda planning their next TikTok while Blake lists his top ten video game villains—isn't the worst thing that's happened in the last week.

Eleven

Our Fictious Chronicles

Fic: On the Other Side of What If   By **OkayDariusOkay**

Rating: Teen and Up   **Fandom:** Disaster Academy

Pairing: Charm/Reverb   **Tags:** First Kiss, Friends to Lovers, Fluff, Romance, Slow Burn, Mild Angst, Pining, Alternate Universe—Coffeeshop, set after issue 6, barista reverb and dorky iced coffee charm, One True Pairing, more than kissing tbd

Chapters: 4/?   **Likes:** 2182   **Words:** 26,302

Comments:

IMartino210 · June 3 1:01 AM: YOU'RE KILLING ME! LET THEM KISS! THIS FIC IS BETTER THAN THE COMICS I NEED A NEW UPDATE NOW!!!

As much as I wanted the night to end at Memorial Park, it doesn't. After lingering around the gazebo for another half hour, we discover we all have something other than Legends Con in common: insatiable appetites.

I'm exhausted from all this new social interaction, but no one turns down a Mondo Shake. Not even me. Thirty minutes before Twisted Burger shuts down for the night, we pull into the parking lot with individual goals.

F.B. races through parked cars, shouting, "I'm getting sliders!"

Close behind, Blake is singing a song he made up about fries. He pauses midway to floss while chanting, "Bacon fries! Cheese fries! Double bacon cheese fries!" Either he's only part-time vegan or has forgotten, thanks to a contact high from F.B.'s stash.

A goth girl and her girlfriend pass them, holding hands. F.B. stops to happily salute before dragging Blake inside.

"C'mon," Zelda insists, looping an arm around Alix's. "We need Cookie-licious Mondo Shakes ASAP."

Alix hesitates with a blank expression before giving in. I'm learning that resisting Zelda's enthusiasm isn't an option. A smile or two has nudged my lips listening to them talk tonight.

I stay behind. I've already handed F.B. a few dollars for a regulation-sized Mondo Shake. Then, as a precaution, I got his number and texted him the flavor I want. Otherwise, he'll probably forget once he's in line. I should've gone in myself, but I need the quiet.

Tonight's been a lot.

I'm seated on the hood of Camila's Jeep. Clouds hang low in the sky. I can't see the stars anymore. But the parking lot's LED lighting casts a gauzy blanket of bluish ivory over me. It's still warm out as my thumb swipes across my phone screen, unlocking it. There's an unread message from Bella. Well, a photo. It's of Abuelito napping on a gingham-patterned couch. I barely recognize it—the hand-me-down one from Mom's parents we used to have in our living room.

Abuelito's hair is dark, thicker. His face is clean-shaven, his mouth hanging open. I can hear his snoring in my head.

I laugh softly, then inspect the image closer.

Nestled in the crook of Abuelito's arm is a baby. More golden than brown skin, fine curls, a matching open-mouthed expression. For a second, I think it's Iggy. But another text comes through.

> From: Bella
> Look at you & lito! Mom sent this to me.
> 9:33 PM

> From: Bella
> thats going to be you soon Uncle Isaac
> 9:33 PM

A wave of heat flushes my face. I scroll back up to the photo again. In Abuelito's long, thin arms, I'm a popcorn kernel. It's hard to believe I was ever that tiny and delicate compared to him. We're almost the same height now.

And there are days when I feel like I'm hugging him too tight, like he might break.

I fire off a quick reply to Bella's last message.

To: Bella

😑 😑 😑

9:34 PM

Then I consider texting my grandpa. But he's horrible with technology. I could call him. Maybe he's awake. Maybe he's at home, alone, thinking about summer and Abuela and *The Princess Bride*.

My phone vibrates in my hand. An assault of notifications come through. All of them are from my social media apps, each from @theonlydavilucas. He's even sent a follow request to my private Instagram, which catches me off guard considering that account has twenty followers, max.

But it's clear Davi put in the effort to search me out.

I only hesitate over the ACCEPT REQUEST button for a minute. My social media isn't like everyone else's at East Middleton. I don't do automatic follows because we were lab partners or borrowed Algebra II notes off each other. I don't like the idea of random classmates getting that close. There's no shame in my goofy posts, but giving access to the people I went to school with makes me uncomfortable.

Maybe it's the thought that any of them could see my *Disaster Academy* stuff.

I'd be allowing them to make fun of something important to me. Showing other kids so they can drag me on their finsta accounts.

Except I don't think Davi's like that.

One click and we're officially mutuals now.

I admire his profile photo. It's black and white. His loose curls hang just above his eyes, and his smile is as massive as the dachshund puppy he's holding. They're both wearing hockey jerseys.

I laugh into my palm.

His entire grid is hockey- or family-related content. Davi on the ice. Davi with his younger sister perched on his shoulders. Davi wearing a mouse-ears hat from Disneyworld. Photos with his teammates, some of whom I recognize from classes we've shared.

No couple-y pics of him with anyone else.

Not even a photo of him and Callie Hernandez, his prom date.

And, yes, I realize it's very stalkerish to examine all his posts like this, so I tap on a more recent one—Davi and his mom. They have the same deep brown eyes, dimpled chins, faint wrinkles in their foreheads.

It's from December. He's tagged the location: São Paulo.

I've never been to Monterrey. But I love that Davi's vacationed where his dad grew up.

"You're making The Face."

Diego hops onto the hood next to me. He ran inside to pee when we got here. He's still drying his hands on his shorts when he elbows me, eyebrows raised.

"What? No." But my cheeks are achy and hot from an awkward smile. The next denial comes out of my mouth with a stutter: "It's no-nothing."

"Well, it's *not* nothing."

I roll my eyes. Then I mumble, "Just Davi."

"Davi Lucas?"

I nod.

"Wow," he whispers, something uneven about his tone. "This really is A Thing."

"It's not A Thing."

"It is! Come on, say it. You think he's muy lindo."

"You're muy lindo," I tease.

Diego freezes. Something unreadable passes over his face. I guess he's a little thrown off by the way I almost mimicked his accent. Almost.

He recovers quickly. I can hear every bit of the capitalized accusation in his tone when he says, "Isaac Martin, we're full-blown Crush Syndrome here. Should I alert your next of kin?"

Embarrassment seeps into my bones. I wish I could call Bella right now. Tell her about the boy I can't seem to get out of my head. But doing that in an empty burger restaurant parking lot while Diego's next to me seems wrong somehow.

"Hey." Diego's arm curls around my tight shoulders. "¿Qué pasa?"

"Nothing," I say.

I stare at my shoes. They're my favorite pair of chalk-orange Adidas Campus sneakers. Scuff marks have ruined the white soles, and the leather has lost some of its brightness. I've had them since junior year when my feet stopped growing faster than the rest of me. They were a birthday gift from Abuelito. The next day, Diego bought me a matching tangerine *Disaster Academy* T-shirt off Etsy.

I paired these shoes and that shirt so much that year, it was ridiculous. I've already planned to wear them together at UGA. A reminder of the two people I'll miss the most besides Mom.

"I'm thinking about Bella," I finally confess. "About how bad I want to tell her I don't know how to ask a boy out."

Diego's silent. I wonder if he wants to ask the question that I'd ask him: *How is that possible?*

Also: *How are you so pathetic?*

But he doesn't. He waits patiently, arm still resting on my shoulder.

"I mean, I do." I wrinkle my nose. "I've seen a million bad Netflix rom-coms. Asking a guy out is the easiest part."

"It's not." Diego says it so confidently. As if he's taken his shot before and missed. But Diego doesn't date. How would he know?

"It's just—" My jaw clenches shut. A trail of sweat wiggles down my spine. I'm uncomfortably hot. Diego's so close and his arm's suddenly this heavy wall of heat. "I'm *eighteen*. I'm about to be in college, in a brand-new city. But I haven't had sex. Never been in a relationship. Never been on a date." I list everything on my fingers. "I haven't even kissed a boy."

"You've kissed a girl?"

"Diego," I hiss, annoyed.

"Sorry."

"I haven't even kissed a boy." I hunch over, elbows on my knees. "I haven't."

Thing is, I'm not ashamed I haven't had sex. Or been in a relationship. Seriously, I don't know why people focus so much on those things in high school. I was just trying to survive physical education and all those science classes. It was enough of a struggle crawling out of bed extra early so I wouldn't have to ride the bus in the morning.

I was terrified dating would screw all that up.

But here I am now—Isaac Martin, the perfect virginal sacrifice for a cult looking to awaken their world-ending god.

"So practice."

"Practice?" I laugh harshly. "What? On a pillow? A mirror? My hand?"

"No. No. And definitely not." His knee knocks against mine. "We both know where that hand's been."

I exhale loudly through my nose, shaking my head.

As if sensing my frustration, he says, "It's a joke. Sorry."

"This isn't a joke. *I'm* not a joke."

We sit in a silence only interrupted by cars starting up and exiting the parking lot or the occasional sugary pop song whispering through Twisted Burger's doors as someone steps inside. An unmistakable need to call Bella tugs at my ribs. The Crush Syndrome discussions are so different with her.

Not better. Only different.

"I meant me," Diego finally whispers.

I almost believe the voice is coming from inside my head until he says, louder, "You can practice with me."

My eyebrows shoot up, my mouth opening with nothing coming out.

Diego shrugs, nonchalant as ever. "You need to get the nerves out of your system," he explains. "You need to know you can do it."

I search his face. The artificial ivory glow from the lights leaves his complexion pale, but his eyes and the way he holds his mouth is earnest. He's serious.

"It's just for practice, right?" Diego says.

A laugh tickles my tonsils. "What makes you the expert for practice kissing?"

Diego shoots me an affronted expression. He sits up, chest puffed out. "Because I am."

"Who've you kissed?"

"None of your business."

"Wait. So, you have *kissed* someone?"

"Yes." Before I can ask who, he says, "It was a silly game at a party and then we kept kissing after."

"You never told me."

His eyes lower. He tucks his bottom lip under his teeth. "It didn't mean anything." Then, he bumps our shoulders. "The same as you practicing on me. It's just to make you comfortable."

I chew over his words. Silence settles into the parking lot again. There are fewer cars around us. A giant expanse of blacktop marred by bright yellow lines and the occasional Twisted Burger paper bag or empty cup with a red straw saluting the sky. No one's around.

F.B. and the others are still inside.

I inhale deeply, thinking of Davi's profile photo—those smiley lips I want against mine.

A kiss I don't want to fuck up. Not the first time.

Plus, this is Diego the Fearless. My best friend. The one who never leaves me out of anything.

"Sure," I say. "Practice is good."

"Yeah?"

I nod, grinning. "I don't want to be nervous the first time."

"It does kind of mess things up."

Another chorus of *who, who, who* fills my head, but I don't ask him. This isn't some big, unforgivable secret. Besides, Diego's doing me a favor.

"Okay." I fidget on the hood before twisting toward him. "Let's do this." The words come out so confidently, but I freeze. Roughly forty viewings of the same kisses in *The Princess Bride* doesn't prepare you for how you're supposed to initiate one. Or what to do when your palms are extremely sweaty. When your leg is starting to do that anxious bouncy thing it does.

I have no clue when to close my eyes. What angle to come at. What else I should say—

But then Diego's breath, minty from gum I didn't realize he'd been chewing, glides across my closed mouth. His hand is next. It's soft and steady as he palms my cheek.

He leans forward.

I follow.

His lips brush mine. Once, twice. Our noses bump awkwardly. This is terrible. Then he smiles against my mouth and it happens.

He kisses me. I close my eyes and I let him.

It's weird, the way my heart starts to beat like someone learning to play guitar for the first time. The wrong notes, wrong sounds. Everything out of rhythm and horribly clumsy. But something is materializing. It's music: not quite perfect, but it's coming together.

I kiss him back.

For ten seconds, with my eyes closed, I envision this is Davi. Strong shoulders and dimpled chin and experienced hands. Every inch of myself falls into that image. Kissing Davi Lucas. Touching him. Wondering if the stars are watching over us like mythical beings blessings this kiss.

A cool breeze skims the back of my neck. Teeth catch my lower lip. My thumb traces the scar on the underside of Davi's jaw.

Wait. Davi doesn't have a scar under his jaw. He doesn't smell like jasmine fabric softener and diner tacos.

I pull away. Diego does too.

It's an aching thirty seconds of silence. The LED lights shine on us like a spotlight rather than a blessing. My lips are open, but I don't say anything. Diego stares at his hands. A distinct distance has formed between our knees and hips now.

What have I done?

There's a buzzing in my head. Tonight's warmth pours down on me like a thunderstorm.

I kissed Diego.

And it was . . . I can't find the word. *Great?* I spent four years of high school writing and rewriting essays about dead white male authors who "shaped a generation" only to describe my first kiss as . . . great?

Then it hits me. Diego is my first kiss. Practice or not, he's the first.

What does that mean?

I think about *The Princess Bride*. About how long it takes until you finally get that first real kiss between Buttercup and Westley after being apart for so long. And it's perfect. Abuelito always gasps noisily just before it happens. I get all fuzzy every time, even though I know it's coming.

"Isaac, uh . . . so, that was . . ."

He stammers, then stops. Diego's face is a pale rose. His fingers tug at the ends of his curls. A *squeak-squeak* echoes in the parking lot from his sneakers dancing along the Jeep's grill. He can't keep still.

Then he chuckles lowly, thudding my shoulder. "See, dude. No big deal."

This wasn't a real first kiss, I tell myself. *It was practice. Procedural.* I was pretending Diego was Davi the whole time, which means—

I don't have time to analyze what that means because a voice catches my attention: "Isaac!"

I squint in the direction of the restaurant. A boy is running toward me. Sneakers pounding on the pavement. He waves, saying my name again. My breath stalls on an inhale.

That's my name in Davi Lucas's mouth.

That's Davi Lucas, smiling vibrantly as he gets closer. His curls bounce as he comes to a stop in front of me. He's clutching a large plastic bag so stuffed, the contents almost spill out. In fact, he's left a trail of fries from the door to the Jeep. His chest rises and falls rapidly, and I notice his T-shirt.

It's red-and-white striped. Like the one Diego wore to my house yesterday morning.

Diego.

I force myself not to look to my right. But Diego's there, in my peripheral. He's a blurred image of fluffy hair and scrunched eyebrows and a flat mouth.

A mouth that was just on mine.

Did Davi see us?

Panic splits my chest. I almost double over to vomit, but Davi's beaming like he didn't witness a thing. His face is speckled in sweat, glowing. I find a rhythm, a faint *tap-tap* of my heart that reminds me I'm okay.

"You're here."

"Yeah." He laughs as though he's embarrassed. Then he holds up the bag. "Grabbing food for my fam this time." Then, with a glint in his eyes, he leans close. "I might've snuck myself a cheeseburger too. Don't tell my boys."

My snort-giggle rings sharply in the parking lot. I flush, mortified. But Davi waggles his eyebrows, unfazed by the inhuman sound I just released.

He says, "You're here too."

"Mm-hmm." I'm struggling with words, not that it would matter if I had them. Staring at Davi like this, breathless but happy, feels like I'm standing underwater.

Everything is wavy and light and suffocating.

"I ran into F.B. inside." Davi nods back toward Twisted Burger. "He was all like, 'Yo. Captain Incredible is so here! Just chillin', hella mad cool, and BTW you should go see him.'"

His impersonation of F.B.'s SoCal vibe is probably the worst thing I've ever witnessed. But it's also hilarious. I'm laughing again, stomach knotted, eyes watery.

He stands back, grinning. The apples of his cheeks are pink.

"Anyway," says Davi. "That's why I followed you." Then he holds up his phone, showing me all his open apps. My face and tweets and grotesquely outdated Tumblr. "F.B. was yakking my ear off. I didn't know if I'd have a chance to see you."

"You wanted to see me?"

"Of course."

I'm drowning.

"He was suggesting all these cool things I should get for my best friend," Davi continues, pocketing his phone. "He kept mentioning this thing called Legends Con? It's a big deal, right? I remember him going on and on about it that day we were at Secret Planet together."

The water fills my lungs.

"Sorry you're not going. Heard you missed a deadline or something?"

I blink hard. Next to me, Diego scoots forward. I forgot he was there. But now his pinched voice cracks through the fuzziness in my ears to say, "A lottery."

"Ouch." Davi shakes his head. "I remember trying to win some tix to an NHL All-Star game once. My little sister drained my phone battery playing *Candy Crush*, though. I forgot my charger. Couldn't log on in time."

"Is that what happened?"

I'm still not looking at Diego, but he's shifted from the edges of my vision. He's closer, crisper. The disappointment in his face is unmistakable.

"No. My battery was good." But I'm sure Diego knows that. I always keep my phone charged. Diego slides off the hood and I follow. "We were all just talking that day. You know how F.B. gets going—"

"He's intense," Davi confirms, laughing.

But Diego remains silent. His back to me. Shoulders drooped like the heaviness of the truth I've been keeping is weighing him down.

"Just talking. You and F.B. and . . . Davi, right?"

"Yes." I nod slowly. "But you knew that. Remember?"

I already made this confession in his bedroom. But Diego's staring at me like I'd left a detail out when explaining things. Did I?

"That was before . . ." Diego trails off, no longer staring at my face. His eyes flit over Davi. "Never mind."

Davi raises an eyebrow. I don't get a chance to question what Diego was going to originally say, because he's walking away.

My hand trembles at my side, like I should reach for him. Dampness overtakes my vision. Finally, I force my voice to work: "Diego, I—"

But there are no words. How do you explain to your best friend that not only have you ruined their future, but you did it because of a boy?

You can't. In every universe, every alternate reality, you're still the asshole.

Over his shoulder, Diego announces, "I'm gonna grab Ollie a Cookie-licious Mondo Shake. He'd like to know I was thinking about him." It's hard to miss the frown pulling his entire expression down. He clears his throat like he might say more.

But he doesn't.

And I don't either.

Davi says, "Okay. Weird."

I pivot in his direction. He's staring at me funny. As if he's lost on what just happened.

I paste on a smile. "Best friends, right?" I say, nodding in the direction of Diego disappearing into Twisted Burger.

Davi shrugs, then his expression softens. It's a look I've seen him direct toward girls he's talking to. The one he wore while dancing with Callie at prom.

Except . . . it's for me.

"I've got to run before all this gets cold." He holds up the bag. "I'll, uh. We'll talk, okay?" His cheeks pinken again.

I like that color on him. I like the way he's stumbling and I'm fighting a grin and the night seems so big but also so closed in around us.

It's got that *Disaster Academy* Issue #6 energy.

Davi walks to his car in a far corner of the lot. I lower my chin but secretly watch him. He looks back once, then shakes his head. It makes my heart sputter. Until I hear the familiar noise of F.B. and the others.

They're all slurping Mondo Shakes as they approach. I scan the group. Diego's not with them. He's still inside. That's when guilt truly worms its way into my heart.

After a large gulp—and fighting through a brain freeze—F.B. finally says, "So, what'd we miss?"

I wish I could reply.

I wish this night had ended a long, long time ago.

Twelve

GEEKS NATION FORUM

Re: DISASTERS #11 OUT NOW!!!

TheAristotleMendoza: Wheres @ACharmingReverb with his review of DA #11? Hes never this late. DID HE SEE THE LOOK?!

JulianDiazLuvsYadz: mayb thse last few pages killed him? rip #charmverb fans! Lmao

I can't breathe.

My brain is fuzzy. Everything except my fingers are numb. This is *the moment.*

I'm holding *Disaster Academy* #11, the latest issue. I've avoided reading it since the Day Davi Returned—also known as the Day Destiny Sucker Punched Me—because every time I pick it up, I think about the fact that I'm not going to Legends Con. I won't be face-to-face with Peter and Jorge to find out the answer I need to . . . I don't know.

To feel kids like me get the happy ending we deserve.

I squint at the page.

"You did it!" Reverb says.

"*We* did it," Charm says.

They're smiling at each other, hands on each other's

shoulders. Their school uniforms are covered in dirt and debris. Half the observatory is destroyed. But Charm and Reverb are only looking at each other, not the mess they've created defeating Replicant.

"Say it," I whisper when I remember how to breathe.

The next page is a single panel of joy and chaos. I bite my lip, grinning.

Mrs. Zafar, Reverb's mother, is cupping Charm's cheeks with grateful tears streaming down her face while Mr. Zafar shout-laughs "My boy!" to him.

Charm's mom, Mrs. Morris, is bear-hugging Reverb.

Earlier in the comic, the Webster Academy for the Different was celebrating Family Day. Of course the villain decided to attack when Charm and Reverb were meeting each other's parents for the first time.

Now they stand in the wreckage of the school. Over their shoulders, Charm and Reverb give each other this look. The Look. I don't have the bandwidth to process it all, but I know as soon as they escape their parents, Charm will finally say . . .

Bzzt.

My phone vibrates on the beat-up carpet in my corner of Secret Planet. I ignore it, refocusing my eyes on Charm's supergiant-bright smile. Earth science was one of my least favorite classes in middle school, but I still remember Ms. Gallagher going on for a solid week about how luminous those stars are.

Bzzt. Bzzt.

I sigh before finally giving in to my phone's demands. I have seven notifications, all text messages.

We have an official group chat now.

It's the weirdest thing. We haven't hung out since the diner and Memorial Park and Twisted Burger. That was three days ago.

Diego and I haven't been around each other, either, since he dropped me off that night.

We definitely haven't talked about the kiss or Davi.

There's an awkwardness between us now. Not kiss related. I think. Diego's busy working on his gaming ideas, and I don't want to interrupt his research. But I might be avoiding us formally discussing Davi being the reason we're not going to Legends Con.

That also means I'm spending less time with my best friend, which was never the plan.

Bzzt.

Anyway, now there's this group chat. It's mainly F.B. dropping random texts about whatever. Blake comments back. Zelda responds with emojis. Diego's replies are all "LOL," while Alix has made it her mission to grammar check everyone.

I read through everything but rarely reply.

Diego's noticed. He's messaged me privately with GIFs from our favorite movies or the geekiest *Disaster Academy* memes he can find.

At least we still have that.

My phone vibrates with another new message.

> F.B.:
> What about the Six?
> 2:12 PM

> Blake:
> The Six? What kind of 1st gen MEGA MAN name is
> that??
> 2:12 PM

A gray chat bubble pops up with three blinking dots. Zelda replies with several side-eye emojis.

I scroll up to find the current debate is over a group name. Then I crane my neck to look at the front counter, where F.B. is tapping away on his phone. Five feet away, sitting on the thinning carpet with his phone in one hand and a portable gaming console in the other, is Blake.

There are two competing text bubbles in the chat.

"For real?" I groan. "I'm literally right here. In the same place."

Bzzt.

"But Zelda's not here," F.B. says, peeking over his screen.

Bzzt. Bzzt.

"And KonamiCode's MIA too," says Blake, eyes

bouncing between the two devices in his hands. "He's preoccupied with . . ." He doesn't finish, a sheepish expression blooming across his face as he stares at me.

Before I can ask anything, Alix says, "None of us would be opposed to you being unaccounted for too."

I glare at her. She sits, legs folded under her, in her favorite spot on the carpet. A mini stack of graphic novels surrounds her. It's a colorful fortress separating her from the living and breathing. I'm two seconds away from unleashing a marginally acceptable clapback when I notice something: Alix is reading *Disaster Academy*. The same issue I was devouring before my phone went nuclear.

I didn't know Alix read *Disaster Academy*.

But it means nothing. I'm not going to be friends with Alix. I can make small talk with F.B. Be civil with Blake and Zelda for Diego. That's it. And I guess I'm disappointed that he's not here. How can I make it up to him if he's not even around?

The worst part is I know this is what life will be like after the summer. Me, surrounded by people I don't know how to talk to or don't *want* to talk to. And Diego, too busy for anything but the occasional GIF or meme or LOL. The distance between us not only physical, but mental and emotional too.

"You okay, Captain Incredible?"

I lift my head slightly. "Yeah."

My voice sounds distant, an echo in the empty comic book store. I shoot F.B. a tight smile for reassurance. Then I slide the comic into my backpack, grab my phone, and stride toward the door.

Okay is a distant fifth place to what I am right now.

The air outside is scented with a heavy sweetness.

Pineapples and mangoes and berries.

Next to Secret Planet is NRG, a smoothie shop. It promises fewer calories, all fresh fruit, and every bland green vegetable imaginable in your drink. Bella worked there the summer before her senior year. Her clothes always smelled like protein powder mixed with weird chemicals. Iggy hated the overwhelming aroma, so of course Bella picked up as many shifts as possible.

These are the rules of Anti-Iggy squad.

I lean against the sliver of brick wall that separates Secret Planet and NRG. There's no shade here. The afternoon sun beats down on my face mercilessly.

Someone walks out of the smoothie shop. A maroon apron is slung over her shoulder as she passes. She slurps a goldenrod smoothie in a plastic cup with NRG's logo—a lightning bolt paired with text in Comic Sans.

Her smile while reading something on her phone gives me a familiar sensation. Like tearing wrapping paper with your fingers. The thrill of chasing what's underneath.

It reminds me of all the faces Bella made after work while checking texts from whatever boy she met at the shop earlier that day. She'd never tell me all the details. Just the names. Jamal or Andre or Jordan. And what kind of shoes they were wearing. Bella's such a sneakerhead. She never took any of the guys seriously—too focused on school and volleyball and working through her own Mom-and-Carlos issues—but it was still nice to share another thing with my sister.

Iggy, the serial dater, only discussed girls with Mom. Her approval bought whatever girl he liked an extra month at the minimum.

I unearth my phone from my back pocket. It only takes two consecutive *deet-deet-deet*s before my screen is transformed into a sideways view of poorly styled copper hair and some tragic singing.

"Is that . . . Ed Sheeran?"

There's a giggle, then the image goes from shaky to a close-up of my sister's face. "My husband thinks singing to my belly is going to make our firstborn stan wackass Ed Sheeran rather than a true legend like Bruno."

"Our baby will love ginger-haired singer-songwriters," Chris argues in the background. I can see his angled head resting on Bella's plump stomach. "And don't call Ed wack."

"Are y'all on a first name basis now?" Bella says.

Chris blows a raspberry against her exposed belly. Her

giggles intensify to levels I'm certain only dogs understand.

As grossed out as I am, I can't help but smile.

From the moment she finally realized all the other guys she was dating were trash, Bella and Chris have been an epic team. They'd known each other since freshman orientation at South University in Savannah. After those last two years of high school, Bella was dying to get away from city life and our parents' issues. Chris was the local boy, so he escorted Bella and her friends around town on weekends. She didn't catch on that all the times he asked her to grab a coffee, he meant *only her*, until Mom pointed it out. By the end of sophomore year, they were a couple, and married before senior year started. Now Bella plans to finish her studies and graduate a year after the baby is born.

I think that's why I've always liked Chris. He was Bella's reset.

"Hey," I say, making a face. "I didn't call for all this PDH."

"PDH?" Chris asks.

"Public displays of heterosexuality," Bella and I say together, except her voice is dry and unimpressed.

I hold the camera high to capture the full breadth of my smirk.

"Oh. Hilarious." Chris chuckles.

My cheeks warm. As corny as Chris is, I still get a funny feeling when I'm able to impress him with my humor.

Probably because nothing I've ever said has moved Iggy.

Chris, as a brother-in-law, is light-years ahead of Iggy in the acceptable sibling role.

"What *did* you call for?" Bella finally asks. "Miss me?"

"Not even a little bit."

We grin. She knows the truth; I don't have to confirm it.

"I'll be there soon enough," she says, then yawns.

"I know."

But I wish Bella were here now. Even in her constantly tired, pregnant state, I need my sister around. To recalibrate my systems. Fix this imbalance in my life. Yes, I still have Mom and Abuelito, but everything feels lopsided because of Diego.

"So, what's up?"

Bella plays with her curls, waiting for me. I love that about her and Diego. They let me think through my words.

I consider telling her about the Diego situation. Not the kiss. But the Legends Con catastrophe. How the weight of destroying my best friend's chance at achieving his dream keeps me in bed an extra thirty minutes every morning. How I still want to fix that.

"Uh."

Bella and I have a pretty tight relationship, but she's also very close to Mom. I'm not ready for Mom to find out about any of this yet. Not secondhand.

"Isaac?"

"It's nothing." I smile hard.

Even with the momentary distortion on the screen from poor reception, I can still see Bella's eye-roll. She sucks air through her teeth for emphasis. "I don't know who you think you're fooling but—"

"Isaac? Hey."

I almost drop my phone at the voice calling out to me.

It's the same timbre and excitement from the other night.

Davi jogs up to me, waving. Four years of high school together and we rarely shared the same hall space during the day. Yet this is the fourth time we've run into each other in fewer than two weeks. Is it a sign? Or is there a rule that once high school is over, you see less of the people you hate and more of the ones you wish you would've spent more time with?

When he stretches in front of me, Davi's tank top rides up enough to expose a view of his toned abdomen and a strip of dark hair from his belly button to the waistband of his nylon shorts. "Sorry." He points to my phone. "Am I interrupting?"

"No!" I quickly cover the speaker just in case my sister decides to revert to no-filter, seventeen-year-old Bella who would have absolutely zero problems telling Davi that he's *indeed* interrupting. "It's nothing."

"Okay," he says slowly, doubtful.

"Just give me a sec."

I raise my phone. Bella and Chris are whispering and it's clear *who* they're talking about. "Can I call you later?"

"Uh-huh," they say in unison.

Then, Bella says, "You're making The Face."

I hang up before she can say any more.

Davi leans back on his heels, grinning. "So, how are you?"

"I'm so good." The wave of lightheadedness that attacks me says otherwise.

"Well"—Davi looks amused—"that's *so* good, then."

I laugh. I don't know what else to do. Something about Davi, glistening and perfect, makes me feel exposed. A good kind of exposed, though.

"I'm glad I ran into you."

"Again?" I tease, but that one word requires tremendous effort.

He nods. "I realized I didn't ask you for your number the other night."

"Oh." I scratch my eyebrow. "I mean, you follow me on IG and stuff. You could've . . ."

"Slid into your DMs?" Davi laughs, soft and genuine.

There's only one option for escaping this level of embarrassment: hurling my body into oncoming traffic.

But it's a slow day in downtown Alpharetta. Even the local MARTA bus is too slow moving to do the bodily damage required to exit this moment.

"I'm joking." His eyes crinkle. "Mamãe always says we

152

do too much communication via social media. We need to do things the old-school way."

"Right."

"Like asking a boy for his number." There's a pale redness to his face, as if this is just as awkward for him.

I can't imagine it is.

"So . . . mamãe? That's your mom?"

His happy-scrunched eyes answer the question for me.

"Your mom knows about me?"

"Oh, no."

Of course not. Why would Davi mention me to his family? I'm still sixth-grade Isaac, barely memorable tour guide.

Davi digs the toe of his sneaker into a broken piece of sidewalk. "I don't talk to Mamãe about boys. We have this unspoken policy: I don't bring up that I'm bi, and she pretends it doesn't exist when she's around her church friends."

"Sorry."

"Don't be," he says with a sad smile. "Papai is really cool about it. If I keep up the hockey thing, graduate on time with a business degree so I can help when he retires, he doesn't care who I date."

"Nice."

"Most def." His smile returns to its usual easiness. "Anyway. There's this movie coming out tonight and—"

"Which one?" I desperately try to control my thudding heart.

"The spy movie where the guy's really a brainwashed assassin for a corrupt foreign government."

Somehow, I manage to maintain eye contact as Davi speaks. Action movies are me and Abuelito's least favorite. At least, the nonsuperhero ones with massive Hollywood budgets and two hours of cars exploding, unrealistic plot twists, and the girl needing "Insert Hot White Guy with limited acting abilities and a huge case of mansplaining" as an agent to her rescue.

"Are you in?"

I don't know why I'm hesitating. It's a movie with Davi Lucas. But I've never done this. I don't know if I'm *ready* to do this.

"We could grab something to eat after," he offers.

We. Davi and me. In a dark theater where there are reduced opportunities for discussions. Maybe I could survive having a burger or something with him afterward. I did it with the Six—I can't believe I'm endorsing that name—three days ago.

Something about Davi's hopeful expression makes me feel . . . comfortable.

Maybe, if things work out, I can ask him to hang out at Pride.

Maybe he'll kiss me at the end of the night. My first official kiss. Not the practice, off-the-record one with Diego.

In a very chill way, I gaze at Davi's mouth. His full lips

have just the slightest part between them, like words are constantly waiting to escape. I wonder if he's a soft kisser. *Does he prefer slow or fast? Is he okay with tongue? Does he kiss like— No. Shit, shit, shit. Has Diego ruined this for all future kisses? Will Diego's ghost forever linger between Davi and me?*

"Isaac?"

"Yes!" I say too emphatically when my brain realigns. "Tonight. I'd love to."

He passes me his phone. The screen has a small lightning bolt crack. It's kind of endearing that Davi Lucas, star right wing of East Middleton High School's ice hockey club and future American Hockey League Hall of Famer, has a splintered phone screen like the rest of us mortals.

I add my number to his contacts with shaking hands. It takes three tries to spell my name right. When I offer back his phone, our fingertips brush. And, no, there's no electricity when it happens.

There's an apocalyptic thunderstorm.

"Around eightish? I can pick you up if you want?" he offers.

The temporal rifts that might occur if Davi comes by my house are too great to risk. Davi meeting Mom? The possibilities of her turning this into A Thing. Or worse, Abuelito being there and turning it into A—*The Princess Bride*, all caps—THING.

"No, I'll meet you."

We agree to link up at a shopping center three miles from my house. I know it well enough that I can stash my bike behind the pizzeria nearby. This might be the beginning of Davi's journey into my reasonably geeky alternate universe, but I'm not ready to expose my inability to operate a motor vehicle just yet.

Some alter egos should remain hidden.

"Cool, cool." He slips in an earbud, then waves as he jogs away.

I wave to his back for a solid minute before realizing he can't see me. Damn. I hope I'm not this awkward on our date.

"Oh, shit," I say, slapping a hand over my mouth when a father pushes a baby stroller by. He shrugs at me as if it's not that serious. But it is.

I have a date with Davi Lucas.

Thirteen

Young Titans Reviews

Top reviews for *Disaster Academy* #5

@Coopthe4th

★★★★★

Let's be real: this series is all about CHARM. A gay Black superhero with agency, solid growth, and emotional relatability? Love to see it! Also: did anyone peep that smile he gave REVERB? What about when Reverb blushed? Let em go on a date ASAP. Give the Black boy a win!

I meet Davi outside of Young Mario's, a pizzeria two blocks from the movie theater.

"Hey."

"Nice evening," I say. A "hello" or one of those "'sup" head nods isn't simple enough, I guess. It's too bad I spent so much time stressing over what to wear tonight instead of browsing YouTube for basic first date social behavior videos.

"It is kind of nice, huh?" He smiles at everything around us.

The air is warm with the lingering scent of coffee and

pastries from a nearby café. The string lights strung above Young Mario's outdoor seating sway. Someone's car is parked curbside by a furniture store, their hatchback lifted, pouring John Legend's music into the streets.

The perfect date-night atmosphere.

Davi's phone screen lights up and he says, "The movie starts in twenty. We should probably, you know, move."

"Okay."

We walk northward to the theater. Thankfully, Davi does most of the talking. Nerves have sunken sharp fangs into my stomach. As we wait on crosswalk signals to change, he jumps from hockey to television series he's marathoning to a YouTube reviewer his younger sister is obsessed with. He's flawless at carrying the conversation, which is a relief. I can nod and *hmm* and smile at all the right places without appearing too awkward.

That is, until we finally arrive at the theater's parking lot.

We're no longer alone.

"Davi!"

Three boys race up to us. Rounds of fist bumps and complex handshakes and one-arm hugs are exchanged before Davi introduces them.

"Ezra, Jax, and Amin."

But I'm already familiar with them, at least through casual observation. They're current or former—Ezra graduated with Davi and me—members of East Middleton High School's ice hockey club.

"You guys know my, uh . . ." Davi stammers next to me. "Isaac Martin from school."

"Sure." Ezra up-nods at me in that casual way I should've greeted Davi with earlier.

"Yup," Jax says, scanning me with a skeptical smile as if he's probably never paid attention to me until this very moment.

But I can't focus on Jax's first—second?—impression. My mind lingers on Davi's words. One word: *My.*

My what?

Friend? Sidekick? Uncomfortably nervous date?

"Bro, you're late," Jax whines to Davi. His arms are crossed and he has very thick, judgmental eyebrows. They're a shade lighter than his dirty blond hair that's pulled into a hipsterlike man bun.

Davi rolls his eyes, grinning.

"Now, Davi, you know our Jackson isn't down for missing the trailers," Ezra says, curling an arm around Jax's broad shoulders. He's significantly taller than Jax, almost my height, with light brown skin, and a smile made for charming villains.

"Translation: You're a punk. Stop man crushing on Ryan Reynolds," Amin says to Jax. His closely shaved dark hair exaggerates the sharpness of his cheekbones. He's the only soon-to-be-junior at East Middleton to effortlessly achieve a full mustache-chinstrap combo.

I bet he doesn't get carded anywhere.

"Fuck you both," Jax says with little heat in his voice. "Double-R is iconic. He'd make the perfect movie version of Shrapnel."

First off: nicknaming Ryan Reynolds "Double-R" is a no.

Secondly: going by the excitement blossoming in his eyes, this kid seems to have a serious hard-on for an unworthy comic book character.

But then it clicks—Jax is Davi's best friend. He's the reason Davi came into Secret Planet that day. I suppose I should thank him. Then again . . . *Shrapnel*?

Ezra, Amin, and Jax continue their shit talking with the occasional silent stares only true friends can comprehend. Davi nods and laughs by my side. It's nice—his warmth, how unbothered he is by our proximity. But I don't understand any of their inside jokes.

Once again, I'm out of place around so many unfamiliar faces.

It's like the other night with Diego. The same Diego who hasn't responded to my text from two hours ago asking which shirt I should wear. I didn't tell him where I was going. I just wanted his opinion.

I wanted things to be normal.

Now the bright glow of the theater's marquee bounces off the cherry blossoms on the white T-shirt Bella bought me. *But it's still not Diego-approved.*

Why does that matter right now? I'm with Davi. He asked me to go to see an action movie . . . with his friends.

That's not typical first date protocol, is it?

Disappointment seizes my lungs and makes every breath I take harder than the previous one. This isn't a date. It's not even date adjacent.

"Chill, Jackson." Ezra grumbles as Jax anxiously tugs him toward the entrance. "Your obsession with Ryan as a future husband is unhealthy."

"It's mad platonic. Double-R and me are life-mates," insists Jax. "That means I won't have to share my potential 401(k) in the future."

"In our current political climate, you actually think financial security is guaranteed?" Amin asks.

"Obviously. White privilege always wins," Ezra says dryly.

"Ez, we agreed that I'm an ally who recognizes the need for universal equality," Jax says matter-of-factly.

"That's the same shit your ancestors said, Jackson."

I almost laugh at that. Davi does, unrestrainedly.

His strong fingers circle my wrist as his friends scramble for the front entrance. I try not to look surprised. "Is this okay?" he asks in a low voice, even though we're the only two boys standing awkwardly in a parking lot like we're plotting something sketchy.

I want to tell him no. None of this is okay. And that I want to go home, curl up on my bed in a pair of sweats and my orange *Disaster Academy* T-shirt so I can finish my comic from earlier.

I don't want to be around *his* friends.

"Sorry if it's not," he says before I can reply. Not that I was going to. "The guys really wanted to see this movie. Soon, we won't be able to hang out for God knows how long."

His eyes are large, a shine in them that I know isn't from the parking lot lighting.

Davi won't have his boys at college, just like I won't have Diego. It's probably not the same for him, though. Davi's outgoing. Instantly likable. It didn't take him long to make friends in middle school.

The New Kid Curse wasn't a thing for him.

"You can say it's not okay. I promise I won't mind."

But I still don't tell him how I feel. I say, "It's cool." Like a coward.

Davi beams. His fingers slip down my wrist, feather light. They skim my palm. Our fingers nearly catch, then his hand drops to his side. My heart flops into a pool of stomach acid.

"Thanks, Isaac," he whispers, guiding me toward our official non-date.

It's not the worst night ever.

The movie was predictable. Not that I paid much attention to it. I spent most of the two hours with my right knee bouncing uncontrollably, which was hard to hide with my foot sticking and unsticking to the gross theater floor. I sat at the end of the row. To my left, Davi leaned my way the entire time. Every laugh, his shoulder brushed mine. Every explosion, his fingers gripped the armrest, white knuckles and veins so close to my own hand.

During the sex scene, his eyes almost found mine. Almost. But I chickened out at the last second and stared at the bag of Twizzlers in my lap instead.

The pulse of that *almost* lingered until the end credits.

After, Jax was craving mozzarella sticks. Davi gave me this sidelong look. It wasn't a guilt trip, though. There was no obligation attached to his expression. In the creases of Davi's shy smile, I saw something else.

It felt like he didn't want our night to end.

Maybe I didn't either.

Now we're in a corner booth at Cosmos and Java. "I can't believe you dated her," Amin shouts, shaking his head at Jax.

"We didn't date," Jax argues. "We hooked up. Several times."

"Bruh, you dated her." Ezra points a half-eaten mozzarella stick at him. "You cried when she started ghosting you."

"*Sobbed*," Davi clarifies. "On my bed, after practice."

Jax glares playfully at him. That casual, fake animosity only best friends can achieve without it going overboard. They fist-bump across the table, squashing their nonexistent beef.

I slouch low. This war of insults and shaming each other's dating history has lasted thirty minutes. Before that, it was an abundance of hockey talk.

Jax and Amin are on one side of the booth. Davi's squeezed between Ezra and me on the other. Truth is, I feel like I'm at a table by myself. I still have no reference point for their jokes. I know half the girls they mention, but by name only. Part of me wants to know things about their friendships and deep secrets and what other things have made them cry.

But I don't know *how* to ask those questions.

It's disorienting to, once again, be the odd one out.

I browse Geeks Nation on my phone. During the trailers, I may or may not have started a war with two other posters over whether Boomstar was originally supposed to be a love interest for Reverb. Yeah, right. It's bullshit. Peter and Jorge would never.

The thread's picking up speed. The other two posters have gone in *deep* with their theories. But the odds are in my favor.

After all, I'm the creator of the "HISTORY OF CHARM-VERB IN GIFS" thread.

One point eight thousand likes and counting.

"So no one's going to bring up Davi and Hannah?" Jax mumbles, his mouth full of cheese and marinara sauce.

I nearly drop my phone between my legs. Most of the conversation has been dissecting Jax's famed—and questionable—relationship choices. There was a brief inquiry into Amin dating Priya, who graduated last year. But nothing about Davi.

My neck prickles. I'm curious, but also intimidated.

Davi says, "It was nothing. We're cool."

No one argues. They all nod, as if it's a dead subject. But it's not for me. I'm already mentally scrolling through Davi's followers on Instagram. Do I know a Hannah? Did she go to East Middleton?

Davi slumps, his side pressed to mine. He says, "What about Ez and Roy?" with a smirk.

The table *ooh*s while Ezra squints at Davi. "You're gonna go there?"

"First-class tickets booked, bro."

Ezra rolls his eyes. His complexion is nearly as brown as mine, but his blush stands out against his cheeks in this almost maroon hue. He shrugs. "Roy was definitely worth it."

Everyone laughs at that. Davi's face is turned enough that his breath tickles my jaw. Then he stays there, his head almost on my shoulder. Amin starts showing off old YouTube clips of *Steven Universe*, reciting every scene word-for-word. And Davi never moves.

My phone vibrates in my lap. I peek down at it.

The group chat is active. But there are also a few missed texts from Diego I frown at.

After five hours, he's finally decided to reply. He offers opinions on my outfit and asks what I'm up to before rambling about his mom.

Davi's laugh shakes me. I close out Diego's texts without responding. But I don't lock my phone. Instead, I open a new message.

> To: Bella
> I think I'm on a date??? IDK.
> We're with his friends.
> 10:48 PM

It takes less than a minute for the gray text bubble to appear, the ellipsis blinking as Bella types.

> From: Bella
> Do you feel awkward?
> 10:49 PM

I exhale quietly. Bella knows me so well.

> To: Bella
> YES!!! 😱
> 10:50 PM

Jax and Ezra are arguing over dessert choices. Davi, still

against me, gently reminds them about dietary restrictions and summer training. Amin records it all on his phone.

From: Bella

Is this crush syndrome from earlier? Give him a chance . . . it doesnt have to be permenent.

10:52 PM

I roll my eyes, trying hard not to correct Bella on her spelling. I refuse to be Alix Jin.

"Hey, hey," Davi says, straightening up. His warmth disappears. But his eyes are on me, wide and twinkling. "I'd love to hear Isaac's opinion on Shrapnel."

Jax sits up. Ezra rubs his chin, waiting. Amin leans back with this shit-eating expression as if he knows I'm about to go in on Shrapnel and is anticipating the moment Jax's face inevitably falls. But it's Davi peeking at me through his long eyelashes that unravels that uncertainty I was just texting Bella about. He's opened a portal into their world, allowing me to join their conversation.

"Tell us," Amin says.

Davi's arm gently slides around my shoulders. He gives me a squeeze.

Give him a chance.

"Okay." I clear my throat before angling to face Jax. "First of all . . ."

"Did you see the look on his face?"

Davi laughs so loud, people passing us raise their eyebrows as we walk back toward Young Mario's. He doesn't seem to care. We left his friends outside of Cosmos and Java. Amin mentioned something about a party. What's a summer without a kickback and alcohol and the nauseating scent of regret the next morning? But Davi wasn't interested in going. No one gave him crap about it either.

I have this weird feeling Davi's the alpha of their group.

"I can't believe it. Jackson Riley, shut down by Isaac the Phenomenal."

I grin. He thinks I'm phenomenal.

The inky black sky above us is endless. No stars, no moon. But all the possibility is there, as if within that long stretch of space, a hundred million realities exist. The kinds where Davi and I hold hands instead of keeping just enough distance that the elderly couples around us don't stare.

A reality where he bites his bottom lip because he wants to kiss me.

Another world where my heartbeat is low-key instead of thundering away when he cheats a look at me as we pause at a crosswalk.

"They weren't too much, were they?" Davi rubs the back of his neck. I've learned it's a sign of his anxiety.

"Your friends?"

He nods with an offbeat smile.

"They were—"

"Extra?" He laughs again, but it's subdued. That unsure one where you've made a joke but think it's going to fall flat. "That's why I like them. Without my boys, I'm too serious. All I think about are the goals people like me aren't supposed to achieve. But I have to."

"I get that."

Truth is, I know it can't be easy for Davi. He'll never be like Jax, who, despite his unwavering determination to break systemic cycles, will always automatically be the default to everything. Straight, white, male—the holy trinity.

"Yeah, I guess you would, Isaac."

The crosswalk light finally changes. We hesitate. I look at him. The ivory glow of the walk signal frames his brown eyes. He rubs his neck again, then stops and grins.

"Come on."

We wander through back roads but stick to sidewalks and paths visible by streetlight. Black and brown boys strolling through quiet, suburban communities isn't something that goes unnoticed—for all the wrong reasons, even in a city I've lived in for my entire life. If Jax were here, it'd be a different story. But Davi confidently leads me along a different route from the one we took earlier.

Maybe he doesn't want our journey to end.

I'm fine with that.

The night opens around us like a pair of arms waiting to catch our free-fall into something new. Neighborhoods are lit honey by streetlamps. Roaring cicadas and restless dogs behind cedar fences are the soundtrack of our walk. We pass darkened houses with old cars leaking oily drool down the driveways. Our steps fall into rhythm as Davi explains what it was like coming out to his coaches, then the team.

"Everyone's been mostly cool," he says.

"Why wouldn't they be?"

His right eyebrow lifts. "You'd be surprised. Like, no one's ever said anything to my face or anything, but those three?" He motions behind us, as if his friends are still nearby. "They never let any homophobic shit go down. Not in the locker room. On the ice. Nowhere."

We cross over another street, back onto the main road.

"I mean, I still have to call Jax out for saying 'that's gay' when something's corny or ridiculous," he continues. "But I'm comfortable in every situation as long as they're there."

It's hard to shrink the size of my smile. Ezra, Amin, and Jax—yes, even Jax—seem like good friends.

"I guess it helps that Ez is pan." He pauses at another crosswalk. "You know, pansexual?"

"Yeah, thanks. I'm super versed in sexual identities."

He bumps my shoulder with his, smirking.

"The only one I don't understand is that heterosexual thing," I say. "When are people going to realize it's just a phase?"

"Right?" Davi says. "I think they're confused."

"Maybe they haven't met the right person yet?"

"Hopefully, they'll grow out of it."

"But what if they don't?" I gasp dramatically.

That sets us off. We crack up, somehow drifting closer. Davi says, "I wish Ez was going to Pride with me."

"He's not?"

"No. His family vacations in Orlando around that time."

I nod, frowning. I don't know why I'm disappointed. Briefly, I imagine Davi and Ezra hanging out at Pride with Diego and me.

"Anyway," he says, "Ez has offered—more than once—to set me up with someone."

There's this tiny echo in my chest like my heart's skipped a few beats.

"I'd never let him, though," Davi says assertively. "I think I've made some solid dating choices in the past."

Like Hannah? I want to ask, but that's not fair to him or Hannah. I'm a certifiable asshole for even considering it.

"Jax would disagree, though."

"Jax has wet dreams about Double-R." I make a face. "Bad nicknames aside, though, he seems like a reasonably good best friend."

"Really?" There's something about Davi's voice, as if he's searching for my approval.

"He's no Diego, but . . ." I let the words hang, flashing him a teasing smile.

"No." Davi stops again. "Diego's a hard guy to . . ."

He doesn't finish. I scan his face. It's serious for a second, then he blinks and he's beaming again.

We're outside Young Mario's. I have no clue when we got here.

It's dark inside, but the neon red HOT PIZZA sign hung in the front window gleams off the curious curl of his lips.

I want to kiss him.

"This was cool," he says.

"Yeah?"

He nods once.

Damn, I want to be that boy who just takes risks. I want to be like Buttercup and say what's on my mind. The kind of person who's spontaneous and falls hard and doesn't constantly worry about the what-ifs.

No one ever tells you that the what-ifs never go away. They change shape, go from loud to quiet. But they never truly disappear.

"We should do this again," he says. "Soon."

"Soon," I repeat softly.

What if I just inched closer and—

Then he's here. One hand on my shoulder, the other

carefully touching the back of my neck. I'm sweating. And I'm hard, which is awkward considering how close he is.

Davi's fingers creep into my hair. I almost flinch away, out of instinct. It's weird having someone's fingers there, other than Bella's or Diego's.

Why am I thinking about Diego?

Why am I watching Davi's mouth, wet and soft-looking, and remembering Diego's lips?

Why am I replaying a high-def version of our kiss, Diego and me, on repeat? The clumsiness. The smell of burgers in the air. His teeth. My fingers against his scar.

Davi's breaths are slow, deep.

I close my eyes. My brain's singing a new song: *kiss me, kiss me, kiss me.*

And it happens.

Davi Lucas kisses . . . the corner of my mouth. Practically my cheek. "Thanks, Isaac," he whispers, backing away. "Text me when you get home."

Then he's gone. His warmth and voice and everything.

I'm left standing in front of Young Mario's with the ghost of a first—*real*—kiss that never happened.

Fourteen

Our Fictious Chronicles

Fic: On the Other Side of What If   By **OkayDariusOkay**

Rating: Teen and Up   **Fandom:** Disaster Academy

Pairing: Charm/Reverb   **Tags:** First Kiss, Friends to Lovers, Fluff, Romance, Slow Burn, Mild Angst, Pining, Alternate Universe—Coffeeshop, set after issue 6, barista!reverb, dorkcustomer!charm, One True Pairing, more than kissing likely

Chapters: 5/?   **Likes:** 3001   **Words:** 34,751

Comments:

IMartino210 · June 16 00:12 AM: Sorry you've been busy with family stuff but: this chapter was so short. and they still didn't kiss. nothing. they should kiss at least once by now. more-than-kissing stuff too. lots of it 😊 charm wouldn't just . . . let reverb walk away like that. HE'D KISS HIM!

The next morning, my phone and the golden light outside my window wake me far too early.

"You look like shit."

I sneeze twice before squinting at Diego's sideways face on the screen. He's wearing his headset, which means his phone is propped somewhere on his bed while we FaceTime. I peek at the time. It's barely 8:00 a.m. and he's already playing video games.

"Thanks," I say, throat scratchy.

"I'm always here to give you honest takes on your face," he teases with scrunched, exhausted eyes.

I yawn again, then flip him off.

I didn't sleep much after my non-date—and consequent non-kiss—with Davi. I can't seem to shake the disappointment. Did I say something wrong? Maybe I should've made it clearer that I'm into him.

"So . . ." Diego starts, but doesn't finish. The volume in the background is loud enough for me to hear the soundtrack for *Beyond the Valley of Stars* playing. It's accompanied by the *click-click-click* of his fingers on the controller. I let it fill our silence. Diego's eyes flick back and forth between screens.

When our eyes finally meet for more than three seconds, I ask, "Is something wrong?"

"What? No." He laughs clumsily. Then he says, "You didn't reply to any of my texts. Or any of the group chat messages either."

"Yeah, uh . . ."

"Was your phone dead?"

"No." I can hear the sharpness in my voice.

Diego studies me. His hand brushes over the top of his

hair. He does that when he's thinking. Involuntarily, I do too. In a bottom corner of the screen is a small box with my face in it. I need a haircut.

I need Diego to be upset or normal or whatever about all this, not impassive.

What I really need is for him to stop being so busy with video games and act as if this summer is as important to him as it is to me.

Instead, he rubs his jaw. His thumb rests against his scar.

I've touched that scar.

I've kissed Diego.

I'm so stuck on that fact, I wonder if I would've even *enjoyed* a kiss from Davi.

"We were, uh, trying to meet up last night," he finally says.

I read all the messages when I got home. A long string of gray chat bubbles from F.B. about food and Taco Tuesdays even though it wasn't Tuesday. Blake rambled in all caps. Zelda exhausted the side-eye emoji. Alix ended the discourse with a classic *New phone. Who's this?* Grammatically correct as always.

In the middle of it all were three messages from Diego:

Isaac.

Isaac Martin.

ISAAC MARTIN.

"Yeah, sorry," I mumble, swallowing half of the second word.

"Were you busy?"

Intense heat consumes my face. I hate that Diego is interrogating me. That he's doing it while playing a video game and sounding so chill. I can't even call him out for ignoring my texts because at least he eventually replied. I kept him on read all night.

"I was occupied."

Diego snorts. "Is that code for reading some suspect Charm and Reverb fanfic while—"

I cut him off. "I was with Davi."

Silence overtakes us. The game is paused. He lifts the microphone piece away from his mouth but doesn't say anything. All I hear is his breaths. Or maybe they're mine.

My heartbeat's cranked to max volume.

I stare off at a corner of my room. A new tower of boxes has accumulated, climbing halfway up the slate gray wall. Mom's been in here packing. Piece by piece, she's stuffing my world into cardboard, dismantling everything I've known since I was old enough to have a room to myself. She's shoving me at warp speed into the future while I'm trying to stay rooted in the present.

Above the boxes is the dry erase board I used to

countdown the days until Legends Con. It's remained on 21 DAYS since the Davi Lucas Incident.

I finally look at the screen. The tension in Diego's jaw could cut flesh.

"Qué padre," he says, shrugging.

"¿Qué padre?"

He ignores the uncertainty in my voice. "That's tight. Did you have fun?"

"I guess." Then I remember sitting at the diner, going in on Jax's obsession with Shrapnel while Davi's head rested on my shoulder. "Yeah. I did."

"Did you kiss him?"

I cough violently, blinking away the tears fogging my vision. "What?"

"Did you," he says, slow and deliberate, "kiss him?"

The phone slips from my hand, thudding facedown on the sheets. Diego's laugh is loud and vibrant through the speaker. I count to three.

"Dude." He's still laughing when I turn the phone back around. "It's not that serious."

I don't speak.

"I just want to make sure all my skilled teaching didn't go to waste."

He smirks. This is a joke. My tragic non-date with Davi is a gag to him. *Poor Isaac; he can't climb out of his own shell enough to date anyone. He's nothing like Charm.*

"Isaac?"

But maybe I am like Charm. We're over ten issues into Disaster Academy *and he still hasn't said shit to Reverb about his crush. He hasn't owned up to his feelings.*

We're both pathetic.

"It doesn't matter." I glare at that dry erase board and the blue smudges where I've repeatedly wiped, then scribbled a new number. Today, I'm going to change it: a countdown until I'm at UGA and closer to the true version of Isaac Martin I want to be.

"Dude, what's up?"

"Nothing, man."

"It doesn't sound like 'nothing, man.'"

"Well, it is," I say, my frustration steadily building. "It's nothing." Something catches in my throat before I can say *I'm nothing.* It's as if someone strikes a match and the flame in my chest is seconds from escalating to a wildfire.

There are three soft knocks on my door, then it opens.

"Morning," Mom says, beaming. "Abuelito's downstairs."

"He is?" I ask, confused.

"I thought it'd be a good idea for you two to spend more time together before summer's over."

Before summer's over. But wasn't it just starting?

"He wants to take you to breakfast. Then maybe the park?"

I smile sadly. Out the corner of my eye, I spy Diego's pursed mouth and lowered eyebrows.

"I need to shower and brush my teeth first."

"And do something with that hair," teases Mom.

In her hand, Mom's phone rings. But it's not the default ringtone she assigns to everyone. It's not the Sencha melody she uses for Iggy, Bella, and me, either. Instead, an old-school, up-tempo Beyoncé song plays. Her face brightens when she peeks down at the screen, teeth biting into her lower lip.

"Who's that?" I ask.

She swipes to answer but doesn't put the phone to her ear, pressing it to her chest. "Don't be long," she warns.

I stare at my closed door after she leaves. The finger snaps and Beyoncé's shouting about someone putting her love on top bounce around in my head. *That's a strange ringtone for a client. Maybe it's someone else? Someone I don't know.*

But Mom only ever talks to us . . .

A throat clears. I lift my phone to face level and stare at Diego. "I gotta go."

Before I can end the call, Diego says, "Isaac . . ." He pauses, swallowing. "I'm happy for you, okay? I know it's not easy for you to be around new people. I know you're not . . ."

He blinks and blinks. I wait for him.

"I mean, you're amazing," he finally gets out. "Davi

would be a high-key jerk if he didn't see that."

I watch him pull on his hair. The corners of his mouth lift, only a little. It's Diego's way of apologizing.

"Whatever," I say, pushing the awkwardness out of my voice. "Go find another Imperio Stone, nerd. I'll text you when I get back."

That's my apology, too, I guess.

His grin is still shallow, but it's there. I smile back.

We're mostly okay.

"The sky's so blue today."

We're sitting in Memorial Park's gazebo, Abuelito and me. There are hardly any clouds overhead. It's a limitless stretch of cobalt. Sunlight drapes warm arms across the grass occupied by scattered families having picnics. In the distance, the light kisses the top of my unforgiving enemy, the wire fence. The same fence that, in another time, another reality, I climbed—and nearly died on—with Diego.

Diego.

I can't stop thinking about him.

We're cool, better than we were twenty-four hours ago, but I can't quite escape that slow-blooming tingle in my nerves. Something's not right. Our smiles, our words, our laughs—it's like we're functioning at seventy percent. Maybe less. It doesn't feel normal.

A hushed breeze comes and goes. June is the perfect

time for sitting here. July is an endless heat wave in Georgia. August is only slightly better. Abuelito leans against me, exhaling.

When I was younger, I'd spend hours tucked into his side. I remember resting my ear on his chest to count his heartbeats. I'd hold my breath until I could time my inhales with his. Beat for beat, I wanted to be just like him. Someone who loves unapologetically.

"Do you know why the sky's so blue?" asks Abuelito.

"Why?"

Our legs are stretched out onto the discolored wooden beams leading out to the green-blue lake. A man around Oscar's age is teaching his daughter how to fish at the end of the dock. She squeals every time his line jolts. A smile pulls at her father's cheeks like he can't ever imagine a world where he wasn't by her side. After a minute, I have to look away.

Abuelito clears his throat, a pre-speech habit. "The sky's sad," he begins. "It holds all our secrets. All day, it keeps them inside with no one to tell. Only at night, when the world's asleep, is the sky free to whisper those secrets into the empty blackness."

I grin at tips of sunlight crawling up our shoes. It's so ridiculous, so poetic. Abuelito pulled this story right out of those fairy tale fantasies he loves.

José Martin is the narrator of all the best happy endings.

My favorite is when he tells me about the moment he realized he was in love with my grandma: *"It was our third or fourth date. We saw* The Princess Bride. *I loved it! But your abuela was so quiet the whole time. Until after—her face was like sunshine."* He always takes a deep breath at this part. *"She couldn't stop talking about it. That look in her eyes—oh, Chiquito, it made me believe I'd found my storybook love. My happy ending!"*

It's hard to imagine one single moment can define how you fall in love with someone. But the way Abuelito tells that story makes me want to believe.

Now he tips his head back. "There's so much magic and mystery in the sky."

"Yeah."

"Summer, Chiquito." He fiddles with the cuff of his button-down shirt. It's the color of a blue jay's feathers and contrasts with the rich brown of his eyes, the gray of his mustache. "So many things happen in summer."

I never met my grandma. She died two years before I was born. But I've seen dozens of discolored Polaroids. Her warm smile and animated eyes. All the pretty dresses she owned. The way she pinned her dark hair up.

Abuelito's told so many stories, I feel as if I knew her. But I don't know Leticia Martin, not the way the rest of my family does.

I only know that Abuelito's still so ridiculously in love with her.

And that after someone dies, you only get to keep the memories and the photos and the songs you danced to.

You never get to keep the person, only the loneliness their absence leaves behind.

Abuelito sighs gently. "Your mother says we need to change our annual *The Princess Bride* rewatch," he says rather than asks.

I slouch against him. Humiliation twists its thorny fingers around my organs. I didn't ask Mom to tell my grandpa for me, not intentionally. I was going to. But every time I scrolled to his name in my phone, I couldn't follow through.

I hated the idea of changing an important part of our history for a small part of mine.

"It's for Pride, yes?"

"Um." My throat begins to close. It's allergies, that's all. "Yeah, I'm sorry—"

"Chiquito," he cuts me off, tucking an arm around my stiff shoulders. "Por favor no te disculpes."

It takes me a second, but I know what he's saying: don't apologize.

Abuelito only uses this much Spanish with me when it's serious. But I can't help wanting to ask for forgiveness. *The Princess Bride*, Abuelito, and I are a unit. A tradition that has never experienced a break in the cycle.

He says "Another day" as if time is endless.

But that's not true.

I try not to think about how Abuelito is in his mid-seventies. About how Abuela is gone, and, one day, he will be too.

So, no, there isn't infinite time. I'm not Charm. This isn't a comic book.

"Pride is a big thing," he says, like he's read my mind. "Much to celebrate. It's a place where you get to be yourself, fully, correct?"

I grin so hard, my eyes squinch.

"I've seen the news. The parades." He winks, then says, "I've watched that *Drag Race*. The *Queer Eye*. I'm cool."

A choked laugh escapes my throat. "The *Queer Eye*? Abuelito, no bueno."

"No está bien," he gently corrects. "Gay Pride is important, Chiquito. Just like pride in being Black and Mexican is. It's who you are."

He lightly taps his index finger against my chest.

"You should be there to celebrate."

Absorbing the intensity of Abuelito's face as he looks at me—with immeasurable love—is near impossible.

"And since you've not yet met a nice boy at church"—the implication in his voice unleashes a new wave of prickly heat across my face—"maybe there are nice boys at Pride too."

"Uh. I guess."

I know there will be nice boys at Pride. Boys I'd never imagine talking to under any other circumstance. The Crush Syndrome kind.

My phone vibrates. I discreetly unlock the screen, peeking down. I can't believe it. It's as if I'd somehow channeled all of Charm's reality-bending powers to make this happen.

I have three new text messages.

> From: Davi
> I had so much fun last night!
> 12:01 PM

> From Davi:
> Cant wait to hang again
> 12:01 PM

> From: Davi
> Mayb @ Pride?? If youre still going?? I hope so 😌
> 12:02 PM

My organs shift, realigning under my skin. I'm not even annoyed like I usually am when the person texting you can't seem to compile all their thoughts into a single, coherent message instead of multiple bite-sized ones. Davi wants to hang out again. At Pride. This almost cancels out the embarrassment and disappointment of our non-date.

"Possibly, at Pride," Abuelito says, knocking his elbow against mine, "you'll meet your Westley?"

I flush, then laugh softly. I don't have to look at Abuelito to know he's peeping over my shoulder, reading my texts. He's probably grinning as hard as I am.

"My Dread Pirate Roberts?"

He gives me a wink, and a slight nudge in my side.

I text Davi back the smiley emoji, then pocket my phone. There's no way I can let my grandpa see how laughable my flirting game is.

Instead, I convince him to tell me about the time he asked Abuela out for their first date. He's repeated it enough times over family dinners or on their anniversary that I can quote it line-for-line like *The Princess Bride*, but still. I love the way he tells it.

I rest my head on his chest and try to mimic the flutter of his heartbeat when he says "As you wish."

Fifteen

I don't like secrets. They destroy everything.
Friendships, family, relationships. If you're not
careful, they can destroy you too, Daniyal.

—Charm, *Disaster Academy* Issue #4

Three things are permanently programmed into my memory.

One: all the lyrics to Bruno Mars's *Doo-Wops & Hooligans* album. Again, entirely Bella's fault.

Two: my mother's password for *everything*—Lilah051002. It's a combination of the three Martin children's birth months: Iggy, May. Bella, October. Me, February.

Three: the route from my house to the Santoyos.

Diego's house is less than a five-minute bike ride away. I'm grateful for that today because the heat in Georgia isn't kind at noon. Or anytime the sun's out.

I catch a strong breeze gliding down the hill on Westin Place. Then I whip around the corner on Jupiter Road. A left, then a sharp right onto Rosa Avenue. At the end of the street is a pale yellow, split-level house with peach-painted shutters, a gravel walkway that snakes past a

garden of sunflowers and marigolds before I'm at the Santoyos' mahogany door.

I knock hard twice, then softly three times. It's my Hi-
it's-me-Isaac knock. I never use the doorbell.

Except, it's not Diego who answers. It's Oscar, drying
his hands with a tea towel, grinning the same way his son
does. "Hi, Isaac."

"Hey."

"I was hoping you'd be by too."

Too?

Behind Oscar, I hear the echo of Diego's laugh. Then
other voices. Ones that feel familiar but new. They're
invaders coming from inside the Santoyos' home.

Oscars sighs, but his smile doesn't slip. "They all just
got here." He motions with his head into the house.

I pull tightly on the straps of my backpack. Is that Blake
whining? That can't be right.

Diego and I hadn't planned to hang out today. It just
happened over text an hour ago. We haven't seen each
other in a few days, but it feels like weeks. I've missed his
laugh and his obsessive video game playing while I read
comics. I've missed *him.*

So I told him I was going to come by and bug him. He
replied quickly in all caps and with seven million excla-
mation points.

I got slightly delayed showering. Then grabbing comics
for the inevitable Diego-*BtVoS* Time. On the way out the

door, I heard Mom on the phone again, giggling. Pitching her voice so low I couldn't make out the words, only the sweetness in her tone.

It could've been Bella. Maybe Iggy. But I couldn't tell without giving away that I was eavesdropping.

"Come on," Oscar says, stepping aside to let me in. "They're probably waiting on you."

There's not supposed to be a "they." Only Diego and me.

I hesitate on the doorstep. Oscar raises an eyebrow, studying me. A voice that's distinctively Zelda's comes from inside. The collar of my T-shirt feels too tight. My skin's on fire even after I step into the comfortably air-conditioned house.

The living room goes quiet the second I'm inside. The rest of the Six is spread out across the Santoyos' furniture as if they've been here a dozen times before. Their eyes lock on me. I can't stop pulling on my backpack straps.

Suddenly, I'm the stranger in a place I've practically lived all my life.

Diego leaps up, swallows me in a hug, almost concussing me when our foreheads knock. It's strange staring into the brightness of his eyes, inhaling the coconut scent of his shampoo with others around us. I watch the curve of his mouth. His hands rub my shoulders.

Our closeness is different now. Not bad, just different.

"Isaac, Isaac, Isaac," he says softly. "It's you."

My voice catches as I say, "It's them."

Diego clears his throat. "Uh. Yeah." He steers me fully into the room. Involuntarily, my feet put up a fight, my spine stiff, but Diego's bony exterior undersells his strength. "The funny thing is—"

Before he can finish, Zelda says, "Isaac! Thank Whitney you're here to save me from these complete bores."

I freeze, my mouth twitching.

"Captain Incredible saves the day," F.B. concurs from where he's draped across the Santoyos' family sofa. Something tightens around my stomach as I watch Cloud Strife nap contently on his chest. She's already taken to him despite usually being opposed to all strangers.

"Is anyone going to save him from his pathetic wardrobe choices?" Alix wonders.

Even *her* presence hasn't compromised the infrastructure of the Santoyos' home. She sits in a corner, on the floor, playing on her phone. A dark curtain of hair covers most of her face.

This is . . . all wrong.

"Come. Sit," Diego almost pleads.

But I don't think I want to. Actually, I want to turn around, hop back on my bike, and ride until my legs are numb and I can't think about how this keeps happening to me.

"Isaac." Camila stands in the kitchen doorway with her warm smile. "Stay. I'm making snacks."

"The *healthy* kind," mumbles Diego.

Camila squints at him. "Yes, the kind I'd be sending you off to college with in a few months if you were—"

"¡Amor!" Oscar says, tugging on Camila's elbow until they disappear behind the kitchen door. But I can still hear their angry whispers as it swings shut. The frown stretching across Diego's mouth says he can too.

"Can we get back to the game?" Blake's settled on the floor in front of the Santoyos' moderately-sized flatscreen.

I don't think I've ever seen them use it. Diego spends most of his time in his bedroom alone or with Ollie by his side. Oscar's not a big sports spectator—other than the LBPRC, the professional baseball league in Puerto Rico—and reads the news on his laptop or phone. The rare family movie nights are usually a joint affair between the Santoyos and Martins at my house. But Blake's planted, scowling at the paused video game on the screen, and there's a waiting controller by Zelda's hip on the azure loveseat.

I sink to the carpet in front of it. A heaviness weighs down my bones.

Diego wiggles until he's next to Zelda, his knees bracketing my shoulders. He's practically surrounding me. One false move and I could headbutt his junk. Not that I'm planning to. Not that I want to think about how close my head is to my best friend's dick.

"Let's do this, Level_Zero."

I unpack my comics and try to pretend like this is any other day. Diego and his video games. Me and *Disaster Academy*. Pieces of our bodies connecting us: knee against shoulder, calf to bicep, ankle to hip. But it doesn't work.

F.B.'s laugh is too loud.

And Blake grumbles accusations, breathing through his mouth as if he's got a stuffy nose.

And Alix's demonic vibes make the hair on my forearms stand up.

And Zelda's humming . . . well, that's nice. I like their humming.

"What song is that?"

Zelda measures me with eyes darker than rich soil, framed by thick eyelashes. It's intimidating. "Sweet baby Bobbi Kristina, how do you not know 'How Will I Know' by our Lord and Savior Whitney Houston?"

Thanks to Mom's affinity for classic soul, I know some of her songs, but not this one.

"My dads raised me on her music, her style, her legacy." They smile broadly. "Every fourth Sunday, we communion with popcorn, Dr Pepper, and a viewing of *The Bodyguard* or *The Preacher's Wife* or *Cinderella*, the Brandy Norwood version."

"Sounds intense."

"It's euphoric."

They don't have to explain it with more words. Their

expression says enough. It's that faraway look in their eyes. The same one Abuelito has when explaining *The Princess Bride*. The same one Diego says I have when I talk about Charm and Reverb.

There's no questioning the laws of that kind of love.

After I finish an old *Disaster Academy*, someone sits next to me. Ollie bites his thumbnail, staring down at the pile of comics in my backpack. Unlike Diego, Ollie's hair is perfectly straight, almost blue-black. Camila loves to comb her fingers through it, leaving Ollie with perpetual bedhead. It works on him.

"Hey."

He doesn't answer. But his lips move just a little, like he might smile.

I dig through my collection. "Want one?"

He nods slowly. Another nonverbal response, but I take it as a sign to hand him *Disaster Academy* Issue #4. It's a solid starter for anyone looking for a reason to fully commit. Lots of action, smart dialogue, and an exceptional cliffhanger.

"Don't try to recruit my little bro into your cult."

Diego grins down at me, his eyes scrunchy. We stare at each other for a second too long. Something catches in my chest.

"You better pay attention, KonamiCode," says Blake, *BtVoS* paused on the TV. "We're almost to the Ruins of Tezcatlipoca."

"I'm on it, Blake."

"*Level_Zero*," Blake corrects him sharply. Then, a wry smile crosses over his mouth. "Besides, you don't want Mel roasting you the next time you two—"

"Shut it," Diego hisses.

I trade stares between them. Blake wears a mischievous expression and Diego is . . . I don't know. His eyes are narrowed, his nostrils flaring. He doesn't look back at me.

"Who's Mel?" F.B. asks.

"Melanie," Zelda replies just as Diego whispers, "Nobody." But the distinct flush to his cheeks says otherwise. He plays with his curls in that shy way he does when he's thinking hard about something—someone—he likes. It's a full-on Isaac Martin, Originator of Crush Syndrome, Thing.

I wait for him to crack. But it doesn't happen. Melanie remains a mystery.

It's another rift in our reality, the one where Diego and I don't keep classified information from each other. I know about the García twins. He knows the passcode to my phone, my MacBook. I know where he got the scar on his jaw. He knows about the one and only time I cried over Carlos.

But I didn't know about his first kiss, so maybe there's more.

A thick knot tightens my stomach. Are Diego and Mel a *thing*? Or is it like Davi and me—Diego wanting some reality-bending miracle to happen between them?

"Let's just—" he starts, but Alix cuts him off.

"Melanie Bricio," she says from her dark, hellmouth corner. Then, to my surprise, she holds up her phone for me to see. I think this is the first time Alix's done something positive *for me*. The distance between us doesn't allow me a sharp view of the girl's Instagram grid, but she appears attractive and fun and dateable.

Suddenly, the only thing I can hear in my head are Diego's words from yesterday: *I'm happy for you, okay?*

Of course he's happy as fuck for me. He's met someone and doesn't have to feel guilty about ditching me if I've got Davi to occupy my time.

"Mel's not up for discussion," Diego says snappishly. There's a finality to his tone that everyone accepts.

Everyone except me.

Anger bubbles inside me. I'm not jealous. It's good that Diego's interested in someone. And I have no room to complain. After all, I haven't exactly told him I've agreed to meet up with Davi at Pride.

Another secret piled on the others.

The jarring silence keeps all my questions buried. Diego's abandoned his spot on the loveseat, pacing in front of the TV, chewing on his lip. Zelda pretends to be interested in their phone but keeps peeking at him. Blake's openly staring. Ollie is too. Out of the hundreds of things

I could focus on, my eyes keep falling back to Diego. His wrinkled expression. The uneasiness when his hands shift from his hair to his sides, finally playing with the hem of his T-Shirt.

This awkwardness feels everlasting.

Thankfully, the quiet is replaced by music. Something upbeat seeps in from the kitchen. A calypso song I know, thanks to Abuelito.

"¡Ay, Dios mío!" Diego covers his eyes with one hand, head tilted back. But he's laughing. I can't contain the chuckle that inches up my own throat. It only takes a few seconds before Diego and I share a look, thinking the same thing.

This can't be happening.

Just like that, we're Isaac and Diego again. Best friends from the photo above his TV. All the guilt from the secrets we're keeping temporarily erased.

"Is that the song from *Beetlejuice*?" F.B. asks, sitting up and dethroning Cloud Strife. She hisses, scurrying away.

"Beetle-what?"

F.B.'s jaw drops. "Seriously? It's one of Tim Burton's defining cinematic gifts to the world of film and—"

"Can you spare us the origin story?" Zelda requests.

Ollie runs excitedly into the kitchen. Laughter bursts like a loud *pop* when the door swings back and forth. "No, no, no," Diego says as he follows his brother's lead. I'm right behind him. The Six stampedes and nudges until we're all squeezed into the kitchen entryway.

Camila and Oscar are dancing to Harry Belafonte's smooth voice telling Senora to shake her body line.

"Look at them go," Zelda says, awe in their voice.

I grin, pressed against Diego.

When we were much smaller, Camila and Oscar found a new way to ignite the flame in their marriage: ballroom dance lessons.

Twice a week, Diego camped out on my bedroom floor while his parents attended a local instructional class. A month later, Diego and I were no longer the sole live performers.

Their favorite dance was the samba.

Once, Mom and Carlos dared to attend class with the Santoyos. The night ended in Mom spraining her ankle and Carlos grumbling as he carried her upstairs. Maybe it was another sign that their romance was incapable of maintaining a fire. But the Santoyos kept at it, winning a handful of dance competition ribbons.

It all came to a halt around the time Ollie popped up in Camila's belly. Despite what Diego wanted to believe, Ollie was no immaculate conception. Nonstop months of sexy dancing was clearly the instigator.

Here they are again, hips swiveling, their bodies spinning and twirling around the hardwood. Their feet move in a blur. The horns and percussion and all of us clapping from the entryway guide their steps.

My heartbeat always kicks up a notch watching them. They're in sync, unabashedly happy. They're also everything I never got to see at home.

"¡Ay! C'mon now," Camila shouts breathlessly. "Don't just watch."

"¡Vámonos!" Oscar turns his wife in a violent circle. "¿Les gusta bailar?"

"I don't know what he's saying, but it sounds hot," says Zelda, hands on their swaying hips.

"¡Mijo, ven!" Camila giggles as Oscar dips her. "Get out here."

"Mamá, no." Diego chokes on laughter. "¡Basta ya!"

I roll my eyes.

All Diego's stammering and blushing is an act. Secretly, he loves to dance with his parents. I've witnessed it. He lacks their rhythm, a fact Oscar loves to point out. But Diego's offbeat talents are made up for with truly ego-driven resolve.

I know he wants to join them. I also know, like every good Bruno Mars performance we've ever given, he needs a push.

Or maybe a pull.

I grab his hand and lead him to the middle of the floor.

We begin our typical awkward shuffle. Oscar's lifted a

squealing Camila above his head, her arms spread, body perfectly vertical in a move Mom refers to as the *Dirty Dancing* Emergency Room Lift. I don't get the reference. I'm only proficient in *The Princess Bride* and the required '90s movie-related content for BuzzFeed quizzes.

Our steps are not as elaborate as Diego's parents. No spins—because I get dizzy easily—or fast footwork. Mostly, we try to stay on beat.

"¡Más rápido, más rápido!" Oscar yells.

Diego and I wobble like androids. Sunlight from the kitchen window tints Diego's face gold. All that tension from five minutes ago is eradicated.

I can't stop laughing.

Not when F.B. and Zelda join our uncoordinated troupe.

Not when Ollie slides across the floor in his socks, crashing into his parents.

Not when they grab his hands and turn their duo into a trio.

Not when Blake claps so out of rhythm, he might as well be creating a new song.

Not when Alix, blank-faced, doesn't walk away. She watches.

"¡Ay, mijo!" Camila says, rounding us. "It's all in the hips."

"Yeah," I say with a teasing smirk. "It's in the hips." My fingers find Diego's waist. I guide his hips, rotating them around like the turn of a washing machine. Diego drapes his arms around my neck, hands clasped. The look in his eyes—euphoria framed by his dark eyelashes, pupils tripled in size—steals the air from my lungs.

I remember the kiss. His teeth, my fingers, our clumsiness.

My phone buzzes in my pocket. I stumble out of our dance. Harry Belafonte's infectious voice directs us to continue jumping in the line, but I can't stop staring at Diego as all our realities crash, then splinter.

The phone vibrates in my hand. I'd ignore it if it were Carlos. But it's not.

It's Davi.

Sixteen

bennathan @iwishyouallthebestest · Jun 17

tbh all I want is for someone to look at me the way reverb looks @ charm at the end of #disasteracademy 11 with their parents RIGHT THERE lmao like its just too real #lgbtqsuperheroes #charmverb #boyfriends

Isaac @charminmartin · Jun 17

Replying to @iwishyouallthebestest

This is such a mood

"What about this one?"

"It's . . . nice?" I say.

"Nice? That means it's tragic."

"I didn't say that."

"Your eyes did."

I cock an eyebrow at Davi. I doubt my eyes said anything other than that I'm not a qualified fashion stylist. My entire wardrobe consists of comic book graphic tees, athletic joggers, jeans that may or may not be designer-ripped, and hoodies. Lots of hoodies.

That's a lot to confess with my eyes.

"It's fire," I finally say.

Davi rolls his eyes, smiling. "Now you're trying too hard."

I want to tell him the outfit he's wearing—pastel pink shorts that stop mid-thigh, a one-size-too-small T-shirt with PRIDE AF splashed in rainbow colors across his chest, and a red headband—is trying too hard, but I don't want to offend him.

Also, my hormones are triggered by the slightest peek of ab muscle under the T-shirt's hem when Davi stretches.

"What else . . ." I can't speak around the lump in my throat that matches the one in my joggers. "What else do you have?"

Davi sighs, then wiggles his eyebrows. "Outfit number five!"

We've been holed up in the H&M dressing area for thirty minutes. Davi walked into a changing booth carrying an armful of clothes with one goal: finding an outfit to wear to Pride.

It's why he called me yesterday. He needed a second opinion.

The real endgame is the soft pretzels bites and slushies he promised me after I help.

I've been killing time between outfits on my phone, checking the weather and my UGA email. I avoided update notifications from Nerds Anonymous and the Legends Con app—I can't believe I forgot to delete it—about the con. That led to some very uncomfortable creeping on Peter and Jorge's social media for updates on their panel.

I countered my doomscrolling by visiting Geeks Nation

for a few minutes. The *DA* threads are mainly dead since we're between issues, but there's a lot of speculation about what's going to happen next. The Charmverb squad obviously believes Issue #12 will be The One. Issue #11 left off with Reverb talking to Charm's mom about what to get him for his upcoming birthday. He wants to show his appreciation for Charm helping him adjust to life at Webster Academy. I'm not saying that I started the discussion, but . . . well, I did.

The forum blew up with all their Charmverb opinions, but I logged out before becoming too consumed.

Now I'm thumbing through the Six's group chat, avoiding the five private texts I have from Diego.

He's been asking if I wanted to come by for dinner. Camila is making pastelón. Diego knows it's my favorite.

We're in a quiet war of message bubbles with ellipses appearing and disappearing. I don't know what to say.

How are you?

Is Mel a friend or more?

Oh btw I'm out with the guy I fucked up our summer for and he's going to be at Pride also, so maybe we can meet up with him but just in case I already made plans to?

"This is the one."

Davi stands in front of one of the long, deceptive mirrors in the dressing area. I never understood their magic. They appear ordinary, but the reflection makes every piece of clothing look great on you, even when you know it won't look as amazing after purchasing. Maybe it's the bright white LED lights running vertically on either side. Is it the length? Is it the shape?

Changing room mirrors are a sensory overload of perfection.

One glance at Davi's current outfit says this particular mirror has been enchanted by a Disney witch.

He's in an ivory lightweight cotton hoodie, half zipped. He's shirtless underneath. I force myself not to stare at his collarbones, but the material's so thin it's like I can see every inch of his chest and torso. Running vertically on the sleeves are symmetrical rainbow stripes matching the Pride flag. It's kind of cool. But he has on a pair of denim shorts, and tricolored socks pulled to just below his knees like a soccer player. They're pink, lavender, and blue.

Davi looks down. I guess he could sense my confusion about the socks. "Dope, right?"

"They're definitely a"—I don't mean to pause for so long—"choice."

He grins. "Bi flag socks."

"Oh. Nice."

"I just . . ." He pauses, nervously tugging at the hoodie's sleeves.

I hate that self-conscious feeling when you're trying to be vulnerable with someone about who you are.

"I want to make a statement. Not everyone takes my sexuality seriously. It's like, coming out is supposed to be this huge declaration. But then no one hears you when you say you're bi. They think it's a phase."

The speakers in H&M are humming soft music. Lorde's "Perfect Places." He taps his sock-covered feet to the melody.

"It's not," I say.

He almost smiles. "Some of my family back in São Paulo, a few guys from school—they don't believe it because I haven't dated or kissed a guy. But, like, getting a hard-on looking at another dude, just like when I look at a girl or *anyone*, is suddenly . . ."

He trails off.

"Invalid."

"Exactly!" Davi laughs but it's vacant, missing that fullness he unleashes around his friends. "They say 'You *think* you like guys,' like it's all in my head."

I watch him play with the hoodie's zipper. Up, down. Repeat.

"When I finally do date or kiss a guy," he stops again, words hovering. His eyes trace my face like they did in front of Young Mario's. My brain spins for a second—did Davi want to kiss me that night? Maybe we were both too nervous? An unacceptable amount of heat invades my cheeks at that concept: a boy anxious about kissing me.

He finally says, "People will probably say something like, 'He was gay all along.' As if bisexuality is just this in-between to being gay or lesbian."

"Queer purgatory," I tease.

He smiles in that way people do when your joke is amusing, but not quite perfected.

"We have to work extra hard to prove who we are to everyone." He sighs, then looks down. "That's why these socks are dope. They're my 'Here you go fuckers, this is me' statement."

There's an honesty in his voice. I can tell he's wanted to get this off his chest forever. I get it. Being anything other than straight means performing your queerness for everyone, all the time, for validation. But that's stupid.

Queer people don't have to prove anything. We are who we are.

"Keep the socks," I finally say. "But the rest"—my eyes skim over his outfit—"has to go. You're doing too much."

"I thought 'doing too much' was the way of the unstraight." He grins.

"I mean." I walk over to him. "It's not as bad as outfit number one—"

"That look was the bomb dot com."

"Shut up. You're not cool enough to say that."

He gasps noisily before playfully punching my shoulder.

In my defense, outfit number one was atrocious. He'd paired a floral-print button-down shirt with board shorts that practically touched his shins and flip-flops with socks. All the signs of a legendary douchebag-in-training.

Davi sizes himself up in the enchanted mirror. "Outfit number two had a lot of swag, though."

"You mean that sunshine romper?"

"Isaac," he whines. An electric shiver zips up my spine. I just barely manage to hide it from him. He says, "That was not a romper."

"Whatever it was, it was awful." Behind him, I make a face in the mirror.

"What about number three? That fit was nice."

"Nobody in Atlanta wears all black in the months of March through November. That's a death wish," I tell him. "Also, the fedora? A disgrace to the gay community."

"You know, you're cute when you snark," he says, that smile from the other night returning.

For a full ten seconds, our eyes meet in the mirror. Everything under my skin ignites—blood, cells, the fine tissues of my heart. I should kiss him. Not on the corner of his mouth. Not a peck. A full, struggling-to-breathe-after kiss.

He clears his throat.

I flinch, then rub the side of my head. "That shirt from outfit number one," I say, "plus the shorts from outfit number four."

Little wrinkles like on the surface of Memorial Park's lake crease his brow.

One of my hands awkwardly squeezes his shoulder. "And those socks." I point in the mirror so he can see and hear my support.

"My bi-as-eff socks?"

I nod. "But no flip-flops. And definitely no fedora."

Davi laughs so loud, two different H&M employees with clothes in their arms peek in on us. He doesn't seem bothered, so I ignore them too. I'm too in love with my ability to pull that sound from him.

"We can go shoe shopping," I suggest.

He turns to face me. "Are you sure? I don't want to take up your whole day."

"You're not. I like hanging with you," I say, my voice steady. That's growth, right?

My brain only briefly drifts to Diego and how I haven't replied to his texts. Maybe that's what I should be doing instead of hovering in a changing area with my crush.

Davi unzips the hoodie, peeling it off. "I like hanging with you too," he says. His chest is this perfect canvas of muscles, his stomach toned. "Here, you should wear this at Pride. I'll get it for you. You can be . . ."

"Gay-as-eff?"

"Exactly."

I shake my head. "I can't."

"Yeah, you can." His fingers gently grab my wrists. He turns my hands over, pressing the hoodie between them. "Thank you for all of this, Isaac."

There's a strong possibility I'll never stop beaming at Davi.

Seventeen

GEEKS NATION FORUM

Re: Disaster academy 2

abbyontheonbeat: I still think they should've let Charm save his dad in this issue. Show how powerful he is. Big mistake.

ACharmingReverb: No its perfect the way it is. Just because Charm CAN change the past doesn't mean he should! Not saving his dad is how he ended up at Webster. He might not have met Reverb if his dad was still alive. or become a superhero. Grief and loss are important. I can relate. Yeah it sucks but Reverbs helping him thru it 😏

infinitysnap: @ACharmingReverb dude its just a comic

A relentless heat blankets Alpharetta at four in the afternoon. The kind that sears the back of your neck. Where the pavement is scorching. Perspiration pools in places you didn't realize had sweat glands. White clouds stretched thin and translucent like spider's webs remain stationary as the sun sits on its cyan throne in the middle of the sky.

I'm drenched from riding my bike. I didn't let Davi drive me home after shopping. Too many emotions swirled in the pit of my stomach. My blood feels like it's filled with those exploding rock candies.

I need space from Davi and his smile and the little ways he looks at me now.

I need a cold shower.

It's too bad I'm unable to step into my own house.

Parked in our driveway is a copper SUV with one of those BABY ON BOARD decals in the back window, except instead of an infant's footprint, it's a dog's paw. As in Valentine, the far-from-infantile English bulldog. It's Carlos's Toyota Highlander.

Carlos is at our house. The house I grew up in. The house he once lived in, until . . .

No.

My hands tremble on my bike's handlebars. Sharp, metallic flavor sits at the back of my throat. I'm biting my lip too hard.

I refuse to blink. I won't let the tears fall.

Rage crackles like lighting in my veins. Bella told me anger is poisonous. Once it's in your system, it's hard to remove. Other than exerting so much energy, you're too exhausted to contain the resentment. Or simply crying it out.

But I'm not crying over Carlos and the shards of our family he left behind.

Why is he here? Why does Mom let him visit? Why do

they sit at our kitchen table to talk? The same table my grandpa reads his newspaper at with lukewarm coffee. The same one Bella and I sit at during the holidays while Mom and Iggy argue over what we're having for dinner.

Why do I have to pretend this fury inside me, supernova hot and seconds from exploding, doesn't exist because Iggy—and maybe Mom, maybe Abuelito—wants me to talk to Carlos?

I don't understand my own anger, my pain.

I climb back on my bike. Instinct says to go to Secret Planet to hide in my corner of the store and read comics until it's too dark outside to care. Or I could ride to Memorial Park.

Neither of those places will clear my head.

Instead, I glide down the hill on Westin Place. Around the corner onto Jupiter Road. I take a left, then a sharp right onto Rosa Avenue. To the split-level house with the peach-painted shutters, gravel walkway, and Camila Santoyo's summer garden of sunflowers and marigolds.

I don't even know if Diego's home. Maybe he's busy with Mel.

I knock anyway.

"Isaac? ¿Mijo? ¿Qué tienes?"

It's a phrase I've heard Camila direct at Ollie enough times for me to know what it means.

She guides me inside, holding my face to inspect it. I can barely make out her expression through my blurred vision. I'm trying so hard not to cry, but I can feel the wet trails slipping down my cheeks, hanging on my jaw.

"I'm sorry," I manage to say.

"For what?" She touches my arm, worry creasing her brow.

I can't get the words out or control the way I tremble.

"Oh, Isaac." Her voice is this soft melody, calm but concerned. She brushes the tears away. My sinuses are in rapid collapse as I sneeze twice, wiping my nose with the back of my hand. I feel gross and mad and lost.

Why am I even here?

But Camila must know. She yells "Mijo. ¡Ven aquí!" while smiling gently as if it aches to do so.

"Sí, mamá." Diego's voice drifts down from his bedroom, a hint of annoyance in it.

I should go. There are a million other places I could be instead of the Santoyos' foyer with tearstains on my cheeks, hands shaking, and a heart that's torn in half without anything to stitch it back together.

Is that what hate feels like? Being ripped in half? Unfixable?

I freeze at the sound of clumsy footsteps on the stairs. Then he's in front of me, in a pair of old swishy basketball shorts and a secondhand T-shirt with a Nintendo logo on it. Soft, bedhead Diego, his bright eyes filled with questions.

He never asks them.

Instead, he says "Allergies?" with a wry smile.

Something that feels like a laugh but tastes like pain escapes my mouth.

"Yeah," I reply.

He nods once, as if he understands. As if Diego Santoyo, Latent Telepath, knows all my secrets. Everything I've tried to keep buried. He grins before grabbing my hand. Our fingers interlock in a hold that I hope never breaks, and he leads me upstairs to his bedroom.

Ollie's in the middle of the floor with a lapful of my *Disaster Academy* comics. I must have forgotten them yesterday. He looks at us but doesn't speak.

I follow Diego to his bed. He sits first, then motions for me. Our quest to avoid discussing the Big Issues continues, as does our childhood psychic link. He leans against the wall, a small stack of pillows supporting him. His knees shift apart and he pats the open space between them.

Reluctantly, I shuffle into place.

My spine is cushioned by his chest and stomach. He brackets me with his legs and arms like yesterday. He doesn't care that I'm damp with sweat. I breathe him in. Camila must have changed their fabric softener.

Why am I thinking about that?

Sometimes, I don't understand my own brain. The way it drifts. It gets caught in the static of my emotions, helpless, like a fly stuck on one of those sticky traps.

I stare at my hands. They're not really shaking anymore. Only mild vibrations like Reverb's when he's using his powers. Diego fumbles around for one of the game controllers. In the background I hear the *Beyond the Valley of Stars* theme music.

"I don't want—"

He cuts me off. "I know." There's a smile in his voice, but I'm not looking at him. Only at my hands, unsure what to do with the controller he's placed between them.

The opening chimes of a familiar game start up. *Mario Kart.*

I sigh halfheartedly. "You know I suck at video games."

"Yup." His laugh tickles my ear. "Sometimes you just have to be bad at something. Sometimes, you have to accept it's bad."

"What for?"

"So you can enjoy it without stressing over winning." His arms curl around me, his chin resting on my shoulder. "Sometimes, it's okay to just enjoy something for what it is."

I sniffle. Another sneeze is looming. My eyes are heavy, painfully dry from the dam of tears running out. But the fight is gone. The anger is dormant once more.

"Okay," I whisper.

"Good. Choose your player."

Two hours later, Mom leans in my bedroom doorway. "I made enchiladas." She's smiling, but it's a fatigued one.

"I know." Their scent lingers in the kitchen, but I could

barely smell them when I finally walked into the house. A stronger aroma hit me at the door—woodsmoke and bergamot. Carlos's cologne.

"Are you hungry?"

"No."

Mom nods. I don't tell her I had a small bowl of Camila's pastelón while Diego and I avoided talking about the Big Issues again. But that silent hope that this is the *last time* Carlos comes by clung to my lungs the entire bike ride home.

Her gaze drifts to a corner of my room. She eyes the shower caddy that's nearly filled with toiletries. Something weird passes over her face, though she tries to smile it off. I know that look. It's the same one she wore when she let a friend convince her to put auburn streaks in her hair a few months after Carlos left.

Regret.

What's there to regret?

"It's late, Isaac," she finally says.

"Do I have a curfew now?" I fire back.

"Hey." The firmness in her voice steals my attention from the corner. "I'm still the parent here. Save your sarcasm for Diego. I'm not the one."

Mom loves that saying, "I'm not the one." Don't mess with her. Don't challenge her with sarcasm or a tone she doesn't like.

"Sorry," I whisper.

She shakes her head. "You didn't answer my texts or calls."

"Mom, no one actually *calls* people anymore."

"I do," she argues, but with a giggle. "That's what phones are for."

No, phones are for texting and social media and games and looking up your favorite comic book fan art so you can repost it everywhere. But I'm not going to say anything that might provoke the wrath of Lilah Johnson on any day she makes enchiladas or mac and cheese.

"I was at Diego's playing video games."

"I know," she says.

It's clear where Camila Santoyo's allegiances lie.

"Do you want to talk about it?" she asks.

"Nope."

"Isaac."

"Mom," I say with more annoyance than tolerable.

But Mom doesn't raise her voice or remind me the laws of parent-child relationships. She says, "He's your—"

"He's Carlos," I interrupt.

"Jesus, Mary, and poor Joseph, when are we gonna discuss this?"

I don't know, Mom. When will we talk about him cheating on you? When will we talk about how you tried so hard to keep it together, but the moment Bella and Iggy were off at college, you broke? The perfect, shining saint of the Martin household cracked into a million little fragments and I had no clue how to put them together?

How was fourteen-year-old Isaac, who could never remember the combination to his locker, supposed to figure that out? The same boy who sat in the hallway outside his parents' former *bedroom while his mom cried in the shower? Who still wakes up in the middle of the night, haunted by the ghostly chants of* Weren't we good enough? Wasn't *I* good enough, Carlos? *in the shadows.*

"I don't want to talk about it," I say. But I obviously do because I ask, "Why do you still let him come here?"

She leans against my doorframe. "We're friends, Isaac."

"*Friends?*" Allergy-related complications is the only explanation for my voice cracking.

"Yes," she says, "we're trying to be. For our children."

For our children. Mom's following a step-by-step manual on guilt trips. There must be an online tutorial only accessible to parents.

"Is that a problem?" she asks, a hint of warning in her tone.

I glare at the framed poster on my wall. The one from Iggy. I scan the boxes, half stuffed with my life and who I've been for eighteen years. All this expectation of gratefulness lingers in my room.

I can't handle it.

"Isaac Jaime Martin, you can be angry and choose not

to forgive him, but is it worth letting one person control that much of your life?"

I shrug.

"I know this is my fault," she says. I don't confirm or deny anything. She tries to smile again, but it doesn't erase the exhaustion in her eyes. "It's better now." She doesn't explain what that means.

My mind coasts down a familiar hill—does *better* mean someone new? Is that who she's been talking to on the phone whenever it rings?

"Are you going to leave for college without attempting to get past this?"

I turn on my side, my back to her. It's the only answer I have.

Her sigh echoes in the silence of my room. "I left a plate for you on the counter. Ginger ale's in the fridge."

"Thanks."

I sense her lingering in the doorway as if she has more to say. The door clicks shut, and I close my eyes. I want to sleep this day away. Most of it, at least. Not the Davi parts. The hoodie he bought me, with the rainbow-striped sleeves, is folded in a bag under my bed. I can't wait to wear it to Pride.

I think about texting him. Or calling, because that's a thing, I suppose.

Instead, I roll on my back, stare at a storage bin in the corner of my room labeled COMICS & DIEGO.

An actual container filled with comic books and items I've collected from Diego over the years exists. Old T-shirts that we used to share before I outgrew them, a baggy pair of sweatpants, Polaroids of him and me from kids to graduation. All these little things that will have to replace his jokes and bad singing and closeness while I'm at UGA.

I squeeze my eyes shut, trying to quiet the noise in my head.

It's decided: every second of today needs to be erased from the annals of time.

Eighteen

You're making friends at this academy, right baby?
There are people you can lean on here? People who
love you . . . for you?

—Mrs. Morris, *Disaster Academy* Issue #11

I can't find a reason to get out of bed the next day other than to brush my teeth, shower, and down my allergy medicine with ginger ale.

The house is quiet. After sneaking an extra helping of enchiladas this morning, I caught Mom napping on the couch. Another all-nighter. She does that sometimes—spends late hours in front of a laptop or her phone, obsessing over a client's controversial misstep on social media and how to fix it before the Cancel Culture Squad comes to eat them alive. But, on occasion, Mom will stay up late because she's upset.

I wonder if I'm the reason she couldn't sleep.

Am I a bad son for not forgiving Carlos?

I'm definitely a terrible person for thinking about throwing the debris of their shattered marriage in her face. But yesterday was just a disagreement. It happens, right?

What Mom said is probably true, though. I'm destined to carry this to UGA with me. I've fortified this wall of distrust inside me because of Carlos. Because of my own unwillingness to "get past this." Maybe the real reason I haven't left this one spot in the middle of my bed is because I know I'll have to acknowledge the things I've been avoiding when I do.

Carlos. Being alone at UGA. Leaving Mom and Abuelito. Diego.

Nope. I'm staying right here with my stash of *Disaster Academy* comics and a fully charged phone and a cold bowl of leftover enchiladas until summer ends. Or until my massive consumption of ginger ale overfloods my bladder. Either way, this is my day.

Diego's MIA once again. We texted and briefly Face-Timed this morning. He was parked somewhere I couldn't make out, but he never said where.

I didn't ask either.

Most likely something Mel related.

I still feel funny about that. I've never had to share my best friend before. Even with his video games, he'll press pause just to listen to me ramble. With the Six, he still whispers inside jokes with me. Takes time to include me in their conversations. But with Mel . . . he's *gone*.

Here's what I know: I still need to make this up to Diego. Mel wouldn't even exist if Legends Con was still happening. I think. Then again, Davi wouldn't either. The way he looked at me in the mirror yesterday—bright-eyed and grateful—left me restless last night. Unfortunately, the images in my head eventually wavered like heat coming off a blacktop, and all I could see was Diego's face in Twisted Burger's parking lot when he realized my crush on Davi was the reason I screwed up.

Curled up in those dark, noiseless hours of the night, I obsessed over YouTube videos. It only took one search—"how to sneak into a comic convention"—for me to fall down a rabbit hole. Video after video of schemes. Some were just the standard Reddit tricks—badge switching, hiding in a large crowd entering the exhibit halls—but others were far more complex. Full-on seven-member heist stories where groups fooled security and met their favorite creators.

In London, this one Black boy snuck in by impersonating a former Power Ranger. He even spoke on a panel with former TV actors. No one noticed.

I spent an hour afterward, delirious from lack of sleep, picturing it: Me and Diego getting into Legends Con. Maybe the Six would help. I'd meet Peter and Jorge. He'd talk to Elena. Both of our destinies fulfilled.

But that's not how things work in this reality. I'm no YouTube hero.

Okay, Isaac Jaime Martin, stop. I shake my head.

There must be another way to help Diego. One that won't get us arrested.

I busy myself with rereading this month's *Disaster Academy*. The full-page spread of Charm and Reverb being hugged and congratulated by each other's parents stares back at me. The way they look at each other without saying a word liquefies my organs.

Their smiles shared from across the room remind me of one thing: nothing can come between people who love each other.

Someone knocks on my door. Not a Mom knock. This one's unfamiliar, and I panic for five whole seconds thinking she's ambushed me with an unannounced Carlos visit.

Instead, Iggy shoulders the door open. He shoots me a judging expression.

"Lazy as ever."

I roll my eyes.

Thing is, I didn't recognize Iggy's knock. I should have. It was mandatory after he accidentally walked in on me getting friendly with certain parts of my anatomy when I was thirteen. The early stages of Puberty Isaac were pretty awful. And, let's be honest, ridiculously fun. But he hasn't visited my bedroom since moving out for college.

He studies me from the doorway like Mom did last night, dressed in a creased black T-shirt with an artistic rose emblem on the chest. It's paired with drawstring khaki pants cinched at the ankle. Iggy's attempt at casual somehow still manages to look sophisticated.

"How many naps have you taken today?"

"None," I snap.

One point five, actually. But that's classified information.

Iggy smirks. "Liar."

I sniff, then unlock my phone. My fingers blur over the keyboard.

> To: Bella
> Iggy is here. SAVE ME!
> 2:52 PM

> From: Bella
> Yay! Tell him i said 🖕💀
> 2:53 PM

I snort into my pillow. For a mom-to-be, Bella's ruthlessness remains intact. Good for her.

A few months after Carlos left, I remember channel flipping through mindless television programs with her on a Saturday. Neither one of us could settle on anything. Honestly, I think we were both just looking to alleviate all the tense silence around the house. Iggy was home from college that weekend. He demanded we watch anything other than the cooking show Bella landed on.

By then, he'd refused to join our We Hate Carlos Alliance.

"Sure, mano," Bella replied sweetly. Then she cranked the volume on the television, removed the batteries from the remote, and tossed it to him. "Enjoy!"

He stomped out of the room.

For three straight hours, Bella and I watched the misguided, country-loving, redheaded host create flavorless meals, never saying a word to each other. But when Iggy finally left to meet some friends, I heard it: The sniffles. Her frustrated sighs as she wiped her face.

The Iggy and Bella who ate McDonald's together with Abuelito had ceased to exist.

> From: Bella
> No seriously do you want to facetime? get him to
> leave you alone?
> 2:54 PM

I smile down at my phone. My sister's the true MVP, I swear. As I compose a reply to her, Iggy clears his throat. I glare at him. "What're you here for?"

Iggy's usual fracturing of our twenty-six-miles-apart agreement typically happens early in the morning or on weekends. He's risking unearthly amounts of city traffic on his return trip to stand in my doorway at this hour.

He says, "I'm taking Abuelito to dinner."

"Just the two of you?"

He snorts. "It's a thing we've done for a long time."

Abuelito's never mentioned having dinner with Iggy before. Is it because he thinks I'll feel neglected? Maybe, without me saying it, he knows all that time Iggy and Bella spent with him when we were young, living with him and learning Spanish, made me jealous.

The entire Martin family has things to get past.

"You should take him out sometimes," Iggy suggests.

"I do."

We have the diner, even though Abuelito always drives. And pays. But we have our time together.

"Good." Iggy plays with the hem of his shirt. "He needs it. I hate . . ."

I wait but Iggy doesn't finish. He stares at the ground. I know what he wants to say: *I hate him being alone. I hate him being without Abuela.*

Watching this side of my brother is strange. He's being . . . sincere. Thoughtful. I never figured those words could apply to Iggy. I never figured I'd see him care for anyone unless it meant gaining leverage in his own world domination.

He looks up. A smile almost appears. "Anyway, got here early, so I came by to check on Mom. I don't think she's eaten today."

Guiltily, I peek at the half-devoured bowl of enchiladas. *Should I have left some for her on the coffee table near the couch? Shouldn't I—the son who lives here—be in the kitchen cooking her one of Abuelito's world-famous, delicious dishes?*

Once again, Iggy earns a check in the Best Son column.

Iggy probably doesn't even consider me competition. He probably knew he won the moment I was born.

"I figured," he continues, sizing me up. "I've got time to go grab her something at Twisted."

He's quiet for a beat. Then he says, "Thought maybe you could come with? I could let you get some driving practice in."

I blink at him, confused.

"We could take the back roads. Just go over the simple stuff."

"I'm sorry, what?"

"It'll be good for you."

Iggy rubs at the shadowy stubble on the lower part of his jaw. It's not as gloriously pronounced as Amin's; more like how my face gets when I forget to shave, but cleaner. He says, "Let me teach you."

"Why would *you* teach me?"

His expression darkens. "You need to learn."

There he is—Iggy, part-time older brother, full-time clone of Carlos Martin. He took on the role of brooding, strict father figure after Carlos moved out. But I've never wanted it. I don't know if Iggy did either.

"No, thanks," I say, looking away.

He exhales, the irritation almost at full boil. "You can't bike your way home from Athens," he says. "Mom's not gonna make that trip back and forth every weekend just so you can be here. Abuelito's definitely not."

I scrub at a sauce stain on my sheets. He's right—Mom's not big on long-distance driving. It's why she rarely goes down to Savannah to visit Bella and Chris unless Iggy volunteers to come along. And, as much as I know he wants to, Abuelito can't. Not even for a weekend of *The Princess Bride* viewing.

"How will you get home?" he asks like it's a test.

"Public transportation. A bus or something," I say without lifting my eyes. It's crossed my mind, like everything else. But I haven't found a reasonable solution yet. "Maybe I'll ride with friends."

"Friends?" The way he says it—part amused, part disbelieving—stings. "Last I checked, Diego's not going to UGA. Do you have some other secret stash of besties I don't know about? Ones that'll be in Athens with you?"

A sharp burn forms a volatile liquid barrier over my eyes. I bite the inside of my cheek to stop the tears. I don't want Iggy here in my bedroom reminding me I'm useless when it comes to making friends.

"Isaac," Iggy says gently. "I didn't mean—"

Now I snort. His attempt at an apology is weak. "It's cool. You're right."

"No," he says adamantly. "It came out wrong. Can we start this over?"

I roll onto my back, blinking at the ceiling. The tears have receded.

"Whatever."

"Do you want to come with me to Twisted Burger to grab Mom some food? No driving lessons. No more Iggy Martin being a complete dick." I can hear the humor in his voice. "Just us forgetting whether Mom likes extra mustard or mayo on her burger."

"It's extra mayo."

"Light on the pickles."

"And make sure they don't forget the jalapeños," we say at the same time, imitating Mom's voice. Then we chuckle.

It's bizarre to see Iggy smiling at me. He looks so youthful. His hair's perfect, waves and all, something that earned a lot of attention from girls at school.

"Did you get a fresh cut?" I ask.

"Yup. Darrell hooked me up."

"You still go to Darrell?"

We've been going to the same barber since Iggy's freshman year. But I assumed he stopped after moving to the city.

Iggy cautiously runs a hand over the top of his head. "Why would I stop?" Then he gives me a hard look. "When's the last time you saw him?"

Self-consciously, I brush my hair too. "A few weeks." Iggy scoffs and my face heats up. "Not since graduation."

He laughs, loud and high-pitched like I remember hearing from across the hall years ago. "You need to change that ASAP."

I keep expecting him to take his true form again. To shed this happy, jokey, alternate-reality Ignacio Martin for the one I've fought with for an eternity. But he doesn't. He says, "Come on. Mom's probably starved."

Her words from last night echo in my head: *Are you going to leave for college without attempting to get past this?*

I think about what I would've said to her—*I want to move on, but I'm not sure how yet*—if I wasn't being so stubborn. It's exhausting, letting people have so much power over your life. And here's Iggy, waiting patiently in my doorframe, offering me a chance to move on, at least for now. Maybe it's time for me to take it. Not for my brother.

For me.

"Okay." I nod, swinging my legs off the side of the bed, searching for my shoes.

Then Iggy says, "Before we go, please change that shirt. You've got a massive chalk stain on it. I can't risk bumping into someone I know with a brother who's incapable of using antiperspirant for his sweaty, foul armpits without getting it all on his clothes."

The Crown Prince of Darkness has returned.

I'm kind of surprised at how full Twisted Burger is when we arrive. It's early for the dinner crowd. Most of the booths are occupied, and the ordering line is moderately long.

The speakers are blasting my least favorite music—

dance-pop. Every lyric is about heartbreak, set to pulsing beats. Beside me, Iggy hums a Selena Quintanilla song. He's a fervent fan of old-school hip-hop, preferably Southern rap groups—Outkast, 8Ball and MJG, Goodie Mob—but his love for Selena is clearly influenced by Abuelito. Another rare side of Iggy often overshadowed by his natural assholery. I like it.

On the drive here, we didn't speak much. The occasional nod or singing a chorus at the same time. Even now, in line, we stand awkwardly, surrounded by a wall of terrible music, staring at the menu as if it's changed even the slightest since we were younger. It hasn't. Neither has the barrier between us.

"Wow, I haven't had a Mondo Shake in years," says Iggy.

"Really?"

"They don't have a Twisted downtown." He frowns. "Anytime I'm back here, I always go where Abuelito wants."

Which is definitely not Twisted Burger. To be honest, if it were up to Abuelito, he'd cook every meal. But he gets exhausted standing at a stove for too long now. I'm lucky he even lets me help finish the chicken tacos for *The Princess Bride* rewatch. Burgers and Mondo Shakes are not high on José Martín's list of favorite things.

"Do you still love the Scorcher?" I ask, my voice almost a whisper amid all the noise.

The Scorcher is a double-patty burger loaded with lettuce, finely diced jalapeños, bacon, pepper jack cheese, and slathered with fiery BBQ sauce and an avocado spread. As much as I'd like to wear the crown, Iggy is unquestionably the king of spicy foods in the Martin bloodline. He could challenge Diego any day of the week.

Iggy cocks his head, smiling. "You remember?"

I shrug. "It's a pretty basic order."

"I just didn't think . . ."

"What?"

He doesn't answer, turning back to the menu. But that look on his face leaves my cheeks burning. We shift forward. A minute passes before he says, "You still like the TB Original? With extra jalapeños?"

"And extra pickles."

"I knew that." His voice hardens a little, a determination behind his words. Is this another competition? Memorizing each other's food orders?

Sorry, Ignacio Martin. I've won this round.

We're two customers away from the register when he says, "Hey, I need to take a leak. You can handle Mom's order, right?" He passes me his credit card. It's new-looking, his name still perfectly printed across the front.

I wonder what the spending limit is.

Also, when did my brother become such an adult?

I'm almost to the front of the line when a familiar giggle cuts above Twisted Burger's unforgivable playlist. I freeze. My spine locks up. My shoulders are so tight, it hurts to turn my neck. But I do, just enough to look at a corner booth.

It's Zelda.

They cover their next squealing laugh with both hands. On either side of them are two people I vaguely recognize. Zelda's dads. They're not dressed in drag, but it's easy to distinguish the smirks, sharp cheeks, and effervescent personalities.

"Daddy! Papa!" Zelda shakes their head. "Don't start!"

"What? You know it's true," says the one I know as Anita, his mouth stretching into the kind of smile that is equally teasing and proud.

"Anthony, hush," the other one—Havana—chuckles. He has a bronze complexion and dark hair teased into a Bruno-worthy pompadour.

"What about *that one*?" Anthony points at a guy head-bopping at the condiment station. The boy has a large Afro, his face eye-catching. He looks about my age and has dark brown skin.

"Daddy, no," Zelda asserts.

"Fiiiine." Anthony sighs. "He would've made a classic Luke Cage, though."

My heart's achingly loud against my tongue. I avert my eyes. Already, my leg wants to shake nervously. Zelda's at Twisted Burger with their dads, which isn't strange. Plenty of people are here, obviously.

I should be able to walk up to their table, say hi. We're friends, right? I mean, we don't text directly or even follow each other on social media. Out of everyone in the Six, Zelda's the coolest. A level above F.B.'s status, but not in Diego's realm.

That's the part that makes this a million times more difficult—Diego not being here. He's the one who always facilitates these kinds of interactions.

My entire body is ready to shut down at the *thought* of starting a conversation with Zelda and their dads.

How the hell do I expect to survive at UGA?

"Just in time."

I flinch, but it's only Iggy. He swipes back his credit card as the girl at the front counter says, "Can I help you?" I glance back over my shoulder to check if Zelda or their dads have clocked me, but they haven't.

After ordering, Iggy asks, "Do you know them?"

Again, I wince. Before I can formulate an acceptable response, Zelda's walking toward us, cheeks glowing with the size of their smile. Their retro Whitney Houston T-shirt is as vibrant as their eyes.

"Hey, Isaac!" Zelda up-nods me. I return the gesture, almost grinning. Then Zelda's eyes are on Iggy. He stares at me expectantly.

"Uh, this is—"

"Iggy, his bro," Iggy says, intercepting the conversation like a pro. He shakes Zelda's hand. "Nice shirt."

"Thanks. I'm Zelda."

"Like the video game?"

Zelda nods, their mouth twitching more and more. Why am I surprised? That's just who Iggy is with strangers, charming and approachable. He can read the room with one quick glance.

I hang back while they chat as if they've known each other for years, not seconds. Zelda rattles off a bunch of gamer things. Iggy grins along, even though neither of us is into them. But he's able to hold a conversation without fumbling.

Easy-freaking-breezy.

How am I related to him? He's never without words or struggling to maintain eye contact. Iggy goes with the flow while my instincts force me to fight it.

"Isaac," singsongs Zelda. They poke my shoulder. "Would you like to meet my dads?"

"Uh. Sure."

We all stand together in the middle of Twisted Burger. Zelda's dads are Anthony and Gabriel, officially. Anthony is stunningly tall and graceful. Iggy's six foot four and still shorter than Anthony. Gabriel has this low, melodic voice and hazel eyes.

Iggy doesn't miss a beat with Zelda's dads. He has them instantly laughing. It's frustrating how normal this is for him. Bella does the same thing. She has random, friendly exchanges with strangers in the checkout line at a grocery store. She compliments someone's shoes, their outfit while she pumps gas.

Why didn't I inherit that Martin gene?

I glance down at Zelda's shoes. Another so fresh, so clean pair of Jordans. They're black high tops with red near the toe of the sneaker, a blue Nike swoosh to match the accent on the heels. I don't know what edition they are. But Bella would.

"Sick kicks," I say, my voice stiff.

"Thanks." Zelda rotates one shoe from side to side. "The UNC to Chicago edition. Papa woke me up at six a.m. to stand in line for them." Something bright passes over their eyes. "It was a ridiculously cold January morning, but he insisted since it was my birthday."

I smile with them. "My birthday's in February."

"Aquarius?"

I nod. "You too?"

"Nah. Straight up Capricorn. G.O.A.T. all the way."

We laugh together.

Zelda's eyes fall on their dads, their expression dimming. We're standing away from them and Iggy now.

A minute later, the girl at the register calls our number. Mom's food is ready. Cautiously, I elbow Zelda. "Hey. Wanna come make sure they didn't scam my mom on the extra mayo?"

Immediately, the brightness returns to their face. It radiates so intensely, heat spreads from my hairline to my toes.

I check Mom's burger at the pickup counter while Zelda manages to haggle their way into a Mondo Shake refill. As clearly outlined in the Twisted Burger Rules, printed across an offensively yellow sign in blue lettering, REFILLS ON MONDO SHAKES ARE PROHIBITED, NO EXCEPTIONS. But Zelda's smooth, and the girl behind the register, evidently fed up with absurd mandates, obliges.

I fail to mute the awe in my voice when I say, "You did that, huh?"

Zelda winks, slurping on their shake while heading back to join their dads as Iggy approaches me.

A piece of me wishes I'd known Zelda before now. Before I was weeks away from moving to another city where I wouldn't know anyone.

As Iggy and I walk away, he leans close to whisper, "Zelda? They're pretty cool."

"Yeah. They are."

Over the noise echoing throughout Twisted Burger, I hear Anthony say, "Those eyebrows. That hair. Good skin. Oh, Zelda, your friend would make a flawless T'Challa."

Zelda replies, "Nah. He's more of a Miles Morales."

My cheeks prickle. The smile on my face isn't awkward or forced.

It's natural.

Nineteen

Our Fictious Chronicles

Fic: On the Other Side of What If   By **OkayDariusOkay**
Rating: Teen and Up   **Fandom:** Disaster Academy
Pairing: Charm/Reverb   **Tags:** First Kiss, Friends to Lovers, Fluff, Romance, Slow Burn, Mild Angst, Pining, Alternate Universe—Coffeeshop, set after issue 6, barista!reverb, dorkcustomer!charm, One True Pairing, more than kissing likely
Chapters: 5/?   **Likes:** 3001   **Words:** 34,751
Comments:

IMartino210 • June 18 09:34 AM: hey sorry for my last meltdown. i just . . . I think charm and reverb's friendship is really important. so is taking things slow. I just want . . . . . . **something** to happen. I want charm to tell reverb how he feels. idk. I love this series. really hope you and your family are okay.

The sun sits heavy across the back of my neck as I glide down the hill on Westin Place. To my left and right, kids are flooding out of their houses for games of tag or to draw all over the sidewalks in bright-colored chalk. Nearby, someone screeches "Cannonball!" The pool water's splash is louder than my heavy breaths as I pedal faster. My endorphins are buzzing, but it's more than just the exertion from the bike ride.

It's been less than forty-eight hours, but it feels longer since I've seen my best friend. Since it was just me and Diego. Not the Six. Not teary, snotty Isaac carrying all his Carlos baggage into his limited time with Diego. Just us.

After Iggy dropped me off yesterday, I tugged Mom away from her latest social media crisis to eat together in the kitchen. Then, we watched an old rom-com on her laptop. I even cleaned the kitchen. We didn't talk about our argument. She didn't bring up Carlos. It felt like the old us—the way we were when Bella left for college. Before she started packing my own things for UGA.

For now, we're good. At least, I think we are.

Anyway, I collapsed after that. Spending time with Iggy requires too much energy. I didn't even hop on Geeks Nation to search for the newest *Disaster Academy* preview Jorge usually drops on social media.

Before I fell asleep, I checked my notifications. No missed calls or texts from Diego.

I decided today would be our time.

As I make a sharp right on Rosa Avenue, my body's point five seconds from an allergy overload, thanks to all the pollen.

Camila answers the door. "Isaac! ¡Buenas tardes!" Most

of her hair is piled on her head, but a few pieces fall around her face like black vines. She's in light purple scrubs with sunflowers on them.

"Hey," I say a little self-consciously. The last time Camila greeted me at the door, I was a mess. Now I'm combating an itchy nose and increasingly damp armpits.

The Excruciating Fall of Isaac Martin continues.

"Come in, come in," she insists, flagging a gingham-patterned tea towel at me. "It's unbearable out there."

The Santoyos' house smells like peaches and maduros, lightly fried, ripe plantains. They're one of my favorite snacks, though Camila's made them less and less since Oscar's hospital incident. Today, their scent floats victoriously in the air.

I bite the inside of my cheek. *Food later.* I have a mission.

"Is Diego upstairs?"

"No." She sighs, dancing around me. "Oscar's out with Ollie, so he rushed me home from my shift to use my Jeep. He acted as if the world was on fire."

I hesitate before following her into the kitchen.

"Can you believe he was impatiently waiting on the front stoop when I pulled into the driveway?" she continues, wiping at a spot on the granite countertop near the stove. "Like I was on *his* clock. ¡Dios mío!"

I nod along, but my brain is on autopilot.

Diego's not here. Again. He hasn't called or texted or anything.

Is this my fault? Is he avoiding me or is he just . . . moving on?

Camila's voice snaps me out of the sludge corrupting my skull. "Are you hungry? Thirsty?"

"I'm okay."

"I just made maduros," she says, guiding the white ceramic bowl toward me. The browned plantain slices sit on a stack of paper towels, shiny from the oil with a fine dusting of salt. The temptation is almost unbearable.

"No, thanks."

Camila pops one into her mouth without flinching. She's one of those moms who has taste tested enough still-hot foods before serving her children to have developed an immunity to excruciating temperatures.

"I'm really glad you're here."

She lifts a hand to rub my cheek. She's done that for as long as I can remember. For a while, it bothered me. Only because of all my acne. I couldn't imagine anyone ever wanting to touch my face, but Camila always did, as if she were immune to my flaws. Never once did she offer unsolicited advice about how to treat my skin like Bella and Carlos did.

She made me feel normal.

"I worry about him, Isaac," she says, smiling through her defeated tone. "He goes and goes for this video game *dream* of his. He won't listen to me or Oscar."

Her hand lowers, then her chin. She scrubs at a different

place on the countertop, searching for new spots. But there are none.

"Ugh. He's so stubborn!" She blows tendrils of hair out of her face. "He's so much like me."

I grin. It's true.

"I've begged. I've yelled," she says. "You know, he wouldn't have to bug me so much for *my Jeep* if he agreed to take courses at Georgia Tech. He'd have his own car!"

I'm not sure what to say, so I nod.

"He has all these plans mapped out. None of them include the things Oscar and I advise him about." She folds her arms, then drops them at her sides. "Why does he think he has to do all of this on his own?"

I whisper, "Because he's Diego."

"No lo soporto."

When I give her a confused look, Camila explains, "I can't stand it." She laughs sadly. "I had dreams too. But I knew the only way I was gonna achieve them was with an education. Not one from YouTube. An honest-to-God college degree. There aren't a lot of opportunities out there for . . ."

She doesn't finish, but I hold up my arm and point to my skin. "For us?"

"For us."

Silence eases its way into the kitchen. I stare at Camila; she watches her shoes. An achingly loud part of me wants her to ask me to persuade Diego to pursue his goals at UGA. They're not one of Georgia's top five video game design schools, but it's a start. Another piece of me wants her to ask because I need an excuse to tell Diego that I'm lost without him. He's more than my best friend—he's my compass on this journey toward being the version of me I want to be. All of this is less terrifying when he's by my side.

Unfortunately, Camila never asks. She pastes on a hopeful expression, then says, "I'm so glad you're spending the summer together. It's good for you both."

"Yeah," I mumble. But I guess we're not since he's not around.

"He's so excited about Pride."

"Me too."

My eyes drift away from Camila's gaze. I need to tell Diego about Davi and Pride. He's not going with us, but I'm determined to meet up downtown. It's time for that non-kiss I think we were both disappointed with to be replaced by a long, unforgettable, real one.

One better than my practice kiss with Diego.

"You'll look out for him, yes?" She tucks strands of hair behind her ear. "I know how those things can be. Festivals. Celebrations. I was young once."

It's unreal to think about parents as *young*, ever.

"People will want to talk to him. Or . . . more."

I snort. Diego is oblivious to those kinds of things. Fact

is, he's always been single. Anything that resembles a relationship isn't his thing. He didn't even *attempt* to find a date to senior prom.

We're complete opposites: Diego's everyone's friend, while I want to fall head over clumsy-ass feet in love like Charm does with Reverb. He doesn't seem invested in that kind of thing.

"Yes," I finally say, smirking. "I'll watch out for him."

"Thank you, Isaac."

I shrug. There isn't anything to thank me for. I'd never let anything happen to Diego Santoyo.

"¡Mamá! I'm back!"

The front door slams. Keys rattle against the small table in the Santoyos' foyer, followed by shoes thudding against the hardwood. Diego walks into the kitchen, as Camila and I chew on maduros. My resistance waned seconds after we awkwardly chatted about Pride.

Diego's barefoot in a pair of tropical-print board shorts and a plain black T-shirt, but his hair's impeccably swoopy and tame on the sides, as if he put effort into styling it. He blinks at me for a moment, confused.

"Hey," I say.

A giant smile wrinkles his face. "Isaac!"

He hugs me, rubbing my back in these quick, soothing circles. He smells like summer's heat and a thin layer of something else—a strange combination of grapefruit and apple. Not like a body wash. More like a perfume.

"I was going to text you," he says, pulling back. I try to mimic his enthusiastic expression, but it's hard. Camila's Jeep never smells like grapefruit and apple. Neither does the fabric softener she uses on Diego's clothes. This is someone else's scent on him. It initiates this bizarre chemical reaction inside me.

Diego scoops up the bowl of maduros, pausing to peck both Camila's cheeks before walking back to my side.

"You better wash all the dishes," she says, sounding briefly annoyed. "Including the ones in your room."

"¡Sí, sí!" he agrees, steering me toward the foyer.

"Diego!"

We're halfway up the stairs when he leans over the banister, a picture-perfect grin in place, to shout, "¡Te amo, Mamá!"

Diego's bedroom is the typical war zone—piles of clothes everywhere, a plate with last night's dinner chilling on his desk, empty energy drink cans set up like bowling pins in a corner. The floor is covered in notebooks with design ideas scribbled between the wide-rule lines. Diego will never change. At least his *bedroom* will never change.

We find a clean landing strip on the carpet by his bed. His pleated shades are pulled up, pouring sunlight over us. It's stuffy, but we're too lazy to open the window. We sit shoulder to shoulder, knee to knee, our backs propped against the side of his bed.

I try not to inhale too deeply. For allergy-related rea-sons. Not because grapefruit and apples are consuming my thoughts.

Diego pops two plantain slices in his mouth. "How long have you been here? Long enough for my mom to talk you ear off?"

"I like talking to her."

"Oh yeah?" His lips twitch upward. "What'd you talk about?"

You waits on my tongue. "Pride." I steal a slice for myself. "She wants me to look out for you."

He coughs into the crook of his elbow. "Excuse me?"

"Can you believe it?" I almost chuckle. "Like you're going to Pride to hook up."

"Right."

"I told her there's no need to worry." I watch him care-fully.

Diego pops two more pieces in his mouth before wip-ing the grease on his shorts. I wait for him to mention Mel. To confirm she's a friend, that he wants her to be something more. But Diego slouches, wiggling his toes at Cloud Strife as she passes us on the way to her laundry throne. He says nothing.

Disappointment and relief fill my stomach.

He stares up at the ceiling. "Is that all you two talked about? Sorry I made you suffer through—"

"We also talked about you and college."

Diego goes rigid. His eyebrows furrow. "What?"

"I mean, your mom did all the talking, but—it was nothing bad."

"It is bad. It's annoying. It's fucked up." His chest rises and falls in these quick beats, his shoulders drawn close to his neck.

"Diego, chill. She just needed to—"

He cuts me off again. "We've had this discussion. We made a deal. She doesn't need to talk to *you* about it."

"Fine," I say, my hands raised, palms out. "I didn't know we were breaking best friend code by being polite and chatting with each other's moms."

"It's not that serious, dude."

"Obviously it is, *dude*."

My ears burn. That hunger for time with Diego is rapidly giving way to frustration. "Also, my bad for coming here to hang out and you not being around. Again."

"Isaac—"

"Where were you?" I clear my throat, my jaw stiff as I say, louder, "You weren't here."

Something flashes in his eyes. "No. I wasn't. Does it matter?"

I shrug one shoulder while my body screams *YES! YES! YES!*

"¡Dios mío!" he groans, his hand reaching up to finally wreck his flawless hair. The hair he apparently styled to hang out with Mel and not me. I don't know why that makes me so angry. It makes me sad too. "What're you, my mom now? Are you worried I was out ruining my future? ¿Qué pasa?"

"I . . ." But I can't finish. I can't confess that I'm not worried about Diego's future, just my own.

"Everyone's all in *my* business. Mine."

"I'm not—"

"You are." He huffs, his pupils two dark moons expanding. "What, is there not enough happening in the geek forums for you to focus on rather than the fact that, yeah, I'm a little busy? Dude, I'm not your best friend only when you *need* something. What about what I need?"

"What do you need, Diego?"

"For everyone to stop throwing all these expectations on who they want me to be," he says through his teeth.

I lean back, examining him. The color in his cheeks reminds me of the strawberry jam Bella loves to spread on her toast. There's spittle on his bottom lip. His legs are pulled close to his chest, his forearms resting on his knees. Every breath is rapid and uneasy.

Suddenly, Diego's an alien to me.

He's acting as if I'm stressing him out like his parents. Maybe I am.

"I'm sorry." I stand. My foot scoots a pair of boxers aside. I blink at the carpet, unable to make eye contact. "I didn't mean to—"

"Wait, you're leaving?"

His fingers curl around my wrist. I wonder if he can feel the lightning under my skin. I wonder if he knows how bad I want to jerk away from his touch.

"No. Sorry, it's my fault. I'm just wound up about . . ." His voice fades as his hand drops away from my wrist to reach back for a small remote control lost in his sheets. I wait a beat as he queues up a movie streaming app on his TV. Does he expect me to stay? Does he want me to go?

Then he pushes the white ceramic bowl with maduros in it toward my feet.

He never asks me to sit with him, but I do anyway. I reclaim my spot on the carpet, coiled into a lopsided ball as he picks a film. We don't mention the unusual space between our hips, the distance between our shoulders and knees.

It's the most abnormal afternoon I've ever spent with my best friend.

Twenty

I get it. You trust Charm. But you barely know each other. Be cautious about who you call *friend*. You let the wrong person into your world . . . and they'll destroy it.

—Pica, *Disaster Academy* Issue #5

The Six Group Chat
Today 1:09 PM

F.B.: Squad we need to hang out!!!

Level_Zero: Yasssssssss!

Misty Munroe: SIR, that's queer appropriation! 😡😡😡

Level_Zero: Who said I'm not hear???

Level_Zero: *queer

Unknown Number: Why are you HERE?

Level_Zero: SHUT UP ALIX!

F.B.: back on topic! whos dwn to hang today? I'm off at 5. THE PARK??

Misty Munroe: 😎🍔🌭🍅

Level_Zero: Ill be done kicking Konamicodes ass by then.

Diego: 👍

Unknown Number: I'LL. Use an apostrophe.

Level_Zero: Alix your a dick.

Unknown Number: YOU'RE. Thank you.

Misty Munroe: Can someone pick me up?

F.B.: OTW at 5!

Diego: Mom says I can get the car after dinner. 6 okay?

Diego: Isaac are you in?

Diego: ISAAC?!

Me: ok

Golden glitter reflects off the lake's surface. A hint of smoke lingers in the air, no doubt from someone's afternoon grill down by the field. Crickets begin their evening orchestral performance. Charcoal clouds gather in the sky over Memorial Park. They look hungry to absorb every inch of waning light left.

I can smell it in the air—the coming rain.

We're at the gazebo, the Six, lost in our phones while passing around a community bag of fries F.B., Zelda, and Blake picked up from Twisted Burger on their way here. I can't take my eyes off Zelda, who has a cape on over a silver-sequined jacket that glows like a beacon out here. I'm not as concerned about a patrolling cop spotting us as I am about the potential heatstroke Zelda will suffer under all those layers. It makes my skin itch.

"Aren't you hot in all that?" I ask, gesturing to their ensemble.

Zelda twirls once, the cape fanning out in a dramatic tornado. It's a deep plum, long and flowing, made from a sturdy fabric. "I've decided not to give up on my dream," they say. "Since LC is a wrap, I'm gonna design the hell out of some dope cosplay to fill up my SCAD portfolio. I started an online donation account for my followers to help with supplies."

My eyes widen. "That's awesome."

Zelda smiles self-consciously at their Jordans.

"Can you, uh . . ." I hesitate. A knot of guilt forms in my stomach. "Send me the link?"

Diego reclines against me, his spine pressed to my left arm. Considering what happened the other day, it's odd to be this close. I'm careful with my next words: "I have some money I can donate. Since, y'know, I didn't actually get to buy passes to the con."

I wait for Diego to react, but he's lost in some app on his phone.

"*For real* for real?"

I nod.

"I can spare a little money too," says Diego, leaning away from me. He doesn't have to explain why he has extra cash. The shame has already made a permanent residence inside me.

"Thanks," whispers Zelda.

"Damn it, my service sucks out here," grumbles Blake. He desperately waves his phone over his head trying to catch a bar or two.

Diego's mouth curls up into a smirk as he says, "What's wrong? Can't hack DigiSoft's database to decode a way to beat *BtVoS* before me, Blake?"

Blake flips him the bird. He asks Zelda about a new video game they're both playing. On my other side, Alix tells F.B. and Diego about a Chinese soul mates drama on Netflix I've never heard of. I try hard to find my place in the discussions. I'm a leftover screw in a giant IKEA furniture project—no one knows what to do with me.

But then Zelda compliments my shoes, and I smile at them. The *thank you* and *I like yours too* feel so close to my tongue.

Instead, I stuff my mouth with fries before cautiously holding them out to Diego.

Our fingers brush as he accepts the bag. "Not really that hungry," he says. "My mom made a ridic dinner today."

A rapid fire of *ping-ping-ping* prevents me from asking what magnificent meal Camila prepared for the Santoyos. My phone screen illuminates with competing notifications. The chimes are like the opening chords of my favorite song: *a new message from Davi!*

From: Davi

IVE MADE THE BIGGEST MISTAKE! HELP!
8:59 PM

From: Davi
Ez tricked me into driving out to Stone Mtn to hike
the mountain. In. the. summer. WTF!
8:59 PM

From: Davi
Hes a monster!!! 😈◀ EZRA
9:00 PM

From: Davi
Wish u were hre 😖
[media attached]
9:00 PM

In the last message bubble is a photo. Davi and Ezra
are cheesing at the camera on top of the mountain with
an orange sun sitting like a cherry on a pink-sky sun-
dae. They're both holding up two fingers, a peace out to
another humid summer day. Ezra is caught mid-laugh.
Davi's tongue is out, drenched curls hanging over his eyebrows.

And he's shirtless.

The angle of the shot captures his slick chest. The
beginnings of his lean torso. Ezra's in a loose tank top.

I focus on that. Not on the glow across Davi's bare skin. Not on the promise of what's not shown in the image.

I struggle to breathe properly.

Is this Davi flirting? He said "wish you were here" in the text. There, with him . . . shirtless.

It's all I think about. I'm hard, which is really awkward since I'm in public with the Six, so I curl forward to try and hide it.

"Whoa, Captain Incredible," says F.B., swooping in to snatch the bag from Diego. He polishes off the fries with one handful. "You're very"—he chews and chews, then takes a swig of cherry Coke. It's followed by a noisy burp—"popular."

"Sorry." Quickly, I download the photo and close out the message app. My cheeks are hot. I blurt, "It's Davi."

"Davi *who*?" Zelda asks, one sharp eyebrow rising.

"Davi Lucas," Alix says flatly. "The Guy."

F.B. hunches over, striking the most unrealistic hockey player pose—gritted teeth and arms taut as if he's holding a hockey stick. "Davi from high school. From SP. That guy you have zero chill about."

"Excuse me?!"

My heart races as I scramble to figure out *how* they could possibly know about Davi and my crush on him.

Blake shrugs. "KonamiCode told us about him."

If the fireflies were close enough, they could build a nest in my open mouth. My eyes flit to Diego. His long eyelashes flutter against the tops of his cheeks, his brow pinched. Nonchalantly, he says, "I didn't say anything bad."

"But you said something," I snap.

Crush Syndromes are sacred. Then again, Diego and I don't have those kinds of secrets anymore, do we? He has no problem discussing Davi and me—not that there is a "Davi and me"—with the Six. He also has zero issues with telling them—not me—about Mel.

"He didn't drop any new details," comments Alix. "It was pretty obvious the other day when you two were talking outside Secret Planet."

"You were spying on us?" My voice cracks.

"One, you're far beneath my espionage skills," Alix says, frowning. "Two, the inhabitants of Neptune saw those heart eyes you were serving him."

I *pfft* at her. Complete bullshit. I have never been anything but calm, impassive, and smooth around Davi Lucas.

Also, lying to myself about boys is an underrated skill.

I shift back around in Diego's direction. He bites his thumbnail, avoiding my eyes. Is he seriously not going to explain himself?

Fine. I reopen Davi's text. I reply with a smiley emoji, a GIF of Alexis from *Schitt's Creek* sarcastically saying "Oh! Fun!", and that "no thanks" Drake reaction image saved in my camera roll. All the corny things you send a boy who you hope elevates your relationship past platonic levels. Soonish.

"I don't get it," Blake says, stealing my attention from the gray text bubble under Davi's name. "If he's such a big deal, just ask him out. Go on one of those Olive Garden dinner dates."

"Yuck!" Zelda gags. "You should *cook* him dinner. That's romantic as hell."

In the background, I can hear Alix dry-heaving, which must be a positive sign.

"Our Lord and Savior, the divine Whitney Houston, gives you her blessings." Zelda confers the sign of the cross at me.

The thought sticks: *Invite Davi over to my house for pozole with romantic music and candlelight. The ambiance alone should make my feelings obvious, right?*

Diego clears his throat. "Great. Cook him dinner." His jaw flexes as if he's grinding his teeth, sharpening his canines. "Invite him to Pride too. It'll be the perfect happy ending." The edge in his voice knifes right through my skin, straight to the bone.

"Uh, I mean . . ."

I can't finish, but Diego's large eyes tell me I don't have to.

"Wait, you invited him to Pride?" he says, sitting up, "*Our* Pride?"

"It's the entire metro Atlanta teen population's Pride," I correct, trying to inflect a degree of humor in my voice.

It doesn't work. Diego's face remains tense. I swallow. "He's not going *with* us. We're just going to meet up. It's NBD."

My right leg is shaking. I don't like discussing this with Diego in front of everyone.

I add, "He was gonna be there anyway."

"Awesome," Diego says, eyes narrowed. "So, he'll be there, we'll be there, and you're going to what? Ask him to be your boyfriend?"

"Maybe."

"Since when has getting a boyfriend been one of your priorities for the summer?"

Since Davi Lucas walked into Secret Planet and noticed me.

Honestly, what's wrong with that? If Davi and I meet up and something—*anything*—happens, then shouldn't my best friend be excited for me? Why is Diego being such an ass about this? All his spare time's dedicated to Mel instead of me, anyway. I don't see the problem with wanting what everyone else, including him, has. What's wrong with me getting the real-world version of what Charm and Reverb should already have?

Why can't I have Davi *and* the summer I wanted with my best friend?

"Whoa, whoa." F.B. leaps into the middle of the gazebo, arms extended as if he's creating a wall between Diego and me. Too late. That barrier was established the moment I ruined our Legends Con plans. "Let's not go all Nicki versus Cardi B here."

Diego scowls at his lap. I cock my head at him, anticipating an explanation about where his hostility is coming from. But that never happens.

F.B. claps three times until we're all looking at him. "Why don't we go to teen Pride as a group? We can hang out, enjoy this good summer vitamin D, and celebrate who we are." He points at himself. "As a straight ally."

Then he points at me. "As the coolest gay geek."

To Diego: "The most celebrated bisexual gamer."

To Zelda: "As a fabulous nonbinary cosplay legend."

Zelda fans out their cape, chin tipped upward like a true superhero.

"As a . . ." F.B. raises an eyebrow at Blake. "No pressure to discuss your sexuality here. That's for safe spaces. In fact—"

"I'm undecided," interrupts Blake with a shrug.

"Which, by the way, is also sweet. Decide whenever you're ready. We support you." F.B. turns, holding a hand out in Alix's direction. "And . . ."

"I refuse to conform to society's insistence on self-identifying in order to belong to a community based on their own black-and-white views of what is an acceptable sexuality," Alix replies.

"Right on!" F.B. fist pumps the air. "Stick it to the Man."

"That's not what I'm communicating. Also, that's highly problematic—"

"Let's do this," F.B. says over Alix's argument. "The Six Takes Over Pride!"

No. This wasn't my plan. Not at all. I'm still adjusting to being around the Six. Diego's right—Pride is one of my summer goals. *Our* summer goals. Then Davi got added on. Now the Six is tagging along.

It's too much.

"Captain Incredible?"

All their eyes, including Diego's, are on me. Nausea unsettles my stomach. As much as I want to reject F.B.'s request, I don't want to look like an asshole. So now I'm caught up in a situation that's completely opposite of what I imagined. I say "Sounds dope" with a smile that lasts less than three seconds.

"Awesome!" F.B. shouts. "We're doing this."

The sky darkens, the clouds drooping lower. Thunder growls above us. Whispering drops of rain hit the surface of the lake.

"Yeah," I say to Diego. "We're doing this."

There's something about a nighttime summer storm. The crackling sky competes with raindrops plinking on roofs, the scrape of windshield wipers. Tree branches sway with the wind, their green muted against the gray.

A chill R&B playlist hums gently in Camila Santoyo's Jeep. It's the only interruption in the silence between Diego and me. We're parked outside my house. I've undone my seat belt but haven't opened the door. Diego drums his fingers on the steering wheel but hasn't shifted gears into reverse.

We're stuck in a stasis field. In a universe that's not ours.

"I love the rain," he says.

I nod, though he's not looking at me. "Good for naps."

"For listening to music when we're supposed to be sleeping," he says, a sideways smile overtaking his whole face.

I can't help the way I grin back.

At a different point in our timeline, when our clumsy feet were too big for our bodies, we did this—listened to music at night. Usually on my bedroom floor with shared earbuds. One for me, the other for Diego. We put on Bruno Mars, discussing Bella's plans for the next big family performance. Diego would go on and on about a new video game he wanted for his birthday. I would brag about my last comic book haul.

Yawns and smiles and feet tapping to the melody while a storm pounded down on the world outside.

"It's still gonna be fun," I say. "Pride is still about me and you."

"Is it?"

"You know it is."

But Diego doesn't confirm my statement. He lets the music play for a beat. Then he says, "You should text him."

I turn my head against the headrest, blinking at him. The light over the garage breaks through the misted-over windshield to smear a champagne glow across his face. His expression is blank. His hands are white-knuckled on the steering wheel. Tension unrolls a trail of veins up his arms.

"Invite him over." He laughs. It's hard, nothing like the one I've known my whole life. "Cook him dinner. What's it gonna hurt, right?"

"Diego—"

"Just do it."

His voice has an unmistakable sharpness to it. The world outside is blurred, bringing Diego's simmering even further into focus inside this enclosed space. I don't know how to respond to him, so I unlock my phone, scrolling to Davi's last message. He was ranting about Ezra's body odor and his dinner plans. Our texts remain nonchalant and meaningless. But I like that.

Every other thing in life is way too imperative these days.

"Come on, Isaac."

My thumbs clumsily wrestle for the right letters. I start, then stop three times. I hit send before regret strangles my motor skills.

"Done."

Diego's smile rests awkwardly on his lips, as if it's not supposed to be there.

Like his mouth against mine that night at Twisted Burger.

"Good for you and Davi," he whispers, an edge to how he says Davi's name. It reminds me of the pitch Camila uses when she's fighting with Diego. That prove-me-wrong tone. Suddenly, I realize what's happening.

We're fighting, Diego and me.

And I'm losing.

Twenty-One

He said YES!

Well, Davi texted "yeah." But that's irrelevant. He's coming over and I'm going to cook him dinner and I'm more than a little nervous about it.

Mom's at Whole Foods, alone, picking up last minute supplies. I couldn't afford to fidget and overthink while pushing a shopping cart through the produce section with her. I'm still kind of shocked I survived telling her about an official Crush Syndrome. Informing Lilah Johnson I'd invited a boy over for a home-cooked meal was a major lesson in How Not to Tell Your Mom You're Dating.

I decided spending all day in my bed staring at the ceiling gave my mind too much freedom to revisit that shirtless selfie in my camera roll. The idea of inviting Davi upstairs after dinner was overwhelming. Would he sit on my bed? Put his hand on my leg? Would he laugh at my officially licensed *Disaster Academy* socks while we made out?

Too many weird thoughts were happening. Then my hand started drifting, and—no.

DJ smiles at me as soon as I walk into Cosmos and Java. "Usual table, love?" she asks, balancing a plate on each hand. Early afternoon sunlight diminishes the wrinkles around her eyes. "Or would you like to sit with your friend?"

I freeze. *My friend?*

She must sense my hesitation. "You know, from the other day?"

I follow the direction her head nods in. In the middle of the diner, sipping an iced coffee as dark as her soulless insides, is Alix. She's alone, head down, scrolling through her phone.

"Uh."

"Come on," insists DJ, easily walking backward without tripping. "It'll save me cleaning up another table."

I wait near the door. Someone clears their throat behind me, but my feet don't move. A young couple maneuvers around me, the guy shooting me a sideways glare as they pass. DJ waits with an impatient expression crowding her face. I struggle to catch my breath.

It's only Alix. We coexist at Secret Planet all the time. There's a required fifteen feet of physical distance involved, but we manage.

Lately, I've thought a lot about how this could happen at UGA. Eating with strangers or pretentious, brownnosing classmates I'm forced to be in group projects with. Who knows, maybe I'll have an archnemesis in Athens too. Dining at The Bulldog Café with a table full of Alix Jins could be my inescapable future.

"Okay," I whisper to DJ, following her with heavy feet.

"Stop staring at me," Alix demands. "It's disturbing."

Congratulations, Isaac Martin, you've finally unlocked your Worst Idea Possible.

"You're disturbing," I mumble.

She rolls her eyes. "Superior comeback. Did your critical thinking skills help you achieve any national titles for East Middleton's debate club?"

Before I can hit her with another searing—see: *lackluster*—response, she grunts "Just stop looking at me" while lowering her chin to adjust her messy ponytail.

"There are far more entertaining things to look at than you, Bane."

It's true. We're seated in the middle of the diner. I'm still a little amazed Alix agreed to let me share a table. Technically, she glared at me when I walked up with DJ. And I might've sat down without invitation. But she hasn't formally expelled me yet.

Around us, tables are filled with parents trying to appease their bored children with plates of fries. Solo diners are occupied by their coffees and laptops. A woman in a corner booth watches the door. She's wearing a navy-and-white checkered blouse, her chestnut bob elegantly styled.

Every thirty seconds, she anxiously checks her phone.

In my head, I play a guessing game. Is she waiting on a date? A friend? Maybe a potential job interview that'll change her life?

Two tables over, a youngish hipster dude with the kind of mustache-beard combo only seen on Instagram ads smiles at a guy in a suit across the diner. Suit Guy is casually holding hands with a pretty girl too oblivious to realize what's happening behind her back.

A secret affair? Harmless flirting?

"Trust me," I finally say. "I'm not looking at you."

"Great." Alix types away on her phone. "It's tragic enough being seen in public with you. I'd hate for you to think we're going to engage in a tête-à-tête."

"What?"

"Never mind."

She sips on her iced coffee. I pick at the burnt remains of the grilled cheese I ordered. Under the table, my leg jiggles to the opening theme for *Star Trek: The Next Generation* playing overhead. She sighs. I cough.

Yeah, this is the best way to spend my last summer before college.

At least I'm no longer freaking out about Davi coming over in a few hours. I consider texting my mom to ensure she grabs all the ingredients needed to make Abuelito's world-famous pan de elote. Then I remember it's Mom, former sous-chef to the legendary José Martin. I'm in good hands.

Alix props her chin on her knuckles. A few strands of hair fall across her round cheeks. She checks something on her phone.

"Hold up." I reach for it before the screen goes dark.

Alix lurches to snatch it back. "Personal property."

She's right, but I hold the phone above her reach, examining the screen. "Is that Pica?"

"As if you'd know." Alix manages to knock the phone free from my fingers, catching it. "Figured you only had eyes for your precious Charm and Reverb."

"Facts. But I'm a fan of all the Webster Academy students."

Pica is a *Disaster Academy* character who can alter any situation in her favor through telekinetic manipulation. She's Korean American, sarcastic, and asexual. Instead of the school-mandated Webster Academy crimson-and-navy striped tie every student wears, Pica has a black, gray, white, and purple one.

"Is she your favorite?" I ask.

Alix glares hardcore at me before nodding.

"Are you . . . ?"

I know not to ask the question waiting on my tongue. Someone's sexuality is their own. Coming out shouldn't be forced just so you can have something in common with another person. It's for someone to share when they're ready.

For some reason, I suddenly want that connection with Alix.

She sighs, then pushes up one sleeve of her red hoodie. On the inside of her left elbow is a small bird outlined in black ink. A magpie, like where Pica gets her name. It's shaded in with gray and purple ink.

I've never noticed it before.

I've never witnessed Alix wearing anything but loose-fitting, long-sleeve tops.

She's only seventeen, but I don't interrogate *how* she got the tattoo. It's Alix—she probably knows an underground, unlicensed person. But I say "I think Pica's awesome" with a wide, all-teeth grin.

"Of course you do. Everyone does."

I bite at the straw bobbing in my glass of ginger ale. "I didn't expect . . . *you* to be so into *DA*." She snorts, and I realize I might've just called myself out a bit. Okay, I've seen an issue or two of *Disaster Academy* in Alix's collection of comics when we were at Secret Planet at the same time. But it's a popular series. I never thought it was her *thing* like it is for me. That she'd have a favorite character, one that she relates to enough to ink on her skin.

But I guess I've made a lot of assumptions about Alix since we've never really talked one-on-one.

"Congratulations," she says. "I've known a lot of four-star losers, but you're the first five-star loser I've met. Your mom must be so proud."

I smirk, flipping her off.

"Yes, I'm 'into' *DA*," she says, air quotes and all. "I'm

not an android like my brother, Henry."

Henry Jin, former East Middleton High School Class President, Valedictorian, National Honor Society member, AP Scholar, State Blah-Blah-Blah winner of Achievement in Something-Something.

I recognize the tension around her eyes. The nervous way she plays with her hoodie's sleeves. It's virtually identical to the way I get when explaining Iggy to anyone.

"He wasn't that big a deal."

"He's an eighteen-year-old sophomore in college," Alix deadpans.

I chew my thumbnail, trying to do the math. "He skipped two grades?"

"Almost three." Alix's eyes focus on a water spot on our table. "He's the family G.O.A.T. Every comma in my parents' bank account is invested in his future presidency. I have to save up for my own tuition by working part-time at my uncle's restaurant."

"The House of Jin, right?"

Alix gives me a thumbs-up and an eye-roll. "My parents expect that I'll only live up to half of Henry's legacy."

I frown into my cup. Heat rises up my neck. Weirdly, I want to say "Sorry" to her. I know what it's like—to have a dysfunctional family. To have issues with your parents. But I've never had anyone who wasn't Bella to talk to about it. No one's ever talked to me about it happening to *them*.

The Santoyos, despite Diego's current situation, are

flawless. I know he listens when I rant about Carlos, but I don't think he *understands*, not fully.

DJ breezes by us with a tight smile, marching over to a group of noisy diners. Alix blinks so many times, I think she might cry. She doesn't. And I'm brave enough to say "Henry or not, you'll always be number one at destroying someone's feelings with one look" before she can return to phone-staring.

"Ha." It comes out dry, but Alix smiles.

"It's true." I finish my ginger ale. "And I know what that's like. The brother thing. The parents thing too."

She makes a face, which lights a fire in my cheeks, but I say, "Seriously. It's not . . . easy." She doesn't immediately respond, only studies me. Then, she nods.

I exhale, feeling good. Small victories.

"Um, hey." I nudge my cup aside, trying to buy time while I relocate that courage from a minute ago. "Who's Mel?"

"Melanie?"

"Yes." My eyes look anywhere but at her face. Something tugs hard on my ribs. I shouldn't be asking *Alix* about Mel. Nor should I have spent part of this morning searching her name on social media. Turns out there are quite a few Melanie Bricios in this world. Her Twitter's a dead zone. Her Insta is private.

I should just ask Diego, but . . . why hasn't he volunteered any information?

It hit me after sitting in silence with Diego in his mom's Jeep. Why he's been angry. Why our distance continues to grow. Watching his face in the broken light of the storm, I saw a Diego I remembered from the Twisted Burger parking lot. The night of our practice kiss. When Davi came up to us. When he saw how deep my Crush Syndrome really is.

That's what has Diego so annoyed. He thinks my crush on Davi is taking up all my time. The time we planned to spend with each other.

But I don't understand why, especially since he's always with Mel.

Alix sniffs. "Uh, Mel's a girl. A gamer. She lives here, on Earth."

"Thanks for the basic fact sheet." I stab at the ice in my glass until it breaks.

"Shouldn't you be asking—"

"No. You're right," I reply. It was a silly thing to bring up. "Forget it."

We're quiet for so long. Alix grabs her phone and starts typing. Holy Nightwing, if she's texting Diego, I swear—

"Remember when Boomstar first joined the team?" She lays her phone down on the table. The screen is bright with color and sharp lines and familiar faces. I recognize the panel from *Disaster Academy* Issue #2. Reverb, with his tall, spiked hair and friendly grin and terra-cotta skin tone, talking to an electric Boomstar.

In the next panel, Charm's glaring at Boomstar with

a sour expression. At first, he wasn't her biggest fan. It was never specifically stated, but all the *DA* fans know he was jealous of her—totally platonic—relationship with Reverb.

"Who doesn't remember?" I sigh. "There was a monthlong war on Geeks Nation about it."

I didn't start that one. But I might've participated. Often.

"Did she end up a being a legit threat to their friendship?" Alix asks.

"No."

"Did she dismantle your desperate wet dreams of a Charm and Reverb future?"

I snort. "No."

"Was she anything other than this epic, doesn't-need-a-romantic-storyline-to-exist badass?"

"No," I reply begrudgingly. I know what she's implying: Mel isn't a threat. She's just a secret my best friend's keeping from me.

Before this summer, it was impossible for me to imagine Diego having genuine friends in his gaming community. Finding out that they're more than gamertags and quests to beat a final boss, that these are *real* people Diego hangs out with, has been unexpected. There are others who get the best—and maybe the worst—of the one person outside of family who *understands me*. He has relationships with them that extend past KonamiCode.

I didn't think any of that online stuff translated into real-world friendships. That's why it's always been easiest for me to socialize on forums like Geeks Nation. I can geek out. Say what I want when I want. No expectations to carry a conversation. No one's two feet in front of me, judging every piece of who I am with their expressions or snorting or eye-rolls.

That barrier makes me feel safest.

Thing is, I'm sitting here with Alix, and I feel a little bit more like the Isaac that only my family or Diego knows.

Talking to Alix about comics, face-to-face, isn't any different from doing it with the people in the online forums. She gets me. Kind of. She certainly gets the *DA* side of me, maybe the family side too.

Alix plays with the ends of her hair, finishing her coffee. I consider ordering her another. It'd be my way of saying "Thanks" and "You're not the worst person ever" and "We should do this again."

But I'm not there yet.

She squints at me. "Don't get the wrong idea about today. We're not buddies. This isn't a peace treaty."

I grin. "Back on your I-hate-Isaac bullshit?"

"Never left." But her mouth twitches into a dangerously authentic smile. It's enough.

We're not friends, but maybe we're not really enemies either.

Twenty-Two

Rufus is reading DA @theybothliveatthebeginning · Jun 4

whoa just finished #DisasterAcademy 10—joining team #charmverb after all that sexy tension in the vent! love their friendship too. they're always there for each other. any good fics about these two??

Isaac @charminmartin · Jun 10

Replying to @theybothliveatthebeginning

Welcome! 🏄 Start here: https://www.geeksnation.com/DisasterAcademy/jwk8maw/charmverb_fic_masterlist/

Our kitchen is a battlefield.

Onion remnants leave a trail toward the hacked-up leftovers of a chicken. Spilled cumin powder creates a chalk outline around a murdered garlic clove. The cutting board is a bloodbath of sliced vegetable juices. Someone—possibly me—spilled chicken broth on the floor. The sink is piled high with more dishes than necessary to create pollo rojo.

My planned menu of pozole and pan de elote was rejected by Mom. "Keep it simple," she told me. Pozole takes hours to cook, which is why Abuelito only makes it on birthdays or the new year.

"Pollo rojo," Mom insisted. It's a delicious red pepper chicken.

We agreed on cilantro-lime rice as a side dish with store-bought gelato instead of sopapillas for dessert.

Mom hums Sade at the stove. This evening's song selection is "Smooth Operator." It's a perfect metaphor for her, the way she stirs things, adds spices, and snacks on the mango she cubed before we started cooking. She's barely sweating.

A tiny fountain of perspiration currently dribbles from my forehead to my cheeks. It's from constantly checking the tomatoes roasting in the oven. I'm supposed to wait until they're the texture of Abuelito's hands—perfectly wrinkly.

I sniff my armpits. A shower before Davi's arrival is mandatory.

"You know, Iggy never cooked for a girl he liked," Mom says, smiling.

I sneeze three times. Too much red pepper and allergies. "Has Iggy ever *liked* anyone?" I ask. "He seems to tolerate a majority of the human population."

"Melissa Fuentes," Mom says without missing a beat. "She was great."

"They were fourteen."

"So? Age has nothing to do with love, platonic or romantic." She hip-checks me out of the way to remove the tomatoes from the oven. Her internal chef clock is never late. "Abuelito swore she was Iggy's soul mate."

I roll my eyes. Of course Abuelito did. Iggy and Melissa dated—or whatever constitutes as formal relationships when you're fourteen—for the entire summer.

My grandpa and his summer fairy tales.

Out of nowhere, Mom says, "Is this Davi the One?"

"Wow, Mom, can I get back to you *after* we've had a first date?"

She *hmm*s, then turns around.

I've had the same dream about him since receiving that shirtless photo. Kissing him in the middle of Pride with fireworks overhead. Clumsily inviting him back here afterward. Mom will be out of town. We'll have the house to ourselves. I guess this thing with Davi is a little more than just a first kiss now.

"Focus," Mom instructs, waving a wooden spoon covered in red sauce in front of me. "Don't burn the rice!"

It's 7:22 p.m.

The pollo rojo is done. On the stove, a lid covers the pot of rice. Mom washed all the dishes before leaving me alone to finish. I've cleaned and sanitized the war zone that was once Battle: Dinner Date. I'm showered, wearing jeans and a newish, red polka-dot button-down.

Keep it simple.

I've restarted my phone twice. Just in case there's something wrong with the service. In case my notifications haven't updated. Like a new text. Maybe a missed call.

Davi and I agreed to have dinner at seven.

At 7:24 p.m., my phone pings. The Six group chat.

I ignore it.

The Martin household has an official dining room that we rarely use. When Bella and Chris are in town, we'll sit there for pizza and rounds of Mom's favorite card game, spades. At the end of October, Abuelito wrangles all of us, including Iggy, in there to help set up an altar for Día de Muertos. He insists we sit at the table for Thanksgiving dinner, just the way he and Abuela used to. Around Christmas, it's just Mom and me in there while Abuelito and Iggy spend the holiday at Carlos's house.

The long mahogany table is set with two plates, two wine glasses—Mom's idea, even though I only have ginger ale for Davi and me—and a lit single-wick candle. Another one of Mom's suggestions.

All this for a dinner date that I'm clearly not having.

At 7:32 p.m., multiple texts come in.

> From: Davi
> Sorry!!! Last min invitation to play @ hockey exhibition DTATL!!
> 7:32 PM

> From: Davi
> I'm on ice with stars! Pros!! 😊

[media attached]
7:32 PM

From: Davi
Rly srry. Meant to text earlier. Waaaaay earlier.
Don't have me.
7:33 PM

From: Davi
*Hate. Plz have me over for dinner in the future 😔
7:33 PM

From: Davi
Make it up to you @ Pride! Xx
7:34 PM

I scroll back and forth through each of his messages. My brain examines every emoji, every word, every letter. For a fleeting second, I smile at the "Xx," because I know what it means. Kisses, like the kind I expected from him tonight.

When it comes to other people, expectation is one hell of a disaster waiting to happen.

I squeeze my phone until my fingers ache, then drop it on the counter without replying to Davi.

A large portion of my heart is begging to cry, but I refuse. Even if my eyes burn from fighting it. Time to keep it simple, like Mom said. I walk calmly to my room, inhale the scent of citrus until the tears retreat, then change into my favorite *Disaster Academy* T-shirt.

"I'm going out," Mom announces when she walks into the kitchen. Her arm is extended in front of her as she talks into her phone. A tinny, familiar giggle rattles through the speaker.

"Are you FaceTiming Bella?"

"Hey, Isaac!" shouts Bella.

When Mom turns the camera on me, I wave, then squint at my mom. "Out?"

"Yes. Out, Isaac. I'm an adult."

"Ooh, sick burn," taunts Bella.

"I really hope your child inherits Chris's sense of humor," I comment as Mom carries the phone with her to the table. She lays it down to slip on a pair of metallic bronze heels. I wrinkle my nose. "You're an adult? Since when?"

Mom shoots me a look while picking up her phone again. The I'm-not-the-one look. She's wearing a turquoise-and-gold blouse, dark skinny jeans.

My mom in skinny jeans? That's fifteen kinds of wrong.

"Who're you going out with?" I ask.

"None of your business," Bella says as Mom hands me the phone. I immediately scowl at Bella. She's slouched on her sofa, a tub of vanilla ice cream sitting on her belly.

"I'm going with Camila," Mom finally says. She fixes her headscarf. It's yellow with a beautiful sunflower pattern spread across the fabric. "We're having a girls' night out."

"Girls' night out? Doing what?"

"Ohmygod," Bella says around a spoonful of ice cream.

Mom shakes her head, grabbing her wallet. "The movies. Dinner. A club."

"A club?!"

"Mom's gonna be dabbing to Post Malone!" Bella squeals. Seriously, my sister is on an eight-months-pregnant sugar high.

"No one does that dance anymore. And no one likes Post Malone."

"Chris does."

"Point proven."

Mom clucks her tongue. "I'm going out to have fun." She kisses my cheek, rubs my hair. She doesn't ask about Davi or why he hasn't arrived yet, but there's something in her eyes. Far from pity. It's soft, empathetic, as if Carlos has disappointed her enough times that she can recognize it in someone else.

She knows now is not the time to talk about it.

Someone knocks loudly at our front door. "I'll be home late," Mom says as she exits the kitchen to answer the door.

"She told you," Bella teases, scooping up more ice cream.

I bite back the need to remind Bella she's a mom-to-be, not a three-year-old.

"Now, give me my phone," Mom says as she reenters the kitchen. "You have a visitor."

I lean sideways for a better view. An erratic throb reverberates in my chest. Mom carries Bella away, stopping in the kitchen doorway. Her heels give her the perfect height to kiss Diego's cheek.

"FaceTime me later, Isaac! We have some things to discuss!" is the last thing I hear from Bella as she and Mom disappear.

"Smells good in here," Diego says.

I stare at him for a minute longer. We haven't seen each other since Camila's Jeep, caught in a storm. Since he insisted on me texting Davi.

Did Mom call him? Tell him that Davi ghosted me? Now he's here to what? Throw it in my face? That I finally shot my shot with the boy that ruined our summer plans and missed?

The way he's standing there with one of those Diego smiles, so easygoing, maybe that's not it at all. He doesn't look ready to drag me because Davi's not here. His gaze keeps darting around, eyebrows coming together in the middle of his head like he's confused as to what's going on. After my shoulders drop, realization slowly relaxes his expression. The need to unleash all the sharp anger growing inside me—the kind that should be directed at Davi or myself—flees.

"Uh, dinner date didn't quite work out," I say, barely controlling the disappointment in my voice.

I don't want Diego's pity.

"Oh." He raises his eyebrows. "Well, Mamá tried to test a new low-fat, saltless recipe on me. I think tofu was used." He dry heaves, then laughs.

An unexplainable relief moves like vapor through my lungs. Diego's here. He's not Davi, but I realize he's the only person I want around in this moment.

His eyes survey the pollo rojo, then he peeks under the lid of the rice pot. "Soooo . . ."

We sit on the counter—a cardinal sin in Mom's rule book—eating off paper plates with our hands. Bits of rice cover my T-shirt. Diego's fingers are stained red from sauce. Neither of us cares. We chew and bump elbows and talk about nothing at all as if we're still tweens living every day of summer like it's our last.

After, we share gelato while sitting on the floor. One carton, two spoons.

"Blackberry?"

"Wildberry," I say.

The kitchen smells like cinnamon and vanilla bean from the candle I forgot to blow out. On the edge of the counter, my phone recycles through Mom's Sade playlist.

I still haven't texted Davi back. Truthfully, I don't think I will. Not tonight.

"By Your Side" hums over us. We pass the carton back and forth, fingers slippery from the condensation. Our bare feet tap out the melody. Unplanned synchronization.

"Ollie's in love with your comics," Diego says.

"A win for Team Isaac."

"Mamá loves it." He frowns, eyes downcast. "I hear them. My parents. Late at night, they talk. Mostly about how they're worried it's going to be difficult for him after this school year. You know, once he starts high school."

Diego's eyelashes fan against his cheeks when he closes his eyes. They're long, like Camila's. He whispers, "I don't know, though. I think Ollie will be okay?"

I nod, taking another bite of gelato.

Diego flexes his bony fingers over his kneecap. "I know high school's probably not gonna be easy, but I don't want him to think it'll suck because he's on the spectrum. He's Autistic. That doesn't mean he should feel like he's . . . different."

I hate the way Diego has to swallow around that word. The way people use it as a negative. As if it defines a flaw. Different isn't bad or wrong. It's not a space you drop someone into because they fail to fit the mold of normalcy dictated by other people. It's certainly not a place I want anyone to put Ollie in.

Different is important.

Different is something to aspire to.

I elbow him. "He'd fit in perfectly at the Webster Academy."

Diego's shoulders lift as he lets out a breathy chuckle. "You really think Ollie's gonna be okay?" he asks, looking at me expectantly.

"He'll be more than *okay*, Diego," I confirm. "We're talking about Ollie Santoyo. He's already fucking amazing." I don't know why, but I press my fingertips to his knuckles as if that one connection can make my words more powerful.

He nods.

The song ends. Our conversation does too. But Diego stays right here, by my side, until we finish the gelato and the cold silence creeps back into our friendship.

Twenty-Three

Mrs. Morris, Charm—*Aaron*—is my best friend.
But what do you give someone who already has
everything at his fingertips?

—Reverb, *Disaster Academy* Issue #11

Thursday morning, the heavy scent of dark roast coffee clings to the air. The kitchen floor's cool beneath my bare feet as I stand over the stove. Abuelito's smooth, deep voice fills my ears as he croons all his favorite songs. Between Luis Miguel tunes, he calls out instructions to me like he's a master chef and I'm his line cook.

I don't mind.

Anticipation is pulsing through my bones.

It's T-minus twenty-seven hours until Teen Pride Day in Atlanta. By noon tomorrow, I'll be surrounded by people dressed in every variation of the rainbow imaginable, all of us celebrating the same thing—our awesomeness.

I can't wait to see Davi in his bi socks and new shoes.

I can't wait to stand shoulder to shoulder with Diego and watch the parade.

"Chiquito," Abuelito says from the table with his

lukewarm coffee and newspaper. "¡Presta atención! Check the sauce."

A fire rises in my cheeks at the same intensity as the one below the saucepan. I can't mess this up. I've already ruined enough things this summer.

After sitting in this kitchen with Diego a few nights ago, I couldn't shake the sadness in his eyes when we said goodbye. Or the countdown in my head. Saturday is Legends Con, the most epic event we're not attending. While I cleaned up our mess on the counter and floor, my mind drifted back to *Disaster Academy* Issue #11. Those last few pages where Reverb is asking Charm's mom for help.

It was right there. An answer to a mystery I've been trying to solve for weeks.

I need Mom's help.

"Well? How is it?"

Quickly, I dip a wooden spoon into the sauce to taste it. I wince as the heat singes my tongue. "Perfect," I say over my shoulder to Abuelito. It's not as good as when he makes it, but it's a suitable replacement for today.

He nods. "Bueno."

I ignore Abuelito's disapproving grunts when I add store-bought tortillas rather than homemade ones to the sauce. Time is a factor. At least I cooked a fried egg, Mom's favorite part.

Her latest product freebie—The Enchanted Blade VII,

a state-of-the-art blender—is a behemoth that obliterates fruits and vegetables and probably small woodland
creatures. All her favorite ingredients are shoved into the
plastic blending pitcher: kale, mango, mixed berries, pea-
nut butter, and whey protein, along with soy milk and ice.

"You have one mission," I whisper to the appliance.
"*Work.*"

I press the start button. Surprisingly, it whirls to life,
chopping and crunching, then humming happily.

"Chiquito, did you turn off the stove?"

Shit. I hurriedly shift the pan to one of the unused burn-
ers before the sauce is ruined.

"Morning, Isaac," Mom says loudly as she marches into
the kitchen, pausing at the table to peck a kiss to Abuelito's temple. "Morning, Abuelito."

"Buenos días, Lilah."

Mom surveys the counter. It's not as disastrous as when
we cooked for Davi—well, for me and Diego—but it's a
mess I'll undoubtedly be cleaning up alone in an hour.

"Chilaquiles rojos." I offer her a loaded plate, then a
glass full of puke-green contents. "And a smoothie. Enjoy!"

Mom narrows her eyes at the drink. "You're way too
cheerful. Have you been sneaking Abuelito's coffee?"

"Ha." Abuelito raises his mug, saluting us.

"Nope!" I paste on a synthetic grin.

Credit to her—Mom doesn't vomit all over the floor

while drinking the smoothie. But her right eye twitches a little when she lowers her glass. "This is a trap."

"What? No." I shake my head.

"It's a trap," Abuelito says from the table.

Traitor. Sold out by my own kin. But I'm not surprised. Carlos proved the loyalty runs thin in the Martin bloodline years ago.

Mom bites into the chilaquiles. She doesn't gag, another tiny win. "Spill it, Isaac," she says while pointing her fork at me.

"It's about Legends Con," I say. She chews and waits. I practiced this next part multiple times in front of my bathroom mirror last night. But that doesn't steady my heartbeat. "It's about Diego. Actually, it's about a lot of things, but mostly him."

Mom has a green mustache from her smoothie, which almost makes me laugh. If Bella was around, she wouldn't hold back. I wish she was here. She's always been a nice buffer when I've had to tell Mom something serious.

Eventually, it all falls out of my mouth in a stream of nonsense. No punctuation, no breaks. Only quick breaths and more words. I explain to her how I fucked up trying to buy our Legends Con passes. How I let myself and Diego down. I rant about the Six, then Pride, then the Six *and* Pride.

I don't mention how terrified I've been to step onto

UGA's campus without Diego, but I whisper how much I already miss him. Because I do. Everything's changing in hyperdrive.

Then I ramble about *Disaster Academy* and why meeting Peter and Jorge was so important in the first place. "I never see relationships like that, Mom." I blink at her, then at Abuelito. "I haven't seen it anywhere else. Not for kids like me."

When I'm done, the dam holding back my tears is nearly cracked in half.

Mom's fingers brush over my hair. Her thumb strokes my temple.

"Is that how you really feel, Isaac?"

"Kind of," I say to my feet, shrugging. She continues to brush my hair. Once I know I won't cry, I lift my chin. "All I want is to make sure I fix this for Diego."

Mom studies me for a long moment. Her mouth moves like she might comment on my failures concerning Diego or my uneasiness with new people like the Six, but she smiles instead.

"I need your help, Mom."

She's nearly finished with her food and smoothie as I show her my phone. I already have Elena Sánchez's social media accounts up, pointing out the similarities between her followers and Mom's clients, begging her to find a way to link up Diego and Elena while Elena's in town for

Legends Con. Mom doesn't speak as I once again rattle on. She chews and raises an eyebrow and twists her mouth sideways.

After I finish, she clears her throat. "I'll try," she says, "but I can't make any promises."

I sag against the counter. Across the kitchen, Abuelito beams at me. Mom will try. It's not a solid answer, but it's good enough.

"Any other confessions you want to drop on me before my trip?" she asks, arms crossed.

"No," I say, half grinning. Her flight's scheduled to leave in less than four hours, which means she should've already been at the airport. It's a well-known rule you must arrive two weeks in advance to navigate Hartsfield-Jackson's notoriously disorganized TSA lines.

"Good," she says, carefully wiping her mouth in an attempt not to smear her lipstick.

That's when it hits me. Mom's not dressed in her usual travel outfit—running shoes, yoga pants, and a ratty UGA sweatshirt. She's wearing a rose-gold V-neck blouse and pinstripe slacks. Her hair's not hidden beneath a scarf. Instead, it's down, twisted into a braid that looks like it took more than thirty seconds to create. Under the aroma of chilaquiles and green upchuck smoothie is the scent of cherry blossoms. Mom's signature perfume.

I size her up. "What's happening here?"

"What do you mean?" she asks sweetly.

"This." I wave a hand wildly at her. "I thought you were going on a business trip."

"I am."

"Deception. Fabrication. Bullsh—"

"Isaac Jaime—"

Her phone rings on the counter. Beyoncé's "Love on Top." A tender grin smooths over her lips as she reaches for the phone. She hides the caller ID before I can see the name, then silences the song. But her hand stays there, like maybe she regrets not answering.

"Mom." I draw out every single letter until she looks at me. "Are you . . ."

The rest of my question waits in my throat. I briefly glance at Abuelito. I think I'm afraid to ask this in front of him, as if he's clinging to this secret hope that Mom and Carlos will somehow find each other again.

Frankly, I'm afraid of how the answer will affect me.

Mom smiles at Abuelito, then me. Again, she brushes fingers through my curls. "I'm the adult here," she says, like always. "I'm taking care of myself."

"But—"

She shakes her head. "Just because you haven't seen it yet, doesn't mean those kinds of happy endings *can't* happen for us. For you."

I remain still. Her words from the other week, when

we fought about Carlos in my bedroom, echo in my ears: *It's better now.*

Is Mom done carrying the weight of Carlos's betrayal around? Maybe we get second—or third, fourth, tenth—chances with love. Our hearts break, but breaks heal over time. Still, the possibility of my mom dating again scares me. I want to keep her in this strong, bulletproof glass case where no one can disappoint her again.

Clearly, she's not giving me that opportunity.

"It's summer!" Abuelito announces with his own mischievous smirk.

All three of us crack up.

"Okay. Enough about . . . this." Mom has her all-business face on. "Are you set for Pride? Everything is—you're fine?"

I watch her. Her feet shuffle, heels scratching the kitchen floor. She's nervous about me like I am about her.

"Mom," I say, smiling. "I'll be fine."

"You're sure?"

I grab one of her hands, squeezing. "Yes. Diego will be with me. It's all good."

"Good." She inhales deeply. "I just—I want you to know I'm proud of you."

She looks like she might cry. I hope she doesn't. To be honest, I hope I don't.

"I know that's corny," she says, her voice thick. "I

know Jennifer Garner killed it with her monologue in that one movie. You know, the one with the gay son who was being blackmailed."

I fight off a laugh. "Yeah, Mom. I know."

"I'm not one of those cool moms who buys their kids booze, pretending to be their best friend or whatever."

"That's perfect. It's all you need to say."

"Okay."

"But about that booze thing—"

"Not on your life, Isaac."

We grin at each other. Mom doesn't cry, but she squeezes my hand back like Morse code.

I love you too.

Abuelito shuffles up to me, dropping an arm around my shoulders. He kisses the top of my hair. "Chiquito, remember—when you find a nice boy, ask him one question," he says. "What are your thoughts on *The Princess Bride?*"

"Abuelito!"

"What? It's nonnegotiable. ¡No hay excusa!"

Abuelito and his unwavering fondness for nostalgia. His belief that we all fall in love the right person at the right time, just like he did with Abuela.

Mom pulls away. "I'll be home Sunday afternoon." She grabs her keys, phone, the messenger bag with her laptop in it. "Check in with me when you get down to the park tomorrow. And let Abuelito know when you're leaving."

"Yes, Mom."

"Don't forget that Bella and Chris will be here Sunday night."

Endorphins flood my system. Bella, home again. Finally.

"We're having dinner with Iggy—" Mom points at me the second I suck air through my teeth "—on Tuesday. All of us. Abuelito too."

"Fine."

I'm more worried about how Bella's going to be around Iggy than I am. At least Mom didn't add Carlos to the equation.

"Don't forget Monday, Chiquito," Abuelito adds.

Monday is our rescheduled *The Princess Bride* viewing. My stomach growls. Mexican corn salad and inside jokes and Abuelito.

I lean my head on his shoulder. "As you wish."

Twenty-Four

Charm, I hope you know you can always be who you are with us. You're different. You can do things no one in this world can. You're a Disaster. And you'll always be one of us.

—Halo Boy, *Disaster Academy* Issue #3

This is a dream. One bursting with so many vibrant colors and fluttering flags and smiling faces, I hardly know where to look. At just after 10:00 a.m., Piedmont Park is already filling up. The park, northeast of the city, is the heart of Atlanta. An emerald landscape where metropolitan life meets nature.

Where the queer youth of Georgia gather to—*finally*—be who we are, inside and out.

"Wow." Blake stands next to me at one of the entrances off the main road. His eyes are huge with excitement. "This is . . . epic."

We arrived early so there'd be time to walk around before the parade at noon. It was the first thing on me and Diego's itinerary before this became a group project. On this side of the park, a giant lawn is cluttered with people sitting on blankets, dancing teens, and small tents where volunteers are handing out Pride paraphernalia—buttons, stickers, flyers for the Trevor Project and the Human Rights Campaign. One end of the grass is occupied by an enormous stage. A DJ plays music between sporadic performances from local artists.

Lady Gaga blasts from the speakers. Her voice reaches for miles, like a call to prayer.

A symbolic vigil the entire city of Atlanta needs to be a part of.

Three kids that look younger than Blake strut past us with glitter-painted faces and the kind of confidence I've only seen on TV. This involuntary grin pulls at my mouth. I'm wearing the rainbow-striped hoodie with a *Disaster Academy* T-shirt underneath. Already, I'm realizing this might've been a huge mistake with the cloudless sky unleashing all the sun's heat on us. But I have yet to acquire the conviction Davi possesses to go shirtless. Plus, I didn't want to make him feel bad if I didn't have it on when we see each other.

This morning on FaceTime, Mom asked if I was going to mention anything to Davi about what happened the other night.

I'm considering it, but . . . I'm not like her. Or Iggy or Bella. This is my first time doing any of this. I need to take things one step at a time. It's too early for drama.

Besides, today's all about enjoying Pride.

Diego elbows me. "Dude, this is a lot." A baggy white

tank top hangs off his slim frame. BORICUA AF is repeated vertically down the front, the letters outlined in pink, lavender, and blue. The sun is already bronzing his exposed light brown skin. He smiles goofily at me. "Think you're gonna be able to hang with this crowd?"

I peek at my shoes. Mom special ordered a pair of authentic Pride Converses for me. "Yup. These are my people."

"Our people," Zelda insists.

They pirouette in front of the group. Today's iconic outfit is inspired by "Her Majesty Whitney Houston, circa 'I Wanna Dance with Somebody' era," according to Zelda. Golden curls bigger and fuller than a lion's mane are held back by a silver headband. Pink and blue eyeshadow, bold scarlet lips, cheeks dusted purple—everything enhances the richness of their dark brown skin. They wear a long lilac tank top over gray tights. Airbrushed on the front of the shirt is I WANNA PRIDE WITH SOMEBODY . . . On the back: . . . WHO LOVES ME!

Zelda is so secure about their body. Their curves, their arms, the way clothes fit on them. No fucks given.

I'd kill for five percent of that coolness.

"Come on." F.B. hooks arms with Zelda. "Lots to see, kiddos."

We follow a gravel road that borders the lawn. The air is spiked with electricity. It buzzes in my system.

Around us, everyone moves with the same energy. *Freedom.* Young drag queens still learning the feel of their heels against the sidewalk, teens holding hands, a boy around Ollie's age waving a rainbow flag with glassy eyes.

I clinch my fists. I hold onto this moment.

Home, home, home.

We climb a small hill into the shade of trees. The park's set up street-fair style: Rows of booths selling food and alcohol-free beverages and merchandise. Most of Piedmont's 185 acres are covered in tents stretching in every direction. Signs advertise youth groups and harm-prevention centers. In the middle of the main road's vendors is a photo booth where you can pose against a green screen while someone gives you information on LGBTQ-centered social media apps.

Diego tugs me inside.

I pick a cheesy rainbow backdrop. We pose back-to-back, arms crossed over our chests, mugging at the camera for the first one. In the second, he hops onto my back. We nearly fall over before the flash. The next is us holding up peace signs like Davi and Ezra in that photo I still have saved in my phone.

I can't believe we're finally here. Me and my best friend. Our *first* Pride. And we're okay. The distance between us has finally closed.

In the final shot, Diego throws his arm around my shoulders. I'm grinning at the lens when he leans up and kisses my cheek. A wet and messy one. He disappears to examine the photo strip the girl working the booth hands him. He holds it gently as if he might ruin it, then carefully tucks it into his drawstring backpack.

Something about Diego being that cautious with a silly strip of photos tugs at my stomach.

My phone buzzes in my back pocket. I don't reach for it. Diego glances over his shoulder at me with scrunched eyes, cheeks red. My own cheek is still damp from his lips.

"Should we keep exploring?" he says.

My brain finally resets. I check my phone.

Three excited, all caps texts from Davi await me. I scan through them:

> From: Davi
> HOLY SHIT THIS IS AWESOME!!!
> 10:59 AM

> From: Davi
> 🖼️🖼️🖼️
> EVERYWHERE! SO. MANY. PEOPLE. BUT NOT YOU!
> ISAAAC!
> 11:00 AM

> From: Davi
> WERE ARE YOU???
> 11:01 AM

A smile bubbles over my lips. Another text comes in

with a photo from Google Maps. It's a nearby destination.

F.B. drags Zelda away from a queer comic artist's tent back to us. Blake returns with bottles of water for everyone. Alix leans against a nearby tree, people watching.

Diego says, "Isaac, where to?"

"Um, yeah," I stammer. "Let's go this way."

The winding walkway leads us to a building that stretches for nearly a mile. Once-white bricks are gray with age. Stepping into the Piedmont Park Aquatics Center is like strolling into a candy store while an army of primary schoolers is there on a class field trip. Kids leap off the pool's edge, cannonballing into the water. Lifeguards yawn from their ivory towers, shaded by blue umbrellas. Lounge chairs are occupied by teens pretending they don't want to get wet.

Over the chaotic noise, a voice sings to me.

"Isaac! Yo, Isaac!"

My stomach knots when Davi rushes toward me, violating the pool's policy about no speeds greater than one mile per hour. He's in his pre-approved Pride outfit. The top three buttons of his pink, floral-print shirt are undone. Bisexual socks, pulled to mid-shin, match his shoes—a pair of suede Pumas, mostly black with a cool pink-paint-splatter design.

I beam at him until I notice Davi's wearing that damn fedora.

You can't win every Pride outfit challenge.

"You made it," he says.

"Duh. I mean, of course."

In classic Crush Syndrome form, I fail to sound like this isn't that serious.

Davi is two steps from me. No, one step. He's right in front of me, easing a hand behind the back of my head.

He kisses me.

Right here. In the middle of Piedmont Park Aquatics Center, in front of three dozen shouting children and too-cool-for-summer teens, Davi Lucas kisses me.

My brain short-circuits. I gasp against his parted lips. He tastes like cinnamon gum and cherry Gatorade. A weird combination, indeed.

Why am I thinking about what his mouth tastes like?

Why, for two point five seconds, am I weighing his kiss against the one I had with Diego?

I hate that my first kiss with Davi will always have an asterisk next to it. A footnote about what happened between Diego and me in Twisted Burger's parking lot will be underneath it. Deep down, I know all kisses hereafter will be compared to Diego's, not Davi's. No matter what, this thing will exist between us. Case in point: Davi's kiss is firm and precise, not clumsy and understated.

As I'm thinking all this, I wonder, *Why am I not kissing Davi back?*

Autopilot finally kicks in, but Davi's lips are gone. He

grins awkwardly at me, his cheeks a pale pink as he rubs the back of my neck. I tense self-consciously when a few boys nearby catcall.

"Whoa," whispers Zelda.

Davi mouths the same word, exhaling. "Sorry. I mean—uh . . ."

Happiness vibrates intensely in my chest. I've left Davi speechless.

"I'm happy to see you," he finally says.

I nod robotically. "Me too. Like, really happy."

Davi tips back the brim of his fedora. "You're *all* here." He up-nods at the Six. For a long moment, he holds someone's gaze over my shoulder. His jaw clenches, then releases. I don't have to turn around to know it's Diego. I'm not ready to see his expression.

"Are you going to the parade?" Davi asks me.

Unlike the morning Pride parade that happens in October, the Atlanta Teen Pride parade is an afternoon activity. Somewhere, in a thermo-cooled conference room, the city's adults decided the queer teens could endure the extreme heat conditions of a march around the city in late June. We've survived the thoughtless, homophobic, racist, privileged decisions of the highest governmental representatives, so I suppose their assessment is accurate.

"Of course!" F.B. replies.

"Cool," Davi says. "It's gonna be wicked."

"Davi! We're rolling out."

Behind Davi, a small group of guys, either shirtless or shirtless adjacent, stand in board shorts and sunglasses. I don't recognize any of them. No Jax or Ezra or Amin. But they're all social media hot. "OTW," Davi calls back, then his eyes find mine. "We'll meet up later, okay?"

"Cool."

"We'll walk around and stuff."

My brain translates his "and stuff" to: *and hold hands and make out.*

Maybe that's more my hormones than my brain.

His hand inches forward like he might grab mine. But he pauses midway, shakes his head, then jogs toward the Insta Crew.

I swallow down the disappointment like a pill.

"Well, watching that was . . ." Alix trails off, twisting hair around her index finger.

"Unexpected?" Blake suggests.

"I was thinking more like nauseating."

After a breath, I finally pivot to stare at Diego. His expression is blank. His mouth is flat, but his jaw keeps moving under his skin like he's biting his cheek.

Neither one of us says a word.

From Peachtree Street to 10th Street, all the way back to Piedmont Park, the teen parade ignites the city. People and floats and cars move down the sun-soaked streets. In a cacophony of music and unified voices and contagious energy. Two whole hours of young, queer glory.

We watch from behind wobbly metal barriers on 10th Street. Mascots from all the Atlanta professional sports teams march in rainbow jerseys and kits. QSA clubs walk with handmade banners and shirts. Local businesses carry their logos embossed in the Pride colors with pageant-waves and practiced grins. It's obvious they're meeting their Support Your Local Gays quota for the year, but I don't give a shit. They're here, filling out the infinite line crowding the street.

On my left, Diego's mostly silent until a troupe of hip-hop performers glides by. One carries an old-school boombox on their shoulder pumping out Lizzo. A dancer with rainbow dreadlocks points at Diego, encouraging him to join. He laughs, then—gracelessly—dances for her.

"Where's your rhythm?" she shouts, giggling.

"I left it at home!"

That makes her laugh harder.

To the rear of the parade, a convertible slowly eases along. Sitting on the trunk, wrapped in a skintight, glittery outfit, is a teen drag queen with hair as high as the Westin Peachtree Plaza, the fifth tallest building in all of Georgia. Havana Niceday would be proud. The car blasts Whitney Houston's "So Emotional."

Zelda nearly knocks down two barriers to get to the other side.

The drag queen stumbles while climbing down from the car to join Zelda in the middle of 10th Street. Hands clasped, they scream every lyric at the sky. It's as if they're shouting at every person that has denied them their right to be fierce, fearless, and fantastic. When the song ends, a volunteer in a fluorescent yellow vest gently asks them to get out of the street.

Zelda Elmore has halted the entire Pride parade.

The crowd roars as Zelda squeezes back behind the barrier. But not before the drag queen blesses them with a purple lipstick-print mark on their cheek.

"It's a good omen," I whisper to Zelda, resting an arm on their shoulders.

Today is everything I imagined. The parade. Pride. Knowing that, somewhere in this sea of people, Davi is probably experiencing the same thing we are.

Diego's hand brushes mine. Our pinkies interlock, holding on.

At fourteen, I don't think we were ready to admit how big it was to come out. We were two boys saying the words casually. Terrified of how the other would react. Friendships don't come with guarantees, even the closest ones. I know how lucky I am that neither one of us made it this epic, life-altering moment. Still, I wanted more back then. Maybe Diego did too.

This is the moment we didn't give each other then.

It's years and years of waiting to feel . . . normal. Thing is, normal isn't what the everyone tells us it is. It's what we make it. Normal is finding the place where you belong.

Sometimes you find it early. Sometimes it happens late.

In the middle of the afternoon, in the unforgiving summer heat, I know this: finding your normal is the best feeling ever.

As the parade fades, we follow the crowd back into the park. I clumsily bump into Alix. A miracle happens. She doesn't curse my bloodline. Eyes squeezed shut, Alix's bottom lip quivers before she frees a genuine, visually blinding smile.

Thank you, Whitney Houston.

Twenty-Five

I don't have any real friends back home. Not anymore. Not after they found out what I am.

—Charm, *Disaster Academy* Issue #2

The sun coasts from its pink-skied kingdom, moving toward the horizon as we walk the park's huge landscape for the third time. We cross the bridge over Lake Clara Meer. Through a maze of people watching the parade's dance team perform on the promenade. Away from the massive lawn where an a cappella group belts their way through an Ariana Grande medley. Past the aquatic center where the screams and splashing have died down to a whisper of moving water.

Rinse and repeat.

As I lead the way, I never confess I'm searching for Davi. He hasn't responded to my texts. I'm sure he's still somewhere nearby, thinking of me. The hoodie he bought me is tied around my waist now. I think about the ways his fingers skimmed the sleeves earlier.

Hours later, my lips are still humming from his kiss.

"Okay. Stop," Alix finally complains. She leans over to rub her ankles. It's clear the sandals she chose to wear today aren't meant for marathon laps around a park. "Phys ed doesn't start until August. My body is opposed to all this exercise."

"Shouldn't we head home?" Blake suggests. "I'm starved."

"True that," F.B. agrees, even though he's working his way through his second bag of cotton candy. He lifts one arm, sniffing. "A shower would be good too."

"Isaac," Diego says gently, stepping closer. "We're beat, dude. I have to get up early tomorrow morning."

"For what?" I ask, my voice harsher than I intend.

Diego runs a hand over his hair. It's sticking to his forehead, curls falling just over his eyebrows the way Davi's do.

"It's not like we're going to Legends Con," I say, shrugging. "What's so important about tomorrow that you—"

Diego cuts me off. "None of your damn business."

I flinch. The words hit like a punch to the ribs. Diego's face reddens, and my hands shake at my sides.

"Why would it be?" I clear the trembling from my throat. "Why would you share that kind of info with me?"

"Why are you being an ass?"

"Why are you rushing me out of here?"

"Listen. Today was fun, but—"

"Today's not over." I hold my phone inches from Diego's face, the screen lit to display the time. "This is our first Pride together. Our last summer before . . ."

I don't squeak out those final words, but Diego's left eye twitches as if I spat the reminder at him.

People around us stop and stare. Alix nervously rubs her arm. F.B. stuffs a handful of cotton candy in his mouth. Diego gives me a lower-your-voice look that I almost obey until a guy with a two-toned Afro says, "Honey, it's not Pride without drama!"

Diego inhales so deeply, his chest doubles in size. "This is about *him*." He doesn't elaborate. He doesn't need to.

"You don't get it," I whisper.

How could he? Diego has Mel. He's spent his entire life avoiding relationships while I've been desperate to find one for myself, and now I have a chance.

"No, please, educate me, Isaac," he says. "Tell me all your theories about finding love at Pride with some guy you barely know. Who ignored your existence in school. He's the very reason we're *not* going to Legends Con."

A growl slips from between Diego's clenched teeth.

"Tell me why our summer is all about you chasing some dude—"

"He's not some dude, *Luis*."

The fire inside me can't be contained. It climbs and climbs, singeing the inside of my mouth. It eviscerates every molecule of understanding left between Diego and me.

"Oh?" Diego *pfft*s. "Is he your precious Dread Pirate Roberts now?"

"Don't be a dick."

"Me? *I'm* the dick?"

"I never wanted this." I shake my head, my jaw tense.

It's like I've been biting down on things for so long that now they're fighting back. "Pride—this whole summer—was supposed to be about me and you. Not hanging out with people I barely know." As soon as the words leave my lips, I feel the others' cold, unforgiving stares on me.

Anger is bitter to swallow on its own; it doesn't need to be chased by the sharpness of betrayal too.

"I thought these were our friends," says Diego.

Our friends, the ones he knew, other than F.B., from gaming. The ones who know his secrets when I don't. Friends he'll probably hang around when I'm sixty-one miles away in Athens. I'll be replaced. Actually, maybe that already happened.

"I did this to make you happy," I blurt, still not looking at the others. "But I didn't think it would substitute all the time we were supposed to spend together. You've been MIA for *weeks*."

"Like you haven't?" He snorts. His arms cross, then unfold, dropping to his sides. Something flashes in his eyes before he spits out, "You've been so distracted by Davi—who, BTW, doesn't seem like he wants to hang with you."

I step back, eyes wide. My heart thumps against my ribs, trying to escape its fragile cage. Somewhere, buried in a dark pit inside me, I knew Diego felt that way—that Davi wouldn't want to waste his time with me. That it wouldn't work out.

I wonder how long he's been chewing on those words.

Since the night Davi ghosted our dinner date?

Before then?

"If you'd let that—let *him* go, we'd have more time together." His tone is hard, unbending. "We'd be going to Legends Con tomorrow."

There it is. Just like I thought: Diego is mad about the time I've spend with Davi. All the small moments I could've been with him. I'm a terrible friend because he thinks I chose a boy over our friendship. Part of that is true. But it's not fair for him to unload this on me now. To not say anything before today.

"I fucked up, okay? I own that." My voice cracks, but whatever. If he's cool with flinging the things he's been holding in at me, then I can too. The inferno in my chest is fully raging. Swiftly, it's decimating fourteen years of friendship and geekery. "Is it going to matter in a few months when I'm at UGA, alone?"

His face cringes the way it does when you're unexpectedly hit in the cheek with a snowball. He's flushed, speechless. But I'm not done.

"Maybe that's how I should've spent today—by myself," I add tensely.

He squints at me, head tilted like he can't believe what I'm saying.

There's a piercing ringing in my ears. But I can't stop myself. "Might as well get used to it, right?" I hiss, my chest heaving.

Dust. Slow-cooling ash. Whatever barrier between Diego and me, the one we never acknowledged but both knew was there, is a crumpled heap of the words I allowed to live inside me since March.

"You really believe that?" he asks.

Through the thin tunnel of my throat, I say, "Yeah, I do."

I'm exhausted. Every muscle and bone and cell inside me has carried those thoughts for weeks and now I'm empty. I don't have enough energy to brace myself for the inescapable crack in Diego's exterior when he stares at me. It happens in slow motion. He hiccups, a glassy shield forming over his eyes. Then he shakes his head before walking away.

He's gone.

All that's left behind is the ruins of something I've loved so long, I didn't know it could cease to exist.

I've finally unlocked my true superpower: destruction.

"Not cool, Cap," F.B. murmurs. "Not cool at all." He jogs off in the direction Diego's escaped to.

Blake tugs on Zelda's hand. His eyes never meet mine. "Let's go. He's our ride home."

Zelda's mouth opens, then closes. Their face falls before they follow Blake.

I deserve that.

What I don't deserve is Alix's silence. This moment, like any other day, is one built for her sarcasm. For her ruthless, cutting, debilitating words. But she doesn't provide them. She sighs, drags a hand down her face, then punches my shoulder, hard. "That's not what Charm would've done."

Alix leaves me in the crater I created. The aftermath of my frustrations. Crowds shift around me, bumping my side, laughing and talking.

All these people and, just like I requested, I'm completely alone.

When it's dark enough, the Pride organizers erect a colossal screen on the main lawn. Teens spread out on blankets and towels over the grass. Volunteers pass out boxes of popcorn and bottled water. Projected on the screen is a movie about two boys who meet-cute at a post office in New York City when one of the boys is trying to ship off a box of his ex-boyfriend's things. It's hilarious and adorable and exactly the kind of movie I don't need.

Lost near the edge of the lawn, I continuously check my phone. Nothing from Davi. No signs of life in the Six's group chat.

Radio silence everywhere.

I press the heel of my hand against my left eye to stall any tears from escaping. In the middle of Piedmont Park, among a hundred queer teens, no crying is allowed unless it is movie related.

Ten feet in front of me, the crowd laughs at something on-screen. But I only hear one cackle behind me. One so loud and genuine and memorable that my heart speeds up. I follow that noise. Away from all the people watching the movie, I find Davi near an abandoned tent, its nylon flaps shivering from a breeze. He's doubled over, cracking up. His eyelashes are wet, cheeks a bright crimson.

One of the sunglasses-and-board-shorts boys from earlier is with him, smiling. His hand squeezes Davi's shoulder until Davi straightens up. He says something I can't hear. The boy nods.

Then Davi kisses him.

Not a friendly kiss. Not the cautious way he kissed me earlier. A real, cinematic kiss with tongues.

I can't take my eyes off them. As much I try to force myself to breathe and blink and *move*, I don't. All that happens is my mouth opening to say, "Oh, shit."

Davi shrinks away from the boy. Not by much. There's a minimal amount of space between their chests and, well, other regions. But it's enough for Davi's wide eyes to locate me.

"Isaac?"

I run.

I stumble up a hill, into a thicket of trees. Branches reach out, snagging the hoodie's material. One swats my cheek. The sting is nothing compared to the burn in my lungs from running. I slip on a rock, barely managing to steady myself before I eat dirt.

A breathless "Isaac" comes from behind before Davi's fingers catch my elbow. I jerk from the loose grip.

"I'm fine."

Looking at him is excruciating. That crease in his brow, the gentleness of his eyes, the tug of his lower lip. His exhales are almost as heavy as mine. Tentatively, he raises his hand to my face. I don't recoil. I allow his palm to cup my cheek.

"Hey," he says, not quite smiling. "Why did you—are you okay?"

The struggle to swallow hurts. A prickling burn spreads through my other cheek from the impact of the branch. "I'm . . ." I sniffle, tipping my head back until I know the tears won't break through. The taste of my sinuses draining into my throat is nauseating. "I'm—You can just . . ."

Go.

I can almost say it.

"Isaac," he says in that way that I hate. Pity. "I'm sorry."

"There's nothing to be sorry about."

"He just—we've been hanging out all day. He's cool. And—"

"It's not that serious." I choke on every word, retreating from his grip.

"Then why are you so upset?"

I drag the back of my wrist across my nose. Then, without thinking, I spit, "Why'd you kiss me? Why'd you kiss me in front of my—"

Friends. Were they my friends? It doesn't matter. Now they're those people who despise my very existence.

"I don't know." His eyes close for a moment. I can't read Davi like I can Diego. I don't know what this wrinkled expression means. "I like you. You're so damn cool."

I snort. "Yup, that's me. Isaac, too cool to be anything other than a friend. King of the friend zone. Sole ruler of Friendlandia."

"It's not like that."

"What's it like, then?"

Davi sighs, shoulders collapsing. "I just came out a few months ago. I've never had anything but one serious girlfriend. No dates, no hookups." He kicks at a rock until it's unearthed from the soil surrounding it. "I've spent so much time trying to be this perfect, one-dimensional person. I hid who I am to make everyone else comfortable. All my life, I haven't known the real Davi."

As much as I don't want to, I nod slowly.

Sometimes, it's so dark in the closet, it's as if you've never seen what you truly look like. The person you truly are.

"I kissed you because"—he pauses, shuffling his feet—"because you made me feel like I see myself."

"And the other guy?"

"I still want to explore. I want to know myself without—"

"Attachments?"

"Without the fear of messing up." He steps closer. "Being out of the closet is like learning to play hockey all over again. I want permission to mess up and learn and, eventually, get it right. I don't want to be the MVP the first time I step on the ice."

"So . . . was I a mistake?"

Crack. Sizzle, whistle, then bang. *Crack-crack-bang.*

Before Davi can answer, fireworks light the night sky. Greens and reds and oranges, explosion after explosion above Piedmont Park. A chorus of cheers erupts from the lawn. Davi closes the miniscule gap between us, tucks his hand in mine. This is everything I wanted for today: fireworks and applause and Davi holding my hand.

Yet it feels so wrong.

I wanted Diego too. By my side. Joking and smiling and being who we really are outside the four walls of our bedrooms.

"You're my friend." Davi must notice my grimace, because he squeezes my hand tighter. "You're the coolest fucking guy I know. You make me feel comfortable. Kissing you was, I don't know, my way of saying thank you."

"You could, you know, *say it* next time."

He chuckles. "Noted."

We stand there, under a series of glittery manmade stars, in silence. He watches the fireworks; I watch him. Once again, I witness my reality collapse into a black hole.

Thing is, I did the same thing when Carlos and Mom's marriage disintegrated. I saw her stumble and fall and, over time, get back on her feet. I never knew how she felt on the inside. I didn't know what it was like to finally open yourself up to someone only to have them shred your heart into confetti.

I didn't know this would feel like the sky falling on me. Like the ground beneath me is on fire.

Like the world is ending.

Eventually, our hands separate. Davi backs away. "Are you . . ." He gazes over his shoulder. "Are you going to be okay?"

"Yeah." I smile sadly. "I'm gonna be good. You can go back to your friends."

"What about—"

"I'll find mine," I lie.

But I won't. There's no Diego to run to this time. No soft, familiar bed to crawl into and forget everything by losing myself in comics and the sound of *Beyond the Valley of Stars* in the background. For so long, I didn't feel like a true Martin. I've always been more like Mom than Carlos. But he's in my DNA. There are pieces of me that are his, including the part that's good at hurting the ones that I love most to be around people who make me feel good in the moment.

I sit on a bench near Legacy Fountain Splash Pad, a splash zone for children—or overheated adults—to play in. But the only ones around at this hour are two girls giggling and kissing on the bench opposite mine. The water's colorful, dramatic display is left completely ignored.

It's 10:00 p.m. and I'm stuck downtown. Diego was my ride here. I consider getting an Uber home, but I'm not sure I want to be alone anymore. Not fully. If I call Mom, she'll panic, maybe catch an earlier flight home. The late hour instantly removes Abuelito from the equation. Bella can only comfort me over FaceTime, then plot to cyberbully Davi for the rest of his life.

I blink and blink until my vision blurs. A fresh knot tangles my stomach. I lean over just in case all the fluids inside me decide to evacuate their current residence via my mouth.

My thumb swipes through all the contacts in my phone before pausing to hover over one unexpected option.

Will he even answer?

I press the call button. He picks up on the second ring. With a planet-sized lump in my throat and tears finally kissing my cheeks, I stutter, "He-hello? Uh. I need you."

"Where are you?" Iggy asks urgently. Before I can answer his question, he says, "I'm on my way."

Twenty-Six

Peter Heinberg @peterthewriter · Jun 21

Good morning #LegendsCon! @jorgepradosofficial and I can't wait to meet everyone + answer DA questions! (No spoilers plz) Today's a good day to be a disaster and a hero. In the words of CHARM: "Let's make history together!!!"

Iggy's sofa is the worst.

It's one of those IKEA construction nightmares. A modern sectional design with granite polyester fabric to match Iggy's—or his girlfriend's—trendy color palette: ultra bland. As with all IKEA products, the sofa's cool to look at, super uncomfortable to sit on. Or, in my case, sleep on. It's supposed to be a foldout, but deciphering its complex functionality last night after Iggy picked me up from outside Piedmont Park wasn't happening. I barely remembered to tug my sneakers off and keep my shorts on before I collapsed on it.

Sleeping mostly nude on my brother's scratchy sofa, in the open space of his apartment, wasn't on the agenda, especially since the pleated blinds covering the balcony's glass French doors were still up.

Downtown Atlanta isn't ready for that much Isaac Martin.

Sunrise peeks in through the doors, sharp orange light striking my closed eyes. I groan, rolling onto my stomach. But the sofa's mound of decorative pillows can't hide me from the sock-covered foot kicking my hip.

"Get up."

"Go away, Death. No one invited you here," I croak, my throat dry and useless. I feel wrung out. Is this what it feels like to be hungover? Weak and dehydrated and off-center?

I don't remember how long I cried in the passenger seat of Iggy's car last night. But, in a rare moment of restraint, Iggy allowed me to sob it out. Legends Con. The failed Davi Boyfriend Project. The demise of Diego and me.

My ideal summer finally dissolved in a flood of tears.

"¡Despiértate! ¡Levántate!"

It's a combination of words Iggy's shouted at me a hundred times before when I was about to be late for school. He snatches the pillow from my face, whacks it across my spine.

I rotate onto my back, rubbing at my sticky-crusty eyes. The aftermath of unwiped tears is quite possibly the grossest optical-related thing. Once I'm done, I check my phone. There's seventeen percent battery left.

Last night, after Iggy gave me a blanket and cut off the lights, I scrolled through all my texts from Davi. I don't know what time it was when I finished. After midnight?

I pushed through a fresh set of tears to analyze every misspelled word, overexcited punctuation, all the emojis. It was all right there: *our friendship.*

Other than that one "Xx" nothing else read like our relationship was anything other than sociable. Even the shirtless photo—which I deleted—wasn't a sign of a future romance. It wasn't as if it was him, alone in his bedroom. It wasn't a dick pic. He was with Ezra, climbing a mountain in the unforgiving summer heat.

He was simply sharing a piece of his world with me.

Anyway, my nearly dead phone is on power save mode. Giant white numbers greet me when I blink at the screen. "What the hell, Iggy," I whine. "It's not even seven o'clock."

He claps loudly. "We're going out for breakfast."

"Why are we going out?" My voice cracks from sleep deprivation. "Because you can't cook?"

"Shut up." He cups a hand around one of my ankles and pulls. "We're leaving in twenty minutes."

I struggle uselessly against Iggy's firm grip before sitting up. I sneeze twice. It always takes my sinuses a moment to get used to new places. I can't remember the last time I was in Iggy's apartment. Everything is so contemporary and mediocre. Not an ounce of personality anywhere.

"Did, uh . . ." I realize I don't know Iggy's girlfriend's name. Not this one, at least.

"Shamari," he says, frowning.

"Did Shamari help decorate?"

He shrugs. "This is mostly me."

I raise my eyebrows. Not impressed, more confused. When we were younger, Iggy was a lot like me when it came to the colors in our bedrooms—anything loud and eye-catching. Shades that remind you of vintage comic books, all the reds and yellows of *Zap!* and *Pow!*

His apartment has a millennial Bruce Wayne vibe.

"There's an extra toothbrush on the sink in the bathroom," he says. "Towels on the rack. Don't use too much of my body wash. Stay away from the cologne."

Discreetly, I lift my arm, sniffing. A shower is imperative. It's a shame I'm still in yesterday's shorts and boxers. The hoodie Davi bought me is a wrinkled ball on the floor next to my shirt. I don't think I'll ever wear it again.

"Hey, uh."

Iggy stops picking up the pillows I knocked onto the ground while sleeping to look at me.

I can't put the words together. This would be so much easier if it was Bella.

I wish I could step back six years into the past, maybe further. Find a younger Iggy, the one that was on the verge of unleashing his true asshole form. I wish I could remind him that, in the bedroom across the hall, there's a younger me that admires him. A younger me who remembers

Iggy's favorite order from Twisted Burger, who didn't mind wearing all Iggy's hand-me-downs because it made him feel almost equal. That there's a kid who will need him in the future.

A kid who will want to say *thank you* but won't know how.

But I can't time travel.

So I stumble toward the bathroom without a word.

The diner we drive to is light-years behind Cosmos and Java in ambiance. It's in downtown Atlanta, one of those vintage designs with a long Formica bar lined with steel stools, their plastic red vinyl tops cracked. The stink of grease hits you the second you walk through the door. The food appears light-years behind Cosmos and Java, too, not that I'm eating.

I'm not hungry.

I haven't eaten a full meal since yesterday, unless you the count concession snacks at the park. Occasionally, my stomach growls, but I'm too sad, angry, and disoriented to eat. In the past hour, I think I've experienced every dreadful emotion a human is capable of.

"Eat. Something." Iggy points his fork at me, the crease between his eyebrows deepening.

I pick an edge off the toast on the small plate in front me. Mouth wide, I chew for Iggy.

"Ha. Ha." He rolls his eyes, returning to his business-person-on-the-go order of toast, bacon, oatmeal, and a fried egg. Periodically, he checks his phone. It vibrates and lights up on the table. Maybe it's Shamari—he mentioned she was out of town for a modeling gig. Or maybe it's work related.

"Do you work weekends?" I ask.

There are so many things about Adult Iggy I don't know.

"Sometimes," he says between bites of egg. "I try not to, but it happens."

"Like Mom."

He smirks, shaking his head. "Mom has no choice but to work weekends. That's when her clients do the most on social media."

I pick another edge off my toast. "But she tries not to."

"Abuelito always said I'm a lot like her."

I guffaw. "You remind me more of . . ."

"Dad?"

Each molecule in my chest contracts. They rub together, creating friction. In my mind, a countdown begins.

"I don't want to do this."

Iggy wipes his greasy fingers on a napkin. "No shit; you never do."

This is why I shouldn't have called him. This is why twenty-six miles of distance is needed.

"It's true, though," I insist. "You're just like Carlos."

More than I am, I almost add.

"Dad—"

"No. Carlos," I snap, cutting him off. "*Dad* left five years ago after he cheated on Mom. You act as if he's this god who makes forgivable mistakes."

My breath hitches, then I hiccup.

"You didn't see her. You weren't there." Supernova Isaac Martin is burning brightly. "She didn't want to get out of bed or shower. She didn't . . ." Another hiccup. "She didn't want to be Mom anymore."

Iggy rests his elbows on the table, seats his chin on his knuckles.

"He's not a hero, Iggy. He's a piece of—"

I stop myself. Not because Iggy narrows his eyes. Not because our waiter discreetly slides the check under one of the plates, ducking away. Not because the rage has finally exhausted.

But because I can't take that word back after it leaves my mouth. I'm worried that one day, I will regret saying it out loud. Even though a large chunk of me believes it.

I don't hate Carlos. I hate the space he occupies in my brain.

Iggy says "I almost dropped out my first semester at UGA" with an even voice. He reaches for his coffee as I stare at him, jaw unhinged. "I came home late one weekend. You were asleep. And Mom was crying on the kitchen floor."

Pain flashes in his eyes. Like the memory's right there.

"She couldn't stop crying. She begged me not to tell you or Bella." He clears his throat several times as if something is stuck there, something that refuses to leave. "Do, you know the real reason Bella doesn't talk to me like she used to?"

I shake my head.

We've never discussed it. I just assumed Bella and I were Team Mom while Iggy's always been pro Carlos.

"She almost didn't graduate high school because of what was going on." He sips his coffee as if he didn't just unlock a secret Bella never shared with me.

I swallow my own spit, too numb to reach for the sweating glass of water the waiter put on the table thirty minutes ago.

"A few of her teachers contacted Mom. With everything that was going on, she couldn't handle Bella too. So I did." Iggy exhales, that knot returning between his eyebrows. "I called Bella every morning. Made sure she went to school. Asked her about classes, tests, whatever. And when she didn't answer the phone, I called her friends."

"What?"

He nods slowly. "Four years later, with a baby on the way, Bella still gives me shit for daring to get involved in her life."

I snort. As much as I want to take the glory, out of the three of us, Bella's the real professional grudge holder.

"Hate to break it to you, Isaac, but you're not the only

person who's been burned by what happened between Mom and Dad," he says, and I don't correct him. My stubbornness, my anger, is thinning.

"I know all about loss," he continues. "I was old enough to remember Abuela dying. I've watched what that's done to Abuelito. What the affair did to Mom. I've held both their hands. I still hear their crying in my head sometimes."

We sniffle in unison.

"Last night, I watched the same thing happen with my baby brother."

Baby brother. I can't remember when he last called me that.

He stares down into his mug of black coffee. "That night, after I made sure Mom got to bed, I called Dad. I went in on him. No fucks given. And do you know what he said?"

"¿Pinche pendejo?" I guess.

Iggy blinks at me for a second. I can't tell if he's unmoved by my weak joke or impressed with how easily I replied. "He cried and apologized," he says.

I finally reach for the water, my hand trembling as I nearly choke trying to drink half of it. Carlos Martin cried. He felt *something*. For years, all I've thought about is how easily he packed up and left us. This empty, emotionless goodbye he gave Bella and me as he walked to his car and drove away.

That's the Carlos I remember most.

Selfish. Unmoved by Mom's tears. His vacant farewell.

In those late hours of the night, after listening to Mom hide her whimpers, I'd stare at my ceiling and think nothing could be worse. I'd pretend it didn't hurt that Carlos left *me* so easily. He's always been this number in my phone, another call to ignore without guilt because he felt no remorse about what he did to us.

But he did.

The pieces of Carlos I've known, the ones I realized were polluting my bloodstream yesterday, are just that— small fractions of who he is. It's not all of him.

"Dad's not a god or my hero." Iggy smiles. "He's just our dad."

"Doesn't mean he's a good one," I mumble.

Iggy laughs. "True that," he says. "But he's family. You don't have an option when it comes to blood. That doesn't mean you have to be him. Or Mom. Or me. Just because someone you cared for burned you this time doesn't mean you're doomed forever."

"He didn't—"

"Davi *did*," Iggy says, cutting me off. "Whatever you feel for him *is* real. Trust like that is hard to give someone. As someone who's never had a relationship longer than eight months, I know."

I sigh. "That's what I get for wanting a boyfriend."

He *pffts*. "No offense, I don't really know this Davi guy,

but I always thought you had better options."

I barely have any real friends, probably down to zero after last night, and Iggy thinks I have options?

"Oh, yeah," I say, eyes rolling. "Friendless Isaac is just drowning in romantic prospects."

"Okay, yes, I'll admit what happened yesterday would probably make me less inclined to be around you too," he agrees. "Plus, thoughts and prayer for this offensive hairstyle you've got going on."

He reaches out, brushing a hand over my curls the same way Bella does. He's never done that before. *Or maybe he did when we were younger, but my brain's been filled to capacity with all the vengeful, petty things Iggy's done that it has no room for the nice ones. Maybe things like that autographed poster on my wall are more than a reminder of who Iggy could be.*

It's a reminder of who Iggy is if I'd give him a chance.

"Based on the way you were sobbing like a two-year-old last night," he says, ignoring when I flip him off, "I'm guessing you had a decent group of friends. More than just Diego."

I did. Zelda and I are Mondo Shake–loving social media mutuals. F.B. has always been open and honest with me, even though I wouldn't let him past surface-level conversations. Blake, Level_Zero, whatever he wants to be, is like the kid brother I didn't know I'd want. And, in another part of the multiverse, Alix is my friend too. We have *Disaster Academy* and family issues and a silent understanding when the other needs space.

Pride—before my Davi meltdown—was fun because of all of them, not just Diego.

"I messed that up," I whisper.

"You know," Iggy starts, jutting his chin in the direction of my phone on the table. "A public apology goes a long way."

I press my phone awake. No new notifications. No life in the group chat.

I glance around the diner. All around, people are dressed for Legends Con. A booth stuffed with four generations of Anakin Skywalkers—preteen Tatooine Anakin, over-dramatic Jedi Anakin, Darth Vader, and Force ghost Anakin. At the bar, a girl Goku sips from a mug. Two guys stumble through the door as Ash and Pikachu from *Pokémon*, followed by a Harley Quinn.

It's a Geekpalooza here. We're only a twenty-minute walk from the convention center where LC is being held.

"Hey." Iggy taps my hand. I focus on him. "How about this: I'll take care of the check. You use that outdated phone of yours to text your friends for a meetup . . ."

I snatch my phone from the table, clutching it to my chest as I glare at him.

He checks the time on his own. "Then we'll head over to Linden Avenue to watch the cosplay parade before I drive you home."

"Really?"

"For sure," he says, twirling his keys on his index finger. "Unless . . . you want to try driving us back?"

I squint at him, frowning.

"We can take the back roads," he says, just like he did that day in my bedroom.

"But that'll take us over an hour."

He shrugs, then grins. "What's wrong? Can't stand to spend that much more time with your big bro?"

"No," I say, smiling. "That actually sounds . . . nice."

It's the most honest thing I've said in weeks.

Twenty-Seven

Premiere Previews—Comic Book News & More

DISASTER ACADEMY #12

Incredible Comix

JULY

Writer: Peter Heinberg   Artist: Jorge Prados

It's Charm's birthday and all hell is about to break loose for the students at Webster Academy! Charm is missing. Reverb has a new secret. Breakups, new loves, and distrust cause friction in the team. But first, the Disasters must survive their toughest threat—final exams!

32 pages/Rated Teens and Up

> The Six Group Chat
>
> Today 9:03 AM
>
> Me: Hi. Can we meet at SP around 3? Plz.

There's a line outside of NRG that tails off just before the corner. One Saturday a month, they have a BOGO special that inundates the tiny shop with people craving cups of organic fruits and sugar. I'm glad Bella's not here. If she saw this crowd, she'd revert to rage-infused, seventeen-year-old Bella who always went off on anything or anyone after working a BOGO shift.

The line is filled with moms and strollers, a pack of tweeners recording Boomerangs on their phones, a few people in business attire constantly checking their Apple watches while waiting, and gym fanatics still glossy with sweat, their earbuds pumping out fast beats that match my hammering heart.

I'm five feet away from Secret Planet. The adjacent parking lot is empty. I don't know why I expected anyone to be here—not on the day of Legends Con. But even F.B.'s hatchback is missing, which is what started my ten-minute waiting game on the sidewalk.

Maybe the Six decided not to show up.

Heroes for Hire has these giant, wide storefront windows that give every potential customer a clear view of the interior, the cheerful employees, and the wandering patrons browsing the hundreds of comics. It's the perfect FOMO strategy. But Secret Planet's windows are mid-sized, the blinds habitually closed. The only invitation to step inside is the OPEN sign taped to the smudgy glass front door.

I haven't seen anyone enter or exit since I arrived.

There's zero activity in the Six group chat, and I'm starting to think maybe they started a new one without me. The Five. I can't blame them.

The thing about apologies is you can't force the other person to listen, no matter how badly you want them to. You can only gather the words, hold them in your heart, and hope the person on the other end will meet you halfway to hear them. Once you've hurt someone, wanting to fix things is the easiest part.

It's the waiting on acceptance that truly destroys you.

Standing here, I wonder if that's what it's like for Carlos when I don't answer his calls. *Is that me slowly demolishing his hopes? Does he feel like this? Nervous and sick with guilt and terrified no one's there to hear his words? Does he want to turn back time?*

Does he want to cry?

A Jeep pulls into the lot and my chest tightens. But it's not who I want it to be. It's only an excited family joining the NRG line.

I double-check the lock on my bike, then wipe my clammy palms on my shirt. Silence greets me when I check the group chat one last time. But I find that single pocket of hope still under my ribs. I latch on, then walk on jelly legs to Secret Planet's front door.

The sad, pathetic *womp-womp* of the de-energized motion-sensitive door chime echoes throughout the shop when I walk in. It's followed by a ghostly, cold hush. Not the kind of quiet I'm used to around Secret Planet where you can still hear that distinct noise of a page turning or someone clearing their throat, that soft inhale of excitement when a reader's favorite comic hero does something cool on the page.

This is nothing. It's like I'm standing in a dark void just like Charm in Issue #6. The emptiness deflates me so quickly. It confirms my fears: I'm not one of the Six anymore.

Was I ever?

My right leg is starting to vibrate in place. I don't know what made me fall for that tiny spark of hope that they'd be here. That F.B. would still see me as Captain Incredible and Zelda would want to quote all their favorite Whitney lyrics at me and Blake could make fun of my lack of gaming knowledge and Alix would be in her favorite spot on the carpet, ready to judge me for whatever, but with that new little smirk she showed me at the diner. That maybe, in an upside-down universe, Diego would be in the middle of it all.

It hasn't even been twenty-four hours since Meltdown Isaac ruined Pride. Why would they be ready to hear out an apology? I'm not sure I'm ready to forgive myself for what I said.

There's a noise beyond the front counter that makes me jump a little. It also reignites the fading ember of optimism inside me. But it's quickly snuffed out when I see Big Winston's shiny, bald head peep outside his office door.

"Oh. Thought I heard someone." He crams into the

doorway with a small grin. Big Winston's a towering, kind of imposing guy. Thick muscles and a scarily deep voice. But his smile reminds me of Gramps, Mom's dad, who loves to make jokes at all the wrong times. "Sorry, figured all the customers would be down at LC today. Did you need something, Isaac?"

It's weird to hear him say my name. We've barely inter-acted over the years. But the look in his eyes is like the one F.B. gives me.

Like he *knows* me.

Blush stings my cheeks. "No," I say around the thick-ness in my throat. But I want to tell him yes. I need to apologize. I need to fix things.

Big Winston raises an eyebrow at me. I jam my hands into my pockets, forcing out a pathetic smile.

"Okay," he says nonchalantly. "Browse around. Do your usual thing. The others went out to celebrate. They'll be back soon."

This time, my eyebrows shoot up. *The others will be back soon? They went out to celebrate?*

But before I can get any of those questions out—as if I could, even on a good day—Big Winston is slipping back into his office, gently shutting the door.

And I'm left alone. My heart *tick-tick-tick*s in my ears. I stare at the carpet, trying to mute the unforgiving chorus of words that keeps trying to accompany the soundtrack in my head: *I never wanted this.*

But here I am, in the middle of my favorite place in all of Alpharetta—other than Diego's bedroom—ready to cry over something I *did* want. I just couldn't recognize that not everything we want in life comes in the form we expect it to.

I don't move from this spot for ten minutes. Maybe less. Possibly longer. It's enough time to consider finally giving up on my plan when the whining motion detector behind me goes off and laughter echoes into the store. Voices and feet shuffling and someone's singing follow. It all crashes into me like a cold breeze in the middle of December.

I take a second to calm the trembles in my hands before turning around.

It's eerie looking at the rest of the Six for the first time since yesterday evening.

Actually, the rest of the Six minus one.

At first, no one speaks. F.B. scratches his scruffy chin, then drags a hand through his freshly dyed teal hair before claiming his usual stool behind the counter. Alix glares at me while forming her mini fortress of graphic novels on the floor. Blake joins her, sitting cross-legged, trading glances between me and his phone.

And Zelda is . . .

Zelda leans against the front counter, eyes narrowed, dressed as the most epic, badass Nu'Bia from the Wonder Woman comics. Their black leather jacket has stars on the sleeves, the cuffs rolled up to reveal silver bracelets. Their curls are picked out into a massive Afro. The fluorescent lighting hits their silver tiara, nearly blinding me. They even have a gold lasso attached to their navy leather pants.

F.B. clears his throat. I snap out of my holy-shit daze.

I'm not particularly good at speeches. Truthfully, I suck at them. After the Legends Con parade, Iggy tried to coach me through what to say, but nothing stuck the moment I got behind the wheel of his car. I'm a solid multitasker, but practicing driving and strategizing a way to apologize required too much brain activity.

"Uh." All the things I want to say feel thick and clumsy, gathering at the back of my throat like a car wreck. "So. Yesterday. That was bad. The ending sucked. I mean, uh, okay—" Everything in my brain is scrambled. Everyone's eyes on me doesn't help.

Zelda's sharp glare shreds any confidence—which is to say none—I had before walking in here.

"I shouldn't have—like, I didn't mean to," I stumble.

"Mean to what?"

My mouth's dry as I gaze at Zelda. I'm desperate for the words that'll erase that hardness in their expression. But I'm coming up empty.

Then, F.B. yells "Yes, we forgive you! Welcome home, Captain Incredible" with open arms.

"What? Hell no." Zelda shakes their head. "I did not leave early from the convention center, looking this fierce, for some half-ass, puppy-dog, sad-face, weak attempt at an apology."

From the many screenshots of a carefully phrased "I'm sorry for . . ." transcribed in the Notes app, then posted by one of Mom's clients on social media after they did or said something problematic, I know Zelda's right. I might be nervous and terrible at verbalizing in front of people, but they deserve better. And I want to be better at this. For them and for me.

"What did you expect from a boy incapable of maintaining any semblance of personal relationships outside of his own absurd, delusional connection with two fictional characters?" says Alix.

Leave it to her to confirm my ineptitude.

"Wow. We didn't discuss how brutal we were going to be with him, but okay," Blake says. He levels me with a scowl. "In that case: You're an asswipe. And you've got deodorant on your shirt."

I peek down. Yup. A broken line of white chalk across the left side of the green, vintage *Legend of Zelda* T-shirt I unearthed from a box in my bedroom. It's Diego's. The moment I saw it, I knew I wanted to wear it, even though it's tighter than I remembered.

I also knew Diego wouldn't show up for this. If the roles were reversed, I'd probably do the same.

Exhaling, I say, "I know I messed up. Bad."

"Bad?" Zelda's voice breaks. They stomp over to me,

poking at my chest with their index finger. "Yesterday was my first Pride without my dads watching over my shoulder. *My first Pride.* Just me and my friends." Their glassy eyes widen. "I was having the most fun I've ever had until you decided to go all Kanye West on us."

I wince.

"I thought we were friends, Isaac."

And that's why their tone hurts. Because at some point, Zelda did become a friend. They all did, Alix included.

I chew the inside of my cheek, then say, "I was a certified dick to all of you yesterday. I'm not good with people. I don't . . ." The air heats up in my lungs. "I suck at making friends. It scares me to let people in. I have a lot of issues—"

"We all do." F.B. offers me a petite grin.

But I shake my head. "What I did was foul. I acted like Pride was all about me, and what I wanted . . ." I pause, staring at the empty spot next to me. The spot where Diego would be standing. "I forgot that I already have what I want. Friends."

Zelda *hmmphs* in front of me.

I close my eyes. "At least I *hope* I still do."

It's so quiet, I can hear the hum of the air conditioner. The snores coming from Big Winston's office. And my own heartbeat, *thud-thud-thud,* is the loudest of all.

"So." Zelda curves up one dark eyebrow. "Was that the apology?"

This wet, ugly laugh escapes my throat.

"Because I didn't hear an *I'm sorry* in there."

"I think it was implied," F.B. says.

"Oh, honey, no. Zelda Elmore did not sign up for *implied* apologies. I wanna hear it."

I wait until our eyes meet, then I say the words, "I'm sorry."

"That it?" Zelda sizes me up. "No glitter falling from the ceiling? No choreographed performance of Her Majesty Whitney Houston's 'I Have Nothing'?"

Everyone laughs. It's this boisterous, unremorseful sound that resonates through the shop. Blake's red faced. F.B.'s fallen somewhere behind the counter. Even Alix is giggling hard enough to almost drop her graphic novel.

I wipe away the warm tears at the corners of my eyes. Zelda steps closer and I don't jump when they pull me down into a hug. I hold them close, resting my head on their shoulder, careful not to ruin their curly Afro.

I whisper, "You're a great friend."

"Damn straight," they say, squeezing me tighter.

We stand around the front counter, talking. In fewer than twenty-four hours I've missed so much. It's strange, because the nerves are still there, buzzing under my skin. But the noise in my head softens. I can focus on all the conversations. I'm beginning to learn when to ask questions.

I still wish Diego were here. Not to be the conduit

between me and these people, though. I'm not going to keep leaning on him. I can manage on my own. One breath at a time.

Zelda spent the morning outside of the Atlanta Metropolitan Convention Center, the castle of glass and iron where Legends Con is being held, with other cosplayers and members of their Patreon. They scroll through all the new posts on their Instagram.

It's like entering another world.

Every photo is of heroes and villains and aliens and monsters. Stormtroopers and orcs stand in the background as Zelda poses with two kids that look around Ollie's age. Black Lightning and Iron Man flank Zelda's sides in another post. The next image is of a girl with flawless brown skin whose pale-yellow hijab completes her Sailor Moon costume.

"Oh, I got this one for you," Zelda announces, tapping on another picture. "Even though I was still pissed."

Gathered around Zelda are seven teens wearing matching navy blazers and crimson-and-navy striped ties. The official Webster Academy for the Different crest is ironed onto the breast of their jackets. They're the Disasters, smiling and holding up peace signs. In the middle of the group, a boy who could pass as Charm kisses another boy—a Reverb look-alike.

My heart thunders, eyes fixed on those two boys. It's perfect. I manage to pull my thoughts away from the photo to listen to Zelda talk about all the new followers they've amassed. It's not a flex—they've earned the respect of the geek community.

"I love this journey for me," says Zelda.

Level_Zero announces he's beaten two otherwise unconquerable games in the last fourteen hours, which sparks a discussion about video games that I don't quite follow. But I don't drown in the noise either. I nod along, mentally clocking terms and names I can Google later. I'll be prepared for next time.

I love that there will be a next time.

"You're also looking at the future employee of the month at SP, my friendos," F.B. adds, ruffling Blake's hair. "Once he turns sixteen, of course."

Blake flushes, eyes lowered. It's the first time I've noticed he's wearing a soft, powder-blue T-shirt with the Secret Planet logo on it. On the back, in block letters, it says TRAINEE.

"He's going to be big time around here," says F.B.

"Because the long list of previous employees of the month is so riveting," Alix says flatly.

It's true. Behind the front counter is a large, wooden plaque. Every month has the same photo and name: PETER PARKER. Except . . . I zone in on June's employee.

Francis Bean Lowell.

"Seriously?" I almost shout.

F.B. explains that Vee Johnson, queen of Heroes for Hire and heir to the Legends Con committee throne, left out one key detail in her planning: she didn't invite any of the local artists, writers, and creators to be a part of this year's con.

To counter her major error, F.B. organized his own independent Legends Con to be held at Secret Planet with the homegrown talent in August.

"Tentatively titled Herolopolis." F.B. beams. "Sick, right?"

I rub the back of my neck. "It has . . . potential."

I check my phone. It's 4:56 p.m. I should get home and set up Bella's old bedroom for her and Chris's arrival tomorrow so Mom won't have to. Maybe I'll call Iggy. Give this whole "thank you" thing another try.

Really, I'm looking for excuses to avoid the one thought throbbing against my temples: I haven't heard a word from Diego since yesterday.

I'm obviously giving off some form of stage-one clinger vibes, because Blake says, "KonamiCode's probably just—"

I cut him off. "Nah. It's all good." I stare at that empty spot next to me again. The cold, unnerving sensation in my sternum isn't longing. It's just . . . weird. I guess I'll have to adjust to it eventually. In the fall, Diego's ghost will follow me all around UGA's campus.

But maybe it won't be so bad.

My eyes shift around the group. I have friends. Maybe I'll have more in Athens too.

"I better go," I finally say.

"Me too," Alix says, stuffing her graphic novel collection into a black JanSport backpack. "Family stuff," she mumbles as an explanation.

I maintain a respectable distance as I follow her to the door, but we almost collide when Zelda shouts, "Hey! Don't forget we're meeting tonight after your shift."

Alix pauses, shoulders falling a little.

"You're still down to model for my IG, right?" asks Zelda. "You're the only badass friend I have that can pull off these looks."

Alix's lips open and close like a goldfish. Then her brow furrows, her cheeks pinkening. She scuffs the toe of her Vans on the carpet, unable to look at anyone. It's almost adorable how self-conscious she seems.

She briefly glances my way, searching my face as if I might call her out. But I'm not going to. Finally, she grunts "Yeah, sure. Whatever" before shouldering out the door.

"Hey."

Alix walks up to me as I'm unchaining my bike. She's backlit by the sun as she approaches, a golden halo surrounding her. "I guess you haven't seen what's happening on Geeks Nation yet."

I shake my head. I haven't looked at my screen other than to check the time. Or for those nonexistent texts from Diego I keep hoping for.

She digs her phone out of her backpack, unlocking it. "Please remain calm when you see this, Nerdstradamus."

"Who?"

Alix scowls. "Whatever," she says before thrusting her phone in my face. "Just look."

I study the screen. She's logged on to Geeks Nation, and the pinned post at the top—the one with nearly three thousand likes despite the thread going up only two hours ago—is a screenshot. It's from Jorge's official, blue check verified Instagram account. He's posted a sketch of two characters. Clean, unbroken black lines, nothing colored in. But it's obvious who they are—Charm and Reverb. Behind them is a star-filled galaxy like on the cover of *Disaster Academy* Issue #6. Reverb's arm is curled around Charm's neck. One of Charm's hands holds the back of Reverb's head, fingers threaded into his dark hair.

"The nerd squads are going nuts," Alix says, a smile in her voice. I can't take my eyes away from the sketch.

Charm and Reverb are kissing.

I blink and blink, the shock of it all springing fresh tears to my eyes. Surprisingly, I repress them. "How?"

Alix's thumb scrolls the screen. "Basically, a bunch of other *DA* fans bombarded Jorge and Peter during their LC panel. They all wanted to know if Reverb felt the same for Charm. They pressed Peter about finally giving two non-white, queer teens the happy ending they deserve."

I try to follow all the comments, the likes, the hundreds of red hearts and crying emojis in the thread, but I can't. Warmth pools in my belly. I lose count of how many times I've been tagged, but it's at least twenty-five. My swelling heart presses against the confines of my ribs.

"And?" I ask, throat dry.

Alix shrugs. "Peter said he wasn't allowed to confirm anything." She scrolls back to the image. "So Jorge did this."

It's all I ever wanted. For these two pining boys to get to this point. And I don't know why, for so long, I wasn't sure it'd happen. I don't know why I thought because I hadn't seen it, it couldn't happen. Or why I spent so much time trying to make it happen for myself with Davi.

It's right here. Two hopelessly-in-love best friends kissing.

Something twists, then releases in my lungs. *It's right there. Two best friends, always there for each other when no one else understands them. Unafraid of being vulnerable with each other. The way Charm looks at Reverb and the way Reverb makes Charm laugh and—*

My breath catches. Alix lifts an eyebrow. I force myself to look back at her phone before my brain spirals into a place I don't quite understand.

The hashtags under the photo are too epic to ignore.

#CharmandReverb

#QPOCHeroes

#MyDisasters

#ItsReal

The last one is in Spanish. #EsVerdad.

It is true.

"I'm pretty sure the publisher made Jorge take down the original post, but a bunch of people screenshot it," Alix explains, lowering her phone. "The internet never forgets."

"Why did you . . ." I pause, my numb legs barely keeping me upright. I can't quite say what I want to Alix.

Do you even like me?

Didn't I hurt you too?

Are we friends?

She bites her lip, her shoulders pulled close to her ears. She says, "I know you didn't mean what you said yesterday. Or maybe you did, I don't know. But I get it. You don't just let people in your life."

I nod, sniffing.

"Neither do I."

"So why have you been hanging around us?"

"I don't know." She rubs her temples. "I'm still figuring it out. I guess it's okay to have people you can lean on when you don't feel like dealing with your own stuff."

"You mean friends?" I offer.

"Oh, please don't use that word." Her mouth quirks. "You're all still on probation." She looks at the dwindling line at NRG, groups of strangers talking and laughing and soaking in the summer heat. She whispers, "Everyone deserves a win, Isaac. Even you."

We stand quietly. I twist the ends of my curls between my index finger and thumb while Alix bunches her hair into a messy ponytail. "I'm gonna—" She jerks her head toward the opposite direction I biked in.

"Yeah. Sure."

Alix stares at me for a beat, like she wants to say something else but doesn't. When she cuts the corner and disappears, I tug out my phone. I download that screenshot from Geeks Nation in case it gets deleted like Jorge's IG post, then I type out the longest, most incoherent post ever created before sharing the sketch across all my social media. I don't even care that my ancient Facebook account hasn't been touched since tenth grade.

Finally, I scroll through my contacts and edit the name of Unknown Number: Dark Disaster.

Twenty-Eight

No Capes! Reviews Blog
Top reviews for *Disaster Academy* #10
@queenlizzielighty
★★☆☆☆

I don't get this series. Better yet—I don't get Reverb/ Charm. Two best friends and one can't see the other has a thing for him? FOR TEN COMICS?! They were trapped in a vent together FFS! ISTG they can't be that oblivious. Their friends suck too. I would be in every group chat like YO REVERB WHEN ARE YOU GOING TO WAKE UP AND REALIZE YOUR BEST FRIEND LOVES YOU AND YOU LOVE HIM?! It's. right. there. Boys are useless.

A silver two-door Toyota waits in the driveway when I return home. It has an EAST MIDDLETON HIGH SCHOOL HONOR ROLL STUDENT bumper sticker and a pair of mini–ice skates hanging from the rearview mirror. I can almost smell the interior—cherry Gatorade and cinnamon gum—as I wheel my bike up the drive.

It's Davi's car.

He's sitting on the front steps of my house. His head

is bowed, curls falling over his eyebrows, as he scrolls through his phone. MADE IN BRAZIL is stretched in black lettering across his white T-shirt. My stomach squirms at the way he looks, compact and casual with his elbows on his knees.

I clear my throat. "'Sup."

"Hi." He wiggles a few fingers at me in a cute proximity to a wave. His smile is small, insecure. "How are you?"

I shrug.

"Sorry. Stupid question." He laughs gently. "And sorry if this is all kind of stalkery."

"You mean you showing up at my house? Waiting on my steps?"

His smile softens into the one I saw in the H&M fitting room. The one I remember from walking around on our—now officially official—non-date.

I lean my bike against the garage door. He scoots over, and I hesitate. Flashbacks of him kissing me, then kissing that boy invade my brain. Davi's face falls. His lips part, but I shake my head before lowering myself next to him.

We sit quietly, waiting for the other to speak. He tugs at a loose thread on his black joggers. The thick taste of pollen crowds the back of my throat, but I fight through it. I'm not inviting Davi inside. That would heighten the already awkward state we're in.

"So."

"So," I repeat, eyeing his footwear. Flip-flops and bi socks. I've failed him as a stylist.

"I was gonna text you. But I wanted to do this in person."

I struggle to control my leg muscles as the warmth of his shoulder touches mine.

"To say I'm—"

Quickly, I hold up a hand. "You don't have to. We did this already. Remember?"

"Yeah," he says. "But yesterday was—well, there were a lot of emotions going on and I couldn't sleep at all last night."

I want to tell him crying unconsolably for an hour helps, but my level of petty isn't there.

"I feel like shit." He tenses next to me. "I didn't mean to lead you—"

I interrupt him again. "You didn't." His knee knocks against mine and I finally look at him. His brow's knit. There's this tiny crinkle on the bridge of his nose. I say, "Seriously. We don't have to rehash this."

"I need the air cleared." He chews his bottom lip. "I need to know we'll still be friends because, as much as I love my boys, no one gets me like you, Isaac."

The way he says my name, with affection and sincerity, re-tangles all my feelings about him. Not in a romantic way. When I look at him, all I see is that vulnerable boy standing in front of a perfectly lit H&M mirror, hoping someone understands what it's like for no one else to see the real him: a confident hockey player on the ice and an insecure bisexual boy learning how to walk on dry land.

We truly do contain multitudes.

I fight off another sneeze to say, "So, you want to be friends?"

"If that's okay with you?"

I consider it for a moment. Can I be friends with Davi Lucas, Former Five-Star Crush Syndrome? I think I could. Maybe he's not the kind of friend I'll be sitting on the floor with, sharing cheesecake or maduros. We won't be choreographing routines to old-school R&B tunes. I'm not going to practice kissing—or any other kind of intimate physical activity—with him. But I can see myself laughing on FaceTime with Davi. Taking long night walks while talking about college. Possibly the boys we like.

Maybe not every friend is the one you share your deepest secrets with. Maybe you're that friend to someone else—the one they confide in. Maybe there are friends for laughing and crying and sharing food with while avoiding problems. Maybe every friend plays a different role.

I rub the back of my wrist across my itchy eyes. I hope he doesn't think I'm crying. Honestly, I'm so done crying over boys.

"Friends works for me," I finally say.

He beams and I don't instantly melt. That's growth.

"Cool shirt."

I glance down. "Oh." Of course it's cool. It belongs to Diego Santoyo the Effortlessly Trendy. But I guess it's mine now, seeing as he'll probably never talk to me again.

"Green and white," Davi whispers.

"What?"

His grin is soft and nervous again. "You were wearing a green-and-white striped T-shirt the day we met back in middle school. Those slip-on Vans that I can never find in the right size for my wide feet. They were—"

"Limited edition Hulks," I say, smirking. My geekiness had no chill back then. "You remember?"

"*Pssh.*" Davi shoulder-checks me. "They were fire. You were so cool."

"I was not—"

"Yeah, you were. You weren't like those other kids who asked where I was from and why my hair was so curly." He wrinkles his face. "All that stupid shit you ask when you're that age." He leans against me. "You were always cool, Isaac. Sorry I didn't tell you that."

"Ugh. Enough with the apologies," I tease. Then, quietly, I say, "You were too. We would've made a pretty dope duo."

"Nah." He shakes his head, smiling awkwardly. "I could never compete with Diego."

I don't know how to respond to that. Fact is, he's right. Diego has a place in my heart no one else can fill. Not even Davi Lucas. And that breaks me more than watching him kiss another boy ever could.

"I can't believe Mom keeps my room the same."

I lower my copy of *Disaster Academy* to smile at Bella looming in my doorway. The hallway light leaves a delicate glow against her face. Her usually curly hair is straightened and messily braided, resting over one shoulder. She has a hand gently pressed over her belly. Bella looks tired, but not just from the drive up to Alpharetta.

"I mean, she totally wrecked Iggy's room." She laughs, an easy sound I desperately miss coming from down the hall every night as she FaceTimed with friends. Or when she'd totally ignore my clearly established knocking rule to burst into my room and show me some hilarious meme she found.

I sit up on my bed. "It's a fair trade. He wrecked her car prom night."

Bella rolls her eyes. "And all she did was ground him until graduation, which was a month later. I was grounded for two months when she caught me kissing that boy from MLK High's basketball team."

"That guy was a goon," I remind her. "It's a good thing Chris came along."

"Really?" Bella signals her belly. "Because, some days, this feels like being grounded."

We laugh in this familiar harmony. My chest unwinds.

Bella's home. She's this piece of my history I keep trying to reach back and grab, but my fingers come up empty. Is it always like that? Things from our past, memories we hold so tightly to for so long, eventually turning into ghosts.

"Oh, Mom told me to give you this." She tosses one of those black poly mailers onto my knees.

I tear it open, peeking inside.

"Something cool?" she asks.

I smile. "Kind of." It's a T-shirt I forgot I ordered.

Bella yawns, so I shift my legs out of the way. She struggles to sit, then sighs contently when she finds a semi-comfortable position. I turn on my side to face her. She stares at a candle burning on my desk, then sniffs, eyebrows raised. "Grapefruit?"

"Lemon zest," I reply.

"Same old Isaac."

"Same old Bella," I counter, pointing at the pair of East Middleton High Volleyball Team sweats she's wearing.

"Shut up. They're the only comfy thing I own."

She stretches awkwardly to scrub my hair. Iggy's already scheduled me a visit with Darrell to get a shape-up this week, but Bella eases her fingers through my curls to scratch against my scalp.

"Where's Diego? I'm surprised he's not here, sitting on your floor."

I frown.

Bella notices, tilting her head. Everything about her—

lowered eyebrows, patient eyes, the careful expression—is Mom. I can't lie to her. I could barely keep any of this from Mom when she arrived home this morning, but Bella's different. She's the vault for all my secrets and fears.

So I tell her. Most of it. I leave out the part about the practice kiss, but I rush through every detail about the distance and the Mel thing and the fights. Every horrific moment at Pride. I can't stop.

After, Bella says, "Huh."

"Huh?"

She smirks. "I mean, I always figured you two were . . . *you know*."

"We were what?"

"I don't know!" She giggles, hands thrown up. "Boyfriends. Or casually, you know, doing things."

"Fuck buddies?"

"First of all, language." She emphatically points at her belly. "Second, gross, you're my little brother. You're not having sex. I don't care how much I love Diego."

"Okay, but didn't you have to have sex to make—" I stop short. Both our eyes widen, then we're dry-heaving and laughing and *this*. This is what I mean.

My sister is the gravity that keeps me from drifting too close to the sun.

"I've always loved your relationship with him," she says after our laughter quiets. "You two . . . you just work."

Do we?

I blink so hard I'm seeing double. How could Diego and I work? We're best friends. We don't—love doesn't operate like that. Yes, according to all the laws of the hundreds of romantic comedies I've watched since I could crawl, best friends fall for each other . . . then everything falls apart. Or it's some sad, unrequited love story that never ends happily for one person.

The friend zone doesn't exist by chance.

The regulations of mutual friendship demand you don't add love—or sex—to the equation.

It nearly never works.

But, after Alix showed me the now-viral Charm and Reverb sketch, I couldn't shake the tiny fires moving through my body. It's all I wanted, right? Two best friends, kissing and being in love. It's one of the reasons I fell so hard for these characters—their friendship.

"Come on, Isaac." Bella pokes my shoulder. "You've never thought about it?"

Not until that kiss, but Davi Lucas was still A Capitalized Thing. I could barely sleep last night. All I heard were Davi's words echoing from every corner of my mind: *I could never compete with Diego.*

That's the reality that scares me the most. Davi couldn't. I don't know why I thought anyone ever could.

"You've never pined or swooned over him?"

"Bella, I don't pine or swoon."

"You *do*." She pats my head like she would a puppy.

"Diego is the highest level of Crush Syndrome you've ever experienced. I guess you missed the email notification."

My mouth opens, then closes. I'm confused and sad and oddly relieved.

Maybe Diego is my first Crush Syndrome.

Maybe he's my One True Disaster.

Maybe crushes are disasters, or a thing you get over the next day, or the start of something that builds and builds until it reaches its final form: Love.

"Holy shit," I whisper.

"Kind of crazy, right?"

"What do I do?"

"Go see him. Apologize. Tell him everything." Another smirk pulls at the corners of her mouth. As if this is the most obvious thing ever. "But tomorrow. Tonight's all about spending time with your favorite sister."

She reaches out to drag her fingers through my wild hair. I don't pull away. "But I can't see him tomorrow."

"Why?"

"*The Princess Bride* rewatch with Abuelito."

"That's not an all-day thing."

But it is. It's like a birthday or a holiday. I'm always extra hyped when I wake up, all this humming energy keeping me anxious and incapable of doing anything before my grandpa arrives. Then I help him unpack the groceries. I pretend to assist him in the kitchen, even though I know he'll eventually kick me out until he needs help at the end.

He'll say he works better alone and send me to get the bottles of Jarritos or whatever Mexican lemon-lime soda is available at the corner store. Then I'll stay by his side until he falls asleep.

I need every second with him before I leave.

My eyes drift over to the mountain of college supplies. Stretched across the top of one unfinished box is Diego's green shirt. I haven't touched the countdown on my dry erase board all week. I'm not ready to shove my entire existence into cardboard and plastic. To give up moments like this.

In true sisterly form, Bella reads my mind. "You're going to kill it in Athens." She plays with my curls. Then she frowns, gesturing to the framed poster on my wall. "Taking that with you?"

I stare at it for a minute. An involuntary smile unrolls across my mouth. "I don't know." I can still hear Iggy's voice yesterday, trading off between giving me instructions as I drove and singing along—terribly—to Selena Quintanilla's "Dreaming of You." Underneath his strained notes, I sang along too. Quiet and happy and relaxed. "I don't think I'll have space in my dorm. Maybe I'll keep it here. So Mom doesn't change my room either."

I don't say *So I'll have a reminder of my brother's kindness every time I visit.*

"That won't stop her," teases Bella.

"Hey." I chew the inside of my cheek as she wiggles

on the bed to get comfortable again. "Why did you stop talking to Iggy? You know, back when all the shit went down with Mom and Carlos."

Deep, Martin-gene-shaped wrinkles appear in her brow. She sighs frustratedly. "Has Iggy been running his mouth again?"

"No."

"Liar." She swats my shoulder. Then she glares at the ceiling. "It's not like—I appreciate it now, what he did. But I didn't want my friends involved. I didn't want them to *know*. I was keeping it to myself and handling it as best as I could, but . . ."

I wait for her to finish.

She gently rubs her thumb under her shiny eyes. "Like, who wants their friends to know that side of your life? I was embarrassed."

Diego's the only person I ever trusted with any information about my family issues. Even then, it felt uncomfortable telling him. The Santoyos are so close to perfection, I didn't think he'd understand. I can't imagine having to discuss it with other friends, if I had any back then. I can't imagine trusting anyone not to talk about it behind my back.

But Bella had to deal with that. We both built walls after Carlos left. Problem is, we never learned how to tear them down.

"I don't hate Iggy," she says almost inaudibly. Her voice

shakes a little. "I hate that when he did that without asking me, it felt like he wasn't my brother anymore. More like he was my . . ."

"Father," I say when she can't finish.

She nods, then laughs wetly. "God, this family is so overdue for group therapy."

"Big facts."

"Okay, go. Go. Now," she says, pulling on my arm, then shoving me off my own bed. "I'm tired of talking about the past. This world is gonna collapse without a proper Isaac and Diego duet. Fix it."

"What about our bonding time?"

"Boy, I'm emotionally exhausted." She pats the empty space I once occupied. "I just want your bed now."

I shrug on a thin cotton hoodie and pull on my high-tops. My hands are shaking. Heat prickles beneath my cheeks. But I want this. I roll up the T-shirt I ordered and stuff it into my hoodie's front pocket.

Bella stretches out on the sheets like a happy cat after a meal. She curls her arms around a pillow, eyes droopy. "Ugh. Bad idea. I might never get off this bed."

I cock my head in the direction of the hall. I can hear voices coming from the living room.

"Want me to get Chris?" I offer.

"Don't you dare," warns Bella. "That man is suffocating me."

I grin slyly. "Chris!"

Twenty-Nine

Charm

From Fandom Wiki, the free source for all things fandom
Real Name: Aaron Morris
Current Alias: Charm
First Appearance: Disaster Academy #1
Created by: Peter Heinberg (writer) & Jorge Prados (artist)
Team Affiliations: The Disasters
Relatives/Relationships: Jacqueline "Jackie" Morris
(mother), Keenan Morris (father, deceased), Daniyal Zafar
(Reverb) (boyfriend) [1]
🕐 Last edited 12 hours ago by **ACharmingReverb**

It only takes three knocks, my knuckles halfway
through my usual routine, before Ollie peeks through the
Santoyos' living room curtains. It's late. I didn't expect
him to still be up. Then again, summer's too magical to
sleep away.

When he sees it's me, his eyes widen like inflated bal-
loons. I give him a small wave.

He darts from the window like he's seen a ghost.

That's fair. I feel like a ghost. More like a shitty best
friend who wandered aimlessly down Westin Place.

Around the corner onto Jupiter Road. A left, then a sharp right onto Rosa Avenue. To the split-level house with the peach-painted shutters.

I wait patiently until the door swings open and Ollie's confused expression greets me on the other side.

"Hey."

For a moment, he only blinks. Then his eyebrows furrow. His mouth puckers in that way my own face got whenever one of Bella's crushes dropped by our house unannounced to apologize for being a fuckboy and making her cry.

Even Cloud Strife, hovering by Ollie's bare feet, stares me down. She sits, back straight, her tail lowered. It's not a welcome sign.

"So." I kneel until I'm Ollie's level, then tug the rolled-up T-shirt from my hoodie pocket. He rocks on his heels as I carefully unfold it, then he freezes. "I got this for you," I tell him. "Sorry, I had to guess on the size."

A massive grin breaks out across his face. His fingers pinch the sleeves, stretching out the light gray cotton material so he can have a full view of the graphic in the center of the shirt. It's an officially licensed Disasters team image. Ollie's mouth is this giant O. His eyes have a subtle sheen to them. He's shaking, but in that excited way I've witnessed when Diego compliments him during a video game.

"Do you like it?"

Ollie makes a tiny, sharp noise. It's as if he can barely contain the elation threatening to fizzle out like a shaken soda bottle. I carefully loosen his fingertips from the sleeves, lifting the shirt over his head. His arms instantly shoot up. I laugh while trying to wrangle him into it. The Santoyo forehead creates predictable trouble.

I scoot back to examine him. It's a snug fit, but only because he's wearing it over the T-shirt he already had on. Still, he looks perfect.

Ollie Santoyo, future Disaster.

"Dude, this is so rad!" Ollie's voice is this squeaky-raspy thing, like someone constantly on a sugar rush but also ready for a nap. He sounds just like Diego did at twelve. His fingers spread across the graphic, eyes closed, as if he's already imagining himself at the Webster Academy.

I thread my fingers through his hair, the way Bella does to mine, and say, "It's the raddest thing ever."

"Ollie?"

The shock of Camila's voice drifting from the kitchen forces me to look up. There's an added shadow in the doorway now. "It's late, Isaac." Diego towers over his brother, hands on Ollie's shoulder. He's chewing the inside of his cheek, staring down at me.

I stand. "Sorry."

He doesn't reply, but his expression conveys his impatience.

"Uh." The way his eyes narrow makes me stumble, but

I press on. I have to. "Want to go for a walk?"

Diego looks over his shoulder, to the hallway.

Camila leans against a wall neatly lined with family photos. Oscar and Camila's wedding all the way to Diego and me on graduation day. Camila's hair is coming undone from a ponytail. Her eyes are soft and exhausted. She shoots me an uncertain smile. Maybe Diego's told her everything about Pride. Maybe I'm not welcome here anymore. But she nods at Diego, whispering, "Mijo, adelante."

We walk in an unfamiliar silence. Diego never asks where we're going. But he stays by my side, our shoulders and elbows and hands almost touching. We cross through sleeping neighborhoods, following their orange-lit streets and cracked sidewalks.

We climb Memorial Park's vindictive wire fence. Thankfully, it doesn't attack either of us, but I think it's plotting to. One day, this flimsy structure will be our demise.

In the gazebo by the lake, we sit, rubbing at the crosshatches left on our palms while the cicadas and frogs sing to us. The park is aglow with fireflies and a fully awake moon and a brush of silver stars. I still haven't perfected giving speeches, so I ask "How are you doing?" when our silence becomes overwhelming.

He shrugs. "Same."

"Same?"

His shoulders lift again, this time in a careless bounce. He truly is the most stubborn person ever. "How'd the whole Davi thing work out?"

"It didn't."

His jaw moves as if he's grinding his teeth. His feet swing back and forth, scraping along the gazebo's pavement. "Guess that means you'll be a little less busy."

"Me?" I squeak, scowling. He shrugs a third time. I angle in his direction. "How's Mel? Having a good time with her?"

He flinches, the beginning of a scowl wrinkling his face. "Why do you keep bringing her up?"

"Because I don't know who she is!" A fast-spreading throb attacks my temple. "Maybe I want to know whoever's been taking up all my best friend's time during a summer where *I* was supposed to be doing that. Maybe I don't want to be the only one who's clueless about someone important in your life?"

There's not enough oxygen in this wide-open gazebo for all the heavy breaths I take.

"Maybe I want—" The words I want to say hover in my brain, just out of reach. I'm scared that when I say them, he won't say them back. "I don't know what I want."

We're engulfed by the quiet again. The back of my head aches. Diego's bottom lip is red and swollen from his teeth. It's all wrong. This is not a moment worthy of *The Princess Bride* glory.

#RelationshipGoals is trash.

Diego clears his throat. His knee presses against mine. "Mel's a friend. She's a popular gamer—La Fénix. She's got mad YouTube subscribers." He tugs at the hem of his black T-shirt. "Did you know you can make a lot of quick cash being a streamer?"

I cast my eyes down, listening to him explain.

"We started a streaming channel. *LeftRightLeftRightBA*," he says. "It's a gaming thing."

I'm not surprised.

"It was for fun, at first," he explains. "Then we got a lot of subscribers and donations. Between Mel's YT following and all my social media stuff, we caught the attention of some lower-level sponsors."

"Cool." I'm happy for him. "Was this—did you need the money for your gamer plan?"

He shakes his head. "When the whole Legends Con thing went down . . ." He peeks at me through his eyelashes, waiting. I nudge his knee to continue. "I needed money for something else."

A piece of me panics. Is he in trouble? Did Camila make one final ultimatum—go to college or move out? That's not like her. If anything, she'd probably keep Diego and Ollie at home until they were old and wrinkled. But what else would he need money for?

The moonlight underscores his profile. The length of his nose and the faintest shadow of unshaven stubble, the way his hair stands up because he needs a trim.

"For what?" I finally ask.

"I wanted to buy you a pass to Legends Con," he admits, turning to look at me. His eyes almost scrunch. His lips almost smile.

I can barely swallow. "A pass for me?"

Diego doesn't laugh at the way my voice cracks. He never has. "Isaac, meeting Peter and Jorge was the most important part of this summer for you."

I open my mouth to argue, but he holds up his index finger to stop me.

"Dude, no shade. I'm not butthurt over it." His thigh is pressed against mine now. "Streaming's a full-time gig. Mel had all the equipment, so I was always over at hers. I knew it'd be worth it if I could at least get a stack together and buy you one of those basic, entry-level badges from GeekPass. Then you could meet them. Ask your question."

It's like I'm floating in space. I'm not in my body. I'm somewhere high, stars skimming my skin, everything in the galaxy so small and beautiful, and the only thing keeping me in orbit is this boy, my best friend, telling me he spent weeks trying to buy me one moment with my heroes. He just wanted me to have that.

The thought steals the breath from my lungs, but I manage to say, "So, you've been MIA . . . for me?"

"Yeah, dude." Diego lowers his chin. "I was so close, but I failed."

I want to touch him. I want to kiss the frown off his mouth.

"You were right at Pride," he whispers. "Every day since I backed out of UGA I've felt like shit. I hate the idea of you being alone."

In any other situation, having Diego Santoyo admit I was right about something would be glorious. But not now. Not at all.

"I just wanted to give you something as a reminder of how much you mean to me."

I tiptoe my fingers along my own knee, still wanting to touch his.

"I tried too," I croak, a lump sitting in my throat. "I tried to find a way to make up for ruining everything with the whole . . . Davi thing."

Diego doesn't look at me.

"I begged my mom to find a way for you to meet Elena Sánchez this weekend. As if my mom's some kind of miracle worker," I say, laughing dryly. "Silly, right?"

"It worked."

His words hit me like that first cold spray of water in the shower when you haven't let it heat up enough. I shiver, eyes widening. "It—what?"

He lifts his head. "I met Elena. Today." The left side of

his mouth rises, then he's full-on beaming. "Your mom, she *is* a miracle worker."

I slump back, mouth open. My brain's a hazy mess, unable to compute that Mom pulled it off. She didn't even tell me when she came home this afternoon.

Lilah Johnson, another Keeper of Secrets.

"I got a call last night from your mom. At first, I thought she was going to rip me a new one for what happened at Pride, but it turns out she has a client who went to school with Elena." He's glowing. "Elena had an opening in her schedule this morning. We had breakfast downtown at this sick-ass hotel." He shakes my shoulder. "Dude, I had breakfast with Elena Sánchez!"

"For real?"

This infectious energy buzzes off him, like when he's finally beat a video game. "I almost upchucked my breakfast burrito on her," he confesses.

"Classic Diego Santoyo."

"I was terrified." His voice breaks like mine always does. "I know I seem like I've got it all together. Like I have this genius plan to be the next big thing in gaming, but I'm shitting my pants constantly. What if I fail? What if my parents are right?"

"You won't fail," I tell him.

He exhales. "Elena was so cool. After I finished fanboying, I told her all my ideas. I brought my notebooks and showed her my sketches, characters, all of it. Even the moderately decent ones."

"You don't do moderately decent, Diego."

Something honest and inviting smooths over his face. "She took notes in her *phone*, dude. She gave me some hardcore feedback. Then she told me how inspiring it is to chat with another Latine person, someone who understands how important our ideas are." His chest inflates, his shoulders lifting. "She said, 'We might not ever get the same respect for our work, but keep fighting for what we deserve.'"

"That's so dope."

Diego smiles at his sneakers. He tells me about the advice she gave him. She broke down his options while he's not in school and what to research. Then she subscribed to his channel, followed him on social media.

"She even emailed my parents. It was this long, super official message," he says, his teeth pulling on his lower lip like he's trying to control his ridiculous grin. "They're finally coming around. Slowly, but still. They're taking it—they're taking *me* seriously."

"Wow." I laugh a little breathlessly. "Diego, that's—"

"I told her about you too," he blurts.

"You did?"

He bites the inside of his cheek. "I told her how bad I felt about not going to UGA with you and—"

I cut him off before he can finish. "It's my fault," I say. "I should never have made you feel like you're abandoning me. College is a *choice*. You shouldn't make that choice for someone else—not even your best friend."

"I know, but—"

"Seriously," I say, interrupting him again. "These past few weeks made me realize I'm good on my own. Not saying I'm gonna walk into a party and make best friends for life or anything—"

"You better not," he warns with a smirk.

"But I'm going to be okay. *We're* going to be okay."

It's true. Summer might be moving at warp speed, but at the end of it, I'm confident Diego will still be there. We'll still be . . . us.

"I'm sorry I made all this about me," I continue. "I'm sorry I ruined what was supposed to be the coolest summer by acting like it's gonna be the last time we see each other."

His lips part to say something, but I'm not finished. "I'm sorry about what happened at Pride too. I was an ass. Your friends—they're *our* friends. I just wanted that day to be about what we never got after we came out."

"Me too," he whispers to his feet.

"And I'm sorry about—" A harsh wave of nausea hits me. I hold down the bile, letting the words float up. This is the thing I need to say most. "I'm sorry about Davi. I'm sorry that I . . ."

Problem is, I don't know how to tell my best friend that I've wanted something that I didn't know I always had. It terrifies me.

Once again, I'm like Charm. I didn't mean to create this alternate reality.

And just like Reverb, Diego says the most unexpected thing: "Watching the way you two clicked so easily sucked. Like, big time." His brow wrinkles. He rubs his palms across his shorts. "When he showed up at TB—both times—that fucking killed me. You forgot me so quickly."

"I didn't—" I stop myself before the lie slips out.

I did.

"Then he's all you were focused on at Pride and I lost it."

My brain flashes back to our argument. It was less than forty-eight hours ago, but it feels so distant, some unwanted memory I've boxed up like Mom's done my bedroom. I've put it in a corner of my brain, never to be touched. But I can see Diego's expression and hear his words. He was never mad about Legends Con. It was this brief, throwaway comment as we yelled at each other.

Everything was about Davi.

Davi and me.

"I thought I lost you," he says, his voice lifeless.

"Diego," I start, my breaths uneven. "No one could do that. You'll always be my—"

"Friend," he says, nodding. "I know."

But that's not the word that was going to leap from my mouth. It's true, yes. Except, it's not what I wanted to say. I know this. Just like I know, somewhere in the hollowed-out cavity of my heart, Diego believes we're friends. *I* love *him*. That doesn't mean he feels the same.

I shake off that feeling, though. I refuse to let hope deteriorate any further. Bella's voice is in my ears—*tell him, tell him, tell him*—and this is where Charm and I differ: He doesn't act against the things that scare him. He waits.

And I waited forever to see him and Reverb kiss, scared it'd never happen.

I'm so done letting fear win.

Sometimes, you have to be brave enough to give yourself the thing everyone else won't.

I reach over, my hand crossing Diego's thigh to grab his hand. I squeeze tightly, offering him my most confident expression as he looks between my eyes and our hands. "I'm sorry for one more thing."

"Yeah?" he chokes out, the word losing gas before it reaches my ears.

"I'm sorry I didn't see what I was supposed to see a long time ago."

"What's that?"

"You." I search for the right words. I know where they've always been. Curled in my chest, waiting for me to shine a light on them. "You're my Bruno Mars," I finally sputter.

"Wow," he says, chuckling. His hand is still in mine. "That was really corny."

It was. But it's true. I spent so much time hoping things would work with Davi. He was supposed to be my Abuelito-fairy-tale happy ending. My real life *The Princess Bride*. Truth is, not everything in life has that storybook ending. It's not supposed to.

The Princess Bride is just a film. My favorite, but still.

Disaster Academy is just a comic book. Maybe I didn't need that sketch from Jorge to know all the possibilities that live inside me. Maybe I don't need Charm's superpowers to fix my reality.

I just need to create it myself.

Diego turns to me. Our knees bump. Our foreheads touch. It's kind of gross, because it's humid and we're sweaty, but whatever. He's smiling. I am too.

"You're making The Face," he says quietly.

"I know."

We remain that way for a few seconds more, but there's something else I want to say.

"Diego?"

"Yeah."

"I love you." The pause floats between us like a ship searching for shore. I don't need him to say it back. For once, I'm taking a chance, saying what I feel without the awkwardness or the worry of how the other person's going to react. I'm done hiding behind walls. And you know what? It feels damn good.

I don't wait for a response or reaction from him before I whisper, "Te amo, Diego." I say it slowly. Not because I think he'll correct me. Because I want him to know I mean every word.

Another second passes. Then he says, confidently, "I love you too, Isaac Martin."

I want to ask him why he never said anything. But I'm kind of stuck on the fact that Luis Diego Santoyo just said those three words to me.

And that's it, huh?

People don't just fall in love. No, we stumble and trip and collapse face-first into it.

I lift my chin to close the small distance—because every mile and square foot and secret are gone—separating us. I kiss him. Not for practice. Not for research.

I kiss Diego Santoyo because I want to.

Because I can.

He kisses back without the hesitation we had in the parking lot of Twisted Burger. Like there are no rules holding us back. And this is all I want to do for the rest of the summer. Glide my mouth along Diego's. Touch his scar. Listen to his sharp inhales when we both add more pressure.

Just as we're getting to the amazing part—where he

gently bites my lip, and my hand slides up his thigh, and *we've just exited friend zone and entered a new realm of extraordinary*—my phone buzzes in my pocket. I sigh against Diego's mouth. Fishing it out of my jeans is difficult for obvious reasons, but I manage.

It's Carlos.

I consider the screen for a long moment. His name remains there, an open invitation. I don't answer.

The screen lights up again: Mom's calling. Next is a series of texts. Three from Iggy, then one from Abuelito. My grandpa is *texting* me, which is a new level of reality warping I'm not prepared for.

I read all the scrambled messages, barely breathing.

"Oh, shit. Bella's having the baby."

Thirty

⚑ **Pinned Tweet**

Isaac @charminmartin · Jan 3

One day I'm gonna meet Peter & Jorge @ #LegendsCon and tell them #Charmverb deserve a happy ending. I DESERVE A HAPPY ENDING. Not tagging them cuz im too scared to tell them rn lol #lgbtqsuperheroes #thedisasters #QPOCHeroes

KonamiCode  @theogkonamicode · 10h

Replying to @charminmartin
Your right: YOU DESERVE A HAPPY ENDING! can i be your reverb? 🖤 #esverdad #mydisaster

A. Jin @picasays · 2h

Replying to @charminmartin and @theogkonamicode
*YOU'RE. Also, this is highly offensive and gross. Delete both your accounts.

Ángel Christopher Murphy. Born at 8:07 a.m. on a Monday in the heart of summer.

"He's beautiful," I whisper.

Bella smiles tiredly, eyes drooping, her face ashen but glowing with joy.

When we arrived at the hospital, Diego and I were confined to the maternity floor's waiting area, along with

Abuelito and Iggy. Only Chris and Mom were allowed in the delivery room, as was Camila, but that's because this is the hospital she works at. She picked us up at the park last night on the way here. It was hard to ignore the curious looks she shot us from the rearview mirror. Probably because we were holding hands.

I hope it's not because she spotted us kissing while we waited on her.

I feel guilty about making out with Diego knowing my sister was in labor. But only slightly. I doubt Bella felt any remorse about those times I had to wait after volleyball practice while she and some basketball dude shared a little lip action behind the school. It was, however, gravely embarrassing asking Diego to walk in front of me on the way to Camila's Jeep. The moon wasn't the only thing high in the air yesterday.

I can't wait to tell Bella about Diego Santoyo, Lifetime Best Friend and Newly Updated Status Boyfriend.

For now, I stare at my nephew cradled in Chris's arms as he sits on the edge of Bella's bed. She kisses the crown of Ángel's head.

Ángel is pale, a bit reddish. He's small too. Tiny hands, nose, lips. But he has just enough fuzz on his head to signify his future dark crown of curls, thanks to Mom. He's already loud, too, like Iggy and Abuelito. A true Martin.

I get why people say babies are cute, but my nephew is the cutest of all newborns in the multiverse.

We're crowded into Bella's room even though it's a violation of the hospital's strict two-person only visitation rules. Camila haggled with the desk nurse until she turned a blind eye on us. We're five people over the maximum capacity for visiting a mother and her newborn.

Bella doesn't seem to mind.

Neither does Ángel, who keeps blinking, then falling back to sleep.

I understand. Being in this family is an exhausting journey.

"Abuelito." Chris slowly stands. "Do you want to hold him?"

"Oh, no, no." Abuelito shakes his head, sounding apprehensive.

I've never heard him nervous. It's reassuring. There are things—big and infant-sized—that scare all of us.

"I've got him," Iggy volunteers, stepping in front of Abuelito.

Mom quickly says, "Shouldn't your sister and her husband be the ones deciding who's going to hold him?"

"Mom! You know she's going to ice me out."

"Uh, hello!" Bella says exhaustedly. "I'm still in the room."

"Not too loud." Camila smiles warmly, gently raising and lowering her hands in a universal sign for *calm the hell down.* "We have to make sure mommy and newborn's adrenaline levels are smooth."

I stand at the foot of Bella's bed, grinning. Diego's next to me. Between the minimal space separating us, our hands are locked.

Bella must notice because she tips her head to the left, an eyebrow raised.

My cheeks are on fire. Diego swings our hands back and forth, unbothered. I want a fourth of his confidence.

"Chiquito," Abuelito says with way too much fondness in his voice. "Does he like *The Princess Bride*?"

Before I can answer, not that I have a real response ready because I've never actually asked Diego his thoughts on the movie, Diego replies, "It's *inconceivable* not to love it," and I want to kiss him all over again.

Until Mom says, "I guess that's not all he likes," poking a spot just below my Adam's apple. There's a soft, unyielding ache there. I've already seen the purpling bruise in the Jeep's rearview mirror. With my complexion, I didn't even know I could get a hickey. "We'll be having a door-open-at-all-times-when-Diego's-over discussion very soon."

So, yeah, I kind of want to die.

Iggy reaches out toward Chris with grabby hands. "I'll just hold my nephew while you get in on this, bro. Give Isaac a few tips about taking things from the friend zone to a more . . . intimate level."

"Iggy," I say through my teeth.

"No, no, no. Wait." Bella wiggles, trying to sit up. Chris evades Iggy to return to her side. "As happy as I am for you two," she waves a finger between Diego and me, "You will not steal my thunder today. As the middle child, I never get the spotlight. It's either about Iggy and his ego or Isaac and his issues."

"Hey!" Iggy and I say simultaneously, which earns us a death glare from Camila.

"So, all those Bruno Mars performances weren't about you?" I ask, squinting at her.

"No," she says, huffing. "Clearly, it was my subliminal attempt to get you two together."

Diego squeezes my hand again and says, "Mission accomplished."

"Um, babe," Chris says, lifting Ángel into her eyeline. "Today's about us, too, right?"

"Yeah, yeah. Not like I'm the one who carried him for nine months and pushed him out of my—"

"This conversation is becoming too grown for my ears," I say, interrupting Bella.

Right then, the hospital room door swings open. I startle, thinking it's the desk nurse ready to eject all of us from the room. But it's not, though now I wish it were.

Carlos walks into the room. He's carrying a bouquet of flowers in his arms, beaming as he eases around everyone to get to Bella. Chris stands stone-faced for a moment, like he's protecting her, before stepping out of the way, Ángel in his arms.

There are so many reasons why I love Chris, but that

brief three seconds of bravery is number one.

Carlos leans over to kiss the top of Bella's head, whispers in her ear, then kisses her temple. She smiles. Not a weak or indifferent one. Not a shocked-Isaac-Martin one either. A relaxed smile like the one she'd give him as a little girl.

Before . . . well, that.

Carlos hands off the flowers to Mom and kisses Abuelito on each cheek, patting his shoulders. He turns to Chris with open arms.

"¿Puedo . . . ?"

Chris hesitates, peeking down at Bella. When they got married, Bella made one strict demand: Carlos wasn't to be invited. Abuelito walked her down the aisle. During the parents' dance, she spun around the small, rented ballroom with Mom, then me. She even managed to survive Iggy giving a toast, something Mom insisted on since Carlos wasn't allowed to be there. I watched her throughout the whole speech. All the tears trailing down her cheeks, the occasional glances she traded between Chris's parents sitting together, holding hands, while Abuelito sat on one side of Mom, her own parents on the other, at the main table.

And I'm sure the few guests in attendance thought it was because Iggy, like me, is the worst at speeches. But a fractional part of me, one that I've never told anyone about, knew it was because Carlos was missing. As much as my sister hates everything he's done, she regretted not having him there on one of her biggest days.

He's here now, though, waiting to greet his first grandchild.

Bella opens her mouth, but nothing comes out. Instead, she nods once at Chris. Carefully, he passes Ángel to Carlos.

It's the weirdest thing. Everything cold and distant and informal about the Carlos I remember at thirteen melts away. All the wrinkles around his eyes and his flat mouth and Martin brow seem to fade. He pulls Ángel in close, but not too close. That hollow *goodbye* I still hear in my worst moments is finally replaced by the sound of a content sigh when Carlos presses his mouth against Ángel's forehead. Ángel exhales too.

Family.

Carlos sways back and forth, cradling Ángel like he might run away. Like he's trying to regain something he lost years ago, by being gentle and cautious with Ángel.

"Isn't he beautiful?" Mom asks him.

"Sí," Carlos says, his voice thick.

Despite Iggy's revelation at the diner, I still didn't believe Carlos had the chemicals needed to produce tears. But I can tell he's seconds from proving all my theories wrong.

"He looks like you," Carlos comments, nodding at Mom.

She rolls her eyes. "Shut up."

"He does, he does," says Abuelito.

Mom doesn't fight him on it. Camila has an arm resting around her shoulders. Mom leans into their half hug. Bella, still smiling with drowsy eyes, reaches out for her hand. Iggy and Chris whisper to each other with twin grins, pointing at her.

As much as I'm worried about her being alone, Mom's not. She has the Santoyos and even Carlos nearby. Abuelito is a phone call away. There's only twenty-six miles between her and Iggy. And, though she still hasn't officially told me, I know there's someone else. Someone new to watch over and protect and, hopefully, love her.

One day, Mom and I will stop avoiding the talks we should be having because one of us is too scared to confront what it means out loud.

But not now. Because Carlos is looking right at me.

I freeze.

Carlos's jaw twitches, his lips parting. He doesn't speak, only stares.

After a beat, I nod at him. And he nods back.

I don't understand Carlos Martin. I'll probably never ask him why he shattered something I needed growing up. But I don't hate him. There's not enough room in in my body, in my universe, to hate him. It's exhausting. It consumes too much of the world I've created with Mom and Bella and Iggy too. It hangs, dark and quiet, over my moments with Abuelito.

I refuse to create space in my new reality to hate him.

His eyes lower from my face to my hand twisted with Diego's.

I never formally came out to him. He wasn't around when I decided to tell Mom and the rest of my family. I know Mom called him. I know Abuelito mentioned it. But it was never a discussion we had.

I stand awkwardly with Diego. I don't try to hide it. Diego continues to swing our hands back and forth between us. He's not afraid. Neither am I.

We're a little bit like Charm and Reverb, after all—slow to get there, but pretty damn powerful together.

Carlos doesn't balk or lecture or dismiss us. He turns to Mom with the biggest grin I've ever witnessed and says, "Ha! I told you it would happen. You owe me fifty bucks."

"Ugh. Level_Zero beat *BtVoS* without me last night," Diego groans. "He's overtaken the Gatherer's Guild!"

We walk out the hospital's automatic glass doors into the haloing light of a July sun. It's nearly noon. Sweat instantly tickles my forehead. Diego has his phone in one hand, realigning our fingers with his other. I clutch Iggy's keys in my free hand.

"Are you mad?" I ask.

"What? No. I was occupied with something better. Anyway," he says as I use the key fob to set off Iggy's alarm so we can figure out where he parked in the visitor lot, "he wants to get together later to celebrate. All of us."

I haven't checked the group chat. My phone's dead in my back pocket.

"I can't today, though," I say. "It's *The Princess Bride* night with Abuelito." Not that I don't want to see the Six again, but I'm so ready to spend time with home-cooked food and laughter and Abuelito.

We squeeze through the spaces between cars, refusing to let go of each other's hand. I can't believe Iggy's letting me borrow his vehicle to go on a food run. I offered to only take the back roads and stay under the speed limit, but he only shrugged.

"I trust you, baby brother."

Ignacio Martin *trusts* me.

"Maybe tomorrow?" Diego offers.

"Cool," I say when we finally reach the car. "It'll be nice to hang out drama free. The Six reunited."

"Uh, the Seven." Diego smiles shyly from the passenger seat. He connects my phone to Iggy's charger before setting up the Bluetooth, then he settles his hands in his lap. I crank on the air conditioner, waiting for him to finally elaborate. "I told them I wanted Ollie to join the group."

An unrestrainable grin tugs at the corners of my mouth. "Oh, yeah? What'd they say?"

Diego thumbs open his messages app. "F.B. said, 'Hell yeah, bring him! Little dude is waaaaay cooler than Captain Incredible.'"

I laugh, shaking my head. "Ollie definitely is."

We sit there for a moment. I'm not ready to leave, not just yet. Diego doesn't seem to be in a rush either. I scroll to the playlist I asked Iggy for the other day, the one he had on while we drove to and from Twisted Burger. Selena serenades us about how she could fall in love.

I angle my head in Diego's direction. "We can't stay out too late tomorrow either. I need to do some packing."

He bites his lip, nodding. Then, with a nervous voice, he says, "Do you want help?"

There's no jitters in my system. My leg isn't ready to vibrate uncontrollably. All the knots in my stomach aren't from fear; they're from the way Diego's soft eyes hold my gaze for the rest of the song.

"Yeah," I finally say.

Then, before Diego can say anything snarky, I lean over to kiss him. He cups my cheek, kissing back. We test out the pressure, alternating between gentle and urgent. I try to figure out where to put my hands. He adjusts the angle so I'm not crushing his nose.

Slow and constant, we find our way.

But it's not enough.

I want to remember what Diego likes while I'm away at UGA. I want to experiment and tease and learn everything, so on the weekends, when I drive back—after all, that's why I'm in this car without Iggy's supervision—we won't have to practice first.

Though, I guess practice kisses aren't so bad. Not the kind that involve Diego Santoyo.

"Uh." He exhales, teeth nipping at my lower lip. "We better get moving or your fam's going to wonder what took us so long. Can we continue this later, after you hang with Abuelito?"

Against his mouth, I say "As you wish," hoping he knows what I mean.

By the little flash in his eyes, I think he does.

As I shift into reverse and desperately try not to piss my pants while navigating the hospital parking lot, I ask him to recite everyone's food order. I don't want to miss anything. I only have enough courage for one practice drive today.

When he's finished, I say, "Wait, you forgot to add the Scorcher with no avocado."

"For Iggy?"

"No." I smile unabashedly. "For my dad."

Then I ease the car onto the main road, and we follow the sun all the way to Twisted Burger, just Diego and me and Bruno Mars on the radio.

The End.

Acknowledgments

It's hard to believe this is my fourth time writing one of these, and I still have no clue where to begin. The thing is—this book was a *journey* for me. There are so many people that helped me get from draft zero to what you're holding right now.

I guess we all must start somewhere, right?

To my agent, Thao Le, who took one look at the first five chapters of this book and signed me on the spot. You loved this book from its earliest stages—geeks, Pride, grandparents, parking lot kisses, and all! Thanks for always championing me. To everyone at the Sandra Dijkstra Agency—Sandra Dijkstra, Andrea Cavallaro, Jennifer Kim, Jessica Watterson, Elise Capron, and all the other amazing staff—thank you for continuously supporting me.

To the most incredible editor, Dana Leydig, who saw the heart of this book amongst all the chaos. (Can you believe there was a whole *heist* storyline?) You made me dig deep and what I found changed my world as a writer. Forever grateful for the ways you helped me shape Isaac, Diego, Davi, and The Six's story. In the words of Westley from *The Princess Bride*: "As you wish."

To Ken Wright, Maggie Rosenthal, and the epic team at Viking Children's Books and Penguin Random House—copyeditors Abigail Powers and Cherise Benton; proofreader Esther Reisberg; authenticity readers Claudia Martinez and Clarence Haynes; designers Lucia Baez and Kaitlin Yang; everyone in marketing and publicity, my amazing publicist, Lizzie Goddell; the all-star social media team, from the fantastic Felicity Vallence to the joyous James Akinaka to the dazzling Bezi Yohannes and everyone on the squad; Samira Iravani for designing a dream cover; Daniel Clarke for taking the characters in my head and making them heroes for everyone to see; Theresa Evangelista for all the help in making this cover real.

To the team at Listening Library for producing an audiobook I never imagined having but am incredibly in love with.

To my favorite partner in crime, Adib Khorram. Thanks for sticking by me despite all the crappy drafts I send you. I love that I get to share this journey with you.

To C. B. Lee, who let me rant about this story in my head until I finally turned in a manuscript. From coffee shops to Dragon Cons to Santa Monica—you're like a sister to me.

To my family—Mom, Dad, Piper, Tamir, Lindsay, and especially my sister Sonya. Thanks for always liking my Instagram posts! To my friends and coworkers, for repeatedly asking, "How's that book coming along?" You kept me going.

To the writing community who continues to embrace me despite my extreme levels of nerdiness—Becky Albertalli, my French toast buddy; Leah Johnson, my John Hughes pal; Kelly Loy Gilbert, the only hero who makes me cry. To Nic Stone, Roshani Chokshi, Adam Silvera, Mark Oshiro, Lana Wood Johnson, Julie Murphy, Karen Strong, Tracy Deonn, Patrice Caldwell, Laura Silverman, Saundra Mitchell, Elise Bryant, Ashley Poston (thanks for answering all my gamer questions!), Justin A. Reynolds, Adam Sass, Caleb Roehrig, Alex London, L.C. Rosen, and everyone else who never let me give up. To Natalie C. Parker, Tessa Gratton, and the entire Madcap community—you give me hope when I think there's none left.

To all the independent bookstores, book bloggers, bookstagrammers, booktokers, booktubers, artists, and podcasters who have shouted from the rooftops about me and my books.

To the teachers, librarians, and educators who share my stories—you inspire me.

And to every Black, brown, BIPOC reader waiting on their happy ending—we have the power to change the world. We deserve joy. We deserve magic. We deserve . . . love. I'm rooting for us. *For you.*

DISCARDED